EVIDENCE
OF
LIFE

BARBARA
TAYLOR SISSEL

EVIDENCE
OF
LIFE

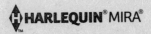

Recycling programs
for this product may
not exist in your area.

ISBN-13: 978-0-7783-1638-1

EVIDENCE OF LIFE

Copyright © 2013 by Barbara Taylor Sissel

For questions and comments about the quality of this book, please contact us at CustomerService@Harlequin.com.

Printed in U.S.A.

HARLEQUIN®
™ www.Harlequin.com

For Michael and David, who remember the way we were.

CHAPTER

1

On the last ordinary day of her life before her family went off for the weekend, Abby made a real breakfast—French toast with maple syrup and bacon. It was penance, the least she could do, given how utterly delighted she was at the prospect of being left on her own for two whole days to do as she pleased. It would sicken her later, in the aftermath of what happened, that she could so covet the prospect of solitude, but in that last handful of ordinary hours, she was full of herself, her silly plans. She set a small mixing bowl on the counter, found the wire whisk, and when Nick came in the back door, she brandished it, smiling at him.

He frowned. "What are you doing?"

"Cooking breakfast, French toast."

"We don't have time. We're going to hit rush-hour traffic as it is."

"It'll be fine," Abby soothed.

He came to the sink still wearing the wisp of blood-stained tissue he'd stuck below his ear where he'd cut himself shaving and the rumpled cargo shorts he'd pulled out of the hamper as if he didn't have a drawer full of clean ones. As if the unwashed pair were the only ones that suited him.

Abby got out a frying pan, aware of his mood, regretful of it. She wished he hadn't bothered with shaving. She wished she'd done the laundry yesterday. Leaving the breakfast makings, she went to him, circled his waist from behind, laid her cheek against his back. *"I'm sorry about your shorts."* The words were right there, but they caught in her throat when she felt him go still.

"Don't," he said, and she backed away. She returned to the stove, absorbing herself in the task of separating the strips of bacon and arranging them with care in the bottom of the pan. As if her care made a difference, as if it could keep her family safe when it couldn't. She ought to have known that much at least. She went to the refrigerator and took out the carton of eggs.

Nick washed his hands.

"I wish you'd tell me what's wrong," she said when he shut off the water.

"Why do you always think something's wrong, Abby?"

"I don't."

"You do."

"Fine," she said. She would not stand here squabbling as if they were their children.

He hung the kitchen towel over the oven door handle, gave her one of those side-of-the-mouth kisses.

"I'm sorry," he said. "Nothing's wrong. I just want to get on the road."

Abby's jaw tightened. She knew better.

"Wouldn't cereal be easier?" he asked.

She broke the eggs into the bowl. "I'd like us to sit down to breakfast together for once."

"What about the mess? You do realize we can't stay to help you clean up."

"I don't mind."

He went to the foot of the stairs and shouted, "Lindsey? What's taking you so long? I could use some help loading the camping gear."

"Down in a minute, Dad," she shouted back. "I had to get ready in Jake's bathroom because the shower in mine is still leaking."

Nick looked at Abby. "I thought you called the plumber."

"I did. He hasn't—"

Nick left. The screen door clattered shut behind him.

"—called back yet," Abby finished.

She whipped the eggs, fuming. She wished she had taken Nick's advice and served cereal. They'd be gone faster. She wished she had said it was only lately that she assumed something was wrong. Because there was something; she could feel it. Nick was distracted, moodier than usual. Too quiet. That is, when he wasn't biting her head off for no reason. And since when did he push her away? Say no to her touch? It wasn't like him.

Abby added powdered sugar and a splash of vanilla to the eggs. She got out a fork and poked at the bacon, aggravated at the sudden stab of her tears, a duller sense of alarm. Whatever it was, she wasn't a mind reader; she couldn't fix it by herself. Why couldn't he see that?

"I can't get my hair to do anything." Lindsey came up beside Abby, her brush and comb in her hand.

Abby composed her face. "Want me to French braid it?"

"Would you?"

Lindsey's hair reached the middle of her back, a thick mane that blended shades of honey blond with darker shades of reddish brown, colors very similar to those of Miss Havisham, Lindsey's chestnut mare. Lindsey said she'd rather groom Miss Havisham's mane than her own, and she conned Abby into doing it whenever she could. Abby didn't mind; she loved the feel of it through her fingers, like rough silk. Deftly, she parted off three sections and began weaving them together. "Should I call you tomorrow and let you know if Hardys Walk wins tonight?"

"Samantha will."

"Is Scott pitching?"

"I don't know. Who cares anyway? He barely knows I'm alive."

"Oh, honey." Abby squeezed Lindsey's shoulder. Scott Kaplan was her first serious crush, the first boy to truly trouble her heart, and Abby was both exasperated and pained by the experience. She wished she could say how little Scott would matter in the long run, but she didn't dare. "Did you bring a rubber band?"

Lindsey handed it over along with a bit of taffeta ribbon, pink with a narrow green stripe. "I don't see why I have to go on this trip when Jake doesn't."

"He has finals," Abby said.

"Oh, sure," Lindsey scoffed. "Like he'd choose

cramming for finals over camping in the Hill Country. Finals aren't until next month anyway."

Abby kept silent.

Lindsey said, "If you ask me he's not going because he doesn't want Dad on his case about law school again."

"Can you blame him?" Abby asked.

Lindsey didn't answer. She was as tired of Nick and Jake's continual bickering as Abby was. Nick was so much harder on Jake than he was on Lindsey. His preference was obvious, hurtful, but if Abby brought it up, Nick denied treating Lindsey differently. "You don't understand about boys," he would say.

"Oh, I think I understand perfectly. He's exactly like you," Abby would say.

Stubborn, she meant. Each one was determined to have it his own way.

"You know I'm right, Mom," Lindsey said.

"At least you won't have to listen to them argue."

"Maybe I'll go to law school."

Abby made a face. Lindsey never passed up an opportunity to remind her parents that she was the better student, the orderly, more agreeable child. "I thought you were going to play pro basketball overseas, travel the world."

"Is there a reason I can't do both?"

"Nope. You, my darling daughter, can do anything you set your mind to, just like your brother." Abby ran her fingers lightly down the length of Lindsey's braid.

"If only I could stay home like my brother."

"Your daddy has gone to a lot of trouble to plan this trip so he can spend time with you."

"I know. I just wish it wasn't *this* weekend."

"There are worse sacrifices," Abby answered, blithely.

"I have finals next month, too. And don't say it's not the same."

"Okay, I won't." Abby centered the griddle over the burner. "Will you set the table and call your dad? The French toast'll be done in a minute." She could feel Lindsey considering whether or not to push.

Please, don't. It was a prayer, a wish, yet one more in the sea of mundane moments from that morning that would return to mock her. To ask her: How could you? Because she would remember that Lindsey hadn't pushed; she'd set the table and left the kitchen without another word.

"What about jackets?" Abby followed her husband and daughter through the back door, onto the driveway. Although it was April, it was still chilly, and it would be colder where they were going.

Colder than home.

"It's supposed to rain," she said. "Maybe you guys should take your boots."

"Dad says it's not going to rain, that the weatherman doesn't know his—"

"Lindsey," Abby warned.

"I wasn't going to say ass, Mom. I was going to say bum or buttocks or what about seater rumpus?"

Abby rolled her eyes.

"He doesn't know his seater rumpus from a hole in the ground," Lindsey finished. She stowed her purse and iPod in the front seat. "Mom?"

"Yep?"

"I wish you were going."

"You do? How come?"

"Because that delicious French toast you made for us? It's the last good meal I'll eat till we get home."

Abby laughed.

"Very funny." Nick hefted his briefcase and laptop into the back of Abby's Jeep Cherokee, shifting it to fit, muttering what sounded to Abby like, "Who needs this?" Or, "Why am I doing this?"

She said, "Why don't you leave that stuff here? You don't have to work every weekend."

"I gave you the keys to the BMW, didn't I?" he asked as if he hadn't heard her, and maybe he hadn't or didn't want to.

"Oh, my gosh!" Lindsey's eyes were round in mock amazement. "Dad's letting you drive his precious BMW?"

"I know," Abby said. "I'm astonished, too."

He straightened. "Hey, funny girl, maybe I'll let you drive Mom's Jeep."

"For real?" She only had her learner's permit, wouldn't turn sixteen until August.

"Do you think that's wise?" Abby was instantly anxious. "She's never driven on the highway."

"She has to learn sometime."

"But they said it might storm."

"Like they know." Nick dropped his arm around her shoulders. "You worry too much."

"Just promise me you won't let her drive if the weather's bad."

"Jesus, Abby, I'm not stupid."

"No, Nick, I didn't mean—"

But he was stepping away, telling Lindsey to get in the car. He wanted to get to the campsite before dark.

She came over to Abby and hugged her. "Never mind, Mommy. You know how stressed he gets before a road trip. If he lets me drive, I promise I'll be careful."

Abby clung to Lindsey for a moment, breathing in her scent, leftover maple syrup and something citrusy, a faded remnant of little girl, the color pink, a lullaby. She said, "I know you will." She walked with Lindsey to the car.

"We'll be back on Sunday." Lindsey settled into the front seat. "Unless we've starved to death from Daddy's cooking."

"I'll make a big dinner, barbequed chicken and corn on the cob. Chocolate cake for dessert. How's that sound?"

"I just hope I'm not too weak to eat it."

"I think you'll survive," Abby said. She looked at Nick over the hood. "Don't be mad because of what I said about Lindsey driving, okay? I didn't mean anything."

"She has to learn, Abby, and it's best if one of us is with her."

"I'm glad it's you." Abby meant it. Nick's nerves were steadier. She went around to him. "I hope you can relax and have some fun."

"Yeah, me, too."

She wanted his gaze and touched his wrist. "Nick?"

"We should probably talk when I get home."

"About?"

"Things. Us. You know. Isn't that what you're always saying, that I should be more open with you?"

"Yes, but—" *What's wrong?* She bit her lip to stop herself from asking.

"Thanks for making the French toast." His eyes on hers were somber.

"Sure, of course. I was glad to. You'll be careful, won't you?"

Instead of answering, he cradled her face in his hands and kissed her, and his kiss was so gentle and tender, and so filled with something she couldn't define. Later she would think it was regret she felt coming from him, maybe even remorse. But then she'd wonder if she'd read too much into it, if her sense of that had been created in hindsight.

He touched her temple, brushed the loose wisps of hair from her forehead. "I don't want you to worry. We'll be fine, okay?" His look was complicated, searching.

"Okay," she said, and she might have questioned him then, but he left her and got into the car too quickly. They reached the end of the driveway, Lindsey waved, and they were gone.

CHAPTER

2

The first time Abby had visited the Texas Hill Country was during the summer after third grade when she went to camp, the year she turned nine. Her mother got the idea from a magazine article that said a summer camp experience could boost a child's self-confidence and help them feel more independent. But the psychology behind it wasn't how she convinced Abby to go. No. What Abby's mother did was to invite Kate Connelly, Abby's best friend, to join her. The girls didn't know it—Kate still didn't—but Abby's mother paid Kate's way.

Camp Many Waters—Many Manures, the girls had dubbed it that first year screaming with laughter—was on the Guadalupe River, near Kerrville. Kate loved it from the first day. Abby struggled with homesickness but not after their first year. Camp was where they learned to swim and ride horses and do the Cotton-

Eyed Joe. Camp was where they napped together in a salt-sweat tangle of limbs in a hammock strung between a couple of ancient live oaks.

The rest of the year they lived a block apart in the same Houston neighborhood and shared almost the same birthday. Kate was older and never minded saying so until they hit thirty. They'd been in most of each other's classes through school and went on to start college together. Mr. Tuttle at Tuttle's Rexall Drugs two streets over from theirs, where they'd bought Jujubes and Superwoman comic books and then their first lipsticks together, had labeled them the Stardust Twins. But where Abby's childhood had been predictable and sure, Kate's had been uneasy; it had wounded her in an unreachable way, like a too-deeply buried splinter. Camp in the Hill Country had been her escape, the one place where every hour was wholly welcome.

So it didn't surprise Abby that when they were grown and married, Kate went there to live. She said there was just something about that part of Texas. She could never define it. Neither could Abby. But then people had been flocking to the Hill Country since pioneer days, and most came away at a loss to describe what set it apart, what made it so special.

But there was one thing everyone did agree on, one thing for sure: It was dry.

Unlike Houston, where Kate and Abby had grown up, where the land began a flattened, flood-prone slide into Galveston Bay, the Hill Country region, near the center of the state, encompassed miles and miles of rumpled, rough-dried terrain. It had been submerged once, eons ago, beneath a shallow, urchin-filled, inland sea, but then the sea leaked out and left behind the skeletal remains of countless marine animals in layers like cake.

That's when the soil became stony and dry.

So dry you could scarcely scratch it with your fingernails.

There were the rare exceptions, the record-making torrential downpours, like the one Nick was driving Lindsey straight into at that very moment. Of course he wouldn't know that for a while yet. He was still in the vicinity of home, having just cleared the outskirts of Hardys Walk, where he and Abby had lived since Jake was a toddler. He was a shade over an hour's drive north of Houston, and the clouds drifting here in this piece of Texas sky were small and as white and innocent as dandelion fluff. Abby noticed them, but only subliminally, as she made her way into the barn to freshen the stalls.

Her mind was still on Nick, her sense of his unhappiness. She was thinking how he used to help care for the horses. He used to ride nearly every day after work, too. Often he and Lindsey had ridden together. Now Abby couldn't remember the last time he'd done anything with the horses other than complain about the feed and vet bills—which were enormous, Abby had to admit. He was always ranting about expenses, though. The way they lived wasn't extravagant, but it wasn't cheap either, what with taxes and upkeep on the house and property, never mind the kids and cars and college. Abby leaned on her rake. It had been her idea to move out here, to the Land of Nod, as her mother called it, and she'd never regretted it. But maybe Nick had. More than she realized. The commute alone was a nightmare, and traffic got heavier every year. On the occasions when she made the drive herself, she always wondered how he stood it.

Abby led Miss Havisham and their other mare Delilah back into their stalls, filled their feed and water troughs and walked back to the house. At the foot of the porch stairs, she slipped out of her wellies, grabbing the porch rail to balance herself. She'd forgotten it was loose and sat down hard when it gave underneath her. Sat looking at nothing, thinking how Nick had once tended to every little chore on the place, but now his mind was elsewhere. She pushed herself up off the ground. Where was elsewhere?

Later on, she switched on the television to the Weather Channel, but there was only a string of commercials and she cut the set off. She wouldn't go near the TV again until Saturday when the flooding in the Hill Country would be approaching near-epic proportions. It would seem unbelievable to her that she hadn't paid the slightest attention. She would wonder what she'd been thinking, doing…with her *delightful* alone time. She was sitting at the kitchen table poring over a seed catalogue when Lindsey called Saturday evening on her cell phone to say they were in Boerne.

"Boerne?" Abby repeated. She went out the front door onto the wide porch and sat on the swing, nudging it into motion with her toe. Boerne was northwest of San Antonio. The campground, on the Guadalupe River, where they ordinarily went when they didn't stay with Kate and George, was farther west.

"What are you doing in Boerne?" Abby asked. "Is the weather bad?"

"We spent last night in San Antonio. Dad says we're taking the scenic route."

"The scenic route? What does that mean?" There was a pause, one so long that Abby had time to think: *How weird.* To think: *Nick never takes the scenic route.*

"Mommy? I have to tell you—" Now Lindsey's voice broke with tears or static. In all the awful months that followed, Abby would never be able to decide.

"It's about Daddy—" something-something— "I'm in the restroom—" something— "Shell station and—"

"Lindsey, honey, you're breaking up. Can you go outside? Is Daddy with you?"

Her voice came again, but now it was as if she were talking through soap bubbles or sobbing.

Abby's heart stalled. "Lindsey! What's wrong?" But there was no answer. Only static. Abby redialed Lindsey's cell number and got her voice mail. She punched in the number again with the same result. She tried Nick's cell phone and listened to his recorded voice suggest she leave her name and number and he'd get back to her. When? Where was he? Where was Lindsey?

A Shell gas station. Was that what Lindsey had said? *I have something to tell you...it's about Daddy.* Abby frowned at the cordless receiver, unsure now of what she'd heard. She put her hand to her stomach. It was too early to panic. Lindsey would call back or Nick would. As soon as they could get a signal.

But the phone didn't ring, not that whole long evening. She finally sat down at her computer and typed out an email in the hope that Nick would switch on his laptop. She kept the television tuned to the Weather Channel. At first tornadoes in Iowa took precedence, but once those played out, the rain in the Texas Hill Country rose to center stage. Warnings were issued for the increasingly hazardous driving conditions and the growing threat of a major flood in the area. The waters in the Guadalupe River and in countless other smaller but no less vulnerable rivers were reported to be flowing over their banks.

Abby thought of calling Jake, but there was no point in worrying him needlessly, and surely it would be needless. She would hear something any minute. But she didn't, and by ten-thirty, when she tried first Lindsey's phone and then Nick's, a canned voice informed her that the mailboxes were full. Of her messages, she thought, each one increasingly distraught. Who knew how many she'd left?

She sent several more emails for all the good it did.

Then at midnight when she called, she got nothing. Not even the recordings. She pressed the receiver hard to her ear and heard no sound. Dead air. It was as if she had dialed into a black hole. She would never be able to describe the sense of desolation that swept through her then. Even the canned voices had kept alive some sense of a connection, but that was gone now, and without it, Abby had no antidote for the panic that came, fiendishly, merrily, as if it had only been waiting its chance. It was a struggle to breathe. She couldn't think.

From rote, she dialed Kate's number, her landline, got a busy signal. Not the usual, steady rhythm of sound, but the rapid-fire drill that meant the phone lines were down. Abby dropped the cordless onto the sofa, dropped her head into her hands.

God...what should I do?

She desperately wanted to call her mother in Houston, but Julia went to bed with the chickens and Abby couldn't bear to waken her. Or Jake. For nothing. It had to be nothing. She was letting her imagination run away with her. *Why do you always think something's wrong, Abby?* Nick's admonition crept through her mind. She felt his palms on her cheeks, the trueness of his kiss when he'd pulled her close. *I don't want you to worry*, he had said, and his tone had been so heartfelt and tender. He'd wanted to make up for before, when he'd been short with her. He hadn't wanted to leave her mad. They'd promised early in their marriage they wouldn't, and they'd tried to stick by it. Sometimes it had been hard, but every marriage, even one as good as hers and Nick's, had hard times.

Abby left the great room and went into the kitchen; she made toast and poured a glass of milk, but then both ended up in the sink. At some point she dozed on the sofa in the den and woke at dawn to the sound of rain pattering lightly on the windows. She sat up, licking her dry lips. For one blessed moment, as she loosened the pins from her chignon and ran her fingers through her hair, she didn't remember, and then she did and the panic returned. It rushed out of her stomach and rose, burning, into her throat. She jerked up the cordless, dialed Lindsey's and then Nick's number. There wasn't even a ring now. She listened, but there was only the rain scratching at the window as if it meant to come in. How she would come to hate it, the sound of rain.

Her mother answered on the second ring. "Abby? Honey, is everything all right?"

"No, Mama." Abby sucked in her breath, almost undone by her mother's loving concern, and when she explained the situation her voice shook. "I'm going out there," she said.

"Abby, no!" Her mother's protest was sharp to the point of vehemence, but then she paused, gathered herself—Abby could see her making the effort—and went on in her more customary moderate fashion. "I don't imagine they're letting people through. It might be best to wait until the weather clears, hmm?"

"I can't just sit here, Mama."

"You'll have your cell phone?"

"Yes. I'll take the interstate to San Antonio where Lindsey said they spent Friday night, and if they aren't there, I'll drive to Boerne."

"And if they aren't in Boerne?"

"I don't know. I'll go on to Kate's, I guess."

Her mother didn't comment on her plan, that they both knew was pure folly. "Have you spoken to Jake?" she asked.

Abby said she hadn't, that she didn't want to worry him. "I'll call you, Mama, and Jake, too, if—when I find them."

It was pouring by the time Abby left the house, but she didn't encounter torrential rain until she was fifty miles east of San Antonio. That's when she began to see more cars and trucks and even semis take the exit ramps or pull onto the interstate's shoulders. But Abby did not pull over. She continued driving west on the main highway, the same way she was certain Nick would have gone. He would never take the scenic route; he was too impatient, and he certainly wouldn't fool around in weather like this. Lindsey had to have said something else.

Safer route? Easier route?

Why had they spent Friday night in San Antonio? Why would Nick pack the camping gear if he had no intention of camping? The questions shot like bullets through Abby's brain.

It's about Daddy....

Had Nick gotten sick? Abby's breath caught. Why hadn't she thought to call the hospitals? But she was fairly certain she'd heard properly when Lindsey said they were at a gas station. A Shell gas station. They could have had a flat tire or engine trouble. An accident? They could be marooned somewhere and unable to call. They could be almost anywhere. Abby searched the roadsides praying to be led to them, to see them, until her eyes burned with the effort. Until the rain grew so heavy the edges of the pavement were lost in road fog.

The lane markings disappeared. Her world was foreshortened to the few feet that were visible beyond the BMW's hood. How foolish she was to be out here. She thought of her mother, left behind to worry. Of Jake and his utter disbelief if he could see her. She thought how the joke would be on her if Nick and Lindsey were home now and she was the one lost.

By the time she reached Boerne, she was bent over the steering wheel, holding it in her white-knuckled grip. There were no other cars. She wanted to stop but couldn't think how. How would she navigate off a highway she wasn't sure existed? Every frame of reference was lost to the fog, the endless sheets of rain. Nothing stood out, not a building or a tree or the road's weed-choked verge. She might have been airborne for all she knew. She had to go on, to reach Kate, the ranch, higher ground. Abby thought maybe Nick had done that. In fact she began to believe it, that when she arrived there, she would find him and Lindsey safe, but when Kate's house finally came into view, her heart-soaring wave of anticipation fell almost immediately into confusion.

There were so many vehicles parked along the roadsides and in Kate's driveway, mostly pickup trucks with boats attached and SUVs. There were a few sheriffs' patrol cars, too, and a couple of ambulances. And incongruously, a helicopter sitting in the north pasture. Abby couldn't take her eyes off it or the dozens of people who were crowded onto Kate's porch. Exhausted-looking official types dressed in all kinds of rain gear with their hoods pushed off their heads, drinking coffee, talking into cell phones. The sense of urgency was palpable even at a distance. The scene was surreal, like something from a disaster movie. Abby felt heavy now with dread. She slowed, hunting for her Cherokee, praying to catch sight of it.

The BMW had barely come to a stop before Kate had the door open. "What are you doing here?" She hauled Abby from the driver's seat and searched her face, both of them heedless of the falling rain.

Abby shook her head, starting to cry from fear and exhaustion. She stammered that her family was missing. "You haven't seen them?"

"No. Oh, Abby." Getting the sense of it, Kate folded Abby into her arms, held her tightly and released her. "Come on," she said. "We're getting soaked."

They went up the front walkway and onto the porch. Kate made introductions as they worked their way through the throng. Abby met neighbors, a lot of them in uniforms, and quickly learned that because the ranch was high and dry, and maintained near-full electrical power from a built-in generator system, it made an ideal base for rescue operations. She was reassured that evacuations and search efforts were ongoing, but then someone mentioned the dozens of people who were missing.

Abby turned to the porch rail and braced herself.

"But not Nick," Kate said. "I'm sure he's found shelter somewhere." Kate brought Abby around, walked with her toward the kitchen door, keeping up a reassuring stream of chatter, and then George spotted them.

It was almost comical the way his astonished glance bounced from Abby to Kate, and once she explained what Abby was doing there, he said, "She needs to talk to Dennis."

"Dennis Henderson is the Bandera County sheriff and a good friend of ours," Kate told Abby.

And then Dennis was there, and once Kate introduced them, he took charge, putting his hand under Abby's elbow, guiding her into Kate's kitchen where it was warm and quiet. He sat Abby down and assured her he would do all he could to help her locate her family. By then, she was shivering, and he brought her a towel and a cup of hot coffee that Kate had generously laced with brandy.

Kate brought Abby a pair of dry tennis shoes and socks, and while she changed into them, the sheriff sat across from her and began asking a series of questions: Why did she think Nick and Lindsey had come this way? Did she know what route they'd taken? What was the reason for their trip? Could Abby describe what they were wearing when they left home?

She managed to give him the physical descriptions, but when it came to the rest, her eyes teared. She didn't know the answers. "I thought they were going to camp out, but they didn't. They spent Friday night in San Antonio. I don't know why." She clamped her lips together, chin trembling. She was horrified. How could she not know?

"Do you know what campground they were headed to?"

Abby shook her head, miserably. "There are several that we've gone to before, but I don't know where Nick made reservations. I didn't ask. How could I not ask?"

"It's all right," the sheriff said. He found a tissue and handed it to her.

She blew her nose and described Lindsey's phone call, saying she was almost positive Lindsey had said they were at a gas station. "A Shell gas station," Abby said, "in Boerne."

Sheriff Henderson seemed pleased with that; he said it gave him a place to start, and he did go there a few days later, once the water receded, and he spoke to the gas station attendant, a high school kid who remembered Lindsey. She was really cute, the kid said. She asked for the restroom key, but he'd gotten busy and couldn't recall whether she'd been the one to bring it back. But it was there, on its hook behind the cash register, so he guessed someone must have returned it. He told the sheriff he thought he saw the Jeep leave the station and head east on Highway 46. And like everyone else, he spoke of the rain. But then no one who was in the Hill Country would ever talk about that April weekend again and not mention the rain.

In the end twenty-six people would lose their lives,

many of them drowned, but many others were rescued. There was one story about a woman, a tourist, who folks heard had been taken out of the water near Bandera alive. Rescuers who treated her said it was a miracle she survived, that her injuries weren't more severe, then somehow, they lost track of her. No one seemed to know what became of her. Some began to wonder if she was real or the stuff of legend, one of those urban myths, but many continued to tell the story and to believe in it for the hope it brought them.

When Abby finally reached Jake, she had to grope for the words to explain, and once she found them, his reaction struck her as odd. Something in the way he said, "Oh, God," made her think for just a moment that he would say he'd known something awful was going to happen. But he didn't. "When did you last hear from them?" he asked.

Abby told him about Lindsey's call and what she thought Lindsey had said and her doubts about it, and her voice cracked.

"It's okay, Mom, I'm on my way. We'll find them."

Abby said, "No, Jake," and paused. Her eyes welled with tears at how calm he was, how he took such care to reassure her—as if he were the parent. "You can't get through," she said when she recovered her voice. "All the roads are washed out. Anyway, you have finals."

"I'm coming, Mom."

The line went dead in her hand. Phone service was still unreliable. She looked at Kate.

"What?"

"He says he's coming. What if he gets lost, too?"

The tears Abby had so far contained spilled over now. "Oh, God, Katie. Where are they?"

It was after nine o'clock on the night of Abby's arrival at the ranch, and she was on the porch alone when a woman wearing a yellow rain slicker approached her. The woman's blond hair was wet and plastered to her forehead and cheeks; she looked exhausted. She looked to Abby like one of the rescue workers, and when she asked if Abby was Mrs. Bennett, the wife of Nicholas Bennett, the attorney from Houston who was missing, Abby nodded and braced herself to hear the worst.

The woman gave her name, Nadine Betts, and said she was a reporter. She gave the call letters of a local television station, too, but Abby didn't catch them. She was terrified of what the reporter would say next.

"Your husband and daughter weren't out here camping, were they?"

Abby could only stare.

The woman inclined her head in a conspiratorial manner. "Look, it's just you and me here, okay? You can talk to me. You're meeting them later, right? Then at some point, your son will join you."

"I have no idea what you mean."

"Come on. You must realize how it looks, Mrs. Bennett," the reporter insisted. "Your husband goes missing within days of Adam Sandoval jumping bail?"

Abby frowned, nonplussed.

"The attorney for Helix Belle? The one they arrested for embezzling—"

"I know who he is," Abby said. Two years ago, Adam Sandoval had been on the legal team for Helix Belle Pharmaceutical when Nick's law firm had brought suit against them for distributing pediatric flu vaccine that had been tainted and caused the death of one child and irreparably damaged the hearts of a number of other children.

"Your husband worked with Sandoval," the reporter said.

"They were on opposite sides. Nick defended those children. He's the one who secured the settlement funds for them. He would have no reason to steal—"

"Oh, there are plenty of reasons, Mrs. Bennett. A half million of them. Surely you aren't going to tell me it's a coincidence that the cash, along with Sandoval and your husband, is missing."

"That's enough, Nadine."

Abby looked around and saw Dennis Henderson, and she was grateful for his support when he slipped his hand under her elbow.

He ordered the reporter off the porch, but she kept pace. "Sheriff, you know who Nick Bennett is. Will you keep looking for him and his daughter under the circumstances?"

"No comment." The sheriff ushered Abby through the door.

The reporter wedged her foot into the gap. "Come on, Dennis, I won't keep her long."

"Back off, Nadine," he said and managed to close the door.

"My husband had nothing to do with that money," Abby said. "He was cleared months ago. I can't imagine why that reporter is asking about that now."

"The San Antonio D.A. is concerned your husband's disappearance and Adam Sandoval's could be related."

"That's ridiculous."

The sheriff said, "Maybe." He set his hat on a nearby table and said, "We had a local boy, Tommy Carr, who got a dose of that bad vaccine. It put him in a wheelchair for the rest of his life. Folks in this part of the state are still pretty riled."

"We knew someone, too, who was injured," Abby said. "That's how Nick ended up representing the families of the victims, but I still don't see—"

"This is a small community. Everybody around here knows Tommy and his parents; they kept a close eye on the case. They celebrated when your husband got Helix to take responsibility. Nick Bennett got to be kind of a household name locally. What happened to Tommy was a tragedy, but it would have been a lot worse if your husband hadn't gone to bat for those kids. The money they were awarded is the only way their families could afford to care for them properly. Now all that is in jeopardy again."

"Not because of Nick. He didn't take that money. Call his law firm, if you don't believe me. Call the Houston police detectives who investigated. He hated what Adam—"

"But they were friends, weren't they? Outside the courtroom, I mean."

"Acquaintances. They knew each other in college. Adam called sometimes when he came to Houston, and he and Nick would go out for a beer. But Nick had no idea Adam was embezzling that money. I remember when he was arrested, Nick said he had financial problems. He and his wife were divorcing. He was going to have to pay a lot of alimony. He was desperate."

"Did you know Sandoval's wife? Did you socialize as couples?"

"Why are you giving me the third degree? My family's out there somewhere, they could be injured, they need your help!"

"There are a lot of folks missing, ma'am, and we need to be certain that we're using the resources we have to assist those whose need is genuine."

"What about my daughter? Do you suspect her, too?" Panic thinned Abby's voice.

The sheriff kept her gaze.

"You know something, don't you?" Abby's heart stumbled. "What is it? What have you found out?"

"Nothing. I'm just trying to figure out what direction they might have gone in."

"Abby? What's going on?" Kate came to Abby's side.

"He's asking me about Helix Belle."

"Why?" Kate asked the sheriff.

"I had a call from the San Antonio D.A.'s office. Obviously the local media got wind of it, since Nadine was here asking questions."

"Nadine Betts?" Kate rolled her eyes. "She's an idiot."

"A call about what? What does any of this have to do with Nick and my daughter?" Abby demanded.

"Sandoval, or a man resembling him, was caught on some surveillance tape on Tuesday outside a bank in San Antonio. He was with another man matching Nick's description," Dennis said.

"No," Abby said, shaking her head emphatically. "There's no way it could be Nick. He was in Houston, working. He was home for dinner that evening."

"You were with him at his office?" the sheriff asked.

"No, but I—"

"I think the drive between Houston and San Antonio is, what? Three, three and a half hours?"

"Dennis, you do realize this is ridiculous." Kate wasn't asking.

He rubbed a line between his eyebrows.

"This is just another ploy," Abby said. "Another way the Helix Belle legal team is trying to get the spotlight off themselves. It's what they did before. They tried to implicate Nick." She spoke strongly over the sound of Lindsey's voice that vied for her attention: *We spent last night in San Antonio,* Lindsey had said. *Dad says we're taking the scenic route.* But the two things, the possibility that Nick had been in San Antonio on Tuesday and again with Lindsey on Saturday, weren't related, Abby told herself. They couldn't be.

"I'm sorry to have to question you this way," the sheriff said, "but it's part of my job to look at all the angles."

Kate slipped her arm around Abby's shoulders. "I'm telling you, I've known the Bennetts a long time, Dennis. Nick may not be perfect, but he wouldn't take money from sick kids and run away with it, trust me."

"He wouldn't run away, period." Abby pulled free of Kate's grasp. "Not with my daughter. You can't stop looking for them. Please—" Her voice broke.

The sheriff stepped toward her; he kept her gaze and reassured her the search would continue. Abby had the sense that he was moved by her plea, that he meant to touch her. He was close enough that she could feel his warmth and smell the starch rising out of the damp creases of his uniform shirt. It was an odd moment, out of time, but Abby was comforted by it. And then it was over. He stepped back, recovering in an instant the aura of his authority, his natural suspicion. He was paid for that, Abby thought. He was a cop, after all, conducting a cop's business. Nevertheless she wanted to believe him, to believe it was kindness she saw in the gravity of his expression.

The sheriff apologized again. "It's procedure," he said. "Routine in these cases," he added.

"Routine?" Abby said. What about any of this was routine?

It was after midnight when Kate led Abby into her guest room and made her lie down.

"I won't sleep," Abby said.

"At least close your eyes." Kate pulled off Abby's borrowed tennis shoes and lifted her sock-clad feet onto the bed.

"I should call Mama and Louise."

"It's late. Why don't you just rest now?"

Abby looked at Kate. "I don't care what the sheriff thinks or that reporter. They're way off base."

Kate took Abby's hand. "But it would be so much more interesting if they weren't. Nadine especially would love it. The biggest thing she ever gets to report is when someone's cow gets loose. Now a celebrity is missing."

"Nick isn't a celebrity. Why do you say things about him like that? Why did you say that before, that he wasn't perfect? Why would you put it that way?"

Kate groaned softly. "I knew you were mad."

"I'm surprised you don't believe he robbed the settlement fund, too."

"Oh, Abby." Kate sounded hurt and half annoyed, and she had a right to be, but Abby wouldn't yield.

She rose on one elbow to peer hotly at Kate. "Maybe y*ou* know something about where Nick was going. Is that it? Do you?"

"I wish I did, but he'd never confide in me."

Abby fell back, crooking her elbows over her eyes. She felt sick with rage and the effort of steeling her nerves to take the next blow. She wondered if she would survive, if she was strong enough. "What if no one finds them, Katie?"

"Oh, Abby, don't. Don't go there."

How could she not go there? Not conjecture? What if Lindsey had been chattering a blue streak or complaining? What if Nick's attention had been drawn from the road? Abby started to see images and plastered her hands over her eyes, but the curtain in her mind rose in spite of her. She saw Nick, distracted, looking at Lindsey. A wider shot of the car picking up speed, sliding into a black, rain-slickened curve. Now, before Abby's horrified gaze, her Jeep slammed through a guardrail and flew for what seemed like forever before it plummeted, bounced end over end between canyon walls until finally it struck the bottom, where it sat with Nick and Lindsey dead inside it. By the time the SUV came to rest, it would have taken on the same contouring as the boulders it had fallen among. Boulders the color of iced champagne. The color of limestone baking in the sun. The same color as Abby's Jeep. It would blend in so beautifully with the rock that no one would ever see it, much less the treasure it contained.

Abby turned on her side, jerking on the sheet, cramming a corner of it into her mouth, and when the cry broke from her ribs, it wasn't louder than a whimper.

* * *

She woke later in a panic, unable to believe she'd slept, uncertain of where she was, and then the sound of the rain reminded her. It peppered the window in wind-driven gusts. Abby pressed her fingertips to her ears, and still she could hear it; its rattling insistence… the never-ending drops forming rivulets, the rivulets making streams, the streams combining into rivers. Rivers rising over their banks. Endless flooding and drowning and dripping and wet. Water sloshing everywhere. She lay staring at the ceiling. Why was she here safe and warm and dry, while her family was out there shivering and alone in the cold and the dark and—

But she couldn't do this, couldn't lie here with her mind spinning through the endless and terrifying loop of her own thoughts. Flinging aside the bedcovers, she got up. There was light coming from the great room, and she went toward it. A man was there, one of the paramedics she'd met earlier. Abby thought his name was Billy. Billy Clyde Coleman. He was sitting on the floor, eating a bowl of chili Kate had made earlier, and watching television. Abby imagined most everyone else was bedded down in the campers she'd seen parked everywhere or else in the bunkhouse. They'd get what rest they could before resuming the search effort at daybreak. But Billy was like her, Abby thought. He couldn't sleep. She started to speak, to make him aware of her presence, but then she heard her name, Bennett, and her eyes jerked to the TV screen.

Catching sight of her, the paramedic raised the remote, saying he would turn it off.

"No!" Abby said. "Please. She's talking about my family."

"—attorney from Houston along with his daughter are among the missing, and at this point they are presumed drowned."

"Oh!" The syllable popped from Abby's mouth, a near shriek. She clapped her hands there. The commentator went on. Abby's ears were ringing, but still she heard it. Heard the woman say the search effort for her family and the others had been downgraded. Now, rather than a rescue, what they hoped for was a recovery.

Of bodies, Abby thought. The commentator meant they hoped to recover the water-bloated remains of her husband and daughter. They would then return them to her for burial. And there was even more to be hoped for, according to the commentator. *Closure,* the woman said. Recovery of the bodies would give a measure of peace to the families and to the community that had suffered such a devastating loss.

Abby shook her head, no. She said, "No!" and repeated it, "Nonono."

Billy came and led her to the sofa. He settled her there and reminded her that the story was unverified. He tried to reassure her. He gave her one of his soda crackers; he brought her a glass of water. She looked straight at him now, at the smooth curve of his cheeks, his relatively unlined brow, and she thought how young he was, not much older than Jake, and she would always believe that was what kept her from weeping. The idea of Jake being put into this position where he would be called on to comfort some hysterical woman.

She drank a little of the water, set the glass down and wedged her trembling hands between her knees, resisting an urge to lay her head there, too. "I'm okay," she told Billy. "You should get some rest," she added.

He nodded and sat on the opposite end of the sofa, and he was still there an hour or so later when morning sunlight burst roughshod into the room, making Abby blink. Billy turned to her, looking astonished. "Am I dreaming?" he asked.

"Do you know who Adam Sandoval is?" she asked.

"The jerk who stole the money from those kids who got the bad vaccine? Yeah, who doesn't?"

"Did you know he was missing? Did they say anything about him when you were watching the news?"

Billy said no. He said he'd heard Adam jumped bail, that he might be somewhere in the area. Billy said, "If that's true, I hope he drowned."

Abby looked into her lap. She would not go there; she would not examine the connection her mind was trying to make between Adam's disappearance and Nick's. There was nothing there. Nothing. Nick wouldn't endanger Lindsey in that way. He couldn't.

"It should get easier now," Billy said.

"Easier?"

"The rescue effort, you know, the work should go faster now that the worst is over." He reddened. "I meant the rain, that it's stopped."

Abby knew what he meant, and she managed a smile. She wouldn't tell him what she thought, that the worst wouldn't be over until her family was found.

CHAPTER

3

It was one of those perfect spring days: a breeze fiddled along under a blue umbrella sky while the sun rose, a butter-yellow balloon above the sodden earth. It was the picture of innocence, a child's crayon drawing. Not one vestige remained of the horrible rain Abby had driven through to get here, and it disconcerted and infuriated her…this weather that lay on her like a blessing, that wouldn't hurt a fly, that would take nothing from anyone. She felt mocked by it. She paced the length of Kate's porch feeling she was the brunt of its joke. An awful noise began to build inside her, and when it pushed into her throat, she bit down hard against it, went back into the house and found Kate in the kitchen. "I have to call Louise," she said. "I can't put it off any longer."

"I can do it, if you want." Kate switched on the coffeemaker. She'd dragged out the big one, the fortycupper that she and George used during roundup or rodeo days when they fed and coffee'd dozens of ranch hands, men who bunked with them, who loved to cowboy. Now a lot of those same men were here in a far different capacity, and Abby was so grateful for their presence. As long as they stayed, there was activity and there was hope.

She opened the dishwasher and began unloading the clean dishes. "As much as I dread it, I should be the one to tell her that her son and granddaughter are missing."

"I'll sit with you then."

"I'm worried she's alone. I wish I knew a friend to call for her, who could be with her. She'll be devastated."

Kate stowed the glasses Abby handed her in the cabinet. "Won't her housekeeper be there? Maybe she'll answer. It might help to soften the news."

But it wasn't Louise's housekeeper who answered Abby's call. It was Louise herself.

"There must be more that can be done," she said through her tears. "You aren't thinking clearly, Abby. Of course, you aren't." Louise blew her nose, and Abby heard the jangle of her bracelets. "I'm coming there."

"No, Louise, you can't."

"What? Of course, I can. For heaven's sake, I'm Nicholas's mother. I'm Lindsey's grandmother."

"I know, but the roads are still closed. They're asking people to stay—"

"I'll fly then. It will be quicker in any case. You can pick me up in Austin or San Antonio."

"The airports are closed, too, Louise. I'm so sorry." Abby meant it. She and Louise had never had an easy relationship, but that didn't seem to matter now. "I'll call you as soon as I know anything. I promise."

"What is going to happen to me?" Louise asked after an uncertain silence.

Abby closed her eyes. It was no surprise really that even now Louise would be most concerned for her own welfare. "Consuelo is there, isn't she? Can she stay with you?"

"Yes, but I mean if Nick is— If he's—"

But Abby wouldn't allow Louise to say it. "They'll find them," she said, and she believed it with all her heart.

Jake didn't make it to the ranch until late on Wednesday, three days after the rain stopped. By then much of the power in the area had been restored, and most of the primary roads and highways were open. Abby saw him from the porch and went down the steps to meet him, and once he was out of his car, she hugged him to her, fiercely, and he allowed it.

"Anything?" He stepped out of her embrace, looked anxiously down into her face.

She shook her head and, reaching up, traced her fingertips across his brow. Although he had her paler coloring, he had Nick's dark hair, and he was as tall as Nick and as broad-shouldered. In fact, Jake's resemblance to his dad had never been clearer to her than it was now, and somehow it hurt her even as it pleased and relieved her. She said, "The helicopter's gone up several times, but there's no sign of them or the Jeep."

Abby had asked the search and rescue pilots to take her up with them. She said she would have a better chance of spotting the Cherokee from the air than they would—it was her car, after all—but they refused, politely. Still, she was hopeful. She thought they would keep going, keep trying, and she was dumbfounded when a few days after Jake's arrival, they packed up and left as if their job was done. Jake was angry. He asked to borrow George's pickup to continue the effort on his own.

"I'll take you," George said. "That way you can look while I drive. We'll go until you want to stop."

Kate said she would drive Abby into town, and they went along slowly, giving Abby ample time to examine the roadsides. Kate's kindness, and George's, their patience with Abby and Jake, moved Abby to tears. She tried to thank Kate, and when she couldn't, Kate took her hand. She knew. She said, "It's all right."

They arrived in Bandera and joined an uneasy crowd gathered on Main Street, where it looked down toward Highway 16, and they stared in dumb amazement at the Medina River still pouring itself out of its banks and over the highway intersection.

A week went by and then another, and the earth baked and dried under a heedless sun and gave them nothing. Abby would never remember much about that time, the losing-hope time is how she would come to think of it. She couldn't look at Jake; she couldn't meet her own eyes in the mirror. She didn't want to know what their sort of despair looked like.

Kate brought it up, though, one day as they were driving back to the ranch after yet another fruitless roadside search. She touched Abby's knee and said, "You know I love you, chickie, right? That I would only ever want what's best for you—you and Jake."

Abby's stomach knotted. *But.* Abby heard Kate's but. And that meant advice was coming, or else Kate would treat Abby to the awful revelation she lived in constant dread of receiving. But it was neither of those things. Instead Kate said she was worried about Jake, worried how long he and Abby could keep it up.

"The search, you mean?" Abby's comprehension was as swift as her sense of offense. "I guess as long as it takes, but I understand if you're tired of it, of us."

"No! Abby, that isn't what I meant at all. It's just it's so hard on you and Jake, going through this day after day. You don't know how long—I'm just saying, it's been almost three weeks. You aren't working now, but Jake has school. Maybe he should go back, try to put some routine back into his life. Please say you aren't mad."

"I'm not." Abby sighed and wiped her face. "I know you're right."

"Oh, Abby." Kate reached for Abby's hand, and when she met Abby's glance, her eyes were brimming.

Jake argued at first. He didn't care about school; he didn't care if he lost the semester. He lay on the sofa in Kate and George's study, his big feet hanging off the end, and said, "I can't concentrate anyway."

"But there's nothing you can do here," Abby said. "Wait, that's all."

Jake sat up. "I told Dad the weather was going to be bad."

"You did?" Abby sat at George's desk. "I did, too. Don't blame him, okay?"

"I wish I'd gone with them."

"Oh, no, Jake. Thank God, you didn't. Why would you say that?"

"If I had, maybe this wouldn't have happened."

"What do you mean?" Abby looked closely at him, feeling somehow alarmed.

"Nothing," he said. "I don't know." He ran his hands down his thighs. "I should have—"

"Should have what?" she prompted sharply.

But Jake either wouldn't explain, or he couldn't. "Nothing," he repeated, and he lay back, folding his elbow over his eyes. He said she was right, that he should get back to campus. "I'll go tomorrow, okay?"

"Okay," Abby answered, but it was too easy. There should have been more of an argument, and somehow the lack of one provoked her into pushing him. "Jake? If you know something—"

"Like what would I know?" He lifted his arm to frown at her.

"What did Dad tell you about the trip? Did he give you a special reason he wanted to go?"

"He just said he wanted me and Linds to go camping on the Guadalupe; he wanted us to hang out and fish like we used to. He said stuff like he knew he hadn't always been the greatest dad. I thought it was weird, if you want to know."

"Weird?"

"It was like he was apologizing. I thought maybe he was trying to make up for ragging on me about law school and for missing freshman orientation."

"He had to be in court that day."

"Come on, Mom. You and I both know if I had signed up for pre-law, Dad would have found someone to cover for him. He would have made it to orientation; he would've broken his neck."

"He was disappointed, that's all." Abby kept Jake's gaze.

"What?"

She hesitated and then against her better judgment said what she was thinking, that sometimes she wondered why Nick was so adamant for Jake to go to law school in the first place. "It's not as if he's always been thrilled with that career himself."

"Yeah," Jake said. "I noticed."

Of course he'd noticed; children were notorious for their perception of their parents. It was foolish to think you could hide much of anything from them.

"Dad was pretty pumped about being a lawyer when he won all that money for those little kids. Remember? He nailed those guys; he put them down. His closing argument—" Jake paused.

"He was great, wasn't he?" Abby said softly.

"Yeah."

Jake and Abby had attended the final day of the trial. It had been Jake's idea. Somehow he'd sensed Nick needed them to be there. Jake had divined—when Abby had not—the extent to which Nick was invested emotionally in winning for those damaged children. In spite of their differences, Abby knew Nick and Jake shared a bond, they understood each other. She remembered in the wake of the trial, Nick had walked on air, and Jake had thought maybe law school wasn't such a bad idea after all. But all that had gone sour last fall when an audit turned up the awful fact that a huge chunk of the settlement money was missing, and Helix Belle had, in an effort to divert attention from themselves, accused Nick of embezzlement.

But he hadn't been himself even after he was cleared, Abby thought. The day he and Lindsey had left, there had been that hurtful moment when she embraced him. *"Don't,"* he had said.

"It isn't Dad on that surveillance tape," Jake said.

Abby wished she could be as certain.

They had looked at it a few days ago. Dennis had driven them to San Antonio and accompanied them into the D.A.'s office. The quality of the film was as poor as everyone had said. The images of the two men had been grainy and distorted, their movements jerky, like puppets on strings. The detective in charge of the case had pointed out that the fair-haired man on the left was the one they had tentatively identified as Adam. Abby had focused on the dark-haired man on the right. She'd asked to have the video replayed twice and watched the man's gestures; she'd studied his posture, the tilt of his chin, convinced she would be able to identify whether or not it was Nick from these small details. But she had not been sure, not beyond the shadow of a doubt, and she'd felt sick inside. She'd felt as if she had failed Nick in a vital and substantial way. And not only Nick, but Jake, too.

"Mom?"

Abby looked up. "I'm sure you're right, Jake. It's not Dad. It couldn't be." She offered reassurance she didn't feel, but Jake took it.

He propped himself on his elbow and said, "He risked everything when he took on that case, you know? He was like a man on fire. His partners would have cut him loose, if he'd lost. He said so himself."

It was true. Nick had said that. Taking on contingency cases like Helix Belle was the same as gambling. You could lose as easily as you could win, and the loss might not be limited to money. It might cost an attorney his reputation, his profession. Abby didn't like gambling. Nick knew that; he chafed against her more cautious nature. But there were their children to care for, always their children who had to be considered. That's what she pointed out to him. That was the authority she invoked.

Jake said, "I asked him once how come he did it, how come he took that case when he never did anything that crazy before, not with his work."

"What did he say?"

"That you can wait too long to figure out what really matters in your life."

Abby tried to sort that out, to make it fit with what she knew about Nick or what she thought she knew.

"Am I supposed to know what that means?" Jake was as mystified as she was.

"You didn't ask him?"

"Why? He just would have started preaching about law school like he always does. How should I know? He's your husband."

Jake made it sound as if he blamed her, Abby thought. For what? Marrying Nick? For failing to convince him that Jake's refusal to attend law school wasn't the end of the world? She considered telling Jake that her and Nick's harshest arguments were about him and Lindsey, but she didn't want to go into it. Abby hugged her elbows. She felt as though the boundaries that defined their roles, hers as the parent and Jake's as the child, were already disintegrating, and it dismayed her.

Jake flipped onto his belly. "I'm really tired. If I'm driving back to College Station tomorrow, I better get some sleep."

But the following morning when they said goodbye, it didn't look to Abby as if he'd slept much at all. He tossed his gear into the backseat of his Mustang. It was vintage, an original 1965 model that he and Nick had painstakingly restored. They'd only finished the project last year, and Abby was still sorry it was over, despite having to fight the grease and the constant sound of tinkering at all hours. She'd loved seeing their heads bent under the hood so close they were almost touching. The occasional rumbles of laughter, even the shouted curses had pleased her.

"I don't want to go," Jake said when he straightened, and Abby was unhinged at the look on his face. She saw the child he'd been, helpless and bewildered beyond explanation.

She said, "I know," and stopped to find her composure, "but you heard Sheriff Henderson; he's not giving up. The search just isn't official anymore. We have to keep the faith ourselves, that's all."

"You'll call?"

"The second I hear anything."

Jake looked off, blinking.

She took his hand, then put her arms around him. "You should get going, okay? It's best for you." She held him at arm's length. "Can you imagine what your sister will say if you blow your freshman year? You'll never hear the end of it."

Jake scoured his eyes with the heels of his hands. "She always has to have the last word, doesn't she?"

Abby nodded, mouth trembling.

"I'd flunk out right now just to hear her."

"Go," Abby said.

And Jake did. And it was only after he disappeared from view that she sank to her knees and cried.

When Louise called Abby on her cell phone the following afternoon, she was alone. Kate was gone to the grocery store, and George was out helping a road crew with repairs. In her old life before the flood— BTF—Abby might have let the call slide to her voice mail. She and Louise had never been close. Louise had seen to it. She'd made it clear from the moment Nick introduced them, that she didn't think Abby was good enough for her son. Louise had never said it to Abby's face, but the sense of Louise's disdain was implicit. Abby had long ago given up on the notion that Louise would change, that they would someday be friends, but now that they shared this terrible catastrophe, Abby felt her heart reaching for Louise. They needed each other, Abby thought. They would help each other.

"Where are you?" Louise asked, and Abby was shaken at how frail she sounded.

She answered that she was still at Kate's. "I keep thinking any day we'll get word, something concrete."

"Lindsey and I were supposed to go to New York this summer." Louise's voice caught on her tears. "I was going to get tickets for the theater. We were going to tour the museums, shop Fifth Avenue."

"I know." Abby went through the house onto the deck. It had aggravated her when Louise had planned the trip with Lindsey as a gift for her upcoming six-teenth birthday. Louise had done nothing so special when Jake turned sixteen. Even for high school grad-uation, he had only merited a small television from Nick's mother. So many times, Abby had wanted to ask her: Do you think the children don't notice how dif-ferently you treat them? But Nick said Louise couldn't help herself, that she had always wanted a daughter, and Abby's compassion for him, for the sore ground of his childhood, had kept her silent.

"How did this happen? Why did it?" Louise de-manded, and she was fuming now and shrill. Abby's heart retreated. Louise would cling to her anger, her sense of offense even in the face of these horrific cir-cumstances. Abby murmured something that was meant to placate, to comfort.

But Louise was beyond that point. "I can't stand it. I'm telling you, Abby, I can't! And as if it isn't enough that my son and granddaughter drowned in that hor-rible flood, poor Nick's name is being slandered again all over the television news. You've heard, I know you must have heard, from that reporter, that odious Na-dine Betts."

"She's contacted you?"

"Oh, yes. She acts as if we're friends." Louise huffed. "As if I would tell that woman or any one of her kind anything."

"You haven't—?"

"No. I might be old, but my brain still works, thank you very much." Louise was offended, but then, she often was. "She's determined to believe that I know Adam Sandoval. She tried to tell me that I'd met him while he and Nick were in school together, as if she could know. I don't see what difference it makes if that were true. I told her my son would never under any circumstances have involved himself with a crook. Nicky was a good man, an honest man, God rest his soul."

"He still is, Louise," Abby said, and she was more curt than she intended to be, but she had so wanted Louise's support to counter her own fear and uncertainty.

"I'll be relieved when this is over, won't you? When we can arrange for a proper burial." Louise went on as if she hadn't heard Abby. "We won't have a moment's peace until then, Abby. Do you know that? Those media ghouls won't leave us alone; they won't allow us to move on, if it's even possible after a thing like this."

"Move on?" Abby straightened. "From what? We don't even know what happened, Louise. I'm not sure anymore why Nick came out here. He and Lindsey spent Friday night in San Antonio for some reason. You don't know why, do you?"

"I know he made the trip to give you time to yourself. He was always talking about how much you treasured having time to yourself."

"He told you that?" Tears thickened in Abby's throat. *Time to herself.* How could she have ever wished for it?

"Yes. Not that he had to. Anyone with eyes could see—"

"You blame me, is that it? You think it's my fault Nick came here."

Louise began an answer, but Abby cut her off. "That's fine, Louise. You're free to think whatever you like, but as you have often pointed out to me, your son has a mind of his own. I couldn't have stopped him if

I'd begged." *Unless I'd never been born*, Abby thought. *Unless I'd never met Nick, never married him.* She half expected Louise to say these things.

But Louise was backing down. She said she was sorry. She said, "You and Jake are all I have left."

But Abby said, "No, we're going to find them, Louise. You'll see." And she wondered when she hung up how Nick's own mother could have so little faith. If it were Jake, Abby thought, she would never give up searching. She would never stop until she knew exactly what had happened to him.

CHAPTER

4

Abby and Kate spent a portion of every day searching the area around the ranch, or they chose a section near one of the rural county roads that seemed to meander in every direction. Abby knew it was complete folly, and she hated that she felt compelled to do it, that she couldn't stop herself. Kate went, too, every time, and when Abby struggled to put into words what it meant to her, Kate hugged her and shushed her and said, "It's all right," or "Never mind," or "You'd do the same for me."

One day, after searching a shallow gorge, they were coming back to the car—they'd driven Nick's BMW that day—and they caught Nadine Betts looking inside it.

"I don't believe it," Abby said to Kate.

"I do," Kate answered.

"What are you doing?" Abby shouted, quickening her steps.

The reporter jumped back. "I was just passing by," she said as if anyone would find that believable. "I saw the car and thought there'd been an accident, that you might need help."

"Oh, right." Abby shot Kate a look.

"But now that we've met up this way—" the reporter ignored Abby's sarcasm "—exactly what are you doing out here, Mrs. Bennett?"

"Do you have nothing better to do than to follow me around?" Abby demanded. "Do you think if you spy on me long enough, I'll do something that's, what— newsworthy? Incriminating?"

Kate said, "Really, Nadine. You need to find another story. Isn't it bingo night at the Knights of Columbus? Didn't I hear that Pratt Street United Methodist Church is having a pancake supper?"

"Very funny," Nadine said. "What have you heard from your husband, Mrs. Bennett?"

"Leave me and my family alone, and that includes my mother-in-law." Abby brushed by the reporter and got into the car. Kate did the same.

"Will she ever give up?" Abby looked in the rearview as she drove away. Nadine was still there, standing inside the open door of her car, watching them.

"She just wants a story, a headline. Her ticket to the big leagues, I guess."

"Maybe," Abby said, but she thought there was more to it, that Nadine's interest was more personal, and it scared her.

On what turned out to be Abby's last afternoon at Kate's, Dennis dropped by. Kate saw him and Abby into the living room, and after she had served coffee, she excused herself and left them sitting on opposite ends of her cream-colored leather sectional. Abby was nervous. She didn't know what to say.

After a moment, Dennis sat forward. His hands were strong, long-fingered and graceful, and he held them in a loose clasp between his knees. He was dressed in jeans and a blue work shirt with the sleeves rolled to his elbows.

She said, "I've never seen you out of uniform."

"I was ordered to take the day off," he said.

"My daughter and my husband have been missing nearly a month," she said.

Dennis's gaze was intent, gentle. "It's possible we'll never find them."

Abby pressed her lips together, feeling heat gather in the front of her skull.

"It was some thirty-plus inches of rain in two days. We lost nearly all the crossings and a lot of the bridges on most of the major roads. There's a lot of wild country, a lot of canyons and gorges. There were rock slides, places where the entire cliff face came down. We've got secondary roads buried under rubble or torn up by the water from one end of a three-county area to the other. Every river flowed out of its banks, and when you get that kind of water raging that way, it gets a hold on things—cars, houses, trees, what-have-you—and it takes them wherever it wants."

Dennis spoke of the water as if it were conscious, as if it had mind and will, a brain. "There's a lot of ground to cover, miles and miles crisscrossed by rivers and streams and creeks, and frankly, there's just a whole lot of it that's not accessible at all, not even on a good day."

Abby studied the pattern of veins on the backs of Dennis's hands, the cording of blue that traced the pale flesh inside one wrist and disappeared into the crook of an elbow, a sprinkling of freckles on his forearms. She looked at his kind face, his hazel eyes. The delicate netting of lines at the corners suggested exposure to sun and laughter. He didn't like having to tell her these things, having to prepare her for the worst. He hadn't liked questioning her in the first hours after her arrival here. She was sorry for him.

He pushed his untouched mug of coffee a little farther toward the center of the coffee table and continued. "Let's say they were on Highway 46 like the attendant at the Shell station said, but they got off for some reason, took one of the ranch roads, by accident maybe, and we don't know that, but if they did, then— Well, there's no telling. Now there are still crews out, clearing and repairing, and so forth. They'll be at it for weeks so it's possible they could come across something, you know?"

She nodded.

"I just don't want to give you false hope."

She thought of saying she would settle for any kind of hope, false or otherwise.

He shifted his elbows off his knees and straightened, looking uncomfortable, and as if he could read her anxiety, he spoke quickly. "It's like I've said before, it would be really helpful if I knew what your husband had in mind coming out here, or where he was headed after he left Boerne, assuming that *was* your Cherokee the kid saw leaving the gas station."

It would be helpful if you *knew?* The retort rose like acid. It brought Abby to her feet. She went to the wall of glass and looked out, seeking relief in the view. The scene was as still, as quiet and lovely as a painting. Even the water was undisturbed by all but the faintest tracing of ripples. It was impossible to imagine that it had ever flung itself over its banks and run amok across ground that wasn't its own. Nature was so full of cruel tricks.

She wondered how she could take on the mystery that the water had left behind, the one Dennis seemed to think she should be able to resolve. He kept asking her questions, all manner of questions, to which she had no answers. What must he think of a wife who didn't know her husband's destination, a mother who would let her daughter leave home without knowing exactly where her father was taking her? *You can make a lot of mistakes in your life trying to figure out what matters.* Nick's line to Jake passed through Abby's mind. What mistakes?

She turned to face Dennis. "We've been over this a dozen times."

"I know, but it's always possible you'll remember something new. So, you mentioned that you and your husband had talked of retiring out here. Could he have been looking at land?"

"No. We couldn't possibly afford to buy property right now." Abby thrust up her hands. "We have two children, one in college, another one on her way there. There's the mortgage, car payments. Nick just bought a new BMW. He's crazy about cars, so is my son."

"He was worried about finances, then."

"I've told you, not more than the average husband and father." Exasperated, Abby crossed her arms. "Did you talk to Joe Drexler, Nick's law partner? Did he tell you how unfounded those allegations are about the settlement money?"

"He confirmed what you said. Helix Belle's legal team is trying to muddy the water, which is what I figured. It's just—" Dennis stopped as if to consider.

"Just what?" Abby prompted.

Dennis met her glance. "Can you think of anyone who might have had a reason to follow your husband? Maybe an associate or one of your husband's clients? Someone who could have had a grudge or just wanted to talk with him? Outside the office, so to speak."

"Why are you asking me that? The firm does mostly civil litigation. Even Nick would say it's boring, not that it doesn't get stressful at times. Some clients can be very—" Abby broke off, looking at the tag end of a memory…a discussion from a few weeks ago, a heated discussion she'd had with Nick about his hours. He'd brought up a client then, a woman who was being difficult about some real-estate matter Nick hadn't adequately represented her interests in or something. Abby hadn't listened really. She frowned now, hunting in her mind for a place where Nick might have mentioned the woman again, not finding it. Why hadn't she paid closer attention? It seemed as if she'd let so many things, little telling details, slip by her.

"You remember something?" Dennis asked.

Abby shook her head. Why go into it? She had no facts, not even a name. "Nick's had his share of difficult clients, but nothing out of the ordinary. He would have told me. We don't keep secrets from each other." *That I know of…*

The words hung unspoken.

* * *

The morning following Dennis's visit, Abby showered and dressed in her own clothes, the ones she'd arrived in. She stowed her toothbrush and the assorted toiletries and underwear she'd purchased in a grocery sack, then changed the sheets on the guest-room bed. She was folding back the coverlet when Kate appeared in the doorway.

"What are you doing?" she asked.

"I have to go," Abby said, gathering the bed linen and the small pile of dirty clothes she'd borrowed from Kate into her arms.

"Go where?" Kate followed Abby through the kitchen into the laundry room.

"Home," Abby answered.

"You can't stay by yourself," George said from where he was sitting in the kitchen having toast and reading the morning newspaper. Abby noticed the headline concerned the cost of the flood damage. Three quarters of a billion dollars so far, it read. Did that figure include the loss of her family, she wondered. Could a dollar amount be put on that?

"It's too soon," Kate said. "We want you here, where we can keep an eye on you."

"I have to go home sometime," Abby said. "I don't like leaving Mama on her own for so long, and there are the horses. My neighbor, Charlie Wister, has been looking after them for me, but I can't expect him to keep feeding them forever."

George and Kate eyed her worriedly.

"Come on, guys. I'll be fine." She made herself smile. "I'm ready. As ready as I'll ever be."

It wasn't true. In fact, she was afraid of going home,

of being alone. *For the rest of your life?* asked a horrified voice in her mind. But there was another voice in her mind, too, a louder one, that kept asking questions, such as what if Nick and Lindsey had amnesia and somehow recovered and went home, and no one was there? What if they didn't remember her cell number and called the home number and no one answered? What if they were already there and Abby was the one missing?

She was convinced, and rationality had nothing to do with it, that if only she were home everything would fall into place. Nick and Lindsey would arrive there, too. Their survival would make headline news. Someone from *Primetime* or *48 Hours* would call to do the story. Even Nadine Betts would say it was a miracle.

But when Abby returned, her house was deserted, the same as the day she'd left it, and Kate was right. It was too soon. Abby wouldn't last a month on her own.

CHAPTER
5

Ordinarily Abby loved coming home, especially in the spring. Every curve of asphalt that led to the house was lavishly dressed in frilled masses of azaleas and camellias under a higher canopy of dogwood and redbud trees. There were drifts of daffodils, too, mixed with oxalis and wild sweet violets. She and Nick had planned the approach to the house deliberately in a way that would cause a driver to slow and take time to admire the view, but turning onto her street now, her stomach was in knots even as her head filled with ruthless, foolish hope.

But the moment she caught sight of the driveway, her heart collapsed into despair. It was a mess, buried under layers of debris, the obvious effects of a storm. She went slowly toward the house, wincing at the sound as the tires crunched over downed thickets of leaf-clotted limbs. Who was going to clean it up? Who was here but her? And what about the rest of it? There were three acres to mind, plus the house, plus the horses and the barn.

Abby set her foot on the brake. She studied the house, noting the pale square of light that glowed from the dining room, and above that, on the second floor, the window that looked into her and Nick's bedroom was cracked open. She didn't recall leaving a light on or a window open when she'd left for the Hill Country, but she must have. No one else had been here since the flood. Not even Jake. When she parked around back and got out, a horse nickered softly. Miss Havisham? Abby's throat closed. She wanted to leave but pushed herself across the driveway toward the back porch, noting the loosened handrail lying where she'd left it on the steps and her Wellies, caked with manure, sitting in the corner where she'd discarded them. She opened the door, and the acrid stench of mildew hit her—from the load of jeans she'd tossed into the washer on Saturday in the half hour before she'd sat down to look at the seed catalogue. In the waning moments of her ordinary life.

The phone rang, breaking the silence, startling her, and she ran to answer it, grabbing it up as if it were her lifeline. "Hello!?"

"Abby?"

"Katie!" Of course it wasn't Lindsey or Nick.

"Are you okay? Is it okay, being there?"

"It's weird."

"Weird, how?"

Abby looked around, unsure how to answer. She passed her glance over the familiar surroundings that no longer felt familiar, that somehow seemed to accuse her: Lindsey's basketball game schedule and Jake's class schedule pinned to the refrigerator, the dish towel hanging askew on the oven door handle. Her dishes in the sink, the seed catalogue open on the table. She looked at the *Texas Highways* calendar over her desk. The picture was of bluebonnets, the month showing was April.

Last month. *BTF*, she thought.

"Abby?" Kate prompted.

"It's fine. I'm fine." She hugged herself, suppressing a shiver.

"Louise called here looking for you. She said you aren't answering your cell."

"She keeps pressing me about having a memorial service." Abby let her fingertips fall onto the pages of her notebook open on the desktop, where she sometimes wrote her to-do list, or her thoughts, or perhaps a bit of silly poetry. There was a line written there from last month: *The first bluebonnets have opened,* she had jotted. *The ground under the oak trees in back is saturated in blue. A pool of blue.*

"Abby?"

"She thinks I'm not handling the situation properly, that I'm not facing facts." Abby closed the notebook.

"You need time, that's all. Listen, I had to tell her you were on your way home."

"Well, she was bound to know sooner or later."

"Just so you know, she told me if you don't answer her calls pretty soon, she's coming there."

Abby closed her eyes and thought how calamity changed everything, how it shifted an entire landscape, a whole solar system that had once been orderly and well-loved, into something that was dark and cold and even sinister. And she realized she was angry about this, and the anger was foreign to her and it filled her with foreboding.

"Abby? I'm here if you need me. You call me day or night. I don't care what time it is."

"Okay," Abby said. "Thank you," she added and clenched her jaw to stop the wretched tears.

"Remember to eat."

"I will."

"Promise me."

"I promise."

"I don't want to let you go, chickie." Kate sounded forlorn.

"Well, you have to. I have mildewy jeans in the washer and I'm going to pass out from the smell."

"Vinegar," Kate said. "Wash them in vinegar and then hang them in the sun to dry."

The sun, Abby thought. She hated the sun almost as much as she hated the rain.

But she washed the jeans using vinegar as Kate instructed and hung them outside to dry. She called Charlie next door and thanked him for tending the horses and mowing the grass. She checked on her mother. There was more of everything she could have done, but she couldn't focus, couldn't organize herself, couldn't think of anything other than Nick and Lindsey. That they weren't home, with her. How could it be? Her bones, her teeth, the sockets of her eyes ached with her need for them, her need to know they were safe.

The following afternoon she went upstairs intending to tidy up, gather the rest of the laundry, but then she didn't get any farther than the doorway of Lindsey's bedroom. Her pink-and-white eyelet bedroom. Too pink, Lindsey had said not long ago. She had wanted to paint it. Yellow? Abby seemed to recall something about yellow. And sunflowers; Lindsey had mentioned sunflowers, but when she'd asked her dad, he had said they didn't have money to redecorate a room she'd be leaving in just a couple of years when she went off to college. Abby had been surprised. Nick almost never said no to Lindsey. He was easier on her than on Jake. Abby had worried about it. It had been a sore subject between her and Nick, one they had argued about on a regular basis.

It seemed to Abby now, in retrospect, that they had argued more frequently in the weeks leading up to the flood. There had been that night in March or maybe early April…he'd had a dinner meeting in Houston with a client and he'd come home late, been wound up and irritable. She'd been in the laundry room folding a load of clothes from the dryer, and he'd come to the doorway to greet her. She saw him there in her mind's eye, staring in at her, gripping his briefcase, looking rumpled and worn out in his suit, tie hanging askew.

"What's wrong?" It had been the first thing out of her mouth. But what other question do you ask when your husband comes home from work looking wrecked?

"Nothing," he'd said. Abby remembered his kiss, dry as an afterthought.

She should have let it go; instead she'd made the mistake of saying it was the third night in a week he'd missed dinner. She hadn't meant anything other than she missed him, missed sitting down to dinner together, but he'd treated it like an attack.

"Do you think I like working my ass off?" he'd demanded. "How else do you think we're going to pay for all of this?" He'd gone on, enumerating their expenses, lumping in the prospect of Lindsey's college tuition.

"She could get a scholarship to play basketball somewhere. Everyone seems to think she'll only get better," Abby had said, following him into their bathroom.

He had yanked off his tie.

Abby leaned against the door frame of Lindsey's bedroom now, seeing it, the way Nick had yanked his tie as if it were a noose around his neck. She remembered the sinking feeling it had given her. He'd looked so tired that night. So—*defeated.* The word rose in her mind. The way he'd looked had made her want to go to him and say, Please, can we drop this? Can we just go to bed? Just lie down and hold each other? But she hadn't said anything. She didn't know why. She remembered that she'd finished cleaning her face, gone to the wastebasket, dropped in the used cotton pad and paused there, hardly listening to the rest of Nick's rant, somehow losing herself in a dream of smoothing the soft skin beneath his eyes, trailing her fingertips over his lips, watching his mouth curl in that slow, sweet smile.

She'd been thinking of the dimple in his left cheek when he'd said her name—

"Abby!"

She'd turned to meet his gaze in the mirror.

"Did you hear me?" He'd sounded so annoyed.

No, she'd wanted to say.

"I said you can't count on Lindsey getting a scholarship. They're not even out of preseason this year and she's already sprained her ankle."

"Slightly. It's not a bad injury."

"This time. But the rest of those girls are gorillas compared to her. Look at Samantha." Nick had brought up Lindsey's best friend. "Twenty pounds overweight, at least. She's a hog."

"Nicholas! That's a terrible thing to say."

He'd brushed his teeth, wiped his face with a towel.

"What is it with you?" she'd asked, and when he'd answered, "Nothing," when he'd said, "Work," or whatever excuse he'd offered, Abby had accepted it and his apology. Because he had apologized, she remembered that now, too. He'd embraced her and balanced his chin on the crown of her head. She was just the right height for it. She used to tease him that she wasn't a chin rest. But not that night. That night he'd been in a mood.

"It's my job to take care of this family," he had said and stopped. Even his heart beneath Abby's ear had seemed to stop, and when she'd looked up at him, when she'd asked, "What is it?" he'd said he didn't know how to explain it. He'd said, "I've made mistakes."

"Everyone has," she'd said.

"Yeah, but— Look, there's this woman, a sort of client, former client, I should say. She thinks I mishandled her interests in some real-estate dealings. She's made some threats."

"Threats?"

He'd shaken his head, looking chagrined. "Never mind. I don't know why I brought it up. She's just some nutcase. It's nothing."

"Are you sure? You sound worried."

"Nah." He'd bent to kiss her, then pulling her close, he'd rested his chin atop her head again. "I mean, yeah, I do worry sometimes. What if I'm not around when you or Lindsey or Jake needs something?"

Abby had been unnerved by that. There'd been an underscore of disquiet in his tone. Or was she remembering it that way because she was desperate for an explanation? Her mind seemed full of tricks. What had she said in response? Something like, "Of course you'll be around," or, "You're just exhausted." Or maybe she'd said, "You'll work it out." It would have been something stupid like that. What was wrong with her? Why hadn't she pushed him, demanded he give her the details, the woman's name at least? But worse: Why hadn't Nick confided in her? Why had he put her off?

Abby pressed her fingertips to her eyes, swept with the hard longing to have that time back. It seemed somehow vital that she understand it. She had the sense that Nick had been trying to tell her something. Warn her? Was she making too much of it now? Should she mention the incident to Sheriff Henderson after all? But suppose *she* was the nutcase?

There were so many questions, too many questions.

Wheeling abruptly, she went downstairs to the kitchen, found Samantha's telephone number, and before she could think better of it, she dialed. It was something she could do, a concrete step she could take, but when Samantha answered and fell into an immediate silence, Abby realized Sam was steeling herself to hear something awful, and she rushed to reassure her.

"You didn't find them?" Sam asked, and the bump of tears in her voice wrenched Abby's heart.

"No, honey. No. I'm sorry if I scared you."

Sam sighed. "I wish I could go there, look for them, do something."

"It's all right, Sam. Maybe you can help me another way."

"Sure," Sam said, but she was wary.

And Abby was sorrier still that she'd called, but she pressed on explaining her quandary about painting Lindsey's bedroom. "You two looked at colors, didn't you? I was hoping you knew the shade of yellow she settled on."

"Oh, gosh. We looked at a bunch." Sam thought about it.

"It's all right, honey," Abby said.

"I just can't remember exactly, but my mom was there. I bet she knows. I'll get her."

"No, don't disturb her," Abby said quickly, but Sam was already shouting for her mother.

Abby waited, feeling awkward and horrible. No one knew how to talk to her anymore. She'd somehow managed to lose touch with everyone who mattered to her. Except for her mother and Kate. And Jake, who blamed her. He hadn't said as much, but still it was there. She was the mother, the adult, after all. She should have prevented what happened to their family. It was what everyone probably thought, that she should have kept them home, kept them safe.

"Abby? How are you?" Samantha's mother Paula's voice came on the line, holding measured notes of sympathy and caution.

"Paula, hi, I'm all right. I'm sorry, I think I scared Sam. There isn't any news. I'm just back from—from my friend Kate's and I'm thinking of painting Lindsey's room." Abby stumbled through the rest of her speech, then, realizing she was babbling, she pressed her lips together.

There was a considering silence. Paula was obviously taking a moment to pick the sense from the rush of Abby's words or more likely wondering how to tactfully suggest Abby obtain psychiatric help.

"I'm afraid I don't remember anything useful," Paula said. "Do you know when this was?"

Abby could hear in Paula's voice that, like Sam, she did truly want to be helpful. Abby could also hear the oh-you-poor-dear-sad-thing lamentation and beneath that were notes of glee, notes that echoed exultation. *Not me*, the notes sang. *Thank God Almighty, it didn't happen to me!* Abby couldn't blame her; it was only human and she did the only thing that made sense; she let Paula go.

Something woke her deep in the night. She didn't know what time it was. The only clock in the den, where she was camped out because she couldn't face the bed she'd shared with Nick, was on the mantel, and she couldn't see it in the dark. She pulled the thin coverlet to her chin rigid with fear. When the sound came again, she realized the telephone was ringing, and she came instantly to her feet, heart pounding. *Bad news, bad news*. The words hammered through her brain, keeping time with her bare feet hammering the floor. In the kitchen, Abby yanked up the receiver, not checking the ID. "What? Yes? Hello!"

Nothing. Breath. A bit of static, then there was the smallest sigh, soft, liquid sounding. Female. Abby was certain of it.

She went still. "Lindsey? Honey, is it you?" The receiver trembled. "Where are you? Just tell me where you are and Mommy will come. Lindsey? Please, honey. Say something…."

Abby waited. Nothing. Dead air. "Nick?" She

slid down the wall beside the desk onto the floor. "Please...?" The connection was held open a fraction longer, and then it broke with a soft click. Abby went up on her knees and switched on the desk lamp. The ID told her nothing. Out of area, it read. She dialed the operator who couldn't help her either. She lowered herself back to the floor, keeping her grip on the phone, willing it to ring again. Finally it was morning, a decent hour, and she called Kate and told her what she'd heard.

She said, "I know it was Lindsey."

"But how, Abby? If she didn't say anything?"

"You don't believe me."

"I just can't stand for you to hurt anymore."

"Is there a way not to? Is there a cure for this other than finding them? One of them called me, Katie. They're alive. Can't you even say it's possible?"

Kate didn't answer.

"I think someone was here."

"In the night?" Now Kate sounded even more alarmed, and Abby filled with even more regret.

But she went on. "I mean while I was gone. Things aren't—"

"Aren't what?"

Abby said she didn't know. She said, "You think I'm insane."

"Honey, I think you're exhausted. I think I should come."

"No." Abby didn't want her. She didn't need traitors, naysayers. "I'm fine," she said. "I'm sure you're right," she added for effect. "Jake's coming home this weekend. I'm making him a meatloaf."

Abby grocery shopped and managed to make a meatloaf—Jake's favorite—before his arrival. To go with it, she made mashed potatoes and carrots she'd harvested from last fall's vegetable garden. She did not plan to tell him about her middle-of-the night mystery caller. But he already knew. He said Kate had called him because she was concerned.

"She shouldn't have bothered you," Abby said. They were repairing the back porch rail. Abby was holding it while Jake filled the sockets with glue.

"She's afraid you aren't telling her the truth about how you are," he said.

"So, what do you think?"

"About how you are?"

"No, the call. Do you think it's possible?"

"I think stuff like that, thinking Lindsey and Dad are calling, thinking someone's in the house—it'll make you crazy."

"According to Kate, it already has."

"Come on, Mom. Let's say it's true, that it was Lindsey or Dad on the phone. Where does that leave us? I mean, do you think they're out there somewhere? Like what? Kidnapped or something?"

"No," she said, but her brain wanted to argue. Sheriff Henderson had questioned her in this regard. He had asked her if there might be someone who was a threat to Nick. Nadine Betts and the San Antonio D.A. had both insinuated they thought it was Nick with Adam Sandoval on the surveillance tape. Suppose it was? Suppose Adam was holding a gun on Nick, forcing Nick to help him? But no one could see that because the quality of the film was too poor. Stranger things had happened. Abby could have said all of this, but she didn't. Jake was right; she would drive herself crazy. Worse, she would drive him crazy. "I'm sure it was nothing," she said, handing him the railing. "A wrong number is all."

He gave her a look.

"What?" she said. "I'm fine. Fine," she reiterated.

The next day, working like demons, they got the yard work caught up and thoroughly mucked out the horse stalls. They labored mostly in silence as if they had no idea what to say or how to be around each other anymore.

At dinner, they sat at the kitchen table in a well of light, silverware clanking monotonously against china. Abby couldn't stand it. "When are finals?" she asked, although she knew, but she couldn't think of anything else, and anyway, it was a normal, motherly-type question.

"Next week," Jake answered.

"I guess you're studying like mad then."

"Yeah."

"But you're okay, grade-wise?"

"Yeah." He forked bites of meatloaf into his mouth, keeping his gaze from hers.

Deliberately, Abby thought, the same as answering her in monosyllables was deliberate. This was not normal. "Jake, is anything wrong?"

His head came up. "Wrong? Gosh, Mom, what could be wrong? Here we are at the dinner table, the two of us, one big happy family with a mountain of food."

She frowned at him. "I knew you'd be starved. You always are when you come home."

"I can't take their place. I can't eat for them. I can't be here all the time like they were."

"I don't expect that."

Jake thrust aside his napkin and stood up; he took his dishes to the sink and rinsed them. He came for Abby's.

She grasped his wrist. "I should have stopped them; that's what you think, isn't it?"

"How? It isn't like Dad was going to listen to you."

She loosened her hold, and he took her plate away.

He turned from the sink, towel in hand. "You aren't going all paranoid on me now, are you?"

Her laugh was uneasy. "Maybe I am."

His smile seemed forced; it seemed pitying. He said, "I'll try and come home more, okay?"

He left for school the next day, and without him the house was dead still again.

CHAPTER
6

In May, nearly seven weeks after the flood, Dennis Henderson came to Abby's house to collect DNA samples. When Abby opened the door, he took his hat from his head and said, "I'm sorry I have to put you through this."

She widened the door, allowing him to enter. "I can't believe it's come to this."

He followed her through the house, and Abby saw how it must appear to him. He couldn't fail to notice the neglect, the musty smell, the dust everywhere, the sheet and blanket tossed in a heap on the sofa in the den where she was sleeping. She thought of making an excuse. Or she could tell him the truth, that she couldn't bring herself to do the household chores, to wash the clothes, to dust and scour. The messiness and smells were all that was left of her husband and daughter, and she clung to them.

"I expected one of your deputies." She poured tea over ice into two glasses.

"I'm trying to give them a break." He put the metal case on the table next to his hat. "We've made a lot of progress since the flood, but it's still pretty much nonstop."

She brought the tea to the table, indicating he should sit. She set the sugar bowl within his reach, and Abby sat down across from him. "I thought you were the boss."

"Yes, ma'am, but the work is the work and has to be done. This has to be done." His eyes were grave, quiet.

"I know you explained what you needed when you called, Sheriff Henderson, but I'm still not sure I understand. On television, the police take hair and—"

"Hair will work, and please, call me Dennis." He opened the case and took out square envelopes made from something transparent.

"We'll have to go upstairs," Abby said, standing.

Again she was conscious of his steps following hers, that she was leading a stranger deeper into her family's private quarters. She felt exposed. Vulnerable. She hesitated in the doorway of the bathroom that joined Lindsey's bedroom to the guest room. There was a scrap of white, lace-trimmed nylon poking out of the hamper door. Abby recognized it was a pair of underwear, Lindsey's underwear, and her discomfiture increased. An athletic sock lay on the floor underneath. She had left it there on purpose, knowing when she picked it up, it would feel crunchy. It would leave a powdering of fine dirt from the barn on her hand.

Dennis saw the focus of her attention and smiled when their eyes met. He was trying to reassure her, to ease her anxiety. She opened a drawer and took a round-bristled hairbrush with a polka dot handle from the jumbled collection. "Her hair is long," she said, "and there's so much of it. She wants to get it cut, but she worries her dad will be unhappy if she does." Abby looked ruefully at Dennis. "I end up having to do it for her about half the time."

When Dennis smiled again, Abby noticed one of his front teeth was chipped. She imagined there were fights in his line of work, men hitting each other. She looked away. "Nick says it's fine with him if she wants to cut it short. Almost anything she does is fine with him."

"Yes, ma'am."

"You think they're dead, don't you?"

Dennis rubbed two fingers near the center of his forehead.

Abby began unwinding long hairs from the bristles of Lindsey's brush, seeing them through the prism of her unshed tears. She tucked them into the envelope Dennis held open.

He bent to label it. "Of all the things in the world that are hard," he said, keeping his eye on what he was doing, "not knowing is the worst. I want to find your husband and daughter, Mrs. Bennett, and I'm going to do everything I can to accomplish that. So will my deputies. I want you to know that."

She brought her hands to her face. He plucked a tissue from the box on the vanity and gave it to her. And he waited for her to mop up and blow her nose as if he had all the time in the world, as if he had been born to wait through a woman's tears.

"I guess you're used to hysterics."

"I don't like this part of the job, ma'am. I never get used to it."

"Abby, please. Ma'am is what my students called me."

"You teach school?"

"I did. I've been thinking of going back."

"What grade?"

"Kindergarten for a while and then second grade."

"Man." Dennis grinned. "Of all the years I was in school, through college, the academy, you name it, my kindergarten teacher is the one I remember. Miss Sneed. She taught me to read. Taught me to tie my shoes. I thought when I grew up, I was going to marry her."

Abby said, "I thought all little boys wanted to marry their mothers."

"I never knew mine," Dennis said. "She and my dad were killed in a bus accident right after I was born."

Instinctively, Abby reached out, touched his wrist, murmured regret.

"It's all right," Dennis said.

Abby led the way into the hall. The bedroom she and Nick shared was to her left, but she hesitated, reluctant to go into that room with Dennis. She said Nick only had one hairbrush, and she didn't think he would have left it behind. "Is there something else that will work?" she asked.

He cleared his throat. "Yes, ma'am."

"Abby."

"Abby," he repeated.

He kept her gaze, and her face heated as she took his meaning, the nature of the "something else" that would suffice. "We didn't." She caught her upper arms in a tight clasp.

Dennis was quiet. Abby stared at the floor. An awkward silence was measured in heartbeats, then Abby had an idea. "Nick cut himself shaving that morning badly enough that he put a bit of tissue on it. I couldn't find a Band-Aid. He was annoyed."

"You think you still have it? The tissue?"

"Downstairs." Abby led the way back to the kitchen. "I emptied the wastebaskets from up here into a bag, but I didn't take it out yet."

The scrap wasn't much, and it was weeks old, but Dennis said it was fine. He said, "We have dental records, too." He repacked his case and they walked to the front door and out onto the porch. Abby thought of telling him about the phone call. She thought of saying that she believed it came from her daughter, but he would only think of her what everyone else did, that she was losing it, and maybe they were right. Maybe she was.

He paused at the foot of the front steps. "You have a real pretty place here," he said, "a nice home."

Abby nodded, and in his quiet presence, she felt somehow comforted. It was almost as if he held her within an embrace.

After Dennis Henderson left, Abby went upstairs and made herself go through Nick's closet and his dresser drawers. She wasn't certain what she was looking for. A confession of lies? A map to his destination with his reason for going there clearly stated? A diary exposing his thoughts? Given his penchant for privacy, she had little hope of finding anything, and she didn't.

Not on his closet shelves, nor tucked into the pockets of his suit coats or slacks. There was nothing in his bureau drawers but the socks and underwear she herself had washed and folded dozens of times.

Back downstairs, she opened the coat closet in the front hall, and her knees weakened slightly at the smell of stale sunshine and wind; the too-familiar scent of her family seemed pressed into the very fibers of their assorted coats and jackets. There were gloves and scarves pushed into cubbyholes—Jake and Nick's ball caps, an old fishing hat. There were the knitted caps Lindsey favored, a riot of color. Her letter jacket. Abby ran her fingertips down the wool sleeve, swallowing the ache of her tears. She touched the cuff of Nick's leather bomber jacket, the one she had bought him for Christmas last year, and before she could stop herself, she pulled it off the hanger and slipped into it, shivering slightly at the sensation of the silk lining against her bare arms.

Closing her eyes, she gathered fistfuls of the leather in her hands and brought them to her face, and breathing in, she could smell him, feel him there with her, just waiting for her to open her eyes. He would be there; he would materialize. She leaned against the wall, willing it to be so, willing her mind to let her believe, struggling not to cry when it didn't happen. It was when she took off the jacket that she felt something in the inside pocket, and her heart stalled, but it was only his checkbook. Nick wouldn't have missed it; they seldom used checks anymore.

Returning it to the pocket, she rehung the jacket and went back upstairs and into Nick's study, where she sat behind his desk feeling sick at heart and weird.

He wouldn't like her going through his things. Once, a few months after they married, she had been gathering clothes from their bedroom to do a load of wash, and when Nick had found her emptying the pockets of his jeans, he'd been upset. It had startled her to have him pull the pants out of her grasp, to have him say he would wash his own damn jeans and stomp out of the room. Within a minute or two, he'd come back.

His mother had done it to him, he'd said. She'd been furious when Nick's father, Philip, had disappeared, and she had taken out her anger on Nick. He was no more trustworthy than his father or any other man, and as long as he lived in her house, she'd felt she had a right to search his belongings and pry into his personal business whenever she felt like it. If Nick had objected, she'd cut off his privileges, made his life hell. Abby had already known by the time Nick shared this with her that Louise was a strong-willed, difficult woman with impossible expectations. She had known Nick's relationship with his mother was complicated, and that he was conflicted about it. She'd sensed it was a source of pain, even resentment. That day she'd gone to sit beside him on the edge of their bed. He'd taken her hand, and it had been as if he was grateful she was there. Abby remembered telling him she couldn't imagine the kind of pressure he was raised under. He hadn't answered, and she hadn't pressed him about it. It just wasn't in her nature to pry.

Now Abby pulled open the top middle drawer of Nick's desk and passed a shaky hand over the contents. Even with so much at stake, she felt somehow disloyal.

"Mom?"

Her glance bounced as if on a string, finally settling on Jake in the doorway.

"What are you doing?" he asked.

"I didn't know you were coming home."

"You sounded pretty freaked the other day when you called about the DNA."

"Dennis just left."

"Are you okay?"

"I'm fine, honey. You didn't have to come home. I don't want you worrying about me."

"I'm not. I've got a chemistry final tomorrow; I came here to study. It's too loud in the dorm." He sat in one of the wing chairs. "What are you looking for anyway?"

Abby ducked her chin. She thought of saying it was none of his business.

"Mom?"

"Just there might be something, you know? To say where they were going exactly."

Jake dropped his keys onto a small table between the chairs.

Neither of them spoke. Morning sunshine from the window behind Abby heated her shoulders. On an ordinary morning in May in her old life, she would have been out in the vegetable garden, maybe with Lindsey, maybe weeding around the tomato plants she'd set out. *How long ago was that? March?* There wouldn't be much of anything left of them now.

Jake propped his ankle on his knee, picked at his sock. "I doubt Dad would leave evidence where you could find it."

"Evidence?" She looked sharply at him. "What do you mean?"

"Nothing, except if somebody's up to something and they don't want you finding out, they aren't going to leave stuff lying around so you can."

"What could he have been up to?"

Jake stood up, flinging his hands. "How do I know? It's not like he ever discussed anything with me."

Abby leaned back and crossed her arms. "I'll be glad when you and Dad iron out your differences."

"There's not much chance of that now, is there?" Jake said.

Abby swiveled the chair around and stared out the window. "I guess you can give up if you want to. I can't stop you."

"Mom, Sheriff Henderson didn't take DNA samples so he could match them to somebody alive."

"I know that, Jake."

"Do you? Because it sure doesn't seem like it to me."

Abby began losing time. She would waken on the sofa assuming it was morning only to discover it was three o'clock in the afternoon, or she would find herself in the barn with no memory of having gone there. Every day she would try to follow a routine, but then she would come to and find herself balled up in a corner of Lindsey's room or standing outside the door of Nick's study, and her face would be wet with tears and she would not know how long she had been there.

One morning in the first week of June, two months after the flood, she was huddled on the kitchen floor by the stove clutching a wooden spoon when her mother appeared. Abby squinted at her. "Mama? You didn't drive on the freeway, did you?"

"Never mind that, sweet." Abby's mother pushed

lank strands of hair from Abby's eyes. "What are you doing?"

"Making oatmeal, the long-cooking kind. It's what I should have fixed for them before they left. It's healthier than French toast." Tears flooded Abby's eyes as if more of her tears could make a difference. As if anything she'd done or left undone could have prevented her car from rocketing off the road in wet slick darkness with Nick and Lindsey inside it. As if cooked-from-scratch oatmeal made from steel-cut oats packed with natural goodness and touched with honey would bring them back.

Abby's mother pulled her up from the floor by her elbow—Abby was always mildly surprised at her mother's wiry strength—and led her upstairs and into the bathroom she and Nick had shared. While Abby undressed, her mother drew water in the oversize tub and tested it with the inside of her wrist. "Jake called me," she said, adding bath beads to the water, stirring them with her hand. "He says he can't come here anymore."

She turned away, and Abby slipped off her robe and stepped into the tub. She drew up her knees.

Her mother opened a cabinet, running her eye over the assortment of linen stacked inside. "It's hurting him to see you this way, honey. He's found a job near campus; he says he's staying there with friends this summer."

"I don't blame him," Abby whispered. "I can hardly stand to look at him either."

Her mother found a washcloth and handed it to Abby, and while she busied herself at the vanity, Abby soaped the cloth and moved it over her breasts and down her torso. She lifted each foot, soaped her calves and in between her toes, and as she worked, the tight icy core of despair in her belly thawed a bit, and the sense of her desolation shallowed in the warmth and dampness of the steamy lavender-scented air. She let out the water, turned on the shower and washed her hair, and when she was finished her mother handed her a towel.

She helped Abby out of the tub and into her robe. "I'm taking you home, Abigail," she said, sitting her down on the vanity stool, drying her hair, "and I won't have an argument about it. I spoke to Charlie. He'll look after things, the horses and so forth, for a while. You can't go on this way. You just can't."

Abby didn't argue. She packed a suitcase and went with her mother, and it grieved her that she was the source of so much consternation. She bent her forehead to the passenger window. "I think Nick was keeping something from me."

"But you didn't find anything, did you?"

"Jake told you. He caught me looking through Nick's desk. I know he was upset."

"He's worried, honey. He wants you to be the way you were. I told him grief has its own timetable." Abby's mother reached out to pat Abby's hand.

"I should be driving," she said.

"No, this once, you can let me."

CHAPTER

7

At the marina, they walk along a pier between rows of moored boats. They're all different sizes, mostly crisp white, trimmed in red or green or blue, like rows of Spectator shoes. Nick carries the cooler with their picnic supper in one hand, the other rests lightly in the small of Abby's back. She's aware of sea birds wheeling overhead, the gentle slap of water against the pilings under their feet, the jostling of boats caught in their moorings. The slight shift and tilt of their masts gives the impression of impermanence. She's anxious. What if she falls?

But Nick's hand is there as if he intuits her unease, a solid prop beneath her elbow, as he helps her over the side of a pretty blue-and-white boat, then hands the cooler to her. Abby manages to hold herself steady, but when she goes forward, he says why doesn't she sit in the cockpit, and she thinks, there. Now he'll know she's ignorant. She had no idea that a boat had a cockpit. Planes. Planes had cockpits.

She sits down, putting the cooler beside her. He frees the knot that tethers the boat to the dock, then steps around doing other things. She would like to help, but she has no idea how. The wind picks at her hair, whipping it across her cheeks and eyes, and she pulls it away, tucking strands behind her ears.

Nick finds her gaze from where he's standing on a step above her. "You've never been sailing before."

"No," she admits, and her heart pecks at her ribs, a nervous bird. She loves the look and sound of water but from the shore. Her pale skin only burns and peels. She never tans. Nick looks as though he was born tan.

He tells her it's okay. "When there's a good wind like today, I can usually single-hand her with just the jib."

She nods. Should she ask, what's a jib? Should she worry about his use of the word *usually?*

"You'll see when we get into open water." He jumps down beside her, and within seconds, she hears motor noise. She hadn't expected that, and she's thankful. They clear the dock area but are still within sight of land when Nick begins unfurling a sail. "This is the jib," he explains, "and these ropes are the halyards." He lets the thick cords play through his hands.

She shades her eyes, watching the white canvas-sheeting rise.

"People think sailing is hard," Nick says, "but for me it's as easy as breathing." He grins at her. "Stick with me, kid, you'll make first mate in no time."

She's laughing when he cuts the engine, then a hard wave slaps the boat, and she grabs the railing. Nick is there instantly, sliding his hand beneath her elbow, telling her to relax, to flex her knees. "I've got you; I won't let you go," he says.

Abby loses focus. Her whole awareness is consumed by her sense of him, the feel of the calluses on his palm, the slow, confident pitch of his voice near her ear. And then it happens: she unlocks her knees as he's instructed and all at once the boat's rhythm takes her, and it is as if her body has become unjointed, as fluid and formless as the water that surrounds them. And she smiles, feeling thrilled. Nick gives her elbow a jubilant squeeze. He bends to tie a rope onto a metal cleat. The little boat catches the wind now and leaps ahead, slicing through the water almost as if it weren't there, as if they were flying.

She tips her face to the sky. The blue seems without end, translucent, an inverted fragile cup, the blue of a robin's egg. The blue of June. Endless blue with hours of daylight left in it. She thinks Nick is right, the predictions for evening thunderstorms were mistaken and she is relieved. Soon he has guided them into a secluded cove. Abby opens the cooler to find one long-stemmed pink rose, a thick lush bud with petals that are just beginning to unfurl. Lifting it out she looks up at Nick to find him smiling down on her.

"I wanted to thank you for coming with me," he says.

"It's beautiful," she murmurs.

"I know." He is looking steadily at her.

Flustered, she brings the bud to her nose, breathing in its faintly heady scent. "It needs water or it will wilt."

"I can take care of that," he says and disappears down the stairs that lead below deck.

Abby sets down the rose, feeling ridiculously pleased, a sensation that deepens as she unpacks the small feast Nick brought for them. There is an assortment of crackers and exotic cheeses, a crusty loaf of bread, peach chutney, a small container of caviar, a bunch of red grapes so flawless they glow like polished rubies in the early evening light. There are tiny cream-filled éclairs for dessert. It occurs to her that he took the time to shop specifically for this occasion, and she is somehow touched by this. It seems so foolish and romantic, so unexpected. She hasn't known him very long, but he seems too serious for romance, too pragmatic.

He comes from the galley bringing a small vase and a basket filled with china plates, linen napkins and crystal stemware. He sets a hurricane lamp on the adjacent bench seat, lights the candle inside it, then uncorks the wine. He watches while she takes a sip, and only after she's pronounced it delicious does he relax. He talks about sailing, and she is happy just to listen to him. She wants to touch the corner of his mouth where he has cut himself shaving, to put her fingertip into the dimple that clefts his left cheek. At the office, the other secretaries call him a player. Her stomach waffles at the thought.

He wonders if she would like to swim.

"I didn't bring a suit." She fingers her linen skirt, eyes her flats. She had come with him straight from work.

He takes her hand. "You don't swim either, do you?"

"No." She can't look at him and looks instead at their enfolded arms. His is dark, olive-toned, hers as white as typing paper. As white as his teeth when he smiles at her. He slides his palm along the ridge of her jaw, cupping her neck, drawing her toward him, and his kiss is gentle, tentative at first, then it deepens and she gives herself to it, shivering in the fearsome thrust of her desire for him. His mouth moves to the hollow of her throat. She arches her back, aware that she is thrusting herself at him, and she is appalled and enchanted. But then, when thunder cracks, she jerks upright, uncertain what has happened. She wipes her mouth, looking wildly about herself.

Nick takes her by her shoulders. "Hey," he says, and it is a moment before she sees him, before she recalls where she is. The wind picks up. Clouds muscle the sky as bunched and ominous as dark fists, and her breath draws down hard.

Nick tips her chin, forcing her gaze to his. "Don't worry. I can beat the rain. It'll be fine, you'll see."

But it isn't fine. Within moments of packing up and stowing their dishes and leaving the little cove, the water goes from choppy to rough. The swells seem huge. Nick switches on the motor, and Abby hears it strain. She flattens her hands on either side of her, spray from the water dampening her hair and her clothes, while Nick moves nimbly, adjusting the ropes, handling the wheel. His face is intent, his expression rapt. He's loving this, she thinks.

A sudden sharper gust of wind heels the Blue Daze over. Water swamps the deck, filling Abby's shoes. Her throat closes. She will not scream, will not be sick and shame herself. Lights finally appear, a necklace of them lie curled in the distance. She blinks to be sure. Yes. The lights are there, on the shore, coming closer. Nick meets her glance, looking exultant.

At the pier, he hands her out of the boat, and when she slips in her wet shoes, he reaches out to steady her, pulling her against him. His gaze locks with hers. "You were afraid?"

He's asked because she's trembling, and at first she nods, then almost immediately, she shakes her head. Out over the water, lightning forks rake the sky. Within a few seconds, thunder growls. Nick disappears over the boat rail and returns with a lightweight blanket. Wrapping her in it, he bends, brushing his lips against her temple, and he is as surprised as she is when her eyes fill with tears.

He thumbs them away, then cups her cheek in his hand.

She covers it with her own and when he softly tells her, "I didn't mean to scare you," she believes him.

CHAPTER

8

Abby answered her mother's phone, heard Dennis Henderson's voice and froze.

He apologized. "I keep scaring you, and it's the last thing I want to do."

"How did you know where I was?"

"Jake. I called him when I couldn't get you on your cell phone or at your home number. He said he's working a landscaping job near A&M, that he's staying there for the summer."

Abby's "Umm," was noncommittal. Their living arrangements were her business.

"Well, I have no special reason for calling. I thought I'd stay in touch, if it's all right with you."

"It's a free country," Abby said, and she didn't really care how Dennis took it.

But he wasn't put off as Abby imagined he might be. He continued to call almost weekly, and after a while, she found she looked forward to their conversations. She learned that he was forty-five and that he'd once been married for twelve years to his high school sweetheart. There were no children.

"She liked the city life in Austin too much to leave it," Dennis said about his ex-wife one afternoon.

Abby thought about it and realized she couldn't picture Dennis in a city. She stirred lemon into her glass of iced tea. "Kate told me you're neighbors."

"We are, but my place isn't near as big. It's just enough to mess around on. I run a few head of cattle, grow a few things."

Abby wondered what he grew, thinking it would be feed corn, something practical.

But he said, "Orchids," when she asked. Someone had given him a phalaenopsis and when it bloomed, he was hooked. He'd built a greenhouse, experimented with hybridization. "It's a hobby, nothing special."

She said she didn't know much about growing orchids, that she'd always been too scared of them to try. "I love to garden, though. Mostly vegetables. It's my therapy."

He laughed. "Cheaper than drugs."

She said she wasn't sure about that, her habit was pretty bad, and when Dennis laughed again, Abby did, too. He had a nice laugh, warm and comfortable. Falling asleep that night, she thought he had a way of making her feel safe; she thought she could trust him.

They didn't talk about the flood. Abby wanted to, and yet she was afraid. She didn't know why Dennis didn't bring it up. Maybe he was sick of it. Maybe he thought it would remind her, as if it wasn't always

there in the forefront of her mind. Whatever the reason
was for their mutual silence on the subject, the sense
of it hung in the off-stage shadows of every conversation, a bad actor awaiting an opening cue. And then
one warm evening in late July, after they had talked a
few minutes, Abby carried her cell phone outside. She
didn't want her mother to overhear. She'd only worry,
and Abby was tired of that, of being the source of it.
She was worn out from trying to pretend she was okay,
that she was moving on. She was sick of the mystery,
of being left, marooned in this weird place with no
answers. She perched on the edge of a wrought-iron
garden chair and asked Dennis about the other survivors, because as little as she wanted to hear their stories, there was something else inside her that needed
to know whether there were other people like her who
were suffering the same terrible uncertainty. As per-
verse as it was, she wanted company in her misery.

But Dennis couldn't help her. It didn't matter how
reluctant he was to answer or that when he did his voice
was filled with regret. The fact was that her husband
and daughter were the only victims whose bodies had
not been recovered. And when he added, "at least not
so far," Abby thought it was out of kindness to her, not
out of any real hope that they would ever be located.
She wanted to leave the awful subject, but now that
she had opened it up, she couldn't. "I heard you mention a woman once," she said, "Patsy something? She
left home when the roads were washing out to go to
the grocery store and after the water went down, you
found her truck, but you didn't find her."

"Oh, you mean Patsy Doggett."

Dennis's voice carried measures of relief, even the

lilt of joy, which could only mean the story had a happy ending. Abby clenched her teeth.

"She got to her sister's place somehow after her truck flooded out," Dennis said. "It was pretty amazing. She's eighty something, did you know? She and her husband Lloyd are coming up on fifty-four years together."

Abby stared into the welling darkness, and she was silent so long that Dennis finally asked if he'd upset her. "No, it's fine," she said. "Amazing, like you said. A miracle, right?"

"More like a fluke. Abby? You shouldn't—"

"I'm not assuming anything, Dennis. Honestly," she added.

Outside of Dennis and Louise, who called weekly, Abby had almost no contact with anyone. She had thought she wanted to be left alone, and it surprised her how much it hurt. She could understand why her neighbors didn't make the drive into Houston to see her, but they could have picked up the phone, couldn't they? And then there were Nick's law partners. Only Joe Drexler, the most senior partner in the firm, had called, and one or two of the other partners' wives had made the effort, but the conversations were brief, perfunctory, and gave Abby a bad feeling. As the summer wore on, their avoidance of her began to feel deliberate, somehow ominous. Her mother excused it. She said they didn't know what to do or say. They were waiting for a sign from her.

To accept what was obvious, Abby thought.

Louise put it bluntly one day at the end of August. "We need to move on, dear," she said. "It's what Nick and Lindsey would want us to do. They would want us to get on with our lives."

"Why do people always say that?" Abby asked. "As if they know what the dead would want."

"Well, surely you don't think they want us to grieve forever, do you? I mean, I know we will, always, on some level. It's difficult, but it isn't as if you're alone, dear. Neither of us is."

"What do you propose, then? What is your advice for how I should get on with it? I don't play golf or bridge." Abby referenced Louise's two favorite pastimes, and she regretted her sarcasm; she hadn't really meant to be flippant. In fact she was glad Louise had these routine distractions to occupy her time; they kept her in Dallas. Otherwise she might have been here, driving Abby crazy.

Louise had fallen silent; something she almost never did, and Abby slid from her mother's kitchen stool, sensing trouble, disapproval, an argument, she didn't know what. A knot of rebellion tightened beneath her breastbone. She put her knuckled fist there. "Louise?" she prompted.

"I've been talking to Joe, Abby, and he thinks we should plan a memorial service. Now I know what you're going to say—"

"No." Abby paced to her mother's kitchen door and looked out.

"But, dear, think of Nick's clients, his associates, they would like to pay their respects. We need to give them a way to do that."

"Why? What do we owe them?"

"It's what people do, what they expect. It's what

convention calls for." Louise's voice quavered with her conviction, her belief that this was so.

"You're worried about what people will think, your church friends. But I don't care what they think, Louise, and I don't intend to give my family up for dead simply to satisfy someone's notion of what's acceptable."

"It isn't only about you, Abby. I want to lay my son and my sweet granddaughter to rest. I want to see them in heaven with God. Please, will you consider it?" Louise's voice broke.

But Abby said, "No," and she might have felt a sharper pang of remorse for how hard she was on Louise, if she had not been so furious at Joe Drexler.

Abby didn't bother calling him. She didn't want to give him the opportunity to refuse to speak to her. Instead, she went that afternoon unannounced to the office, determined to make him talk. Even though she knew neither he nor the other partners would appreciate her barging into their domain; they wouldn't expect it from her. Sweet, quiet, amenable Abby. That was how they viewed her, how everyone saw her. She was compliant. Soft. A creampuff. She hadn't minded before, but it was different now. Everything was different. She'd lost her family, lost herself.

She stepped off the elevator, and her head went swimmy; she felt faintly nauseated. From anxiety, she guessed. The half-panicked state she seemed to live in these days. She pushed open the glass doors to the reception area. Deserted. She found her way to Joe's office, and ignoring his assistant's squeal of protest, she flung open his door.

He had his feet on the desk and his nose in some

file, and when he looked up, Abby watched his surprise morph into consternation. "Abby!" He took his feet down and straightened himself.

"I couldn't stop her," the assistant said from behind Abby.

"It's all right, Jessica." To Abby, he said, "I'm glad you came. I've been meaning to call you. Do you want something to drink? Coffee? Iced tea? Jessica, do we have iced tea made?"

"I don't want any iced tea," Abby said. "I want you to explain why you would discuss holding a memorial service for my husband and daughter with my mother-in-law without a word to me."

Joe dismissed Jessica, asking her to close the door. He asked Abby to have a seat and she did. She wanted to appear cooperative so that he would tell her what he knew. Because he knew something; he was hiding something from her. She was convinced of it.

He spent some time apologizing. He should have been in touch with her, checked up on her.

Abby interrupted him. "Why did Nick go there? Why did he go to the Hill Country in April?"

"What do you mean? I suppose he went to relax, to spend time with Lindsey."

"It's too late for secrets."

"Secrets?" Joe seemed perplexed, but Abby didn't trust him.

She persisted. "You know about the surveillance tape; Dennis—Sheriff Henderson told me you saw it. So did I. It's not Nick; it couldn't be."

When Joe didn't answer immediately, Abby's heart paused. "You don't think it was him, do you?"

"I couldn't say. The film quality was—"

"But Nick was here in his office working that day. He couldn't have been in San Antonio, too."

"I remember he was here that morning, but after that, I don't know."

"You're saying Nick didn't come back from lunch that afternoon?"

"I don't think so."

"Well, he was home at the usual time that evening." Abby said this as if it were carved somewhere in stone, as if her memory of that day were photographic, unimpeachable, but, like Joe, she wasn't sure.

He brought up Adam, as if that might distract Abby, saying it was a mystery to him why the authorities had released Adam on bail. "I heard they didn't even bother taking his passport."

Abby spoke over Joe. "You suspect Nick, don't you? That's why you haven't called, because you couldn't face me!" She could scarcely hear her own voice over the frightened thumping of her heart.

Joe denied it. He said his oversight had nothing to do with who was or wasn't on the surveillance tape. He was annoyed at her now, and while she could see that he pitied her, too, he was struggling to maintain his composure. Abby had worked here once; she could read the signs; she knew patience wasn't his strong suit.

He said, "Look, I told the San Antonio D.A. when he questioned me that Nick was cleared of all suspicion back in December when the business about the missing funds was exposed and Adam was arrested."

"And?" Abby prompted.

"And nothing," Joe said shortly. "But the whole thing with the surveillance tape is up in the air. Even the ID of Adam Sandoval is shaky. Until he's caught or other evidence comes to light, any discussion of who is on the tape and what they're up to is pure speculation."

A taut silence fell.

Abby broke it. "Nick was supposed to testify for the prosecution when Adam was brought to trial."

"Nick and a half dozen others who work here. This isn't about taking out witnesses. You've watched too many movies."

"But who's to say—?"

"There's nothing there, Abby. Trust me."

But Abby didn't. She couldn't, and she looked through the window behind Joe, taking a moment to gather herself.

He said, "I remember when Nick first talked about bringing the suit against Helix Belle. He'd heard from those folks, the Rileys. Friends of your family, aren't they?"

"We knew them, but only slightly. We met them when Jake played Little League."

"I didn't want anything to do with that case." Joe fiddled with his pen, keeping his eye on it. "There wasn't an attorney in town who wanted to touch it. It still surprises me that Nick took the risk. I didn't think we'd see a dime. I remember asking him where he intended to work once he drove us into bankruptcy over it."

Abby didn't like the bitter edge in Joe's voice, but she understood it. She'd been unhappy with Nick, too. But who could have known how complicated it would all get? On that Sunday afternoon two years ago when Doug and Wendy Riley had first appeared on her doorstep with their huge, heartrending story, they hadn't wanted anything more than a referral to an attorney who would be willing to take on a corporate giant like Helix Belle on a contingency basis. By then, their son Casey's medical difficulties had sapped most of their financial resources, and they, along with the rest of the affected families, had been turned away by a number of other law firms. Nick had been their last resort. Abby would never forget how stunned she was, as astonished as Wendy and Doug, as Joe himself, when Nick had offered his services and those of his firm. *Somebody needs to show these guys they can't hurt little kids and walk away*, Nick had said. *Somebody needs to hold their feet to the fire.* He had paced and raised his voice. Abby had been a bit embarrassed by his fervor. She had wondered where it came from.

Wendy had cried, she'd been so relieved to have Nick's legal counsel; Doug had been almost incoherent in his gratitude. But Abby had been disturbed. "Can you really afford to represent them?" she had asked Nick later. "You're always telling me cases like this can take years. You could lose everything."

Jesus Christ, Abby, does it always have to be about the money? Nick's reply skittered down the corridor of Abby's memory. She watched him, in her mind's eye, as he dropped to the edge of the sofa. "Maybe I can make a difference," she remembered him saying. "Do something good for once for people who can really use my help."

That poor family; their poor kid...

Abby had felt awful for the Rileys, too, but she remembered wanting to ask Nick: What about your own family? What about your kids? We can't afford your altruism. But in the end, she had walked away, expecting Nick to sort it out. She'd had plenty of her own issues, like a household to run on a shoestring and doses of altruism. They'd weathered the argument or whatever it had been. At least she'd thought they had, but maybe not. Nothing had ever felt quite right since that Sunday afternoon, had it?

She looked at Joe now. "I didn't want Nick to take on that case either."

"Well, no, but it's got nothing to do with his disappearance."

"Something happened."

"Abby—"

"You don't have to protect me, Joe."

"I have no idea what you're—"

"Nick told me about a client he had recently, a woman who accused him of not handling her interests properly in a real estate case. He said she made threats. What do you know about that?"

Joe sat back. "Nick doesn't handle cases involving real estate, not as a rule. What are you getting at now?"

Joe's annoyance was mixed with bewilderment that seemed genuine. Still, Abby pursued it. "Maybe there was other client trouble. Or maybe something was going on internally here. Dennis asked me whether I thought someone might have been following Nick. He didn't mention the possibility to you?"

"No, because there is nothing. No conspiracy, no—"

"But suppose there was? And it's somehow related to Nick's and Lindsey's disappearance?" Abby said disappearance because she didn't want to say kidnapping, even though she could not get the word, or its possible ramification, out of her mind.

Joe opened his mouth and then closed it, making a flat, disapproving line. He was through talking.

And that was fine, Abby thought. At least he wouldn't toss the idea of holding a memorial service at her. Her visit had accomplished that much. She drew her purse over her shoulder, keeping Joe's gaze as she stood up. "Even Sheriff Henderson asked me to go over certain details with him several times because he said sometimes we will remember something new that can be helpful."

"If I were to remember anything, Abby, of course, I would let the authorities know."

Abby thanked him. Joe said he'd walk her out, that he had to be in court, but she said, no, she was going to the ladies' room. She couldn't stand another moment in his company.

Abby was grateful to find the restroom deserted. Bending over the basin, she washed her hands and patted her cheeks with her damp palms in an effort to cool down, to calm herself, and when she thought she had given Joe enough time to leave the building, she went to Nick's office. The door was open, but she stopped short of crossing the threshold, for a moment convinced she had made a mistake. It was so neat. Even Nick's desk, which was usually buried under a litter of paper, was eerily sterile, design-photo clean. Behind it, the assortment of family pictures he kept on the credenza appeared untouched, and the pair of framed, signed Leroy Neiman lithographs that Abby had bought for him when he'd made partner still hung on the wall. But the clutter that was uniquely his own filing system was gone, as if since he'd vanished someone couldn't wait to tidy up. Abby felt a renewed jolt of alarm like a punch to her solar plexus. Her earlier aggravation freshened its heat. The nerve, that was one thing she thought as she walked behind the desk, but it was tangled with a colder panic, a more distraught sense that despite Joe's reassurances, something awful was happening or had happened that affected her and her family, and she was deliberately being kept in the dark about it.

She set down her purse, picked up a framed photo of Jake from the collection on the credenza, turned when she sensed someone had walked in behind her. It was Nina, but Abby should have expected as much.

"He hates this picture." Abby fought to keep her tone civil. "His skin was so broken out when he was in junior high."

"I know," Nina said.

Of course she did. Nina knew everything. She'd taken over Abby's job as receptionist when Abby quit to marry Nick, and twenty-odd years later, the partners were still Nina's only family. She called them her "boys" in the same smug way she'd said, "I know," and the thing was, she did know nearly everything about all of them. Abby wanted to slap Nina; she wanted to wipe the smirk right off her carefully made-up face. But she wanted answers more; she'd come here to make someone talk to her, and the fact was that Nina's "boys" told her everything. If anyone at Drexler, Davidson, Wilcox and Bennett knew where the bones were buried, it was Nina.

She came around the desk and hugged Abby, then held her at arm's length. "Jessica told me you were here."

"Of course she did," Abby said.

"How are you?" Nina's dark eyes searched Abby's face.

"Better. On some days at least. It's hard."

"I can imagine."

No, you can't. Abby longed to say it.

The phone in the outer office rang. Nina started through the door, but when it stopped, her attention returned to Abby. "No one's touched anything in here—" *Yet.* Nina didn't say it, but the implication was there all the same.

Abby sat down in Nick's chair, feeling with her own smaller backside the round contouring of Nick's larger sitting depression. And independently of her will, her hands recalled the curve of his hip, the flesh there that was lightly haired and how it warmed beneath her touch. The memory started an ache low in her belly, a warm, hard swell of desire that she quickly closed off.

Light glimmered over the desk's polished surface. So much surface. No one had touched anything? Was that a joke? A lie? Abby fingered the blotter, lifting it, shifting the edge. Did Nina expect her to believe that? Did she not remember how many times in the past she and Abby had joked about Nick's mess? They'd shared lunch and commiserated with each other— Abby, the home wife, and Nina, the office wife. Along with the other partners' wives, Abby had been part of Nina's extended "family." But now Abby felt a very unfamily-like strangeness. She felt unwelcome. And it occurred to her that, without Nick, she wasn't one of them anymore. She didn't belong.

"Everything is so tidy." Abby looked at Nina. "You must assume Nick isn't coming back. It makes me wonder what you know that I don't."

Nina's eyes widened. She put her hand to her neck. "I have no idea what you mean."

Abby followed her gesture, noting the strand of pearls that curved beneath the tailored collar of Nina's cream charmeuse blouse, noting Nina's nails, the immaculate French-style manicure. She was like Nick's mother, Abby thought, always immaculate. Perfectly presented. Never a hair out of place, never a snagged nylon. Nina shared something else with Louise, too: a lack of faith; and it infuriated Abby. "You've written Nick off, haven't you? You and Joe and Louise. I don't know how you sleep at night."

"Abby—?" Nina broke off, shaking her head as if in admonishment of herself. After all, Abby was distraught, grieving. Allowances had to be made, if Abby sounded crazy, if she babbled insanely. Nina tried again. "I went through the paperwork on Nick's desk because the sheriff Joe spoke to asked if Nick might have left some record here of where he was going. Since you don't seem to know."

Abby's jaw tightened. How good and righteous Nina was, how superior. If Nina had children, she would never let them go anywhere without knowing their precise location; Nina would never take her eyes off her children. Hooray for Nina.

She said, "I told Joe that if Nick made a reservation at a campground, it would be on his laptop. That's where he kept everything."

"He took it with him." Abby pulled out the top right-hand desk drawer expecting Nina to stop her, half expecting to find it empty. But there were the memo pads with Nick's name embossed on them and underneath, a jumble of what looked like advertising brochures. A few business cards, a half-used book of checks with no cover, toothpicks cased in cellophane from various restaurants. An assortment of pens, paper clips, loose staples. A tiny scrap of paper from a fortune cookie read: *Protective measures will prevent costly disasters.* What did it mean, costly disasters? It seemed almost prescient in hindsight. Why would Nick have kept it?

Nina looked on solemn-faced. Maybe when Joe left for court earlier he'd called her and warned her Abby was loose in the building, and Nina should keep an eye out. Maybe Nina had been told that should Abby enter Nick's office she should be watched and prevented from removing anything that was of a confidential nature. Lawyers were a notoriously paranoid bunch.

Abby closed the first drawer and opened the one below it.

Nina said, "If I'd found a single thing that would help locate your family, hon, I surely would have told that sheriff. And you, too, of course."

Abby smiled sweetly. "Of course." She closed the second drawer and opened a third, thinking: the hell with you. Thinking: I have as much right as any of you do to search my husband's desk. She dipped her glance, saw what looked to be a short stack of legal journals and rifled it. A book of matches wedged between them and the side of the drawer caught her eye. The cover was dark green with silver lettering that read Riverbend Lodge.

In Bandera. Abby recalled seeing it. Edging the highway on the outskirts of town. Pure roadside ambience, low-ceilinged cowboy decor, damp, moldy-smelling air pouring from the A/C unit. Café-type restaurant that featured grits and eggs for breakfast and chicken-fried steak anytime. She and Nick and the kids had spent one awful night there three summers ago. They'd been on their way to Kate's when Lindsey had spiked a sudden fever so high, she had vomited in the backseat of the car, all over Jake. Nick had pulled in at the lodge; they'd gotten a room and he'd carried Lindsey inside. When she wasn't better within a few hours, they'd driven to San Antonio, to an emergency room, where she'd been treated for a severe case of strep throat.

Abby took the matches out of the drawer and closed it. She waited for Nina to ask what she had in her hand, but Nina didn't. She approached the front of the desk and perched on one corner. The ease of her movement suggested habit, suggested Nick's desk ought to be worn on that corner, Nina had perched there so many times.

"Hon," she said, and Abby winced, "I know you've been under a terrible strain, and we are all so sorry. Of all people, you didn't deserve this. But don't you think—?"

Abby toyed with the matchbook, opening the cover, glancing at it. There was a name inside, *Sondra*, and a phone number, jotted in Nick's handwriting. Her stomach dropped, setting off a small explosion of apprehension. She didn't recognize the number. She didn't know anyone named Sondra.

Nina cleared her throat.

Abby opened her purse, tucked the book of matches inside. "I'm sorry?" She looked at Nina. "You were suggesting something about what I should think?"

"Well, I'm wondering whether you might be having a bit of trouble accepting what's happened, if you aren't holding on to false hope. Joe says you seem to think there might have been—I hesitate to use the term—foul play."

Joe *had* called Nina. Abby had been right to think it was possible. He'd probably dialed her number before the elevator door had closed. They were treating Abby as if she were an unreasonable child, a mental case. It made her want to scream, and she gritted her teeth. She made herself breathe.

Nina seemed oblivious; she held Abby's gaze. "Isn't what happened awful enough? It's tragic that so many people lost their lives, but the sad, horrible fact is they're gone, and holding on to the hope that the outcome is something other than that, well, it seems so hurtful. For you, I mean. I'm not the only one who feels this way," she added when Abby didn't answer. "Louise does, too, and she's Nick's mother."

"If you're going to bring up the idea of a memorial service, don't."

"But we'd like you to help us plan it."

Abby shook her head in disgust. "You're talking about a funeral. What are you going to bury?"

"Not a funeral, hon, a ceremony to honor Nick and Lindsey." Nina spread her hands. "People have asked. Nick's clients, his colleagues."

Sondra, Abby thought. Was she a client?

"Louise needs closure. We all do."

"Closure to what? My husband and my daughter are missing. *Mis-sing.*" Abby repeated the word, placing heavy emphasis on each syllable.

"So if that's what you believe, maybe you should check with his father, given the history."

Abby chose to let that pass. She picked up her purse. "It was nice seeing you, Nina."

"I hope you aren't angry with me. I only want to help," Nina said.

Abby walked past her.

"Let me know if you need anything," Nina called after her.

In the parking garage, Abby sat behind the steering wheel of Nick's BMW, fished the book of matches she'd filched from his desk out of her purse and opened the cover. It was definitely Nick's handwriting. The 713 area code was local, one Abby associated with downtown, mostly, everything that lay inside the 610 loop. It was probably the number of a business or another law firm where someone named Sondra was employed.

But suppose it wasn't? Suppose it was something else? Something more personal? A new suspicion lifted from the floor of Abby's mind, unbidden, disquieting, and it confused her. Since when had Nick ever given her a reason to doubt him, his loyalty, his love? She found her cell phone and dialed the number, and in the moment the connection was made, she caught her breath in anticipation of hearing a female voice. Instead, what she heard was the insistent beep of a fax machine.

She pulled her cell phone away from her ear and studied the screen as if it might explain, then set it against her ear again, listening a moment longer to the shrill, rhythmic pulsing.

So it was nothing, she thought, and she was somehow disappointed. But what had she expected? That someone named Sondra had been waiting all these weeks for her call, waiting to answer all of her questions, waiting to lead her to the very spot where Nick and Lindsey could be found warm and safe and alive? A sound broke loose from Abby's chest; she pressed her fingertips to her eyes. Nina was wrong, she thought. It wasn't false hope that hurt her; it was not knowing.

CHAPTER
9

"I think you have to let Louise and Nina go ahead with the service." Abby's mother shook that morning's coffee grounds around the hydrangeas.

"A lot of this thyme has died, Mama." Abby rested on her knees nearby. "We could go to the nursery, see if we can find more. I don't know though, at this time of year—"

"Abby, did you hear me? It's been five months." Her mother came to stand beside Abby in the grass.

She looked at her mother's feet. "You shouldn't be out here in your slippers, Mama. You could fall."

"Abigail, if it were you who had disappeared—" Abby's mother's voice trembled a little "—wouldn't you want Nick and the children to do what was necessary to bring themselves to terms, to find peace? It's what Jake needs, honey. And as much as you resist the whole notion of a service, it's what's done. It's the appropriate thing. It sends a kind of signal, can you see?"

"But we're not religious. Where would it be?"

"Nick was raised Baptist, wasn't he?"

"But he hated it, having to go every Sunday. Louise wanted us to be married in that huge Baptist church she belongs to in Dallas. Nick refused, remember?"

"But this isn't for Nick, is it? I mean in terms of whom it will serve. It's for everyone who wants to show how much and how well your family was—is—loved. It would be a kindness to Louise, especially, I think, to let her have her way in this."

"What does Jake want?"

"Why don't you ask him?"

Abby got to her feet, brushing the knees of her jeans. Jake hadn't come home once all summer, and now classes had resumed. He and Abby seldom talked. He was wary of her now. Like everyone else, he wished she would get on with her life. Stop asking questions, stop jumping for the phone when it rang, stop deluding herself. Go home. Be normal.

"We argued the last time he called," Abby said.

"About?"

Money, Abby thought, but it would only worry her mother to hear it. She would ask how Abby was managing, which would then force Abby to admit that rather than go back to work, she'd been raiding her and Nick's joint savings account to cover her bills. Her mother would then say how unwise it was and ask what Abby intended to do when the savings was gone. Abby didn't know, and, probably even worse, she didn't care. And she didn't need anyone to tell her how dumb that was either.

"Abby?"

"It was nothing, Mama. He needed tires for his car. I took care of it."

"I know your head is full of questions, sweet. I wonder too, what happened, but given how long it's been, I mean without any sign…."

"I know, Mama." *How illogical it is to go on hoping.*

"I think they'll have the service whether you agree to it or not."

Abby looked into thin air. "Nick wants to be cremated." She couldn't let herself think what Lindsey might have wanted. "There's nothing to cremate."

"I know, sweet."

"I don't believe they're gone, Mama. I just can't."

Her mother took Abby's hand. "I know," she repeated.

Abby sat in front of the church between Jake and her mother. Louise sat on Jake's other side, one jeweled hand clutching his knee, the other pressing a lace-trimmed handkerchief to her nose. She was every inch the proper grieving mother and grandmother. Abby admired her for it. Louise would be rewarded as a result with the elusive closure everyone talked about. *Now you can move on,* they kept saying. As if Nick and Lindsey were a town or a vegetable stand, a booth at the county fair. Abby was sick of that advice: *move on.*

A number of people, Joe among them, eulogized. Abby didn't listen. Any moment Nick and Lindsey would come through the door. She felt the possibility run through her blood, cool and light, like quicksilver. She heard the collective gasp from the mourners who were gathered, heard herself say she had never lost faith. She felt the prick of tears, and, reaching into her purse for a tissue, she encountered the book of matches from Nick's desk, the one with *Sondra* written inside it, in Nick's hand. Sondra with an "o" rather than the more familiar "a." Or had Nick gotten it wrong?

Was she here? The possibility skittered through Abby's mind. Suddenly she was convinced that if she were to turn, she would find the woman staring at her.

Abby jumped when her mother touched her arm. "It's over, sweet."

"Thank God," Abby said.

But it wasn't over. On Abby's way out of the church, people approached her. They pressed her hands, murmured their condolences. Several of the women bent their perfumed cheeks to Abby's, and the combined scents were overwhelming and made it hard to breathe. Some were weeping, and they were taken aback, even disapproving to find Abby dry-eyed. It unsettled them, but that was just too bad, she thought. They were wrong to do this, to condemn her family to an eternal rest without proof, without evidence.

She asked to be taken home, but Louise and Nina insisted that Abby, together with her mother and Jake, attend a luncheon at the Metropolitan Lawyers Club in downtown Houston. Abby took one look around the private dining room and thought how Nick would hate it, the tables padded in layers of embossed white linen, the redundancy of silver and china and heavy-bottomed crystal. It would remind him of his childhood, his mother's daily insistence on formal dining.

Abby picked at the main course, a serving of Chicken Cordon Bleu. Beside her, her mother patted her hand. "I'm going to the ladies. Do you—?"

Abby shook her head. "Can we go home when you come back? Have we stayed long enough?"

"I think so. You can blame me," her mother said. "You can say I'm tired."

Louise took the seat Abby's mother vacated as if she had been waiting for the opportunity. "I've opened the beach house," she said.

"When?"

"Last week. I couldn't stand being in Dallas another second. You and Jake should come. A family should be together in a time like this."

"Maybe later this fall," Abby said, although she doubted it. "Have you ever heard Nick mention anyone named Sondra?" she asked.

"Sondra? No, I don't believe so. Who is she?"

"No one," Abby answered. "It's nothing." But if it was so nothing, why hadn't she tossed the matchbook?

Louise smoothed the tablecloth. "Am I a bad person?"

Abby frowned. "Why would you ask that?"

"There are people on this earth who are truly evil, yet I'm the one who is punished. Like Job, I suppose." Louise sighed.

"I don't understand."

"God took Philip," she explained as if Abby were dim. "Now He's taken Nick."

It wasn't true. Nick's father wasn't dead. Even Louise knew it. But she preferred to think of him as dead. She preferred the role of widow to that of jilted wife. It was more socially acceptable. Abby had been appalled when Nick told her the story, that his father had left on a business trip one day and never returned. Nick and his mother hadn't known what had happened to him, and police efforts to find out had proven fruitless. Finally, seven years later, when Nick was sixteen, Louise had the man declared legally dead, clearing the way to cash in his one-million-dollar life insurance policy. She'd been living like a queen ever since. Nick had been in law school when he'd learned the truth, that his father was alive and well and living off the coast of Tampico, Mexico on a yacht with a second wife and three children. Abby could not imagine how hurt and angry Nick must have been, but he'd also felt sympathetic to Philip.

My dad had debt up to here, Nick had told Abby, slicing his hand across his neck. *He had my mother on his back.* "I don't know why he didn't take me with him," Nick had said that, too. He'd been wistful, and Abby had felt incensed on his behalf, that his parents had treated him with so little regard. He'd mentioned the love of sailing he shared with his father. Abby had seen how saddened he was to have lost that along with everything else. She'd wanted so badly to make it up, to love sailing, too. At least that.

But she didn't. She'd tried, but she couldn't take the sun; she was afraid of the water. Nick had finally given up on her and sold the *Blue Daze*. He had said he was fine about it, but suppose he wasn't? Suppose he had left her the way Philip had left Louise, because Abby harped on him and acted the queen and forced him to give up things he didn't want to, like his boat.

Abby turned to Louise. "Do you think Nick is like his father? That he could have—?"

"Could have what, dear?"

But Abby shook her head and said, "Never mind." It wasn't possible. She wasn't Louise and Nick wasn't his father, and Nick's disappearance wasn't a matter of genetics or history repeating itself. He wouldn't have left her, or if he had, he wouldn't have taken Lindsey. When a man did such a thing, when he left his wife, he didn't take his child. Like Nick's father had done, he left his child at home.

At first Abby didn't know what was making the noise. The sound was bleating, dissonant, and she bolted upright, gaze bouncing wall-to-wall in the night-darkened room. She couldn't think where she was. Dreaming? She climbed out from the narrow twin bed where she'd slept all through her girlhood and crossed to the vanity stool where she'd left her purse.

She watched herself pull out her cell phone, place it against her ear. Did she speak, say hello? She wouldn't remember anything except the static that greeted her and then out of that, a voice.

A small voice, a definitely female voice, whispered: *"Mommy?"*

"Lindsey?"

More words came, and Abby struggled to filter them from the background noise. Then, breathily—singing? Crying?— *"You'll never find me, find me, find me...."*

The hair rose on the back of Abby's neck, on her arms. "Lindsey, honey, please, just tell me where you are." She pressed the phone harder to her ear.

But there was nothing. More static. That same liquid-sounding sigh as last time.

"Lindsey, talk to me! Where are you?" Abby could have sworn she was screaming loud enough to wake the dead, but no one appeared. Not Jake and not her mother. Shaking badly, she lowered herself to the side of the bed, fighting for composure.

"Please, Lindsey," she said more calmly. "Is Daddy there? Can he tell me where you are? Mommy will come, I promise."

Nothing. Breath. Abby heard breathing and the low-grade interfering static that was like the hum of insects, like fever. "Lindsey? Please, sweetheart, please, talk to me."

But she didn't, and just as before, after what seemed an eon had passed, but was probably only a matter of moments, there was a click, the softest click, and the connection was severed.

Abby whimpered and pressed her fingertips to her mouth; she kept the phone in place, waiting, waiting, but Lindsey didn't come back. Abby looked at the ID. *Out of Area.* She hit call-back. Nothing. She went into the living room to tell Jake that his sister had called. *See*, Abby intended to say, *I knew they were alive*, but then watching Jake sleep, she couldn't bring herself to waken him. Abby had the same reaction when she looked in at her mother.

And they were both kind the next morning when she told them, when she showed them a call had, indeed, come in at 3:42 a.m. They didn't disagree, but Abby saw in their eyes that they didn't believe it had been from Lindsey.

"A wrong number?" her mother ventured.

"Some crank." Jake was more definite.

But Abby couldn't imagine it. Who would be so cruel?

CHAPTER
10

Out of desperation, Abby turned to Dennis for help, but he said Abby's conviction that it was her daughter who had called her wasn't enough to persuade a judge to issue a warrant for the phone records. A judge would need something more concrete. Dennis regretted it; Abby knew he did. She also knew he didn't share her conviction that it was Lindsey. Wasn't it possible that while Abby had received the phone call—no doubt about that, no one was arguing that—she might have dreamed the rest? Out of terrible grief and longing? And as time passed, as the fall weather cooled and no more phone calls came and no further signs of any kind appeared, Abby felt her certainty slip.

Lindsey's terrified cries echoed from the walls of Abby's nightmares. She was in a dark corridor lined with ringing telephones, and she would run from one to the next shouting, "Hello hello?!" She would scream

Lindsey's name to no avail and eventually wake herself, heart throbbing, in a sweaty tangle of sheets. She began to dread the nights. The sight of her bed made her anxious. Days were more tolerable. At least they had settled into a pattern, proving that even catastrophe can become routine. Abby and her mother did the household chores, they washed clothes and vacuumed. They cleaned closets and manured the flowerbeds in readiness for winter. Abby ran errands. They didn't see much of Jake. He avoided spending time with them— with her, Abby thought.

So when she came home from the grocery store one day in early October and saw his black Mustang parked in her mother's driveway, her heart stopped. She backed her foot off the accelerator and thought: *They've been found!*

Why else would Jake have come here, in the middle of the afternoon, in the middle of the week? When he hadn't once shown his face since the memorial service? When all she'd had from him were excuses?

Nick's BMW crept forward, but then, all at once, a swirl of bright yellow leaves curtained Abby's vision, scattering across the windshield, drawing her attention, and she turned, in relief, to watch them. The way they fluttered and fussed in the pale autumn light was somehow reminiscent of the pert flight of small birds. But then her view cleared and Jake's car was still there. Dark and inevitable. She waited to feel something, panic or anger or grief, and felt nothing but an odd sense of deflation. She had imagined there would be more of a show. A phalanx of patrol cars and flashing lights bearing an entire squadron of uniformed officers. The result of too much television, she guessed.

Was it possible someone—Dennis, maybe?—had just phoned with the news? Could it really end so quietly?

But it wasn't news of their family that had brought Jake home, after all.

When Abby found him in the kitchen, her mother was there, too, and they seemed reluctant to look at her. They seemed guilty. Jake went to look out the window, and her mother set aside the makings of coffee and handed Abby an envelope.

"I should have shown this to you before," she said.

Abby saw that it was addressed to Mr. and Mrs. Nicholas Bennett and that the return address was Texas A&M University. "What is it?" she asked, but, truly she knew. Of course it was more fallout. *Collateral damage.* Additional proof, if she needed it, that when one bad thing happened, a door in the universe opened to let out ten thousand more bad things.

"I'm in some trouble at school, Mom." Jake turned from the window. "I thought maybe Gramma and I could handle it ourselves."

Abby sat at the table and scanned the single page. She raised her gaze. "You were caught cheating?"

"One class. Economics. I can fix it. At least I'm trying to." Jake sat across from Abby.

"This is postmarked two weeks ago." Abby folded the letter, returned it to the envelope and pushed it into the center of the table with her index finger.

"It was forwarded," Jake said, "from home. If you were there instead of here, you'd have known."

"Where I live isn't the issue. I thought you told me you were working with a tutor." Abby was certain that he had mentioned it a few weeks ago.

He didn't answer.

"You lied to me, is that it?"

He didn't deny it.

The pause became awkward. Her heart stumbled at a hectic pace. She thought about the groceries she'd left in the car; the peach ice cream was probably melting all over the floor. She thought if Jake could lie about cheating, something so huge, so shameful and damaging, he could lie about anything. His father, for instance, what Nick had been doing in the Hill Country. Fresh suspicion broke over the surface of Abby's mind. She had tried hard to dismiss it. She had excused as figments of her imagination Jake's odd looks, his avoidance of her, and the sense that he wasn't being truthful when he claimed to know nothing more than she did about what had happened to their family. But now she had proof that he could lie, bald-faced, and she was so gullible, she would believe him.

"Jake?" she prompted, and she did not regret the anger that blistered her voice.

He brought his gaze around, and it was as sharply caustic. "It doesn't matter."

"What do you mean?" Abby blazed. "Of course it matters."

"No, Mom, it really doesn't because I'm quitting school. I'm not going back after the Christmas break." Jake bent toward her. "I can't stand A&M. I can't take the Aggie rah-rah bullshit. You don't have the money to pay for it, and I'm not making my grades anyway."

"Since when, Jake? Last semester you were on the dean's list."

His mouth curled. "See? You don't know a damn thing. I haven't made the dean's list since the fall semester of my freshman year. I screwed up on my finals when you made me go back there last spring, and I've been screwing up ever since."

"I didn't make you go back, Jake. It was best."

"You want life to be the same and it isn't."

"How am I supposed to know you're having problems if you won't talk to me? If all you do is lie to me?"

"What about your problems? You can't even live by yourself."

"So your cheating and lying is my fault?"

"You think Lindsey's calling you all the damn time."

"Oh, no, don't make this about me, mister." Abby rolled her eyes to the ceiling. "Does it never stop? Haven't I been through enough?"

"That's what I'm talking about! You act like it's all about you, like you're the only one who lost your family. But it happened to me, too, Mom, and sometimes I feel like I'm— But goddamn! What the hell am I thinking?" Jake hit his head with his fists. "Dad and Lindsey aren't *dead!* They're on fucking vacation, and every so often Lindsey phones home to talk about her tan and say what a great time she's having."

Abby couldn't breathe, and in the sudden widening crack of silence, she felt weightless, untethered. At the sink, her mother stirred. Abby prayed she would say something, anything. But she didn't. It wasn't her way to interfere.

Jake got up. "I have to get back to campus."

Abby tapped the envelope. "What about this?"

"I'll handle it."

"If you aren't careful, you'll ruin your chance at getting into law school."

"That was Dad's fantasy. Not mine."

"Can't we talk, Jake? The way we used to?"

He looked at her. With pity, Abby thought, and he said, "Nothing's the way it used to be, Mom. When are you going to figure that out?" And then deliberately, carefully, he pushed his chair toward the table, walked over to his grandmother and hugged her, and a moment later, Abby felt his hand on her shoulder, his light, firm touch. But before she could reach out to him, somehow hold on to him, she heard the back door close, and he was gone.

"Should I go after him?" Abby appealed to her mother. But her expression said if Abby had to ask, the opportunity had passed.

The next morning, Abby told her mother she was going home, and when her mother asked, "Why now?" Abby blamed Jake. The sting of his words, the truth in them had kept her up most of the night.

"Thanksgiving is coming," Abby said. "I should cook, try to make it normal for him."

"We could go out to Luby's. My treat."

Abby smiled. "You saved my life, Mama."

Her mother cupped her cheek. "I miss Nick and Lindsey, too, you know. So much. But if they were here, they would say we should go on. They would say we should make a new life."

"But I don't want a new life, Mama. I want to know what happened to the old one."

The house offered her nothing but its history, its record of what had been. She walked through the silent rooms and heard her family's laughter in every creak of the floorboards. She startled at every shift of light. The past hung in every corner, a boogeyman waiting to crack her across her eyes. In the kitchen, the air seemed redolent with the smell of French toast and bacon, the last meal they'd shared. In her mind, Abby walked around the memory of herself from that morning. Her smiling, smug self with her silly plans, her belief—clearly naïve—in the sanctity of her home, her family.

But her memories were no longer the source of joy or comfort they had been, and this house was not her refuge. It was alien to her, a house of questions, of ghosts, mysteries. And she was the one who had disappeared, Alice down the rabbit hole. How could she stay here? What sort of life could she have?

Abruptly, she left the kitchen, swiftly making her way down the front hall, anxious to get outside. She was at the front door when she felt it, an odd ripple of unease that caused her to turn and look up the stairs, and when she saw the light spilling through the doorway of her and Nick's bedroom, the hair on her scalp rose. She wasn't sure why she was afraid, but she was. She had to make herself climb the stairs, hand gripped like a vice to the banister. As if she expected to be attacked…by what? Did ghosts turn on the lights in the houses they haunted? She remembered her brief sojourn here when she returned from Kate's. After the flood…ATF….

That time she had found the light on in the dining room, a room that was seldom used, and a window had been cracked open in her and Nick's bedroom. She had turned off the light and shut the window and hadn't thought a thing of it. Why think anything of this? It was only her sense of the house, that it was so foreign, so unwelcoming of her now; it made her anxious. If its walls could talk, they would ask her to leave. To vanish without a trace like the rest of the Bennetts.

She paused in the bedroom doorway. The lamp on Nick's nightstand glowed like a beacon. She hadn't turned on that lamp. She hadn't come into this room at all except out of necessity, to get a change of clothes, her toothbrush. The sense of the life she and Nick had shared, their most intimate marital moments, was strongest here and made it impossible to linger. She hadn't once been able to bring herself to go near the bed. But now the soft blue duvet cover was rumpled, and Nick's pillow was pulled out of place and scrunched as if it had cushioned someone's cheek.

I didn't do that. The thought whispered through Abby's mind.

But she must have. Who else could it have been?

In her grief, she must have lain there and pushed her face into Nick's pillow. She'd worn his shirts, hadn't she? Put on his leather jacket...

She brought her fingertips to her eyes. "Where is my family?" she whispered.

Presumed drowned in some unknown location more than three hundred miles away.

Presumed...that word.

It left so much room for conjecture, for doubt.

Back downstairs, she fished the book of matches from her purse and studied the raised silver lettering that spelled out Riverbend Lodge and Bandera, Texas. Why would Nick write down a local fax number in a book of matches that came from a location that was a near six-hour drive west of here? But maybe it wasn't a fax number, Abby thought, searching in her purse for her cell phone. Maybe she had misdialed.

Holding open the tiny flap, she carefully picked out the number Nick had written there with the tip of her finger, then she waited with breath held, only to hear the same rhythmic bleating of a fax machine as last time. She tried to imagine the place where it was, in her mind's eye seeing an office, a woman named Sondra. But where? In what location? Houston or Bandera? Abby stowed her phone and the matches in her purse and shouldered it. There was only one thing she knew for certain: She would never find the answers to her questions by staying here. And something else she knew: If Nick and Lindsey were still alive, they weren't coming home on their own.

CHAPTER

11

Before she left, Abby called Charlie and was relieved when he agreed to take Miss Havisham and Delilah off her hands for the nominal sum she named. She'd have given the horses to him, but he wouldn't hear of it.

He offered to keep an eye on her place, and Abby thanked him again and paused, long enough that Charlie was prompted to ask if there was something wrong.

"Just—you haven't seen anyone over here, have you? Any strangers, I mean."

"No one except Jake, and I don't think he goes inside. He just looks in on the horses now and then. Why?"

"Oh, no reason. I'm sure it's nothing." Because it was nothing, she told herself. A bedroom window cracked open, a couple of lights left on. Charlie might not say it was probable that she'd left these things untended herself, but he would think it, and he'd be right.

She thanked him a third time for his trouble, for all that he'd already done, and she was grateful when he didn't question her further. She didn't want to tell him she was going back to the Hill Country. He might have asked what her plan was, what did she hope to find this time that would be any different than the last time she was there, and she wouldn't have known what to say. She had no real plan. The only thing she knew for sure was that the answers she was looking for weren't here.

At the western edge of Houston, when the city's skyline wasn't more than a gilded smudge in the BMW's rearview mirror, it occurred to her that she could go anywhere: California. Hawaii. Farther, she thought: Japan. Kuala Lumpur. Who could stop her? Who was left to wonder where she was? She was like a kite, floating untethered.

It was dark when she saw the sign for Griff's Café outside Sealy, and her stomach grumbled, reminding her that she hadn't eaten anything since the toast her mother had made for breakfast, and she'd thrown most of that out to the squirrels. She could stop at the restaurant and make herself eat a decent meal or go on, find a gas station and a candy bar. As unwilling as she was, as nervous as it made her, she took the exit.

The bell over the restaurant door jingled loudly when it shut behind Abby, and she paused. There wasn't much of a crowd. Two rough-faced men sitting over mugs of coffee at the counter turned idle stares toward her, and she made herself smile as if she had spent her entire life walking alone into places like this at night.

She slid into a booth along the wall and made a lengthy production of setting her purse down beside her, stowing her keys. A husband and his wife and three misbehaving children were stuffed into a booth near the door. There wasn't a waitress in sight, but a man's voice and woman's big-booming laugh drifted through the order pickup window behind the counter. Smoke mixed with steam wafted through the opening, too, along with the smell of old grease. Abby wrinkled her nose. Whatever appetite she'd had deserted her.

"Eat your spaghetti," the mother near the door told her children, "all of you, finish up or no dessert."

"Oh, man," the older boy said.

"It tastes like trash," the other one said.

Abby closed her eyes. She'd delivered the same lecture, how many times? Hadn't she? Her memories of her children, her family, were they real?

A noise at her elbow made her jump.

The waitress grimaced. "Sorry," she said, and her brow furrowed. "You okay, hon?"

Abby touched her fingertips to her face, blinking back tears. The waitress set a glass of water on the table and produced a paper napkin that Abby used to blow her nose. "I don't know what's come over me," she said into the napkin. Her cheeks felt warm. She had so little control, it was a risk being out in public.

"Man trouble, I bet."

Abby smiled.

The waitress—Peg, according to the tag pinned to the white-cuffed pocket of her pink uniform—rolled her eyes. She could deliver a sermon on the subject. She was older, in her sixties at least, but she still had a rollicking gleam in her eyes. Her longish red hair was faded and streaked with gray at the temples, and she wore it tied up in an outrageous pink chiffon bow.

Rhinestones dangled from her ears. A profusion of rainbow-colored plastic bracelets cuffed one wrist.

Nick would have said Peg wasn't ready to hang it up yet. He'd have teased her and charmed her until she laughed her big, sassy laugh. He'd have left her a huge tip, and if Abby had made a comment, he'd have said something about how hard Peg worked, that tip money was the only real money women like her could ever earn. He was generous that way.

"I knew it," Peg said, "the second I laid eyes on you. I told Griff, he's my cook, I told him there's a woman with heartache on her mind." Peg leaned down and wiped a spot on Abby's table with the corner of her apron. "I said she's either going to him or runnin' from him. Guaranteed." Peg's glance narrowed. "Am I right?"

"Honestly, anyone who knows me wouldn't believe I'm here."

"They don't approve."

"They wouldn't. No." Abby realized Peg still believed they were talking about a man.

She ordered a bacon, lettuce and tomato sandwich and a cup of coffee, leaded, she said when Peg asked. While she waited, she didn't know what to do with her hands. She thought how she'd never liked seeing people eat alone. They made her sad.

When Peg brought her sandwich, Abby could only eat half.

"Box that up for you?" Peg asked.

"No, thanks," Abby said.

"Well, how about dessert? The chocolate pie is real good. Griff doesn't make the pies. My sis does." She grinned widely. "Hon, there's nothin' like a dose of chocolate to rev up your spirits, keep you awake on the road." She scooped Abby's plate and utensils onto the tray she balanced on her hip. "You going far?"

Abby glanced at her. *The Canary Islands, Madagascar, Hong Kong, Belize,* the names lined up in her mind. "The Hill Country," she said. "Bandera," she added.

"Figures," Peg said.

Abby raised her brows.

"Your man's a hunter? Right? Gone off to the deer lease and you've had it up to here." Peg passed the flat of her palm through the air above her head.

Before she could think about what she was doing, Abby reached inside her purse, pulled out a snapshot and handed it to Peg. "Have you ever seen them?" she asked.

Peg studied the photograph. "Gorgeous family," she said. "Yours?"

Abby nodded. "My husband and my daughter drove this way last April. They might have stopped here."

"They were going to Bandera?"

"They were headed in that direction the weekend it flooded. They've never been found." Abby slipped the picture back into her purse. "The police think there was an accident, that they drowned."

"Oh, hon, oh, how awful. I'm so sorry. My aunt and uncle have a place out thataway. They lost near everything, but they're alive, thank you, Jesus, Mary and Joseph." Peg shifted the tray against her hip, and the cutlery clanked as if in frustration. She gestured. "I thought I saw two kids in the picture."

"My oldest, Jake, is in college, at A&M. He had to study that weekend."

"Well, thank God, huh? Most of 'em jump at the chance to cut school."

Abby smiled and asked for her check.

Peg thumbed through her pad. "So are you goin' to visit friends in Bandera?"

Abby said, "Not exactly," and was instantly regretful that she'd left herself open to more questions.

But Peg only said, "Shoot, I can't find your check. Must of left it in the kitchen. Back in a sec."

While she waited, Abby used her napkin to mop up the widening puddle of water under her tea glass. What would she do if Peg asked more questions? Would she pull out the matchbook, rattle on about the surveillance tape, say she'd caught her son in a web of lies about a cheating scheme and felt sicker than ever with the suspicion that he was keeping something worse from her? Would she tell Peg about the flood's survivors? The ones like Patsy Doggett? Her husband Lloyd had given her up for dead. But Patsy wasn't dead. She had somehow managed to get out of her truck and swim or somehow make her way to her sister's. Patsy Doggett was alive today, against all the odds. A woman in her eighties...

Abby looked up as Peg emerged from the kitchen and headed toward her, grim-faced and intent, and she wished she'd dropped a twenty dollar bill on the table and left when she'd had the chance.

"Listen here," Peg began. "I'm not one to get involved in other folks' business, but I got one of my feelin's about you and I'm kinda worried."

"Oh, no, please don't—"

"You're thinking of hunting for your family yourself, aren't you? But, hon, what if you was to find 'em—dead and all?" She added this last baldly, even defiantly, as if to awaken Abby to the cold reality of the possibility—the probability—that faced her. "What then?" Peg demanded.

Abby pulled her wallet from her purse. "I should get going."

Peg touched her hand. "I'll be praying for you."

"Thank you," Abby said.

"Don't you worry none about the bill." She wadded Abby's check in her hand. "Dinner's on the house."

"Oh, no," Abby said. "I couldn't."

"Sure you can." Peg turned away, then turned back. "You know, I can call my aunt, tell 'em to keep an eye out. What kind of car was it?"

"Jeep. Jeep Cherokee." Abby shouldered her purse.

"I'm gonna write that down. You know the license? You have a cell number?" Peg set her tray on the table, and Abby followed her to the cash register. It felt wrong giving her phone number to a woman she'd only just met, but what if Peg's aunt did know something? Or what if Peg mentioned Abby's family to someone— other diners, travelers—who knew something? There were stranger coincidences.

When Abby thanked Peg for her kindness, she came around the counter and hugged Abby as if she couldn't help it. Then Abby went outside and sat behind the wheel of Nick's BMW, blowing into the cold cup of her hands, thinking Peg could have just let her go with her prayer. But she hadn't. She had taken Abby's information as if she felt finding Abby's family was possible.

It was a sign.

It had to be.

* * *

Somewhere west of San Antonio, Abby's cell phone rang. It was her mother.

"Where are you?" she said as Abby pulled over. "You said you were going home."

"Oh, Mama, I'm sorry." Abby sensed her mother poised to drive to the rescue again. "I just went through San Antonio."

"San Antonio? Abby, what are you doing?"

"Going to Bandera, then I—" She paused. "People are going to forget, Mama, and I can't let that happen. One way or another, I have to bring Nick and Lindsey home."

"I understand, honey, I do, but I worry about you out there alone, driving around in the dark."

Abby didn't say anything.

"I'm not sure what you can do by yourself."

Abby wasn't sure either. She could have said she would be closer to them there, that somehow it felt imperative to go there.

"Abby?"

"Mama, the law firm wants to buy out Nick's partnership. They're going to ask the court to appoint an administrator."

"What?"

"Joe called me and said they have to move on, that he's *sorry*." Abby pushed strands of hair behind her ear. "He said he'd see to it that Jake's college fund was secure."

"When did he call? Why didn't you tell me?"

"First, they had that awful memorial; now they want to just let Nick go. They want me to say he's dead, Mama. He gave them over twenty years, and they can't give him seven months?" Abby rolled down the window. The sudden inrush of chilly air took away her breath, the threat of tears.

"It's business, honey," her mother said. "The firm has to deal with practicalities."

"I'm not being practical, am I?"

"I suppose my concern is that you're delaying— never mind." She interrupted herself. "You have to find your own way through this, I know."

"I don't know how you've done it, living all these years alone. You're so much stronger than me, Mama."

"Don't forget you're my daughter," Abby's mother said. "And don't forget, I'm right here."

Abby said she knew, that she was grateful.

"Jake is here, honey," her mama said, after a pause. "I'll put him on."

No, Abby thought. She knew he'd be upset with her, but she was surprised to hear Jake sounding almost cheerful.

He'd come to his gramma's to study, he said, and to tell her and Abby that he wasn't going to be expelled for cheating. Instead he'd been put on probation. "They cut me some slack because of the situation," he said. "It's not that I like trading on that," he was quick to add, "but if it saves the semester—" He paused, waiting for a reaction, but Abby didn't have one ready. "Look, I know what I did was crap—"

"You can't let what's happened to us ruin your future, Jake."

"I'm not a little kid. I know what I'm doing. I know what I have to do."

Abby didn't answer. She traced a pattern on the steering wheel.

"Mom?" Jake finally said. "What are you doing?"

That question again. It was like the flavor of the month.

"I'm going to Bandera," Abby said.

"But you told Gramma you were going home. Now you're going to the Hill Country. I don't get it."

She closed her eyes.

"Mom? Are you there?" Jake's voice cracked.

"Yes, I'm here."

"Are you still going?"

"I have to, Jake."

He said nothing for a moment, then, "You know how you always tell me not to ask the question if I don't want the answer?"

"Yes?" Silence. Her pulse resonant in her ears. "Jake?"

"Come home, Mom, that's all. You should just come home."

Near Seguin, Abby stopped for gas. No one else was around, and slowly she became aware of the lateness of the hour and her surroundings, that she was alone in the middle of nowhere. A chilly breeze grazed her neck; she pushed her hands deeper into her sweater pockets. She wondered if Nick might have stopped here last spring. She wondered what he would say if he were to walk out of the woods that pressed in on her from all sides and find her pumping her own gas alone in the middle of the night.

He wouldn't believe it, she thought. Of everyone, he would be the most surprised.

The gas pump clicked off. She holstered the nozzle

and thought about the possibility of turning around, of going home, and she knew that she couldn't. She had to find out the truth.

CHAPTER
12

The lobby of the Riverbend Lodge was empty, but the office door was open and a light was on. Abby peeped inside and saw an old man slumped in a chair asleep in front of a flickering television screen with the sound turned low. She was reluctant to wake him and tried first by clearing her throat. No response. She tapped the desk bell, cringing at the tinny sound, but almost at once that brought a loud snort. Pretty soon the man came shuffling through the door, scouring his face, blinking at her.

Abby apologized and said she hadn't planned to stop here, that she was on her way to a friend's house and had gotten tired. All of which was untrue. This was most certainly her intended destination. Why else had she carried a book of matches from this place around with her since last August? She asked about a room.

"I'm not sure how long I'll be staying. Will that be a problem?"

The old man looked curiously at her, obviously trying to make sense of the discrepancies in her story. "No," he said after a moment. "I guess not." In between taking down Abby's information and swiping her debit card, he said he was sorry Abby had caught him napping. "I'm covering for my son. He owns the motel, him and his wife do, but she's in the hospital. Emergency surgery." He patted his midsection. "Female trouble. Come on her real sudden-like this afternoon."

Abby took the key he handed her and said she hoped everything would be okay. *Do you know anyone named Sondra? She might have been a guest. She might have been with someone named Nick.* The questions hovered in Abby's mind. The answers to them were all she wanted to know. The old man waited, fingers balanced on the desk. Abby noticed their tremor; she noticed his frailty, that his skin was chalky, his face lined with worry and fatigue.

They talked about the flood, and he told Abby the motel had had a foot of water. "It was a mess," he said, "but I'm not complaining. Some folks lost everything. Next to that, it'd be a sin for me to whine about a little water."

They said good-night, and she went around back to the room he'd given her and sat on the bed with her navy canvas tote beside her—the tote she'd packed that morning at her mother's, her going-home bag. The edge of the mattress was brick hard under her and sank toward the middle like a half-done cake. It smelled sanitized, she thought, wrinkling her nose; it reminded her of the color green. Latrine green, with shades of mold and air-conditioned-damp underneath.

The room's furnishings and décor were styled to resemble someone's idea of the Old West, very 1950s, very Hollywood with all the real hardship and deprivation worn slick off it. Sets from episodes of the *Lone Ranger* or maybe *Gunsmoke* came to mind. Only in Bandera, Abby thought. *Cowboy Capital of the World*. She pulled up her hands, pointed her index fingers at the floral curtained window and said, "Reach for the sky," then lay back. The ceiling overhead had a large yellow stain to the left of center. Dark shadows encroached on it from the corners, making a pattern like a herd of horses or a range of mountains with clefts formed by deep gorges. Abby shoved the tote onto the floor and lay down, pulling her knees up against the weight of dread that had settled in her stomach.

Sometime later, through the fuzzy walls of an uneasy doze, she thought she heard footsteps outside her door, and when they persisted, she went to look, parting the curtain slightly, but there was only a paper cup from McDonald's skittering across the parking lot at the whim of an errant breeze. The taillights of a car nearing the exit caught her eye. Dark blue, she thought, although it was hard to tell in the wash of light that pooled beneath the motel's vacancy sign. When the car turned, Abby saw the driver was a woman. Maybe she was related to the old man at the desk; maybe she'd brought news of the daughter-in-law. Abby hoped it wasn't bad.

When she woke again, the glare of morning sunlight edged the curtains. She could feel it needling her eyelids and crooked an elbow over her face. Her head ached, and she felt heavy, hangover heavy. From driving half the night, she thought. From the stress of not having a clue about what she was doing and doing it anyway.

Abby sat up slowly. What did she think she was going to wear while she was here? She looked down her front at her rumpled sweater and Nick's sweatshirt that she wore underneath it. She prodded the canvas tote with her toe. What was in it? A couple of T-shirts. Maybe another sweater, a pullover, some underwear. She couldn't recall exactly what she'd tossed into it yesterday, but she was pretty sure she was wearing the only pair of socks, the only jeans. She would need more than that if she intended to stay. Did she? What was her plan? Would she grill the old man at the front desk, demand to see the guest register, ask all over town if anyone knew a woman named Sondra?

She took a shower, and once she was dressed, she walked to the motel lobby. She was glad when the girl working at the reception desk told her that the old man had gone home to rest and that his daughter-in-law was going to be fine. Abby had breakfast, and afterward she drove the short length of Main Street hunting a shop to buy a jacket, clean socks and underwear. She didn't know what to think of herself. As if it was rational to believe her family had survived the flood and were now—what? Wandering like vagabonds? Or maybe they'd found housing atop some remote cliff and were living off the land.

At Gruenwald's General Store, Abby bought a fleece-lined jacket, bright red, a happy color, two pairs of thick socks and two pairs of underwear, another bra, Playtex, in the box. When she pulled her wallet from her purse, the book of matches came with it. She handed the clerk her credit card and tucked the matches back inside, thinking: Sondra. Thinking: Well, who knew? Could be anybody. A client. Somebody's secretary.

While Abby waited, she thought how little she knew of the people in Nick's professional life. But was that so unusual? Was it any different than other marriages? Families? She had her role to play, Nick had his. Of necessity, their daily routines were separate, involved different places, different people.

The clerk pushed the sales slip across the counter toward her.

Abby signed it and pushed it back. "I'm trying to locate someone," she said.

The clerk waited.

Abby's cheeks warmed. "Never mind. Can you cut these?" She indicated the tags on the jacket, slipping it on once they were removed. Leaving the store, she stowed her shopping bag in the car and walked down Main Street toward the river. Bandera had been settled in one bent elbow of the Medina River in 1856. Now more than one hundred fifty years later, the river still wasn't much of a hike from the center of town.

She crested the hill where Main crossed Maple and dipped toward the junction with Highway 16. Last time she was here, the Medina had been raging over the intersection. Now as she threaded her way around twiggy clumps of possumhaw, buttonbush and gnarled mesquite, her steps raised powdery dust. Dry blades of yellow switchgrass brushed the sides of her boots. Nearer the water, where a thick layer of cypress needles mixed with oak and sweetgum leaves cushioned the ground, she paused to look at the water flowing east.

After the storm, when she'd come here with Kate, she had watched for her Jeep, certain that she would see it with Nick and Lindsey inside. She had imagined diving in. Somehow she would swim against her fear of water, swim against the furious current and save them. A miraculous rescue. Today the water level was normal, the flow sedate. Still, Abby hunted the river's edges for a sign. The sun's glitter off the car's roof, a tire partly concealed in the gnarled fist of a tree's roots. But there was nothing like that. The water passed her, placid, heedless of what it had done, what it had taken. Did she intend to walk its length? If she spoke to it, prayed to it, would it give up its secret? Tell her where it had left her husband and daughter? Would it deny it had ever taken them?

"Abby?"

She wheeled. "Oh, Katie." Abby walked into Kate's embrace. "Who called, Mama or Jake?"

"Your mama, early this morning. She thought you'd be at my house or that you would have at least called me by now."

"I was going to."

"I saw the BMW outside Gruenwald's, and when I didn't find you inside, I figured you were here."

"Your nutty friend."

"Insanity," Kate smiled, "the tie that binds."

"I can't seem to give up." Abby surveyed the river. "Where did you stay last night?"

"Riverbend."

"Oh, Lord, how depressing. Come on." She linked

Abby's arm with hers. "Let's get your stuff. George can bring one of the men later for the car."

The road leading out of town was edged by a thick limestone shelf, and the view shot into the blue, vacant nowhere, down the wall of a canyon that would end in a boulder-filled crevice. Looking out the window, Abby wondered, Was the Jeep there? In this one? That one? The one fifty feet on?

Stop! The word shouted in her mind. She bit both lips to keep it inside. They could go from dawn until dark and never see into all the canyons and gorges. The land was like a rumpled sheet. If only she could, Abby would pick it up and shake it out flat.

Kate said, "I think I saw Nadine Betts in town."

"The reporter? Say you didn't. Say she doesn't know I'm here."

"Umm, not sure. I was coming down the street toward Gruenwald's. Looked like she, or somebody who looked an awful lot like her, was checking out your car. She was gone by the time I found a parking place."

Abby thought of the blue sedan she'd spotted leaving the motel parking lot late last night, too late for it to have been there for any good reason. "What does she drive? Do you know?"

"Ford. Taurus, I think."

"What color?"

"Dark blue. Why?"

Abby explained and then groaned. "How does that woman know I'm here when I didn't even know myself that I was coming?"

"Hah!" Kate said. "You're forgetting where you are."

Long ago, according to legend, in the midst of a terrible drought, a Comanche chief came to the highest bluff near his village in the Hill Country to survey the brown wasteland that lay in every direction. Nothing moved; there was no sign of anything left alive. All the game that had fed his people—the deer and the buffalo, the jackrabbits, even the lizards—had died off or escaped, and now, without adequate food and water, the chief's people were dying. He fell to his knees then and there, and in a last act of desperation, he petitioned the Great Spirit for relief. The answer came swiftly. In exchange for rain, the chief was told, the Great Spirit would accept his most precious possession, his beloved daughter. The chief was devastated. Never was a child so dear to a father. He begged to give his own life instead, but the Great Spirit refused, and the chief went away with a heavy heart.

It was while he was in consultation with his tribal council that his small daughter approached. In her hands she carried her most prized possession, a small doll made for her by her grandmother from cornhusks before the old woman died. In the ancient voice of the wise grandmother, the chief's daughter announced that she had come at the request of the Great Spirit. The girl told how Spirit was so moved by the chief's love of his child, and his sorrow over her impending loss, that He had changed His mind. He would not take her. Rather, the chief must dress the doll in a bonnet made from blue jay feathers and lay it atop the bluff in offering, and rain would come. This was done, and the promised rain fell like a gentle blessing throughout the night.

But the true miracle wasn't found until the next morning when the chief and his people emerged from their tepees to find the hills surrounding their village awash in a sea of flowers. Tipped in white, the tall spires were the same clear, beautiful shade of blue as the jay's feathers. They were called bluebonnets from that day, and the people honored them as they honored their chief, whose unwavering love for his daughter had inspired the selfless gift that had saved them and their land.

Abby had first heard the legend from her mother, and she had repeated it to her children many times when they'd asked. One very hot, dry summer day when they'd been camped near the Guadalupe River at a site not far from Camp Many Waters—sadly, no longer in existence—Lindsey had offered to sacrifice her Barbie doll to bring the rain. Abby had turned away to hide her smile, somehow not able to picture it, Lindsey's full-busted, pencil-waisted Barbie dressed in blue jay feathers. Standing at the window now overlooking Kate's deck, Abby thought if only it did work that way. If only she could leave a doll in offering, and the Great Spirit would return Lindsey to her.

George came up beside her and handed her a glass of wine. "Big difference since you were here last. In the weather, I mean."

Abby looked at the sky, unblemished now at evening except for the moon, a frosted sickle, that hung in one far corner. "You think I'm nuts, don't you? For coming, for thinking I can find out what happened."

George slipped his arm around her shoulders. "I just hope you won't be hurt any more, Abby, that's all."

She thought of saying it wasn't possible to hurt any more than she already did; she thought of asking him point-blank what he knew. Because she sensed there was something. But didn't she sense that with everyone? Was she wrong? Could she even stand knowing?

She sipped her wine. "I'll be fine," she said.

George tightened his grip. "I hope so, honey. I truly do."

CHAPTER
13

A few mornings after Abby's arrival, Dennis stopped by. He was in uniform and looked official; he looked like the police and not at all like the man Abby had come to know through weeks of phone conversations. This man was a stranger. It was difficult to meet his eye; she couldn't say his name. When he smiled, her face warmed. When he asked how she'd been, she said, "How did you know I was here?"

"Kate called me after she heard from your mother. They were worried, ready to put out an APB on you."

Kate brought Dennis a mug and filled it with coffee. Abby offered the pitcher of cream.

He said, "Thanks, but I take it black," and kept her gaze. "I thought maybe you'd like to go horseback riding this afternoon."

"Oh, no. I don't think so." Abby looked at Kate.

"Well, I meant George and Kate, too. We could meet

at my place, maybe pack some wine and cheese, ride downriver, make a party of it."

"Sounds like fun," Kate said, "but George and I have to go into town to the courthouse. We have an issue with this year's taxes." She looked at Abby. "You go; it'll do you good."

Abby made a face. She could only imagine the planning behind this invitation. The discussion they'd all had about her. What could they do to distract her from her fixation? Her obsession? Considering the extent of some of her wild imaginings, Abby might have laughed. They'd lock her up if they knew, she thought. She caught his eye. "I'd like to go," she told him. "It's been a while since I've ridden, and I've missed it."

He rapped his knuckles on the table and said, "Good deal," and from the light in his eyes, she knew he was pleased.

She was nervous later, following Dennis into his barn, but as she stepped around, helping him with the routine of saddling the horses, she became aware of a welling sense of joy. And she paused a moment to study it, this strange, half-remembered, sweet contentment that seemed to be stealing through her. Suddenly she couldn't wait to climb into the saddle, and just as suddenly, tears pricked her eyelids.

How could she be happy?

She didn't notice the rifle Dennis had loaded onto his mount until they were some distance from the corral, and even then, she didn't ask. She didn't want to disturb their silence. Abby had noticed this about Dennis before, that silence between them wasn't uncomfortable or awkward.

They were crossing a field when he asked her if she was aware that Mormons were some of the first settlers around.

Abby answered she hadn't heard that.

"There were German immigrants, too," Dennis said, "and a few Polish families. There was so much timber back then, they built mills and manufactured lumber. Lumber and furniture mostly."

"Huh," Abby said, and they fell silent again.

Above them the day was all blue air, cool breeze and fall sunshine so warm down Abby's back that she took off her new red jacket and tied the arms at her waist. The horses picked their way over the parched ground, around clumps of prickly pear and wedges of brush that Abby decided was some kind of thistle in its dying season.

She said, "I thought this was ranch country."

"Not at first. Not until the late 1800s when the ranchers south of here started banding their herds together. They drove the cattle up this way and stopped on the banks of the Medina, right there in town where it makes that big bend? Guess it seemed a natural place to rest the herds and fatten them before hitting the trail north." Dennis paused. "The land's been overgrazed now in places."

In the distance, Abby saw what appeared to be buzzards circling the sky. Dennis saw them, too. "If you don't mind, we'll ride that way and see what's up."

She shook her head, aware of the rifle again.

"It might be nothing," Dennis said, sensing her distress. He asked about her house. "Didn't you tell me you designed it?"

"Yes," she said, knowing it was an attempt to distract her and glad for it.

"That porch is something, the way it wraps all four corners."

"That was Nick's idea," Abby said. "He very nearly blew our budget on that porch. It surprised me, too. He's usually so frugal. You have to be when there are two—two children to put through—to—" She couldn't finish. She pressed her knuckles to her mouth, blinking furiously. *Please don't cry, pleaseplease.* She felt the horses stop, felt Dennis bend toward her, felt him wondering whether to touch her.

He didn't.

Finally, when she thought she was all right, she said, "I don't know how to talk about them."

Dennis straightened, and they started the horses walking again. He seemed to understand there was nothing he could say.

Abby concentrated on the sound the hooves made as they swished through rough yellow grass. The leather saddle creaked beneath her. She listened to her mount breathe. From somewhere close by four songbird notes shimmered up a scale and died.

"Mockingbird," Dennis said.

"I thought so," Abby answered.

They spotted the blood almost as soon as they entered the thicket. Dennis dismounted and swiped his fingers over the glossy stain in the leaves at his feet. "Fresh," he said. Handing Abby his reins, he unholstered his rifle and disappeared into the woods.

At first Abby could hear him, then after a bit, she couldn't anymore. She jumped when he emerged on her other side, his expression grim. "Oh, no," she said.

"Some bozo shot a doe and left her," he answered. "She's hurt pretty bad. Her fawn is close by." He went to his saddlebag, took out a rope.

Abby dismounted.

"No," he said reading her intention. "Stay here with the horses. They might spook."

"You have to kill her?"

"Nothing else to do."

"The fawn?"

"I'll try and get a rope on it first." He looked disgusted and furious enough to cuss, but he wouldn't, Abby thought, out of regard for her.

He glanced off as if he needed a moment to gather himself, and she thought he would go, but he didn't. His gaze returned to her, and their eyes locked. She could not have said who moved, but somehow they were standing closer together, so close she could smell the sun on his skin, the minty warmth of his breath, a fainter undercurrent of pine. He slid his fingers from her elbow to her wrist, then loosely cupped her hand and she felt her knees weaken. She felt herself sway. The moment elongated, shimmered. It was sensual but not. And then it was over. She caught herself, broke their gaze and stepped back. Or Dennis did. Abby wasn't sure.

He plowed a hand over his head. He seemed abashed, chagrined, some combination.

Abby didn't want him to feel badly. "You've been so kind to me," she said, and she wasn't sure what she meant. More than was on the surface, she thought.

"You'll be all right," he said.

She nodded. Was he telling her or asking her? She didn't know that either.

He left her then, and she watched him thread his way into the woods until he was lost to her view, and then, only a moment later, she flinched when a single shot rang out.

For dinner that evening, George grilled salmon; Kate made scalloped potatoes, and she and Abby steamed fresh asparagus and tossed a salad. While they ate, Abby chattered about her day, ignoring the voice in her head that said she wasn't entitled to have a good day, a relatively happy and peaceful day. She told the story about the doe and her fawn, becoming caught up in it. She assumed Kate and George would have some response when she finished, but neither of them said a word. They didn't even look at her.

Kate stacked the dirty plates and took them to the sink.

Abby looked from her to George, uncertain, a bit on edge. "Dennis brought the fawn home." She carried the bowl of leftover scalloped potatoes to the counter. "He's going to hand feed it until it's old enough to care for itself."

Now George smiled. "He's always rescuing something, isn't he, Kate?"

But she didn't answer, and the look she shot George would have frozen hell.

Abby ducked her head. Clearly they'd been arguing, and she wondered about the cause, hoping it wasn't her.

George found a container for Abby to stow the leftover potatoes in and said he was going to light a fire in the outdoor fireplace.

"What is up with you two?" Abby asked as soon

as he was gone. "I mean, I know it's none of my business, but I'm worried it's me, that I'm in the way here."

Kate rinsed the plates, started in on the silverware. Her back was to Abby, and she kept it that way.

Abby felt a frisson of unease loosen along her spine. "Kate? Tell me."

She shut off the water, picked up a kitchen towel and turned to Abby, looking anxious, winding the towel around her hands. "You're going to be so furious with me. George is already pissed. No way I go with this is right, but you have to know."

"Know what?" Abby's unease flared now into full-blown panic.

"I should have told you when I first remembered, but George said it didn't mean anything."

"What are you talking about?"

"I saw Nick last December in town, the week before Christmas."

"You saw—what are you saying, Kate?"

"I'm sorry, I should have told you before now, but I honestly didn't remember until we—until George and I started talking about the property taxes for this year. That's what I was doing when I saw Nick last year. I was paying our taxes, and I came out of the courthouse and he was just there, walking up the sidewalk. I did a double take. He said he was in town to do a title search on some land. I think he mentioned a client, but I'm not sure." Kate's gaze was distraught, pleading. "I was so surprised, I didn't pay close attention. I'm sorry."

"He mentioned a client? Was he with someone?"

"I didn't see anyone else. I asked about you, why you didn't come, and he said it was sort of a secret his being there. He said the land he'd looked at was going for a song, and he was thinking of buying it as a surprise for you. He asked me not to tell you. I think that's part of why I lost track of it, because I had it in my head I shouldn't say anything. I sort of made myself forget, you know, because it would fall out of my mouth before I could stop it, and I didn't want to ruin it for you."

"But when the flood came, when he disappeared— it's hard to believe you didn't remember then."

"Well, I didn't, and I *am* telling you now, even though George is dead set against it. He thinks telling you is only pouring gasoline on the fire."

"What fire?"

Kate turned away. She wiped the countertop.

"Come on, Kate. This is you and me here."

"It's just, you're having such a hard time getting past it, Abby. I mean, you have all these—I don't know— suspicions or something as if you can't— You don't want to accept the obvious, and my telling you about seeing Nick, well, George says it'll just keep your mind racing."

"My mind is not racing, Katie." Abby regretted ever sharing her doubts with Kate. She ought to have known better.

A difficult silence grew.

Abby broke it. "Did Nick stay here with you and George?"

"Oh, God, no!"

Abby's eyes widened. "Well, I know he isn't your favorite person, but I always thought he was as welcome here as I am."

"Of course he is. That's not what I meant." Kate took a moment.

And Abby thought she could deny it all she liked,

but the truth was Kate had never cared for Nick. "He's not your type," she'd said soon after they met.

Kate found Abby's gaze. "I'd surely have remembered it if he'd come out here, if he'd actually stayed with us. That's what I meant. And I did say something to him about it, but he said he wasn't spending the night. I thought it was odd that he would make such a long drive in one day, but I assumed he was going home, that you were expecting him."

Abby looked at her shoes. Had she been? Had she even known where he was?

Kate pulled a tray and a big thermos out of a cabinet. She poured coffee into the thermos, set it on the tray, added a pitcher filled with cream, a sugar bowl, spoons and three mugs. She disappeared in the direction of the great room and returned bearing a decanter filled with amber liquid. "Grand Marnier," she said. "It's cold outside. We can use a shot."

Abby held her gaze. "Looking at land can't be the reason Nick was here."

Kate picked up the tray. "Can we finish this conversation later? As you said, it doesn't involve George, and I don't want him overhearing. He's mad enough at me as it is."

"No! Kate! For God's sake, my family is missing. No one knows where they are, and now you're telling me you saw Nick in Bandera last December? Why would he be there? He wasn't buying land. Even at the price of a song, we couldn't afford it."

"All right. All right." Kate turned sharply.

Abby steadied the thermos, the cream pitcher.

They were both startled when George came through

the back door. "Can you bring another cup? Dennis is here."

Abby stepped back, putting her fingertips to her temples, running them up to her chignon, pushing at the pins there. She followed Kate and George outside; she couldn't think of a plausible reason not to, and had it not been for Dennis's presence, there would have been hard words said. Abby could feel them heating her teeth. She thought even Dennis was aware of the friction because he immediately launched into a funny story about a cat rescue call he'd had in the neighborhood earlier in the week.

"He's talking about May Dean Hennesey. She lives down the way. She's always calling 911." Kate was explaining for Abby's benefit, to distract her. Abby could feel Kate's glance, the weight of her distress. But Abby would not relent, not this time.

George said, "May Dean's got the hot pants for Dennis. She runs the cat up the tree so she can get him over to her house."

"She's eighty-one." Dennis's half-sheepish protest made Abby smile in spite of herself. He said, "The worst thing was that after I got the cat down, I had to go inside and eat her tuna casserole for lunch."

Kate laughed. "May Dean's tuna casserole is the biggest joke in this county."

Abby didn't laugh; she sipped her coffee. She wanted so badly to turn to Kate and say she didn't give a damn about May Dean whoever and her pathetic tuna casserole. She wanted to say: How dare you keep such a secret? Abby didn't believe that Nick had come to Bandera to buy land. *In December*, Kate had said, *the week before Christmas*. What was going on then? Abby tried to think. Jake would have been coming home from college. She remembered telling Lindsey they'd wait for him to get their tree.

Their last tree. Their last Christmas as a family. She remembered decorating that tree, she and the kids had done it together on the Friday evening after Jake arrived.

And Nick hadn't been there. Abby remembered now he'd gone to Dallas that weekend to take care of some legal business for Louise, something to do with her estate. At least that's what he'd told Abby he was doing. He and Louise had an appointment to see their family attorney and when they finished, Nick brought Louise home for the holiday. She'd spent the week of Christmas with them and nearly driven all four of them insane. How could he have been in Bandera unless he'd driven there first and then gone up to Dallas? And even so, Nick would never have made such a huge decision without consulting her. He would have insisted they do research. They would have looked at dozens of properties, talked to any number of Realtors.

But there was an even more compelling reason why the whole thing was impossible: Helix Belle. Those ridiculous allegations against Nick had been made only weeks before the holidays. He'd been in such a terrible mood, Abby had been afraid Christmas would be ruined. Certainly he'd been in no frame of mind to look at land, much less plan a surprise around buying it.

Abby let her gaze drift. Everything led back to that time, the trouble with Helix Belle. She remembered after he was cleared, Nick said it didn't matter, that there were always going to be people who didn't get the message, who would feel hostile and angry at him, who would hate him. What people? Why would they feel that way? She didn't know because she hadn't asked. Instead, after repeated attempts to buoy his mood, she'd left him alone. She had assumed he'd come out of it, whatever it was—a funk, a bad patch. Everyone had them. Every marriage had them. Now she wondered what she'd been thinking.

"I hate these stupid, jackass, gun-toting yahoos. Most of 'em are from the city and don't know shit about hunting. Pardon my French, Abby."

She blinked in George's direction, momentarily blank. "Oh, the doe. You're talking about the doe we found this afternoon."

"I'm really sorry you got dragged into it," Dennis said.

"I'm sorry you had to put her down," Abby told him.

Kate went inside and returned with more coffee. George put another log on the fire. Conversation lagged, and in the lull, other noises became audible, small scurrying sounds, the night-doings of animals. Far below, at the foot of the slope, Abby could hear the lake water sliding against the shore. The sense of peace was pervasive, and she wanted it, wanted so badly to yield to it, but what right did she have? Everyone wanted her to resume her life. To make plans for Thanksgiving dinner, next summer's garden. But it was wrong. Disloyal. As if she were giving up on her family, willing to walk on and forget them. Willing not to know the truth.

Abby turned to Dennis. "Kate ran into Nick in Bandera outside the courthouse last December when I had no idea he was there."

"You told her? I thought we agreed you wouldn't."

George sounded every bit as pissed at Kate as she had told Abby he was.

"I had a right to know, George," Abby said.

"I told you she did," Kate insisted to her husband.

No one spoke, and when George got up and said he was turning in, Kate stood up, too.

"I don't know what good it does you," George said, not unkindly, when he paused beside Abby's chair.

"I'm just confused about why he was there, what he was doing," Abby said.

"That's what I mean." George squeezed her shoulder. "It only puts fuel on the fire, causes you to ask more questions when what you need to do is to let go, Abby. You need closure. You need to be able to get on with your life."

"Well, maybe she can't, George," Kate said following him into the house. "I mean, can you imagine how hard it is to live with—"

The door closed behind them severing the rest of Kate's argument.

"They almost never fight," Abby said.

"I don't think they're fighting so much as trying to decide the best way they can help you." Dennis settled an ankle atop his opposite knee.

"Kate said Nick was here to buy land. I don't believe it, but I don't know what else would have brought him here."

"You don't believe that's what he told her or—"

"Could we find out? Would there be a record of what he did at the courthouse?"

"Are you sure he went inside? You said Kate saw him outside."

"But we could still ask, couldn't we? You, your deputies, they could—"

"Abby," Dennis said her name gently, so gently she winced. She knew what was coming. "I know it must be hell having so many unanswered questions about what happened to your family and why, but please trust me when I say we have looked very carefully into your husband's and daughter's disappearance, we have gone over every detail with a fine-tooth comb, and there's nothing to indicate anything mysterious or criminal happened other than what is evident on the surface."

Abby felt Dennis's concern. She waited a bit, and when she thought she could speak without breaking into tears, she said, "I wish it were ten years from now." And then she wondered, why ten years? Did she think she would recover by then? She said, "Kate knows more than she's telling."

"Okay." Dennis went along. "What makes you say that?"

Abby shook her head. She didn't want to tell Dennis about Baylor Gates, the man who had broken her friendship with Kate years ago. But that didn't stop the memory from rattling around in her brain, from warning her that friends could be faithless. Friends could betray you. "She thinks she's protecting me," Abby answered. "But I wish she wouldn't. I wish everyone would stop doing that and tell me the truth."

But maybe that was the problem, Abby thought later as she was falling asleep. She was too caught up in waiting for someone to come to her with the answers. Maybe her plan should be to find them out herself. She could talk to the gas station attendant in Boerne, for instance. She could try and find Adam Sandoval's wife. Abby knew Sherry Sandoval, not well. They'd met through their husbands; the four of them had had dinner once or twice years ago.

Abby was up early the next morning. She helped Kate make breakfast, and she was loading the dishwasher when Kate said she needed to go to the grocery store.

"Come with me. Leave the dishes. You've done enough slaving."

Abby straightened.

"You're still mad." It wasn't a question.

"I'm sorry for the trouble I've caused between you and George."

"You haven't caused any trouble, Abby. George'll get over it."

Abby didn't answer.

Kate sighed. "Look, I really did forget about seeing Nick last winter. Honestly. You know how terrible my memory is."

Abby met Kate's glance. It sounded like an excuse, but Abby conceded, saying, "Right, whatever. It's fine," because she didn't want to fight. She didn't want to blow up their friendship. The time for that was past. She couldn't handle another loss anyway. She said, "I want to drive into Boerne."

"What for?"

"I want to talk to the kid at the gas station myself."

Kate groaned.

"I know. It's probably dumb, but maybe seeing me, he'll remember something."

Kate didn't agree. Abby could see it in her eyes. "You go on to the store. I'll go to Boerne. I might pop on down to San Antonio, too. It's not far. I can be back by dinnertime."

"San Antonio?"

"Adam Sandoval lives there, or he did until he jumped bail. I want to talk to his wife."

"Abby, this is crazy! Do you even know where she lives? Weren't they divorced?"

"That's what Nick said, but—" Abby shrugged. She had no idea what to believe or whom, not anymore.

Kate sighed. "Well, if I can't talk you out of it, then I'm going with you. At least we can shop for groceries at Whole Foods in San Antonio."

It was easy enough to locate the Sandoval residence. Abby drove, and Kate read off the directions she'd pulled from Google. Abby hoped they wouldn't be wasting their time here the way they had at the Shell station in Boerne. The boy Dennis had interviewed no longer worked there; he had moved to Georgia a few months after the flood with his family. Abby had been disappointed, but when she'd looked at Kate, she could have sworn Kate had looked relieved.

"Slow down," Kate said. "It's got to be on this block somewhere. There!" She gestured at a ranch-style home, dark brown brick with cream-colored trim on an oversized lot. The house was low-slung, rambling, yet somehow sharply urban in its design.

Abby pulled into the driveway. "It looks deserted," she said, and she wasn't sure why she had that impression. The grass was cut, the shrubbery was trimmed. There was no clutter of newspapers crowding the front door.

"What's the plan?" Kate asked. "Do we just go up

and knock and then what? I left my religious litera-
ture at home."

Abby made a face. "Ha-ha," she said.

They rang the front door bell and listened to it echo
through the empty rooms. Abby walked back down
the porch steps. "I'm going to look in the backyard."

"Abby," Kate protested, "I don't think—"

"Yoo-hoo!" a woman called, crossing the street toward Abby and Kate. "Are you reporters or police?"
she asked as she got closer.

"Friends," Abby said.

"Avon calling," Kate said at the same time, and Abby
gave her a look.

"Well," the woman said, touching her tightly permed
gray hair, "if you're looking for the Sandovals, they're
gone."

"I'm an old friend of Sherry's," Abby said quickly.
"We were in school together, but we've lost touch. I've
just heard of all her difficulties. The divorce must have
been so hard for her. I wanted to stop by, see if there
was anything I could do to help."

"Oh, but she and Adam aren't divorced, dear," the
woman said.

Abby's breath shallowed. "Are you sure?"

"Of course, I'm sure. I've lived here forty-three
years. I brought the Sandovals an apple pie the day
they moved in."

"So they've moved out now?" Kate asked.

The woman looked at her. "Don't you keep up with
the news? Adam Sandoval is a wanted man. He and his
wife have left the country, you mark my word. He went
first and she followed him. I told the police when they
were over here snooping around that they're probably

sipping cocktails on the Riviera about now, living on all that loot Adam stole from those poor children. I'm telling you, you would never have known Adam was that sort from his—"

"Did you ever see this man over here?" Abby pulled the family photograph she had shown to Peg, the waitress at Griff's, from her purse and pointed at Nick. The woman looked closely at it.

"I might have. There was a man with hair that same dark shade over here a few times. Drove a yellow Corvette. It might have been this fellow."

Abby's breath stopped. She could see it, that Nick would rent a car so he wouldn't be recognized. A Corvette would suit him. Hadn't he talked occasionally about owning one? "How—how tall was the man you saw? Do you know?"

"Abby, no. Come on." Kate slipped her hand under Abby's elbow. She thanked the woman. Abby didn't protest when Kate put her into the passenger seat of the BMW and said she would drive.

"That woman is nothing more than a neighborhood gossip," Kate said as they drove away. "It's no good listening to her."

Abby didn't answer; she rested her head against the seat back. Nick had lied to her about the Sandovals. They weren't divorced; there hadn't been money woes, and somehow, knowing this made all the rest of it plausible—that it was Nick the neighbor had seen driving the yellow Corvette, that it was Nick with Adam on the surveillance tape outside the bank. He could have done it, driven here to San Antonio and back home in a day once, twice, a hundred times, and she'd never have been the wiser. *You had to pursue it; you wanted to know.* A voice in her brain taunted her. But she felt sick and so afraid. Suppose he was involved with Adam and she uncovered the proof of it? What would she do then? Turn him in, her own husband?

"Please come with me," Kate said.

They had left San Antonio without shopping for groceries the day before, and Kate was insisting Abby accompany her now, but she said no, that she hadn't slept well and wanted to lie down for a bit. In truth it was another idea entirely that had taken form in her mind, one that she ought to have acted on long ago. She would have shared it with Kate, if she thought Kate would have been open-minded, but she wouldn't be, not after yesterday. "I think I'll have a nap outside on the deck while you're gone," Abby said.

"You'll sit out there and brood. I know you."

"No. I promise I won't."

Kate pulled on her jacket. "Okay. But you can sit by yourself too much. You can think yourself blind."

They shared a stubborn silence.

Kate broke it. "You can read meaning into circumstance that isn't there. That could have been any guy that woman saw, Abby. Just think how many dark-haired men there are in the world."

Abby dried her hands. "I know, but it just seems as if Nick was doing a lot of stuff I didn't know about."

"Like what else?"

Abby shrugged, turned her back and looked out the window at the saddle horses grazing in the pasture. She let her gaze travel from the corral along the drive to the barn that housed the livestock, and the hot bite of resentment she felt against Kate was as burning and unexpected as a sharp stick in the eye. Abruptly, Abby jerked her glance inside to her hands. She was gripping the counter's edge so hard her knuckles were white.

"Abby?" Kate prodded. "What else have you found out?"

But Abby only shook her head, anxious now for Kate to leave. "It's nothing." She made herself smile. "Go on. I'm fine. I'm not brooding. I swear."

"Cross your soul and never cry?" Kate lifted her foot and traced an X on the bottom of her shoe.

Abby did the same. "Never cry," she repeated. It was the oath and sign they'd made up in their school days.

They walked out together, and Abby waited until Kate's taillights had disappeared completely before retracing her steps, going straight through the house, first into the bedroom to get her purse, then down the hall to the study. Sitting behind the desk, she pulled a sheet of white business paper from the stack on the table beside the fax machine. She uncapped a pen and wrote FAX at the top edge. Beneath that she copied the number from the inside cover of the matchbook.

She started to write *To*: and the name *Sondra*, and then didn't. She pressed the capped end of the pen to her mouth, and after a moment's thought, she bent over the desk and wrote: *My name is Abby Bennett. My husband is missing. He had this number.* But something didn't feel right. She crumpled the sheet, tossed it into the wastebasket, drew out a fresh sheet. *My name is Abby Bennett*, she wrote, and after that: *I'm sorry to trouble you.* But some instinct again said no, and she crumpled that sheet, too.

She headed another sheet, again introducing herself. Then: *I hope you can help me. I'm trying to locate a man named Nick Bennett. He's missing. A record of this fax number was among his possessions. If you have any information about him, will you please call....*

She lifted the pen before she could jot down her cell phone number. Instinct warned she shouldn't give that out. It was somehow too personal, and she copied down the fax machine's phone number as the method of contact instead. Of course, now she ran the risk of George and Kate finding out what she'd done, and if they did, which was likely, she would have to explain that she'd sent off a fax to a total stranger asking the whereabouts of a man they believed to their cores was dead. But at least they would agree that she'd been prudent about it. A person could be harassed on their cell phone, but who, other than advertisers, harassed anyone by a fax machine?

Abby loaded the page and sent it before she could reconsider. Even so, the urge to wrest it from the machine was immediate and overwhelming. She had no clue what kind of trouble might be on the receiving end. *Borrow sugar, not trouble.* Her daddy's advice played through her mind. She picked up the message she'd faxed and tore it in half, then into quarters, letting them drop into the wastebasket.

CHAPTER
14

During their sophomore year of college when Kate insisted on setting up Abby's blind date with Baylor Gates, Abby resisted. She said she had to study.

"Bullshit," Kate said.

Abby made another excuse. "I don't have anything to wear."

"Try this." Kate emerged from their tiny dormitory closet and tossed a scrap of black silk at Abby. "It's too small for me and looks better on you anyway. Only blondes look great in black."

Abby fingered the silky material.

"Come on, Abby. This is college, where you are—believe it or not—supposed to have fun."

A pause fell. Abby felt Kate's gaze; she felt the weight of Kate's concern for her, and it made her feel anxious and guilty.

Kate stamped her foot. "Holy Jesus Christ, Abby.

You sat at home all through high school, then you sat in the dorm all last year. I can't stand it anymore. You live like a nun, and it's making me look bad."

Abby laughed and donned the little black dress; she slipped her feet into the impossibly high-heeled sandals and didn't think twice about it. She and Kate had been friends too long for trust to be an issue. And as badly as it would end, Abby would never believe Kate meant to do it. She didn't purposely set Abby up with Baylor to then betray her. What Kate wanted was for Abby to relax and have fun. She had no patience for it when Abby said dating made her nervous.

It was no different that evening meeting Baylor, but then he took her hand, and she grew dizzy at his touch. She felt as if she would float out of the hated shoes, yet at the same time she felt a longing to press herself against him that was all-consuming, unlike any sensation she had ever experienced before. And from that night on, Baylor's pursuit of her was so tender and careful that when they finally made love, it was Abby who initiated it.

Except for their class schedules—Baylor was a business major, Abby was studying elementary education—they were inseparable. For the first time ever, Abby felt she belonged somewhere. She had always been Kate's friend, accepted because of Kate, but as Baylor's girlfriend, she was part of his crowd. It was the same as Kate's crowd, the one that, since grade school, Abby had only skirted the outer edge of.

But dating Baylor, her confidence grew. It was as if she had stepped into a warmer climate, thrown off her old shy self like some old coat. She couldn't imagine life without Baylor, friends, plans, a steady date. She was finally somebody. One of the It girls, the special girls, who got flowers for no reason and late-night, miss-you phone calls.

It seemed only natural when they began to discuss marriage. Abby couldn't believe her luck, and she assumed Baylor felt the same joy in their discovery of one another. It didn't once occur to her that his commitment to her wasn't as deep.

Junior year, their crowd made plans to go to Cancun for spring break. Abby and Kate had packed their bags, and they were waiting for Tim—Kate's latest and greatest, and last, or so she claimed—and Baylor to pick them up, when someone down the hall hollered that Abby had a phone call.

"Don't tell me it was the guys," Kate said when Abby reappeared.

She touched her brow, struggling to marshal the words. "It's Daddy, he's in the hospital. He had a heart attack."

"Oh, no." Kate hugged Abby and, releasing her, looked her over anxiously.

"I have to go home," she said and, eyeing her suitcase, added, "At least I'm packed."

"Shorts and T-shirts, a strapless sundress and two bikinis. Not exactly hospital attire. Besides it's cold out." Kate lifted the suitcase and tossed out the contents on the bed. She went to Abby's drawers and returned with assorted sweatshirts and pullover turtlenecks. Abby added jeans and flannel pajamas. She changed her sandals for socks and tennis shoes.

"What's this?" Baylor spoke from the doorway. Tim was behind him.

"My dad had a heart attack," Abby said. "I have to go home."

Baylor and Kate wanted to drive Abby into Houston, but Abby refused. She didn't want their trip to be ruined on her account.

The first heart attack was mild, scarcely more than a warning. Her father was up and walking the day after Abby's arrival and discharged from the hospital a few days later with a new cholesterol-lowering diet and exercise regimen. He and Abby took walks together around the neighborhood, and she told him about Baylor, about loving him. Her dad was misty-eyed and held her hand. He was more sentimental since the scare with his heart. He said, "Just yesterday, you were having me in to tea with your dolls. I had to wear your grandmother's hat with the floppy rim and big flower. Do you remember?"

Abby squeezed his arm and bent her head to his shoulder. "Maybe soon you'll have a granddaughter to invite you to tea."

"I hope there's going to be a wedding first," her daddy said drily.

Abby laughed. "Of course. It'll be something small and elegant. In the afternoon, I think. You and Baylor can wear gray. It's a much softer color than black." Abby could see it in her mind. The images were as clear as photographs, so clear, it was as if they were already gathered into an album. One so real to her that even years later, when the pain of remembering was only a worn stain on the floor of her mind, a moment would come when she would catch herself wondering what she'd done with it.

* * *

Abby was waiting in the dormitory lounge on the day Baylor and the others were due home. She imagined he would be sunburned and hungry.

"Baylor is *always* hungry," Abby had said this to her mother. She had said she wanted to copy the family recipes. She thought she would purchase those three-by-five cards, the ones with the cute kitcheny designs, and a recipe box to match. She would need a *Joy of Cooking,* too, like her mother's. Abby looked up when the door to the dormitory opened, expecting to see a crowd, anxious to see Baylor, but it was only Kate who was there, and her face when she saw Abby seemed to freeze, except for her glance that darted everywhere as if Abby was the last person she wanted to look at.

Abby felt a whisper of dread, the narrowest ribbon of cold premonition, unfurl from her stomach. She stood up, bringing her hands together. Her mouth opened. The word, "What?" was poised, a question that blistered her tongue. She wouldn't ever be certain if she spoke it out loud.

But Kate answered as if Abby had. "We didn't mean for anything to happen," she said, and it was a protest, a plea; it was all Abby needed to hear to know that the "anything" Kate was referring to meant that everything between Abby and Baylor was over.

Abby hugged herself hard and shrank from Kate's touch.

"I'm so sorry," Kate said, and Abby despised the tears in Kate's voice.

"I knew we were attracted to each other," she said, "but I was with Kevin and then I—I met Tim. I guess I never thought—"

"What?" Abby fired the word like a bullet. "That I'd fall for him? I was just supposed to keep him amused until you were between guys? Have you been keeping an eye on him? Watching for signs of boredom? Figuring the instant you were ready and I wasn't paying attention, you could crook your finger and he'd drop me flat? How could you?" Abby slapped at her own angry tears.

"It just happened. I—I don't know."

"But you've had feelings for him all along, haven't you? Which you never bothered to mention to me. Naturally. It's just like you."

"I never thought—"

"You never do."

Abby stared at Kate a moment longer, and then, stumbling, she turned and ran.

They never shared their room again, nor did they speak. Abby caught sight of Kate with Baylor sometimes on campus, and the pain was so intense, she thought that, like her father's heart, hers, too, was under attack. The wedding was in summer after graduation. Abby wasn't invited, not that she'd have gone. She had moved home, lacking a better plan, and she was there to help her mother nurse her father when he was forced to undergo heart bypass surgery. It was Abby's mother who told her Kate had moved with Baylor to Chicago.

Good riddance, Abby had thought. She couldn't imagine that she and Kate would ever speak again. But then one day, a few years later, on the occasion of Abby's engagement to Nick, Kate called to offer congratulations and her hope for Abby's happiness. Abby was gracious; she could afford to be because she *was* happy, happier than she had ever been in her life. And it was in the wake of saying this to Kate that it dawned on her she had Kate to thank for it. As grievous a betrayal as it was, if Kate hadn't taken Baylor away, Abby might never have met Nick. She might have missed finding the love of her life.

She and Kate both recognized the irony.

CHAPTER
15

Late in the afternoon, they started dinner. Kate washed a chicken, patted it dry and seasoned the cavity. Abby cut limes into quarters and stuffed them inside. They tied the legs with twine, covered the dish with plastic wrap and put it in the refrigerator. Kate went outside to clean and light the grill, and Abby snapped the fresh green beans Kate had bought that morning.

"There's enough here for an army," Abby said when Kate returned to the kitchen.

"We can make green bean sandwiches for breakfast," Kate said.

"Layer them with a fried egg." Abby grinned.

Kate put her hands together. "Add grated Swiss cheese, slap it all between two pieces of wheat toast and voilà."

Abby laughed. They'd used to do it on purpose, see who could come up with the most outlandish breakfast sandwich combination. Pulled pork barbeque on day-old waffles layered with coleslaw, meatloaf and bacon on a croissant. Peanut butter and sweet pickles sandwiched between pancakes. The air was thick with their silly memories.

Abby said, "Sometimes everything feels so ordinary, you know? As if they'll walk in the door and everything will be the way it always was when we came for a visit. Jake will be hunting through the pantry—"

"Foraging." Kate had no trouble following Abby's train of thought.

"Lindsey will have straw in her hair from playing with the cats in the barn."

"That kid would live in the barn if we let her," Kate said.

Abby pressed the backs of her wrists to her eyes, and Kate came and circled her shoulders. She bent her head until it touched Abby's.

"Sometimes I let myself drift—" Abby resumed breaking the beans, stem end, blossom end "—way up. I go higher and higher until the earth is just a tiny glowing speck, and it's as if it never happened."

Kate brought a small mesh sack filled with new potatoes to the sink and started washing them.

Abby leaned her hip against the counter, giving her room. "What was Nick really doing in Bandera?"

"I told you."

"I want to know what you think, what exactly you saw."

"Him. I saw him on the courthouse sidewalk. That's all."

"I don't believe you. I know you think you're protecting me, but you aren't."

Kate scrubbed a potato vigorously, flushing away bits of peeling under the running tap, and then, abruptly, she shut the water off so hard, the pipe knocked in the wall. "He was never the man you wanted to believe he was, Abby."

"He was too experienced for me, right? Little sheltered Abby Carter and Big Bad Nick Bennett. Miss Mouse and the Wolf."

Kate groaned. "Let's drop it, okay? It doesn't matter anymore."

"Why? Because you think he's dead?"

Kate jerked on the water taps and again shut them off. "You have to accept it," she pleaded. "You're killing yourself and I can't stand it."

"Well, it isn't about you, is it? For once. This isn't some college romance, Kate."

"You think I don't know that? God, Abby, can you give me no credit?"

Abby didn't answer. She waited for Kate to finish scouring the potatoes, and taking Kate's place at the sink, she rinsed the beans and put them in a pan. She added water and seasoning and set them on the stove to cook. Somehow they got through dinner and the rest of the evening. Abby went to bed early and, lying sleepless, thought of going home. It wasn't as if she was accomplishing anything here other than wearing out her welcome waiting for a return fax that would likely never come. Curled on her side, she pictured herself going through her own back door, and it was a relief when she didn't feel the customary wash of horrible dread. She could do it, she thought. She could go home. Try and start over. It was the right thing to do, and she felt better for having made the decision.

* * *

The next morning, once she was showered and dressed, Abby scooped her belongings from the chair in Kate's guest room and stuffed them into her canvas tote. She got clean bed linen from the closet in the hall, stripped the bed and remade it. Kate was already in the kitchen, sitting at the table with a mug of coffee, immersed in reading the morning newspaper. Abby hesitated in the doorway, holding the bundle of sheets. The bowl that held the leftover green beans was out on the counter, along with a loaf of wheat bread and the toaster. All they needed were the eggs to make the sandwiches they'd planned. Abby's mouth watered. She'd have hers slathered with real mayonnaise, she thought.

Kate looked up. "What are you doing with those sheets?"

Abby carried them into the laundry room. "Want me to fry the eggs?" she asked, retracing her steps into the kitchen.

"I thought you'd have coffee first."

Abby filled her mug and sat down at the table. "I'm going home. I need to take care of the house, start looking for a job. I think I'll teach again. Maybe junior high this time. How bad could it be?"

"You're angry at me."

"About—?"

"I don't know. Any number of things, I guess." Kate spread her fingers, knuckled them over her mouth looking puzzled, anxious, some combination.

"You keep secrets, Kate. You always have."

Kate's eyes widened. Abby rarely lost her temper.

"Ever since college, I've never known whether I

can trust you. Even before——" Abby broke off unwilling to get into it, how she had always felt the ground between them was wormed with Kate's secrets. She found Kate's gaze. "You lied about Baylor. How do I know you aren't lying now about Nick?"

"You don't. But I'm not this time, Abby. I wouldn't—I learned——" Kate looked away, blinking, and in a moment, her cheek was limned in the silvery light of her tears.

Abby bit her lips, angry still and rueful, too, because she knew what it cost Kate to cry, and she'd always hated being the cause. "I'm sorry," she said, wobbly voiced.

"No, don't. Don't say that." Kate wiped her eyes, sniffed. "What I did was terrible, and I've never said how lucky I feel that you forgave me, that you let me back into your life, let us be friends again."

"You went through so much." Abby hesitated, remembering how fragile Kate had looked the first time they'd met after Kate had returned to Houston. She'd been horrified to hear the suffering Kate had endured at Baylor's hands.

"You felt sorry for me."

"I felt sorry about all of it," Abby said truthfully.

"Think what I saved you from," Kate said wryly.

Abby ducked her chin. She had thought about that, and she had been relieved and then felt shame for it, and for all the times she'd wished Kate ill. She said, "I would have been there for you, if I'd known." Abby had said this before, and it was easier every time she repeated the words. But buried in her mind was a sharp sliver of wonder. *Would* she have listened if Kate had called her about Baylor's abuse? Would compassion have warmed itself in the bitter fire of her hostility? Abby wanted to believe she would have been there for her friend, but she had her doubts.

"How could I come to you?" Kate asked. "When Baylor hit me, I was convinced I deserved it. I felt like I was an awful person and not only for taking him from you the way I did."

"No, Kate. No one deserves that kind of treatment and the truth is you couldn't have taken him if he hadn't wanted to go."

Kate found Abby's gaze and held it. "I have been so jealous of you, so filled with envy each time you were pregnant, holding your babies. Baylor took that from me." Kate's eyes filled again. "I lost my baby, my little girl. I'll never have children because of him and he— he—" Her voice broke.

Abby bent forward, grasping Kate's forearms, swiping at her wet cheeks, murmuring, "Kate, Katie, hush now, it's all right...."

She bowed her head. "I can't believe I'm saying this now when Nick and Lindsey are—but I've wanted to say it for so long. I've always felt as though we never talked it through, never worked it out between us." She looked at Abby. "I don't think I can ever make it up to you."

"That's ridiculous. There's nothing to make up." Abby went for a tissue and handed it to Kate.

She blew her nose. "I'm sorry I ever said anything to you about Nick, as if I was an expert with my track record."

"Look at George. He's one of the kindest men I know."

"I got lucky. Don't ask me how."

Now in the silence that fell, in the wake of Kate's honesty and tears, the air seemed to ease, and Abby was swept with gratitude. She felt lighter somehow and less burdened by doubt. She shook her head slightly. "It's weird that neither of us saw that side of him."

"When we first married and he acted jealous, I thought it was cute. I had no clue the sort of monster he would turn into." Kate went to the sink and filled a glass with water, sipping it.

"He could have killed you."

"You don't know how close he came," Kate said.

Instead it was Baylor who had died. Five years ago in prison where he'd been incarcerated for his final assault on Kate that had resulted in the loss of their unborn daughter. He'd had a massive stroke in his cell one week before he was due to be released on parole. Kate had called Abby to tell her. She'd been confused that at his passing she could feel both elation and sadness.

Abby picked up her mug and set it back down. Kate dampened a dishcloth and pressed it to her face.

"Abby?"

She looked up at George framed in the kitchen doorway. His face was a mirror of consternation, and then she saw the paper in his hand, and her heart sank.

"Abby's gotten a fax," he said.

"What? How would anyone know to fax her here?" Kate came to the table.

Abby took the fax from George. If he noticed Kate's disheveled appearance, her red face, her scoured-looking eyes, he gave no sign that Abby saw. He, like Kate, was looking at Abby.

She looked at the fax. It was handwritten, but she had no trouble deciphering it. *My wife Sondra, has been missing for nearly a year*, it read. *I don't recognize the name Nick Bennett. May we talk in person?* At the end of the note there was a signature and underneath that, a phone number.

"Who's Hank Kilmer?" Kate was reading over Abby's shoulder.

"I don't know," Abby said.

"Well, if you don't know him, how did he know to contact you here?" Kate asked.

"Why is he contacting you?" George crossed his arms over his chest.

Abby explained with as little drama as possible about the matchbook and what she'd been led to do about it. She wanted that to be the end of it and said, briskly, "I need to get going. I want to be home by dark."

"You should have breakfast first," Kate said.

"You aren't thinking of meeting this guy?" George came to the point.

Abby said, "You don't think it's strange that Nick wrote down the name of a woman who went missing too?"

"Abby!" Kate knelt and grabbed Abby's hands; she locked Abby's gaze. "They drowned. They are gone. You have got to accept it."

Abby looked at George. He shook his head. "I'm sorry, darlin'. Kate's right. It's time to move on. I know—"

"No!" Abby stood up, raising her finger at him. "Don't say it. You don't know how it feels." She spun on her heel, left the kitchen and retrieved her tote. She was gone from the ranch within minutes. She did not look back, not once.

* * *

Dennis caught up with her on the highway west of Pipe Creek. She didn't realize it was Dennis who was behind her, not at first. She saw the flashing lights in her rearview mirror, glanced at the speedometer that registered eighty-five and said, "Shit," under her breath, easing off the gas pedal. "Shit shit shit."

She pulled off the road, turned off the ignition and lowered the window. Cold air pushed in around her, blanketed her thighs, pooled around her ankles. She jammed her hands into her jacket pockets, and her fingers closed over the folded edge of Hank Kilmer's fax.

"Abby?"

She whipped off her sunglasses. "Dennis?"

"What are you doing?"

She tossed her glasses into the passenger seat. "Why is everyone always asking me that?"

He leaned down, folding his arms on the window ledge.

She looked at him. Their faces were so close she could smell the mint flavor of his chewing gum. "I could ask you the same thing. Aren't you out of your jurisdiction?"

"Kate called. She said something about a fax?"

Abby felt a stab of irritation. What right did Kate have talking about Abby to Dennis? How much had she said? Had she filled him in on every detail of Abby's private life and her private thoughts and her private pain? Damn her, Abby thought. God damn them all to hell.

"Abby? If you think there's some connection, I ought to check it out."

"No. It's nothing, a mistake."

"Kate's worried."

"She shouldn't be. I'm fine. I'm going home. I'm going to go back to work, start looking after myself." Abby straightened up. "It's what everyone wants, isn't it? For me to accept what's happened? Move on?" She didn't wait for an answer. "Well, that's what I'm doing. I'm moving on."

"Too fast." Dennis shifted, stiffening his elbows, putting an arm's length between them.

"Are you going to write me a ticket?"

"No, I'm going to offer you some advice."

"Slow down, I know."

"No," he said. "Let me do my job. Okay? Let the sheriff's department do what we're trained to do. If there's more going on here the way you think, we'll find it."

"And if there isn't?"

He stood up. An eighteen-wheeler roared by, leaving a curtain of dust and the smell of diesel fuel hanging in the air.

"Dennis?"

He met her glance. "Have you found out something I should know?"

Circumstantial. The word rose in Abby's mind. A cop word, a detective word she'd heard on television. It meant when evidence wasn't solid, when it couldn't connect the dots. Hers didn't. She was dealing in hunches, intuition. Matchbooks and fax numbers. There was the hearsay about a difficult client; there was a tenuous connection to missing settlement money, some fuzzy surveillance footage. There were the phone calls. None of it was proof of anything, and no one, including Dennis, believed the phone calls were even real. And anyway, Abby wasn't so sure she wanted to know the truth.

Because once it was known, she couldn't unknow it. She would have to live with it.

"What makes you think they're not dead, Abby?"

She shook her head. The threat of tears tangled in her throat. If only she could, she would bury her face against his uniform shirt. She imagined it, the starched feel beneath her cheek, the relief of his arms around her. If only she could lean on him just until she could feel her own strength again. If only she could forget a little while.

"I'm going home," she said, blinking in the clear morning light. "I'm going to try to put my life in order and that's all."

Dennis rested his hands on his belt. The butt of his gun jutted from his hip. "You won't do anything crazy?"

Abby shook her head.

"You'll call me first?"

She nodded and started the car, then before he could walk out of earshot, she put her head out the window. "The little fawn, how is she?"

He turned. "Missing her mama," he said and saluted. He'd put on his sunglasses; she couldn't read his expression. But she knew he was unhappy with her as well as she knew he wouldn't stop looking for her family. Because it was his job; he wanted the facts as much as she did.

And he wasn't afraid of the truth.

CHAPTER

16

Abby had her house key in her hand, ready to unlock the back door, but as she came up the steps she saw that the door was already open, ajar by maybe three inches. She paused, and her first thought was Jake, that he was home. But his car wasn't in the driveway. She nudged the door, widening the gap. The floor was tracked with grit, not a lot. What would come in on your shoes, Abby thought, if you didn't wipe your feet. Had to be Jake. She stepped over the threshold and stood in the mud-room, but rather than shouting out his name, she pulled her cell phone from her purse and called him. "Are you home?" she asked when he answered.

"Home?" He echoed in a voice that said she must be nuts. "I'm at school. Why?"

Abby told him, her eye tracking the trail of grit. Maybe she'd dragged it in herself the last time she was here, but when she said that to Jake, he said, "No, Mom, get out of there. Call 911. Somebody's broken in."

"Who would—?" Abby was already backing out onto the porch, and although she told Jake she would call the police, she didn't. She called her neighbor Charlie instead.

"Don't go back inside," he told her. "Wait for me. I'll be right there."

When he came, he examined the door, running his gaze and then his big-knuckled, work-worn hands over the lock mechanism, the frame. "Doesn't look as if it was forced."

"Maybe I forgot to lock it when I left and the wind blew it." In her state of mind, Abby thought, anything was possible.

"Does anyone else besides you or Jake have a key?"

Abby shook her head. "Not that I remember. Maybe my mother does, but she hasn't been here."

"Well, let's go in and have a look around, or maybe you'd rather wait out here?"

"No," she said over her growing sense of unease. She was grateful that Charlie seemed so calm, so frankly undisturbed. She remembered a summer day a few years ago when Jake fell out of a tree. He'd bitten through his lower lip, and she hadn't been able to stop the bleeding. Charlie had come to help her then, too. He'd scooped Jake up, carried him swiftly to his truck, Abby jostling alongside, holding the towel to Jake's mouth, and he'd driven them into town to the emergency room with such an economy of motion. He had talked the whole way. Abby hadn't heard the words, but the quiet rumble of his voice had comforted her just the same. She followed him inside now. Nothing appeared disturbed in the kitchen or in any of the rooms downstairs.

Charlie started up the stairs.

Abby was behind him when the sound of scuffling and then a tiny cry pierced the silence.

Charlie turned to her. "Why don't you wait here?"

She nodded, watching him go the rest of the way, thinking he should have a weapon, a baseball bat, a gun. She might be able to find a bat somewhere, but she and Nick had never owned a gun. Her heart whisked lightly against her ribs. She had her cell phone still, and she was thinking she would call 911 now when he reappeared holding a furry, squirming bundle of orange fur.

"One of the kittens," he said. "Her mama had a litter of six in the barn a few weeks back. This one must have found the door open before we did and decided to go exploring."

Abby laughed in relief. At least that explained the noises they'd heard. "Spooked by a kitten," she said, making fun of herself. She took the fussing, little bundle into her hands, holding it aloft inches from her face, noting the tawny eyes, the white blaze that led to a pale pink nose. "She's adorable. Aren't you adorable?"

Abby walked with Charlie back outside, and handing over the kitten, she thanked him for checking things out. Her gaze lingered on the tiny furry face, and the kitten looked back at Abby, then promptly climbed Charlie's shirt to his shoulder, where he grasped her. She dug her nails into his flesh, and he grimaced.

"I don't think the wind blew the door open, Abby. I'd call the police, let them come and have a look around. And I'd have the locks changed, too, if I were you," he said. "I can do it for you, if you want."

Abby looked off into the distance, remembering a car she'd seen parked not far from the house when she'd turned onto her street just now, a dark blue sedan. She told Charlie about it. "It was pulled pretty far off the road, near the north end of the pasture by the utility easement. Why would anyone stop there?" Although there were probably any of a half dozen reasons, it struck Abby as odd, now that she thought of it.

"Do you know the make and model?"

"Ford Taurus, maybe? I don't know cars very well." Abby thought it was the same car Nadine Betts drove, though she couldn't be sure. She hadn't really paid attention, but now she was spooked. There was something about seeing that car, then finding the door unlocked…and those times when Nadine had followed her around, followed Jake around, when she'd called Louise, pestering them with her endless questions. And there had been the night, at the Riverbend Lodge, Abby had seen a dark blue sedan then, too, leaving the parking lot. She supposed it could all be a coincidence, but somehow she didn't think so.

Charlie said he didn't know of anyone local who drove a Taurus. "You have someone in mind? Who's giving you trouble, I mean?"

"Maybe. I don't know." Abby made a dismissive gesture with her hand. "Never mind. I'm sure it's nothing." She wondered what she was thinking, to bring up the reporter as if Nadine was—what? Stalking her? So desperate for a story she would break into Abby's house to hunt for clues? Abby met Charlie's gaze. "I'll get locks when I go to the hardware store, if you're sure you don't mind installing them."

He nodded. "Just call me. Anytime."

She thanked him and squeezed his forearm and said she didn't know what she'd do without him. Her gratitude was so deep she felt the pull of tears.

"It's what neighbors are for," he said.

"You need to let me pay you."

He grinned. "All right. I'd love a slice of your coconut cream pie then."

That made her laugh, made her happy. "It's a deal," she said and watched him go before turning back to the house. She stood outside the back door a moment, studying it. It worried her, finding the door open, the idea that some stranger had a key and had been inside the house. It wouldn't hurt anything to change the locks, as Charlie suggested, but she couldn't see calling the police. What would she tell them? That she couldn't remember whether she'd shut the door tightly and locked it in the first place? That someone broke in for no apparent reason? They'd think she was a fool.

Inside the house she swept the grit from the floor into the dustpan and flung it out the door. She went to the refrigerator and briskly gathered the old, desiccated class schedules and other scraps of her family's life off the front of the refrigerator and put them in a desk drawer, then she pulled the fax from her pocket and, smoothing it, pinned it in their place.

The handwriting was neat for a man, a precise series of even loops and firm strokes. *My wife Sondra has been missing for nearly a year....* What did missing mean in this case? Kidnapped? Had someone abducted Hank Kilmer's wife? Abby judged the script too neat to belong to a doctor or a lawyer. It might be the handwriting of a CPA or an architect. Someone who admired order, someone for whom control and precision were characteristic. A man with glasses and grooves of worry carved into his face. He would be thin, she thought, with hair as white as chalk.

It would be pointless for her to call him, she thought. He would be looking for a new shoulder to cry on. They would meet for coffee or a glass of wine and speculate about why Nick would have written Sondra's fax number inside a book of matches, and when that exercise ended in futility, they would go on to exchange stories about their missing mates. They would tell each other things they would never say to anyone else because they shared an understanding no one else could. Hank Kilmer would come to rely on Abby to help him keep useless hope alive.

In hindsight, her actions would strike her as ridiculous, even appalling, that she could have thought so little of her own intuition. That she would simply accept the advice of her family and her friends and Dennis over the agitated voice of her own heart. But that was her problem; she was emotionally overwrought. Paranoid. She thought her closest friends, even her own son, were lying to her and that a reporter had broken into her house. Clearly she was certifiable and couldn't separate reality from delusion. She was letting her feelings, her suspicion, override her good judgment, and if she ended up in a straitjacket, it would be her own fault.

She filled the CD player with music: Pavarotti, Bocelli, the Righteous Brothers, Roy Orbison, turning it up so it would fill the house. She opened windows, heedless of the chill. Gathering cleaning supplies and rags in a bucket, Abby headed swiftly upstairs. She scoured the bathrooms, changed the sheets and dusted the children's rooms. The thought that at some point something would have to be done with Lindsey and Nick's belongings poked at her brain, but she finished in each room and left it without looking back.

She was in the laundry room, considering whether she could salvage the moldy contents of the laundry basket, when the phone rang in the kitchen. It was her mother, sounding anxious.

Abby felt awful. "Oh, Mama, I'm sorry. I keep doing this to you."

"Are you all right? What are you doing?"

"I'm fine. I'm cleaning. I just finished upstairs."

"Do you want me to come?"

"No, it's dark."

"Abby, I'm not feeble. I still know how to drive in the dark."

"It's just—" Abby stopped. She would not mention finding the back door open. It would only scare her mother, and the more Abby thought about it, the more she felt there was some logical explanation. "You don't need to come," she said. "I'm fine, really."

"You left Kate's in a terrible hurry."

"She told you about the fax." Abby closed her eyes. Maybe next Kate would take out an ad.

"How important can it be when someone jots down a phone number inside a book of matches?"

"You don't think it means anything."

"Honey, I think if it were something important, a number Nick intended to use, he'd have written it some-place less casual."

Casual. Abby held the word in her mind. As in casual acquaintance? Casual affair? "Mama, did Kate tell you she saw Nick in Bandera last Christmas?"

"Honey, I'm inclined to believe her when she says she didn't remember."

Abby didn't say anything.

"He'd asked her to keep it secret, you know? And then it was the holidays. In all the rush, you can imagine, can't you, that she might forget? It really wasn't important until April."

"I guess." Abby thought how she was always complaining she had too much to keep up with: Nick's schedule, Jake's schedule, Lindsey's schedule. There were days when her brain felt like a basket stuffed full of everyone else's business. There had been days when she'd forgotten things, important things. But that was BTF, before the flood. It would be different now. She would have more room, a bigger mental space to put everything in. Something else she'd wished for that she didn't want.

Her mother said, "Abby, sweet, I think a person can take any combination of circumstances and make them into something."

"I'm letting my imagination run away with me." Here it was again, Abby thought, more proof she was losing it.

"Your mind wants to fill in the blanks. It wants a logical explanation for this terrible accident that has happened, and there isn't one."

Abby didn't answer.

"Kate thinks you're angry at her."

"I'm not angry." It was only partly a lie. "I just realized I needed to be here."

"Are you thinking of contacting that man?"

"No. Even if there was a connection, what difference does it make now? If they're dead, I mean, if Nick and Lindsey are dead?" Abby made herself say it. "I'm thinking it's time I faced the fact that they're gone, lost in one of those canyons or in the river or who knows?"

"But you don't have to face it alone and not all at once."

Abby sat at the table. She drew doodles in the dust. "I've been thinking, Mama, about teaching again."

"That's a wonderful idea, honey."

"I'm going to call Hap Albright." Hap was the principal and Abby's former boss. She'd read that he was assistant superintendent of the district now.

"He's the one who thought so much of you, right?"

"Nick always thought it was too much. But he's harmless."

"Well, it can't hurt if someone in administration favors you a little."

"I just hope there's an opening, that he'll consider me, but if nothing else, maybe I can substitute somewhere."

"Working will help you, Abby."

"Distract me, you mean."

"A little distraction can be a good thing sometimes. It can get you through the worst of the ordeal. Then one day, you'll wake up and the pain won't be quite as sharp. You'll find you're breathing a little easier."

Abby glanced at the fax from Hank Kilmer pinned to the refrigerator. He had four months on her, but she didn't think it had gotten any easier for him.

When she finished mopping the kitchen floor, her back ached and her sorrow seemed wedged permanently at the base of her throat again. But it was late, and she didn't have the energy to cry. Standing at the kitchen sink, she made herself eat, tiny new peas from the can, applesauce from a batch she'd made last fall. She washed her few dishes and climbed the stairs. She changed the sheets on the bed she'd shared with Nick and hung fresh towels in their bathroom, but then she couldn't stay there. She thought the sofa downstairs might become her permanent bed. Maybe she'd buy a pullout.

She showered in Lindsey's bathroom, and it was there, with the warm steam rising around her, that she cried.

It was near midnight when she wakened. She gathered the quilt around her and padded barefoot into the kitchen. In the dark, she went to the refrigerator, took down Hank Kilmer's fax and wadding it into a ball, she tossed it into the kitchen wastebasket.

There is a time when you have to be through with grieving, when you have to accept your fate. Pick up the threads of existence. Go on. There is a time when you have to let go of faith. When it's just flat-out insane to keep on believing.

CHAPTER

17

The old man led his mule through the cedar break toward the bank of the creek where he'd make camp for the night. The sound of the water laced with the breeze was welcome and familiar. If he was lucky, he'd have a fat catfish on the hook before dinner, and if he wasn't, he'd eat the apples he'd filched off those trees a while back. They were his trees anyway, he reckoned. His own granddaddy had planted them. Didn't mean squat to him if the land had new owners.

Blue shambled behind him, head bobbing low, ready to be somewhere settled in for the night.

When they reached the water's edge, the man stood looking its length up and down, and he sighed. The cobble-filled channel was spring-fed and running at a good pace. Sometimes she flooded bad, like last spring. That flood had put water over damn near four counties, the worst in Hill Country history. Lives had been lost; some folks had never been found.

"An' we think we got problems, huh, Blue?" The old man dropped the mule's reins and patted his neck absently.

He lifted his battered ball cap and resettled it, walked a little way beside the water thinking how she'd never had a name that he ever heard of. Somehow that seemed a shame now. His granddaddy'd just called it "the crick". He'd come haul him out of bed of a mornin' and say, "Let's go fishin' down to the crick, kid."

Man, those had been the days. He'd learnt to swim here, too, and spent many a night camping on this very bank. This was his place, his water. He knew every inch of this land and this stream as if it was his own skin.

He bent and picked up a flat pebble, examined the layers of reddish brown and soft yellow, and then side-armed it, watching it skip the water's surface before it sank in a nest of ripples. The bank on the other side was a wall of limestone cut into cliffs that rose sharply from a litter of rock. Seemed to him as if the face was always shedding its skin, shooting off flakes, creating tables or bridges at its feet, the darker mystery of caves.

Somehow the look of the rock face, the way it cracked and buckled, put the old man in mind of himself, how age was breaking him. Rock or flesh or dirt, in the end, time would have its way. In the end everything breaks. Everything dies.

He squinted up at the sun perched in the high reach of the trees that capped the ridge to his left. Wouldn't be long, time would have its way with the last of the daylight, too. He turned to Blue standing behind him and slid his bedroll and a leather satchel that held his gear off the mule's back. Blue flicked his tail and gave a snort of pleasure, then ambled upstream a little way and a few yards inland to a small, protected cove where the grass grew thick and green.

"That's right, old Blue," the man said. And he knew they were both happy.

He gathered driftwood for a fire later, and pretty quick after that had his hook in the water and his back settled against a good-sized log. He dozed some, and when he came to, it was dark. He checked his line. The empty hook dangled. Some varmint had likely got his dinner, the old man thought. He rose stiffly and lit the fire, ate the apples and some of the cornbread he'd used for bait, and when Blue came begging, he fed him some of his meal, too.

"Worse'n a old bitch dog," he said, petting the long mottled gray nose.

Before he turned in, he gathered a few more good-size pieces of driftwood. He'd be up again in the night. Couldn't go 'til morning no more without needing to take a piss.

He woke with a start and for a moment had no idea what had wakened him or where he was. Then he heard the sound of the water running in the creek nearby and remembered. He turned his head until he caught sight of his campfire burned down to embers now, and there was Blue's slumbering hulk asleep on the other side. Danged mule was twitching and snuffling as if he was having some kind of dream. Was it the mule's racket that had wakened him?

He turned his face up, staring into the black bowl

of the sky, and caught a flicker of light from the corner of his eye.

Flashlight?

He levered up on one elbow and peered out over the water, unmoving, unsure whether to be afraid. But his heart wasn't waiting around for orders. He could feel it thumping in his chest like the hind leg of a jackrabbit. There it was again, coming from up in one of them caves on the other side of the stream. Two bright beams, bigger than from a flashlight. More like car headlights. Seemed as if they were pushed back pretty far, wedged at a slant in the rocks. They kept blinking at regular intervals—on, then off—on, then off.

Nearby, Blue stirred again, and the man glanced at him quick-like. He didn't appear more addled or disturbed than before. But what the hell did a mule know?

The man sat up cautiously and cocked his knees, staring intently across the narrow expanse of swiftly moving water. He scoured his eyes, pinched himself. The lights continued to blink. For real, not a dream— he was pinching himself, wasn't he?

But he couldn't make out what they were attached to. Had to be a car. What else?

Spaceship?

He glanced at the sky. No sign of anything, not even the moon. It would be daylight soon. He looked back across the water. His mind said it had to be a car stuck up in that cliff face somehow. But how could that be? Wasn't no way for a car to get over there. Not even a four-wheel drive could ride over them rocks. Wasn't a road around even on this side of the crick, and besides, the cedar trees grew thicker than old Blue's winter coat, never mind the boulders.

The man studied the flickering lights. Was somebody signaling trouble? He'd been a radioman in the Navy, stationed at Pearl in WWII. What the hell was the sequence for SOS—three dashes, three dots? Or the other way? Shitfire if he could remember. He huddled in his bedroll. Wasn't no way he could get over there to investigate anyway.

It was full light, and he was stretched out flat on his back inside his bedroll when he opened his eyes again. First thing in his mind was that he'd never got up to take a piss, then the next thing he remembered was the mystery lights. He sat up, rubbing his face, feeling the growth of stubble on his thin cheeks. He squinted across the water. Dream, he thought. Wasn't nothing more than—

The old man bent sharply forward. When Blue nudged him, asking for breakfast, he said, "Looky there, Blue. Somethin's catching the sun. See it?"

He scooped up his cap, shed his blankets and walked to the water's edge. He studied the cliff face until his eyes teared. But he couldn't make out anything but the pale yellow stone. It was his imagination, he told himself, turning away, rapidly blinking. His eyesight wasn't too good anyway. He hooked his fingers into Blue's scruffy mane and thought about his daughter, how mad she'd be if she found out he was here. Marcy'd say this wasn't his place no more, that his home was with her. He was trespassing, and besides, hadn't he told her he was camping up on the Guadalupe?

The old man rubbed Blue's neck. "Can you imagine what Marcy'd say if we was to tell her what we seen?"

Blue brayed and showed his big yellow teeth.

"Yeah, that's right, you old shit bird. She'd laugh her ass off sure as anything."

He fished till after lunch when the sun dropped behind the cliffs, then packed his gear. He hadn't intended to leave, not for a couple more days anyway. He'd meant to stay as long as the weather was fine, as long as he wasn't discovered and dragged off the place. But somehow that business last night had left him feeling spooked. There was no peace in the breeze, no music in the sound of the water, and he hadn't caught a damned thing. He loaded his bedroll and satchel onto Blue's back and headed into the trees.

But then, before they completely closed the stream from view, he turned and saw it. The car was wedged a little ways up and pretty far back in the rocks and near as he could tell, looked to be about the same color. Only reason it stood out now was from the light being exactly right.

He dropped Blue's lead, walked back to the bank and stood near enough to the water that it lapped at the toes of his boots. He pushed his hat back on his head and stared. No sign of blinking lights now; maybe he had dreamed that part, but it was a car, he'd swear it. He raised his hat and resettled it.

On the way home, he told Blue: "God strike me dead if I open my mouth about it and don't you say nothin' either. Marcy'd have us both in the fruit farm for sure."

CHAPTER
18

Abby found the puddle of water on the floor of the downstairs hallway, and her heart sank. She had forgotten when she used Lindsey's shower the night before that it leaked. One more item on the never-ending to-do list. She was searching for the plumber's telephone number when Hap Albright returned her call. She let it ring. She didn't want to go back to work. To go anywhere. The phone rang again, and she covered her ears. What if she forgot them? What if the day came when she couldn't remember how Nick loved classic jazz and the shape of her feet or that Lindsey loved backrubs and the smell of new hay? Abby saw it in her mind's eye, her forgetfulness rising like water over their images, softening her connection to them, erasing every bond.

The phone rang and rang.

Hap left a message, and when she didn't return his

call, he phoned again that evening. And she realized he wasn't going to leave her alone, that if she didn't speak to him soon, he was liable to appear on her doorstep. He was jovial when she answered. So glad to hear from her, he said.

"I'd love to have you back in the classroom," he told her. "When can we meet?" he asked. "How about tomorrow morning? Say, around ten?"

"Tomorrow?" Abby searched her mind frantically for an excuse, but found none.

"The quicker we get the ball rolling, the quicker you can be back to work." He was cheerful, certain he was offering her the opportunity she wanted.

Abby thanked him; she even managed to sound pleased, but after she hung up, she went to the kitchen sink and stared out the window. She saw them there, the four of them together in the yard. She could smell them, feel them in the air all around her. Her family.

Real. The word dropped into Abby's brain, and she turned, facing the empty room.

It was real, she told herself. "Real," she whispered.

Hunting for something suitable to wear the next morning, Abby went through her clothes, the dresses and skirts, blouses and vests she'd worn when she'd taught before. They looked awful to her now, out of date and frumpy. Finally, she pulled out a navy plaid skirt that fell to the knee and a white tailored blouse. She tossed a navy blazer on the bed, returned to the closet and hunted for shoes. All she found that would work was a pair of scuffed, low-heeled black pumps. She couldn't remember the last time she'd even worn heels.

In the bathroom, she pulled her hair into a chignon, and for the first time in months, applied lipstick, blush and mascara. She examined herself in the full-length mirror. Even with the blouse tucked in, she'd lost enough weight that the skirt gapped. She made a pleat in the waistband and secured it with a safety pin. The skirt bunched over her backside, but with the jacket on, no one would see. Too bad there wasn't a way to camouflage the circles under her eyes or flesh out the hollows beneath her cheekbones. At least she hadn't cried.

The phone rang as she was on her way out. She looked at the Caller ID, and recognizing Nick's office number, her hand rose. She drew it back. It would be Nina calling on behalf of Joe or Joe himself. Now that she was home, there were steps to be taken, papers to sign, financial matters to discuss. In voices thick with regret, they would acknowledge the circumstances were tragic, but the partnership was a business. And as unfeeling as it seemed, the practice was more than the sum of the partners. After all, didn't she know, and better than most, that the needs of the clients took precedence? That Nick, of all people, would want their interests considered before all others—blah blah blah. Abby left the house.

Hap waited for her in the doorway of his office, eyes alight with pleasure, smile warm with sympathy. Too much sympathy. Abby's steps faltered. She didn't want to be embraced by him, and luckily he only took her hand in both of his.

"Girl, how've you been?" he said.

Drawing her inside, he closed the door behind them, motioned her into a chair, propped his hip on the front corner of his desk. "You look good," he said. "Damn good, considering."

She murmured her thanks, made a show of putting her purse on the floor beside her chair.

"I never could figure out whether to call or come by or what."

"It's okay. I'm fine. Really." She wished he'd sit down in his desk chair. She'd forgotten what a big man he was. Bigger now, thicker than she remembered. "I appreciate your taking the time to see me. It's so close to the holidays. I know how busy it gets."

He held her in his gaze. "You know I'll always make time for you."

She felt her face warm and examined her knees. She could see the shiny pointed tips of his cowboy boots, the hem of his Levi's worn white at the crease. Some women considered Hap attractive, and she supposed he was, in a beefy, athletic sort of way. He'd played professional football once, linebacker—or was it running back?—for the Dallas Cowboys, but the muscle under the heavily starched cotton of his western shirt had lost definition.

"How long's it been since you were in the classroom? I was trying to remember." Hap rounded his desk and sat down, and Abby relaxed a bit.

"Not since Lindsey was born."

"Right, right." Hap grinned. "I remember now—" he made an arc with his arms "—out to here when you quit."

Her face warmed again. She didn't know where to look.

He laughed a bit as if her discomfiture delighted him. "I think I've got a place for you."

"Oh?" Abby's heart sank.

"Do you know Charlotte Treadway? She teaches second grade at Clark Elementary where you taught. Same classroom even. Must be something in the walls because she's going out on maternity leave, too, next week."

"So soon."

"It's perfect, don't you think? You'll be comfortable starting there, and who knows, it could turn permanent. Charlotte might not come back for fifteen years either."

"Well," Abby said. "Thank you. I don't know about it being permanent, though."

"We can cross that bridge down the road. How about if we get you started on the paperwork? You can fill in the application online and then I'll call you later in the week to work out a time for you to visit Charlotte's classroom. How's your schedule?"

"I'm flexible," Abby said.

His phone rang. He put up a finger. "Can you wait a minute?"

Reluctantly, she nodded. To use the interruption to leave would appear rude in the face of his kindness. She clasped her hands in her lap, examining them to give Hap privacy. He was making it so easy for her, and she knew why. She wished she didn't, that she could somehow forget.

That awful New Years Eve party when Hap, having had too much to drink, wept and rambled drunkenly on and on to Abby about his poor wife who was dying of brain cancer. Abby told Nick she thought it was Hap's loneliness and despair that had led him to try and kiss her, to put his hands on her. She squirmed a little now at the memory. She remembered her shock, how for a matter of seconds, she had been paralyzed, and when she finally had managed to extricate herself from him, she'd done it quickly, without a word. She hadn't wanted to hurt him, but she'd been so embarrassed.

Hap's call ended, and he sat quietly looking at her, heating her face with his scrutiny.

Causing her to feel even more regret. "Is—is something wrong?"

"I'm happy to find work for you, but I need to know if you'll be staying in Hardys Walk, if you're keeping your house and all, because I have to tell you, I heard different. I heard you mean to sell, move back home with your mom."

"Who told you that?"

He shrugged. "Several folks, but it's not like anyone blames you, Abby. It's a mystery how you can stand up under what you've been through. Not another woman I know can carry herself like you do."

She touched her eyes.

Hap half rose, as if he meant to come around his desk and comfort her.

She lifted her hands. "No, it's all right. I'm all right. Truly." She managed a smile. But she could see he felt badly for her. She could see his bewilderment, too, and his desire. And as she left his office, she thought how much she hated trading on his sympathy, some long-ago feeling he had conceived for her.

"I never imagined being single again," Abby told Kate on the phone later.

"He always did have a thing for you." Kate sounded delighted.

"I'm not interested."

"Not in him, I know, but you're young still."

"Don't go there, Katie."

"Okay, okay."

Abby bit her lip, on the verge of apologizing.

"So when do you start?"

"After Thanksgiving."

"Do you really think Hap will be a problem? Will you have to see him every day?"

"I shouldn't, but you know, he visits the different schools. He sits in on classes. There's almost no way to avoid it." Abby rubbed her forehead. "This is ridiculous. I'm going back to work, that's all. He's just being kind."

"I doubt it, Abby. Now that you're eligible, still very attractive, an experienced woman…ooh-la-la. Who knows what can happen?"

"Ooh-la-la yourself." Abby glanced down to her bare feet. She was still in her blouse and skirt, but she'd taken off her jacket and peeled off the hated pantyhose the second she'd cleared the back door. She had ignored the message from Nick's office, too. She didn't want to talk to anyone, let alone Joe and Nina.

"I thought you were mad at me the way you took off the other day," Kate said.

"Did you send Dennis after me?"

"No."

"But you told him about the fax."

"I was worried. I wanted his opinion."

"He offered to check into it."

"Better Dennis than you. I don't want you to call that man."

"You think Nick was up to something, don't you?"

"I never said that."

"But you think it, and you talked it over with Dennis and with George. Don't say you didn't. You're speculating, which is what you've accused me of doing, and you don't know any better than I do."

"No. But I don't think that guy who wrote that fax knows anything either. You aren't going to call him, are you? The world is full of kooks, Abby."

"I threw his number away. I cleaned. I shopped for groceries, I called a plumber. I'm going back to work. I'm trying to get on with my—aaagh—" Abby groaned.

She looked out the window past her reflection to the barn. "I wonder if I'll ever know," she said.

"You might not, as hard as it is."

"The mystery is what's so hard to take, Katie. Can you understand that? It's why I can't lay it down. I want an answer."

"What if there isn't one?"

"So, is this a test, then? Is this God or the universe or whatever doing this to see how tough I am?" Abby pulled the pins and the rubber band roughly from her hair and shook it out with her fingers. "It seems cruel. I keep wondering, why me?"

"I tell myself that at some point, we'll find the answers."

"When?" Abby flung her arm wide.

"Oh, Abby, I don't know." She paused as if to consider, then said, "Maybe this won't help, it's not the same as what you're going through, but when I found out I couldn't have children I was devastated. I felt so hopeless and furious, too, because it wasn't my choice."

"No."

"So I could hate, be full of anger, and for a time I was, but then what? I had to get past it."

"How? How did you get past it?"

"I don't know exactly. I remember waking up one day not long after I met George, and I had this burning in my gut, you know? I was just shaking and furious. I was that way all the time then, and it was getting worse. There George and I were, seriously in love, everything perfect, except I would never have our children.

"There was no end to my hate for that man. George said we could adopt, but I didn't want someone else's child. I wanted our child. He suggested we could find a surrogate mother, whatever I wanted, he would have done it, but I couldn't have what I wanted, and I wouldn't see reason. I'm surprised now that George put up with me."

"He adores you." They shared a silence before Abby continued. "You never told me how bad it was," she said, as if that were entirely Kate's fault, and Abby knew better. The truth was she didn't want to hear Kate's woes. She didn't want to hear how badly Kate had been hurt. What about my hurt, Abby thought.

Neither of them spoke, then Kate said, "Remember how skinny I was when George and I married?"

"I remember I was worried about you."

"How much have you lost? Ten pounds? Fifteen?"

"Twelve," Abby said.

"I know it's hard to eat when you're sad, but try, would you?"

Abby said she was getting better about it.

Kate said, "We could write a diet book."

"What will we call it? *Sob Your Way to a Slender You*?"

"*Cry Off Those Thighs You Hate*."

"*How to Grieve That Gut to Death*."

Kate laughed. "It would be an overnight sensation."

"Best seller for sure."

"We're living proof that it works."

"I'll see you, Katie," Abby said.

"Promise you won't call that man," Kate ordered.

But Abby didn't promise. She laughed.

The plumber came the next morning to caulk the leak in Lindsey's tub, and while he was finishing up, Abby rooted through her desk hunting for her checkbook. She searched her purse and then, remembering the day she'd put on Nick's jacket and found a checkbook inside, she went to the front hall closet. But the jacket wasn't there. She pushed apart the hangers, searched the floor, poked into the far corners. Nothing. It was gone.

Abby closed the closet door, leaned her backside against it, mystified.

"All set." The plumber came down the stairs.

Abby said, "Good, thank you," and beckoned him into the kitchen, where she opened a new box of checks, tore one off, wrote it out and handed it to him.

She was back inside the coat closet again a few minutes later when she heard the sound of tires and thought the plumber was back, that he'd forgotten a tool. But it was Jake's Mustang she saw when she opened the front door, and her heart lifted. He pulled to a sharp stop. She crossed the porch to greet him.

"Gramma said you were home." He grinned at her over the hood of his car.

Abby leaned on the rail. He looked so pleased to see her here. Then she remembered the trouble he was in at school, and she frowned. "What's wrong?"

"Nothing. I just had to see for myself that you were back. Got anything to eat?"

"I do, as a matter of fact, if it isn't too early for a sandwich."

He came around the front of the car. "Never too early."

He put his arm around her and walked with her into the house. She'd forgotten how tall he was, how much of a man he'd become. Or had this happened in the past seven months and she'd failed to notice? She said he'd just missed the plumber.

"You got the tub fixed?" Jake went to the refrigerator.

"I did." Abby leaned against the countertop. "You didn't, by any chance, borrow Dad's leather bomber jacket, did you?"

Closing the refrigerator door, Jake said, "He'd kill me if I took that jacket. Why?"

"It's not in the closet, and I know I saw it there."

"Did you get the locks changed like Charlie said?" Jake asked.

"Not yet. But you don't think someone broke in here and took it, do you?"

"Is anything else missing?"

"Not that I've noticed. My laptop is there on the desk in plain sight. The TV is still here. Isn't that what crooks take?"

Jake poked his head back into the refrigerator. "Yeah, but I'd call the cops if I were you."

Abby shook her head. She brought down a plate from the cabinet. "I probably moved his jacket myself. Half the time I don't know what I'm doing anymore."

"Tell me," Jake teased. "But you're getting better. I'm impressed."

"With what?" she asked.

"Everything." He hauled out the package of chicken, the small head of lettuce, the tomato. "Look at this place! It actually smells good in here."

"Nothing like a little spring cleaning," Abby said. "I'm even going back to work. Did Gramma tell you? I start teaching again after Thanksgiving."

"It'll be good for you."

Abby tore off a couple of lettuce leaves and handed them to him. She circled Jake's waist and gave him a quick hug. "What about you? How are you doing? Really," she added.

He loaded his sandwich onto the plate she handed him and took a bag of chips from the pantry. They sat at the table, and Abby was relieved when he said a solution to his school woes had been hammered out between his professor and the department head. "It'll mean a lot of extra work," he said, "but I don't care."

"You're lucky they were so understanding."

"They took my circumstances into consideration. I told them I wasn't ready to come back to campus after what happened. I said you pushed me."

"Jake, I didn't."

"You did, Mom." Jake was determined; Abby could see that. He'd been waiting a long time to accuse her.

"It wasn't doing you any good being at the ranch. If you weren't pacing the floor, you were getting George to drive you all over."

"Like you weren't?"

"You were better off in school." Abby raised her

gaze to Jake's, and her breath caught on seeing that his eyes were welled with tears.

"I wanted to be where you were, Mom," he told her, and he was blinking, furious. "I needed to be with you. We're all that's left."

She could only stare at him, at his clenched jaw and the muscles under his ears that knotted and loosened, knotted and loosened. The idiot part of her brain was busy wondering when she'd last seen him cry. Not in years. Not since he was a very little boy. Not even the weekend their family vanished.

"You think it doesn't affect me?" he demanded. "Sometimes, I'm so scared. They were here, now they're gone."

"Oh, Jake." She leaned forward, cupping his arms above his wrists, rubbing them.

"I wish it had been me instead of Lindsey."

"No! Jake, honey!" Abby half knelt, pulling him awkwardly against her. She felt him shaking. "Let it out," she told him. "Go on, it's okay. I'm right here," she promised.

He sagged forward, and, pushing his plate away, he lowered his head to the table and talked through sobs that grew rough and became uncontrolled. His speech was so broken Abby couldn't get every word, but the gist of it was that he was a bad person, and he'd been a worse brother. He'd ragged on Lindsey something awful, and once, he'd left her stranded without a ride home after school because he was mad at her. He couldn't even remember now what he'd been mad about.

Abby tightened her grasp, murmuring words of comfort through the tears that were packed like stones in her own throat. How would they survive? The pain seemed so incredible, so never-ending. When Jake quieted, she hunted around for Kleenex tissues, and realizing she hadn't bought any, she gave him the kitchen towel. He blew his nose, mopped his face. He looked at her, and in his reddened, swollen eyes, she saw a complicated mix of apology and shame, grief and outrage.

"You can't blame yourself, Jake." She sat down. "You weren't a bad brother. You were a typical brother. Maybe you did rag on Lindsey, but you never minded helping her with algebra or telling her when some new hairdo she tried didn't flatter her. If it means anything, I always agreed, especially that time she gelled her bangs into that shelf over her eyebrows."

Jake's grin wobbled.

"You were typical siblings," Abby said. "Nothing out of the ordinary." She glanced away. She would never see now how their relationship might have developed as adults, if they would have been close, if they would have ended up friends.

"I'm not going to law school, Mom."

She whipped her gaze back to his. "What do you mean? Dad would—"

"Fuck Dad."

"Jake!"

"I'm sorry, Mom, but if it wasn't for him, Lindsey would still be alive. We'd still be a family. We could have been a family without him, you know."

Abby might have argued, but instead, she said, "What is it between you and your dad? It's as if you've lost all respect for him."

Jake looked out the window. "Want me to mow before I leave?"

"I want you to tell me what's going on."

He rose and took his dishes to the sink. "Nothing. We didn't get along, that's all. You know that." He came and put his hands on her shoulders, squeezing gently, putting his thumbs into the sore places at the base of her neck. "Tight," he said.

She lowered her chin, stretching, feeling the knots loosen under his touch.

"We have to accept it, Mom." Jake's hands stilled. "Even if they never find them or the car, we can't keep on as if they'll walk back in here any second."

"When I was at Kate's," Abby said quietly, "I went to San Antonio to see if I could talk to Adam's wife, Sherry."

Jake came around Abby's chair to look at her. "Why? What did she say?"

"She was gone. A neighbor seemed to think she and Adam left the country together."

"So?" Jake started to unbutton his flannel shirt. "I'm going to see if I can get the mower started."

"I showed the neighbor a picture of your dad. She thought she recognized him. She said she'd seen him at the Sandoval's, that he was driving a yellow Corvette. Do you know anything about that?"

"Jesus, Mom." Jake flung his shirt over the back of a chair. "No! I don't know anything about that. I'm not keeping anything from you. I'm not," he repeated. But he didn't look at her. He didn't meet her eye.

CHAPTER

19

Abby studied her reflection in the powder-room mirror. She looked okay, she thought, in her black jumper and white, long-sleeved blouse. Not too casual. She looked like an elementary school teacher, Nick would have said. She had always thought he meant it as a compliment, but now she wondered if he would have preferred she wear tight skirts and form-fitting sweaters. She sat on the closed toilet lid. Once she'd been sure of him, his affection for her, his approval. Now she wasn't, and it felt awful. Her breath kept hanging up in her throat as if there were a bone stuck back there. She couldn't imagine facing a classroom filled with second graders. But she had to, or she'd lose herself and Jake, too. He and Mama were counting on her.

She grabbed a few tissues in case her self-control failed her and tucked them inside her purse. In the kitchen, she made toast, ate half and tossed the rest out for the birds. And when she threw her napkin into the trash, she thought of the fax. Buried now beneath yesterday's coffee grounds and the wrapper from the spark plugs Jake had bought to get the mower running.

She fished out the half-damp, crumpled message, unfolded it over the sink, wiping at the stains. Hank Kilmer's phone number was still visible, and enough of the letters stood out from the blots to make sense of the words.

My…Sondra has be…miss…for .early a year I don.. recogn….he name ..ck Bennett. May we talk in…so….

Where was Hank Kilmer's wife, Abby wondered. Who was she? Why would Nick have written her fax number inside a matchbook cover from the Riverbend Lodge in Bandera? Had he and Sondra Kilmer lunched there together that day last December when Kate had seen him in town? Was Sondra the woman who'd been unhappy with Nick over a botched real-estate deal? Abby looked out the kitchen window at the freshly mown yard. She wished she had shown Jake the matchbook. The sight of it might have forced him to tell her what he knew.

Abby glanced at the clock, folded the fax and picked up her purse. If she didn't leave now, she'd be late.

She had every intention of keeping her appointment with Charlotte Treadway, but then drove right by Clark Elementary to the freeway and headed south into Houston with the rest of the commuter traffic. She told herself she was crazy. She saw an exit ahead and told herself to turn around. She passed another exit. *This isn't rational.* Several more exits. *How will you explain it?*

The city skyline loomed. Now what? She had no idea where to find Hank Kilmer; she would have to call him. She glanced at her cell phone lying on the console near her knee. She pulled onto the shoulder, cut the engine. In the distance the cluster of buildings jutted from the horizon. Their tops were lost in swirls of dirty yellow sunshine. The traffic snaked past her, relentless, hell-bent. How had Nick stood it, driving into this day after day?

Her phone went off, jangling through an assortment of mechanical sounds that was supposed to be Beethoven's *Ode to Joy*. Abby picked it up, studied the Caller ID window.

Mama.

Abby could picture her, happily thinking of her daughter on her way to work, on her way to resurrecting her old life. Of course Mama would call; she would want to wish Abby luck. Abby laid the phone in her lap. She wished she could be where her mama and Kate and Jake wanted her to be, in a schoolroom on the road to recovery. Instead, against even her own better judgment, she was here on the side of the freeway, half-scared but determined to see Hank Kilmer. So there was no point in answering the phone. No point in speaking to her mother. Not now.

Once her mother's call went to voice mail, Abby dialed Hank Kilmer's number. Four rings, five. She was trying to decide what message to leave when a man answered sounding breathless.

Abby jerked upright. "Mr. Kilmer?"

"Yes?"

"This is, this is Abby Bennett. We—we have corresponded via fax." Her voice tipped up at the end as if she were asking him.

There was a moment of silence. "Where are you?" he asked.

"I-45 near the Loop," she said warily.

"I'm closer to downtown. Are you familiar? I could give you directions to the house."

"No." Abby wasn't so deluded as to think that would be wise. "Could we meet somewhere for coffee?"

He named an IHOP south of the Loop and told her what he was wearing: a brown sport jacket and an orange-striped tie.

Abby pulled into traffic. What sort of man wore orange?

Nick wouldn't. He wouldn't think this was smart, either, meeting a man she didn't know, regardless of the color of his tie. But Nick wasn't here.

If it hadn't been for the tie, Abby might have missed Hank Kilmer altogether. His skin, even his thinning hair, was as colorless as dust. He wasn't wearing the glasses she'd expected, and he was much taller than she had imagined. Over six feet, but he stooped as if his height pained him. They shook hands, and Abby slid into the booth. Hank folded himself onto the bench opposite her. Even seated, his shoulders slumped forward as if his back were burdened with a sack of rocks. He'd taken off his jacket and rolled the sleeves of his gold shirt into messy cuffs at his elbows. The awful orange-striped tie was loosely knotted at his neck. Everything about him seemed careless and unkempt. Unhappy. Nothing so neat and precise as his handwriting had indicated.

Abby slipped off her own jacket. She glanced around the restaurant full of diners, mostly men, bent over full plates of bacon and eggs. In the booth across the aisle, an older man was speaking intently to a young blond-haired woman as he stroked the inside of her wrist. They looked unnaturally enraptured given the earliness of the hour and the way they were dressed, both of them in business suits.

Not married, she decided. She wondered if they would make it to the office. She wondered if the man's wife had dropped their kids at school and gone to do the grocery shopping. Had she done the laundry, swept their kitchen floor? Had she planned what she would serve this cheating man for his dinner?

"I can't believe you called. I'd given up," Hank said.

"I wasn't going to," Abby told him.

"Well, thank God you did." He sounded fervent, too fervent.

Abby eyed the door, wanting to leave, but when the waitress came, they both ordered coffee.

"So," Hank said when the waitress was gone, "your husband's been missing since April?"

Abby nodded. "But your wife's been gone since February, you said."

"Late February or sometime in March, near as I can figure."

Abby frowned.

The waitress reappeared with their order. She set the cream pitcher and sugar shaker on the table. Abby smiled and thanked her, but Hank Kilmer didn't even glance up. He poured a stream of sugar into his mug, took up his spoon and stirred a series of concentrated circles.

When he lifted his mug to drink, she noticed his knuckles were thick and misshapen. She wondered if it was from slamming his fists into walls. She wondered why he didn't know when his wife had disappeared.

"We were separated," he said as if he'd read Abby's mind. "She'd moved out, but I figured it was temporary, like the other times."

"You've been separated before?"

"Yeah, but she always came back. She doesn't like being apart from our daughter for too long. Caitlin's eight. She and Sondra are close."

"Oh, she must miss her mother."

"You have no idea." Hank stabbed the table with his index finger. "No kid should have to go through this. Sondra is Caitlin's mother, for Christ's sake. She shouldn't do this to her own kid. Just disappear without a fucking—aaagh—" He groaned and wiped his face. "I'm sorry. It gets to me sometimes."

Abby lowered her gaze. She could hear her pulse in her ears.

Hank shoved his spoon around. "I want this nightmare to end. But when you don't know what the hell it's about—" He shot her a hard glance. "You understand, right? You're in the same boat."

Abby did understand, but she didn't want to share Hank's boat or anything else with him. She felt pity for him, this big, moon-faced, homely, infuriated man. She wondered if it was his anger at his wife that had bleached the color from him.

Hank said, "There must be a reason why your husband had Sondra's fax number."

"I don't know of one."

"Well, is he by any chance an attorney? Is he the

same Nick Bennett who represented those kids in the case against Helix Belle?"

Abby said he was, but with reluctance, not liking it.

"I thought so! That's the connection." Hank sounded celebratory.

Abby felt her heart stall in her chest. "I don't know what you mean."

"Sondra was a judicial assistant for Judge Payne, Harold Payne?"

"The case was tried in his court," Abby remembered.

"She went to work for him a couple of months before the Helix lawsuit was filed, worked for him almost two years."

Abby added more cream to her coffee, even though she hadn't tasted it.

"Sondra was wound up about that case," he continued. "She talked about it constantly. She talked about your husband, too, especially after he won. She could practically quote his closing argument from memory. It started to piss me off, frankly. I wondered then if there was some funny business going on."

"No," Abby said, and she was thinking of her marriage at the time, that when Nick won the settlement, their relationship couldn't have been better. Nick himself couldn't have been happier or more content. She certainly had not been wondering about any funny business.

"I'm not trying to say I've got proof of anything between them. But the fact is they apparently worked together, and now she's gone and so is he."

"But they didn't disappear at the same time. You don't even know for certain when your wife left."

"Like I said, we were separated. She moved out last January. She'd rented a house over in the Heights and opened up an interior-design business."

"I thought she worked for Judge Payne."

"She quit after the holidays. She said she was sick of getting hit on all the time. It was kind of a shock, to tell you the truth. She'd seemed so happy, then boom." Hank fell into a fractious silence.

Abby pulled her jacket into her lap; she found the strap of her purse.

Hank put out his hand as if he might hold her in place. "Your husband went missing in April, right? What's the story there? If you don't mind my asking," he added.

Abby gave him the short version.

"Man, that's rough," he said when she finished. "I was out in the Hill Country a week or so after the flood. Things were bad."

Abby already had an idea of what he'd say if she asked why he went there. She sensed—and she'd guess later it was the horrible gift of prescience—that his answer would be the beginning of the end of what was left of her life, the one she believed in, relied on, treasured. But she asked anyway. "You have a place out there?"

"Sondra's granddad left her some land in Kerr County with a cabin on it. It's on high ground, but that was a lot of water."

"It was okay?"

"Yeah, it's old but solid." Hank kept Abby's gaze. "What a hell of a thing, though, your whole family gone."

She said she still had her son Jake. "He won't be happy when he finds out I was here."

"How come?"

"He thinks I'm at work. So does my mother." Abby glanced at her watch. It was past nine. Charlotte Treadway would be wondering what had happened to her. She would call Hap to complain.

"But you blew that off and called me because you have doubts, right? What are you thinking, that your husband and daughter didn't drown?"

"There's no indication that happened. No bodies, not even the car was found." Abby hesitated. She didn't want to say any more, and yet she was compelled. She hated how desperate she'd become, how helpless it made her feel. It had robbed her of everything, even her ordinary discretion, her dignity. "I thought they were going camping," she said and described Lindsey's phone call, the one from Boerne. "I've never been sure what she said, something about her daddy, about how he was taking the scenic route or the easy route. I don't know. I think she was crying."

"Maybe he had a heart attack or something."

"The boy at the gas station said he saw them drive away." Abby toyed with her cup, thinking of the cabin, its remote location. She thought of Nick jotting Sondra's name inside a book of matches in handwriting that was as familiar to her as her own. She could see it, the rushed slant of his "S," the extra loop on the "r" that made its shape seem almost girlish. She could see him smiling over it, smiling at Sondra, and she felt insulted. She felt the awful insinuation that seemed implicit building in her mind, and she tightened her jaw. She looked at Hank. "I'd like to go there," she said even as she was thinking how insane it was, completely insane to involve herself on any level with this man and his problems. Didn't she have enough of her own?

"Go where?"

"To your wife's cabin."

Hank's eyes widened. "You think Sondra and your husband—?"

"I don't know." Abby didn't want Hank to say it, *having an affair*. "It might not be that."

"What else then?"

"She worked for Judge Payne."

"So? What does the cabin have to do with that?"

Abby pulled the book of matches from her purse and pushed it across the table with the tip of her index finger. "Do you know this place?"

"Riverbend Lodge? Yeah. It's a dump on the highway outside Bandera."

"Is it anywhere near your wife's cabin?"

"Not really. You pass it going there, I guess."

"Look inside."

Hank opened the cover. "That's Sondra's fax number."

Abby said, "That's Nick's handwriting."

"This is how you found me?"

Abby nodded.

"But if he wanted to get in touch with her, why wouldn't he just call her? She has a cell phone, or she did have."

"He might have faxed her documents related to the trial," Abby said. "I haven't any idea, really, but there's something else you should know."

He waited.

"My friend Kate ran into Nick in Bandera last winter, not long before you lost touch with your wife."

Hank's brows shot up. "Alone or—?"

Abby shrugged. Kate hadn't mentioned seeing Nick with a woman, but given Kate's history, that might not mean anything.

Hank's gaze considered her. "Your husband—he was implicated when the money went missing last fall from the account that was set up for those kids, wasn't he? But it was that other guy, Helix Belle's own attorney—Sanders, Sandover, something like that—"

"Adam Sandoval." Abby supplied the right name. "Nick had nothing to do with it." She stopped short of saying that she'd gone looking for Sherry Sandoval; she wasn't going to repeat any of what the Sandoval's neighbor had told her. It was as Kate said, nothing but gossip. It couldn't be more....

Hank said he remembered the raw deal Nick got. "Sondra went on a rant about it."

"Did she ever talk about Adam? She must have known him, too, from the courtroom."

Hank kept Abby's gaze, and she watched the wave of disquiet creep over his expression. Her own breath felt uncertain. Even her surroundings, their entire conversation, seemed unreal now, the product of bizarre imagination.

"Jesus, he's gone, too, isn't he? He jumped bail. It was all over the news."

"Last spring, right before the flood, not long after your wife—"

"My wife and your husband took off."

"Nick didn't take off, not with our daughter."

Hank's eyes widened at the bite in Abby's words. She didn't care.

"So what is all this, then?" He matched her hard

tone, spreading his hands. "A coincidence? My wife worked for a judge who oversaw a case where two of the opposing attorneys are now missing, along with a helluva lot of cash. What's next, or maybe I should say, who's next? The judge? Is he going to disappear?"

Abby didn't have an answer. She picked up the matchbook, returning it to her purse.

Hank's sigh was heavy and unsettled the air. "I still don't see what the cabin has to do with anything. Sondra never went there much. She's a city girl, can't stand being stuck in the boonies. She only kept the place because her grandparents loved it, and she loved them. But now that they're both gone, she's talked about selling it."

"It's isolated, then." Abby found Hank's gaze, saw him take her meaning.

"Yeah," he said. "It's a great place to hide."

"Mom? What are you doing?"

"Driving home," Abby said. "Can I call you back?"

"No, Mom. Jesus, Gramma called me. That teacher from the school called and said you never showed. Gramma's been trying your cell phone and the home number all morning. She's about to go up to Hardys Walk."

"Oh, God, Jake, I'm sorry. I wasn't thinking. Hold on." Abby laid the cell phone in the passenger seat and steered the car over two lanes of traffic and onto the shoulder of the freeway. Cars rushed past so close, they shook the BMW. Abby closed her eyes a moment, making herself breathe, then picked up the phone and apologized again.

"But what are you doing?" Jake demanded.

"I realize you're angry with me, and I wish I could explain. I have to do this, that's all. There's just no other way, and I'm so tired of arguing—"

"Mom, stop. You're jabbering."

Abby pressed her lips together.

"You went to see the guy who sent the fax, didn't you?"

"Who told you?"

"Gramma. She figured that's where you were."

Abby danced her fingers along the top of the steering wheel.

"I don't know how you can accuse me of keeping stuff from you," Jake said.

"I haven't accused you, Jake."

"Maybe not in so many words, but you make it pretty clear."

Abby sighed. "Maybe we're both insane."

"Now you're talking. Who is the guy anyway? Does he know Dad or what?"

"He doesn't. But his wife might." Abby waited for Jake to ask who the wife was, to ask why Hank's wife would know his dad. But the silence from Jake's end was profound.

"Jake? Are you there?"

He said, "Yes," but the distinct hesitation before he answered was unmistakable. Ominous. Alarm prickled the fine hairs on the back of Abby's neck; she put a hand there.

"Mom, it's like I said before, you need to go home. You need to build a new life, because the one you had is over. You don't need to be hurt anymore, okay? Just go home."

Abby looked out at nothing, and when she finally said his name, she knew he'd hung up. She was talking to dead air.

Abby's mother met her at the kitchen door.

"Jake said you've been into town to see that man." She followed Abby into the kitchen. "I thought you threw away his number."

"I did." Abby sat down.

Her mother took a cup and saucer down from the cabinet.

"Could I have a glass of water instead?" Abby asked.

Her mother filled a glass and brought it to Abby, then sat in an adjacent chair. She took Abby's hands. "What's going on, sweet?"

Abby's eyes filled. "Jake is pretty upset with me."

"We were worried. We didn't know what in the world had happened to you. Hap Albright called from Clark at nine and said you still weren't there. The school is only a ten-minute drive from your house."

"Hap was at Clark? What was he doing? Checking up on me?"

"I don't think so. He said he just happened to be there."

Abby made a face.

Her mother patted her hands and released them.

Abby said, "I can't shake the feeling that Jake knows something."

"What do you mean?"

"I don't know. He just seems so determined that I should stop looking for answers. He wants me to go home. That's all he ever says—go home."

"He wants you to be okay, honey. We all do."

Abby sighed.

"So, this man, this Hank person, did you learn any-thing helpful from him?"

Abby gave her mother the gist of their conversation. She said, "Clearly, his wife knew Nick, and if she knew him, she must have known Adam, too. They were all working on the same case."

"Okay, but do you really think it's possible the dis-appearances are related, that they somehow involve Helix Belle and the money that was stolen?"

"I know. It seems so far-fetched."

"Abby, it sounds like an episode of *Forty-Eight Hours*."

Abby managed a smile. She said, "I don't know about Sondra, what she might be capable of, but Nick was cleared. He had no part in what Adam did. I know that," she added. But did she? Did she really know Nick at all?

"Maybe you should go to the police."

"And say what? That I think my husband, who they're convinced drowned with my daughter in a flood, is actually alive and involved in some sort of—?" *Conspiracy.* Abby broke off before she could say it, remembering her confrontation with Joe at his office when she'd questioned whether it was possible that Nick had an unhappy client, one who might have fol-lowed him and harassed him. Even when Abby told Joe that Nick had mentioned that very possibility to her, Joe had been annoyed; he'd practically sneered. *There's no conspiracy*, he'd said. But then she'd dismissed the possibility, too, when Nick brought it up to her.

Abby looked at her mother. "I don't think the police would pay the slightest attention to me, Mama. I'm going tomorrow with Hank to Sondra's cabin. Maybe we'll find something there."

"Like what? You don't even know the man. Where do you intend to spend the night?"

"We're not spending the night."

"But the drive is too long to make it there and back in one day."

"But I'm going to, and that's that." Abby stood up. "I only came by to say I'm sorry I worried you and to tell you I'm going."

"But this isn't like you, Abigail. What do you hope to accomplish? What could this woman, or Adam Sandoval for that matter, possibly have to do with Nick?"

Nothing good. The words rose into Abby's mouth. She finished her water and set the glass in the sink. She thought in terms of the result she would hope for if hope were possible, and she might have laughed, but her mother's anxiety was palpable. Abby turned and hugged her close. "I don't know, Mama. That's why I have to go there."

CHAPTER

20

The neighborhood was old, not more than a handful of crumbling dead-end streets and ramshackle bungalows poked into a frayed pocket on the edge of downtown Houston. Abby would never have found it without the map Hank had drawn for her. He'd said the house was a yellow brick one-story, but pulling into the driveway, she thought the color was more drab. She thought it was as drab and sad-looking as Hank himself. Apprehension knotted her stomach. She wondered if she could go through with it, her fool's errand. *It's not like you, Abigail....* Her mother's caution rattled through her mind. Her ordinarily rational mind. But that word... *ordinary...* what did it mean anymore?

Abby got out of the car into air that was thick and still and too warm for November. The cloud cover had thickened, too, and grown darker like a ripening bruise. It would rain later just to spite her. She picked her way across the haphazard row of stepping-stones that led to the front door and paused at the front stoop, a misshapen, flatish chunk of rust-stained concrete pushed against the house. It looked like leftover construction, as if it might have fallen off the back of a truck bound for the city dump. It wobbled when Abby stepped up onto it. She glanced at the BMW and thought of going home. But that seemed as impossible now as staying here, and she turned, ruefully, to the old, metal screen door that rattled obnoxiously when she knocked. Abby expected Hank to answer, but instead it was a woman, a tall, angular, plain-faced, female version of Hank, who said she was his sister.

"Kim." She gave her name, and Abby sensed aggravation and unhappiness.

It must run in the family, she thought. "Hank didn't mention having a sister. It's nice to meet you. I'm—"

"Abby Bennett, I know." Kim continued her scrutiny and her silence, and Abby was unsure what to do.

"Shall I come in?" she asked finally. "Is Hank here?"

Kim's answer was to thrust open the door so abruptly that Abby was forced to step down off the stoop. She looked at Kim in bewilderment, a bit of alarm, but Hank's sister only rolled her eyes. "Come in," she said, "before the mosquitoes do."

Reluctantly, Abby obeyed, losing her vision for a moment in the dark confines of the tiny entry hall.

"Caitlin and Hank have allergies. You aren't wearing any wool, are you?" Kim looked Abby up and down.

"No," Abby said. "It's a little warm today for wool."

"They're very sensitive. I have to be careful."

"Of course," Abby said. She stowed her keys in her

purse, taking her time, uneasy under the weight of Kim's gaze, her intensity that was reminiscent of Hank.

Kim said she was taking Caitlin to school. "I drop her off every morning," she said, "on my way to work. I'm a teller at First Century Bank, the one near Caitlin's school. Hank picks her up after. I don't like her to ride the bus. Too many bullies. Who knows what could happen? I don't trust a single one of those drivers anyway."

Abby nodded, as if Kim's concern seemed natural when it didn't. It seemed possessive, more like fear-driven obsession. But fear of what? Bullies and bus drivers? Abby didn't think so. Some instinct said it went deeper.

"Hank tells me you believe your husband's run off with his wife." Kim said this bald-faced, without so much as the blink of an eye.

Abby's mouth fell open a little.

"We're close," Kim said. "We talk about everything."

You're rude. Abby wanted to say it. "I'm not sure what I believe actually. What Hank and I are doing, making this trip to the cabin, it's probably crazy."

Kim sniffed. "Since Hank brought Sondra into this family, I've had to raise the bar on what's crazy. You know they were separated?"

"He mentioned it."

"Well, did he tell you the sort of work she found for herself after she moved out?"

"He said she opened an interior-design business."

Kim hooted. "That little venture lasted less than a month and cost my brother half his savings to set up. I told him he was a fool. Sondra can't balance her checkbook, much less run a business. She's got the attention span of a gnat, never sticks with anything. As soon as she ran out of money, Hank caught her stripping again, and I'm not talking wallpaper. She refused to come home, even to see Caitlin. Now she's gone. Poof. No one's seen her since. Good riddance, I say." Kim peered at Abby, but if she wanted a response, Abby didn't have one.

"Well, come along then." Kim turned. "Hank and Caitlin are in the kitchen. This way."

Abby followed in Kim's wake. They passed a dining room, crossed the den. The white walls and scuffed floors were bare of any adornment other than a sofa covered in plastic and the vinyl blinds that were pulled low over every window. There was a definite smell of disinfectant that made Abby think of hospitals and isolation, that made her think of loneliness and depression. Her heart tapped nervously against her ribs.

Kim paused before a closed door and rested her hand on the doorknob, facing Abby. "I should warn you Caitlin might be upset. She doesn't like it when Hank leaves, not since Sondra went off. She's afraid of losing him, too."

"We won't go then." Abby was hopeful.

"But you have to. Hank won't see the truth otherwise."

"The truth?" Abby was at sea.

"About Sondra." Kim was impatient. "I've tried since high school when he had the misfortune of meeting her to get him to listen to me, to see reason. We've always watched out for each other, you know? Since we were kids. But he's totally blind when it comes to Sondra. He can't believe a woman like her would look at him twice, much less marry him. As if *she's* the prize. Hah! If you could see her, nothing but blond hair and cleavage. And Hank? Well, we're plain people with simple tastes, that's all."

Abby lifted her hands. "I don't know—" *what this has to do with me.* That's what she intended to say, but Kim huffed a short syllable of disgust.

"Let me tell you something—" she bent toward Abby "—the first time Sondra left Caitlin, the child was scarcely six weeks old, and Hank called me to come and change her diapers. Sondra was gone the day Caitlin spoke her first word, took her first step. When Caitlin nearly died from an asthma attack, who do you think took the time to learn about it and how to protect her?"

Kim thumped her chest. "Me! I'm the one who knows she can't live in a house that's cluttered with the pillows and throw rugs and drapery that Sondra insists on dragging in here. I know green is Caitlin's favorite color, not pink—everything Sondra gives the child is pink—and that she hates the Barbie dolls Sondra insists are her favorites. I keep this house clean and dust-free and see to it that Hank and Caitlin are properly fed and when that—that whore deigns to show up here, she cries to me and promises she'll do better and thank you very much but go home." Kim paused, pressing her lips together. Still, her chin wobbled.

"I shouldn't have come," Abby said.

Kim spoke as if Abby hadn't. "I am the reason Caitlin is alive and well. I am the only mother—decent mother—that child has ever known, and do you know, she made Hank put a lamp in the window and she turns it on herself every night before she goes to bed. 'For

Mommy,' she says. She waits and waits. It makes me sick. Sondra makes me sick. She isn't fit to be anyone's mother, much less Caitlin's."

Raw envy and a threat of tears ached under the hotter current of Kim's indignation, and it worried Abby. It made her sorry for Kim, and she didn't want to be sorry.

Kim pressed her fingertips to her eyes. "Do you want to know what I hope for, what I pray for?" She dropped her arms abruptly. "That she's dead. And in case you were wondering? I don't care if I go to hell." Before Abby could respond, before she could act on the thought of escape, Kim thrust open the kitchen door. "Go on," she said, and it sounded like a dare.

Hank turned from the kitchen sink. The little girl beside him crowded against his legs. Still, Abby saw that she was beautiful, as beautiful as Hank and Kim were homely. Angelic, Abby thought, and yet so solemn beneath her chin-length cap of thick, shiny blond hair.

Hank said, "This is Mrs. Bennett, Caitlin," and he asked if she could say hello.

But Caitlin shook her head. "Daddy, don't go." She was begging him.

"I'll be back before you can miss me, ladybug, I promise."

She stepped in front of him, tugging his hand. "But I already miss you."

Without a word, Abby wheeled and retreated, walking fast, retracing her steps.

Hank caught her elbow near the front door and spun her around. "You contacted me, remember? You set this up. You can't leave now."

She yanked her arm out of his grasp.

He brought his hands up and backed off. "I'm sorry, but, please, please don't go."

"This was a mistake."

"You know better."

Abby eyed the front door, watching herself walk through it. She'd call Hap, apologize for missing her appointment yesterday; she'd say she was ready now to go to work. Ready to get on with her life. And she would do it. In time, she would forget. Everyone said so.

"What if your husband wasn't alone in Bandera last winter like your friend said? What if he was with Sondra, and your *friend* can't tell you because she thinks you can't handle it?"

Hank was talking about Kate. Kate, who never thought Abby could handle anything. Kate, who had lied to Abby in the past. "Everyone I know thinks this is a bad idea," she said.

"But it's not their life, is it? It's easy for them to sit on the fucking sidelines and dish out a lot of bullshit advice about how we're supposed to live with this. Without knowing what happened. As if they could handle it better."

Abby opened the front door, then paused on the threshold. She couldn't have said why.

Hank's voice drilled her back. "How often do you see it on TV, people pissing and moaning about how all they want to know is the truth. All they want is someone to say what happened, how their loved one died. Or they say, please, bring them home, we just want to bury them. Or what about when somebody gets sick and they don't know what's wrong? They go to doctor after doctor. They go crazy, they go insane until they know. How is this different?"

Abby turned. "I'm not sure I can stand to know."

"Yeah? Well, me either." Hank looked intently at Abby, and she couldn't look away.

Because he was right. If she walked out now, she would have nothing but suspicion and conjecture, the half light of maybe. Even worse, she would have to live with the knowledge that she hadn't done every last thing she could to find her family, to find the truth, and she would hate that. Hank would go on his own to the cabin anyway. Abby could see he was resolved, and if there was something to be found there, he would be the one to find it. Somehow she couldn't stand that either. She took in a hard breath and let it out. "All right," she said. "Let's go."

Hank nodded shortly, and when he retraced his steps down the hallway, Abby followed in his wake.

He drove an old-model luxury car, one of those big-fendered boats. The blue was sun-spotted and bleached like worn-out jeans. From the rough sound of the engine, Abby couldn't imagine they would make it to the edge of town, much less all the way into the Hill Country.

"Get in," he said through the open passenger window.

She bent down. "We can take mine. I have to move it anyway for you to get out."

He flicked a glance at the rearview mirror taking in the image of the shinier, newer, pricier BMW. "I can go around," he said, and his voice was inflected with elements of resentment and desire. He couldn't look at her.

And Abby acquiesced because of this. Because he seemed mortified and furious with himself for it, and more protest from her would only unman him further. This man who had already been so unmanned. The passenger door screeched violently when Abby shut it. The seat belt stuck and Hank had to help her with it. He backed down the drive, maneuvering around her car, heedless that he was driving over the front yard. Abby guessed it didn't matter. It wasn't more than a square of weed-choked, scorched earth anyway. She watched the BMW until it was out of sight, wondering if it would be safe, if it would still be here for her when they returned tonight.

Hank said, "Sondra wouldn't be caught dead riding in this car, much less driving it. I'm always wishing I could afford something better. Better house, better neighborhood, better schools for Caitlin, but selling insurance these days, it sucks, you know? I own my own agency, and business is lousy. It's always lousy. I did manage to get Sondra a new car a couple of years ago. Lexus, loaded. Real classy. Cost a fortune. I keep making the payments, too, like I know where it is."

They were at the western outskirts of town when the rain Abby had dreaded began. Hank fiddled with the knob that controlled the windshield wipers. Nothing happened. He tried again, and when the blades picked up, lumbering across the glass, he smiled uneasily as if to suggest that Abby shouldn't put her faith in them. Or him, or this journey they were undertaking at her insistence. But for all she knew, he could have some alternate plan in mind; he could take her anywhere, do anything to her. She couldn't stop him. And if she were to disappear, no one but his sister Kim would know where to begin to search for her. And Abby wasn't certain that Kim was right in her mind.

"I guess you got your ears burned off."

"Excuse me?" Abby turned to Hank.

"I'm guessing Kimmie unloaded on you about Sondra. My wife and sister don't get along, not even when Sondra's acting right."

Abby didn't want to know what Hank meant by "acting right" as opposed to not. She didn't want to hear the history behind Kim's hostility. Kim wasn't "right" either, nor was Hank, really, and Abby was already unnerved enough. "How long have you been married?" Abby asked the conventional question and hoped Hank would follow her lead, that he would confine their talk to matters that were small and of little consequence. But even as she hoped for this, she knew it was impossible, that their situation had already broken every civilized boundary. Abby somehow sensed that Hank would be as hell-bent on spilling the family drama as his sister.

He answered that he and Sondra had been married nearly twelve years, and he went on as Abby had known, had feared that he would.

"I fell in love with her the second I saw her," Hank said, "even though I knew I didn't stand a chance. She was gorgeous. I was nobody. Second-string junior varsity football benchwarmer. She never gave me a second look. She was too busy working her way through first-string."

The pause that came was as disconcerting to Abby as Hank's speech.

"She's that kind of woman, you know? She could dress in a potato sack and guys still wouldn't keep from seeing, from wanting to—" Hank's voice crumpled. He cleared his throat, raised his hand, resettled it. "She wants you to. She likes attention. Craves it, actually."

Abby thought of what Kim had told her, that Hank had caught his wife stripping in a men's club. *Again*, Kim had said, as if Sondra had a habit of doing it. Abby studied the windshield, the one unwipered corner where the rain-formed rivulets broke into fat veins of polished silver. She wondered if Hank would talk about that next. She wondered if she asked, would he stop the car and let her out?

"You probably want to know what she saw in a guy like me," he said. "It's okay. Everybody does. It's because I'm safe, see? She can trust me, trust I'll be faithful, like the family dog." He switched on the radio, punched the row of buttons, got nothing but a voice swimming in static that reminded Abby of Lindsey's call from Boerne. *"It's about Daddy—" "I'm in the restroom—"* Followed by sobbing. Abby was convinced of it now, that Lindsey had been crying.

"Sometimes my wife goes on, like, these benders. She goes to the men's clubs and you know—" Hank broke off.

Their gazes collided and quickstepped away.

He said, "It's what scares me, that some pervert got hold of her. She didn't do it all the time; she's not hardened to that life like a lot of those women. In fact it had been almost three years when Sondra went back to it this last time. I thought she was done with it. She was working for the judge and she seemed settled. She seemed normal, you know what I mean? More normal than I'd ever seen her."

Another pause dithered. Abby twisted her wedding rings on her finger.

"Sometimes I think if I was just a more exciting guy, if I could just keep her entertained, then I think, how can she do it? Why does she? She's so smart. She's got a fucking degree in psychology, for Christ's sake."

Surprised, Abby looked at Hank, then away.

"After I found out she was dancing again, I tried to talk sense to her. I wanted her to come home," he said.

"She wouldn't?" Abby was resigned now. There was something about riding in the car, being pinned up, a captive audience. Somehow it implied intimacy, confession. As if the situation needed further inducement for that.

"Nope. She refused. She stayed in touch with Caitlin, though, through maybe the middle of February, but then nothing. Her house in the Heights was locked up. Nobody'd seen her there or at the club. None of her friends had seen or heard from her either. It was like she vanished right off the face of the earth."

"You called the police?"

"They didn't give a damn. They were like everybody else, they figured she got tired of the wife-and-mother routine and took off."

"Because you were separated."

"Because she's done it before. I didn't think too much about it myself until she didn't show up for Caitlin's birthday last April. Sondra wouldn't have missed that. She wouldn't have."

"Poor Caitlin," Abby murmured, remembering the little girl, her small angelic face, the anguished way she'd clung to Hank. He shouldn't have left her. Abby regretted her part in it.

Hank said Sondra's landlord had called him to come and clear out the house in May. "Took me half a day. Besides all the office equipment and business crap, sample books and fabric and doodads everywhere, the upstairs was stuffed with her furniture. The closet and dresser drawers were full of her clothes, there was makeup strewn everywhere. Even her toothbrush was still there. None of it meant a damn to the cops. They said she could buy new stuff. I told them there was no activity on our credit cards, no withdrawals from our joint account. They said she was making her own money, she could get new cards. They said she probably had a new guy and a new life. Assholes."

After a moment, Abby said, "It's good you have Kim to help out with Caitlin," even though she wasn't sure it was good at all.

"Yeah, we've always been close. Even though she's younger she looks after me. When we were kids, she was always taking up for me and getting whaled on for it. One day when my old man was whipping her with his belt, I went off on him. I couldn't stop myself. I get like that sometimes. Get pushed to a certain point and can't think straight, you know? I just explode."

Abby looked at him. She didn't know.

"I see red. Literally. It's like a mist." He brushed the air in front of his face. "That day? When I took on my old man? He landed in the ER. I was gone by the time they fixed him up. I never went home after that."

Hank fiddled with the buttons on the dash, bumping up the fan speed on the defroster, and Abby looked at his misshapen knuckles; she slicked her gaze along the tight line of his jaw, where a tiny pulse needled the flesh near his ear. Her heart tapped insistently.

Ahead in the near-distance, a huge flock of geese angled across her view, and she focused on them, their undulating vee-shaped flight. Headed for the coast, she thought. If the weather was good and Nick was driving, she'd ask him to pull over. She would say she had to hear their song. The sound put her in such awe. Lindsey, Jake and Nick had always poked fun at her for it. Abby remembered feeling in such moments as if the four of them were knit into a single fabric from one thread. Now her throat knotted with tears.

They stopped for gas and bought cheese and crackers to snack on in the car, rather than take time for a real lunch. Neither of them commented on it when they passed the Riverbend Lodge on their way through Bandera. North of town, Hank turned west on an unmarked asphalt road. A ranch road. The Hill Country was networked with such roads. The natives knew them as well as they knew the creases on their palms. But someone who didn't know the land could get lost, utterly, irrevocably, especially today without even the sun to define direction.

After several miles, the land gained a gentle incline. The road surface changed into a jolting bed of caliche and crushed rock. The rain softened. Limestone outcroppings loomed from the mist, pencil sketches in charcoal and gold. Sound was muted, as indistinct as the view. For all Abby knew, the world had disappeared except for this narrow stretch of road they traveled on.

"Eerie out here, isn't it?" Hank seemed to read her thoughts. "Kind of gives you the creeps. Almost anything could happen. Nobody'd find you, maybe for a long time. Maybe never."

Abby felt the twitch of his glance. Was he making

conversation? Baiting her? Warning her? She didn't know. She left the pause alone.

"I remember once when I was a kid, my old man brought me and Kim out here camping. He took us to see this place called Boneyard Draw. You ever hear of it?"

Abby said she had, that she knew the story behind it, but Hank paid no attention.

"It's where Indians drove an entire herd of wild horses off the canyon edge rather than let the U.S. cavalry have them, and they rotted there until there was nothing left but their bones. That's how it got its name. They say sometimes you can still hear the horses screaming." Hank snicked his tongue against his teeth. "You want to talk about eerie."

No, Abby thought, and she turned to the passenger window, but rather than the view, what confronted her was an image in her mind's eye of all those bones. Bones strewn in careless heaps, unclaimed, unmourned. But it was so easy out here for such things to happen, for an animal or a car—a car with her husband and daughter in it—to fly off the cracked lip of some bluff and tumble into an abyss. And whatever life survived such a fall was then left to suffer horribly and to die alone without comfort.

Despair boiled right under the surface of Abby's skin; she could feel the heated pressure mounting and she fisted her hands. She could not do this, could not lose her composure, not now, not in front of this man, this near stranger. She groped in her mind for something else, a distraction, and remembered the fawn. Dennis's fawn. She wondered how it was doing, if it had grown. She wondered what Dennis would say if he could see her now. He had told her not to do anything crazy. He had said she should call him first.

The car slowed; they turned again to the west. Ground up an even steeper incline. The engine shuddered as if it might stall. Abby glanced at Hank. "Not much farther," he said.

"Are there neighbors?" she asked.

"Not in any direction for maybe five miles."

"So you can come and go without anyone knowing, I guess."

Hank's brows rose as if he wondered what she meant.

Abby wasn't sure herself, only that she felt anxious, but along with that, she felt a certain sense of fatalism, too. She guessed she'd come too far now to be afraid. So what if Hank had dangerous intentions? Life itself concealed dangerous intentions. You could never know them ahead of time. Uncertainty was adversity's companion. Or maybe it was calamity's companion. Hadn't she heard that somewhere?

The car stopped, and the cabin materialized out of the mist, a snug-looking, unassuming little house made of logs. A neatly kept house. A house that looked cared for despite its great age, that even looked loved. Abby could love it, she thought, in some mix of wonder and consternation. She studied the wide front porch, trying to imagine Nick seated on the rough wooden bench by the door. If she put her hand on it, would she intuit his presence? Feel some vibration? But she avoided contact with it altogether when she followed Hank through the front door.

He disappeared through an archway on Abby's left. She closed the door and looked around, bemused. The room had low ceilings with beams that gave it a cozy feel. But it was the way it was furnished that captured Abby's attention, or rather it was the little touches that drew her, how the light coming through the lace curtain hanging in the front window showed off the delicacy of its pattern. She didn't mind that the edges were frayed. It only added to the charm. The wood floor was scarred and uneven, but there were rugs, floral-patterned in soft faded colors of rose and green and gold.

Abby crossed the room to one corner where someone had set a gorgeous seashell, a huge conch, on a tiny ornate table. She ran her fingertips lightly over the unfurled lip that was ruffled and tinged a shade of pink as delicate as the curl of sea foam at dawn. On the wall above it, a small, framed oil painting led her eye through an open garden gate and down a flower-bordered path. There were shelves on another wall filled with books and photographs, and in a windowed alcove that gave a view of the back of the property, a dining table for two in front of the window held a green glass vase filled with dried grasses.

She could have chosen these furnishings herself, Abby thought; she could move into this little home this very instant and be comfortable, delighted even, to live here. She thought of Hank's house in Houston, its drab, sterile environment created by Kim to keep Caitlin well. The comparison to this home, to this shabby but studied, soft elegance, was more than curious; it was disconcerting. Did Caitlin not come here? Abby went around the high, rolled arm of a sofa that was pulled at an angle near the iron-bellied stove. The dark, tufted leather was worn, but the sofa looked well made, heavy and durable. An afghan matching the faded colors of the area rug was tangled among the cushions as if someone might have recently lain beneath it and tossed it aside.

Abby couldn't take her eyes off it. If her nose wasn't full of the smell of dust, if the wood stove behind her wasn't cold, she would think someone was here, that they had only straightened up and gone out for a walk.

Hank reappeared.

"You said Sondra was into interior design. Did she do the decorating here?" Abby asked. "It's so different from your home in Houston."

Hank said she did. He said, "Some of the things were her grandmother's." He crossed the room and picked up the conch. "We found this in Spain, Marbella. Sondra had to have it. Cost a fortune. It's perfect, did you notice? Not a break anywhere. We found the painting there, too. She was on a bender that trip."

"A bender?" Abby remembered Hank had used the word before when he'd mentioned Sondra and the dancing.

Hank put the shell down. "Kitchen's through there." He gestured toward the archway. "Bedrooms and a bathroom are down the hall."

All at once, Abby realized how much she needed a bathroom. "Could I…?"

"Last door on the left," he said.

The bathroom was colder than the rest of the cabin but very clean. The porcelain fixtures, a vintage, claw-footed tub, pedestal sink and toilet, were stained from hard water, from age and use, rust-edged, like the floor tiles, but still, the surfaces had a just-scrubbed gleam.

Abby hung her jacket on an iron hook on the back of the door and used the toilet. A sense of foreboding stood up in one corner of her mind; she pushed it down, washed her hands, patted cold water onto her cheeks, her closed eyes.

She looked into the bedrooms on her way out. A pair of old iron, twin-size beds furnished the smaller of the two, and a handsomely carved, antique four-poster, a double, sat in the larger bedroom. A wedge of ash-colored light fell across the matelassé coverlet. Two flattish pillows cased in crochet-trimmed cotton lay at its head. She didn't want to imagine Nick in this room, that bed, and she left before she could.

Hank had started coffee when Abby joined him. "So, what's next?" he asked. "Do you want to search the place?"

She laughed nervously and tucked her fingertips into the back pockets of her jeans. "Everything is so clean."

He looked around. "Yeah, I guess no one's ever here enough to make a mess."

He went back into the kitchen. Abby studied the collection of photographs. They were mostly candid shots of Caitlin: on the bank of a lazy stream balancing an inner tube around her middle, sitting in a boat with an outboard motor, standing on a dock, dimpled arms encased in floaties, holding a fishing pole. Obviously she came here. Abby lifted a photo that had been taken outside on the porch. Hank was sitting on the bench. Caitlin was on her knees at his feet, holding up a Barbie doll, grinning into the camera. Other Barbie things were strewn around her, half concealed in nests of brightly patterned wrapping paper. It looked like a birthday party. Kim had said Caitlin hated Barbie. But it didn't look as if she did from the picture.

Abby returned it to the shelf, took down another, an

eight-by-ten, that showed Caitlin holding hands with a woman who was dressed in a flamingo-pink bikini top cut low to reveal her generous cleavage and a matching sarong tied to showcase her sleek torso and pierced navel. Abby carried the photo to the window, tipping it toward the light. The woman had to be Caitlin's mother. This was Sondra, slim and lithe and lovely. Abby could see now where Caitlin had gotten her angelic beauty. Sondra's features were as delicate, and her blond hair, like Caitlin's, cupped her finely molded jaw. A wisp of bangs fell provocatively across her dark eyes. Sondra was bent slightly at the waist, gazing adoringly down at Caitlin, who was smiling up at her. A fashion advertisement couldn't have been more intimately posed.

Or a centerfold out of *Playboy*.

She likes attention. Craves it, actually. What Hank had said about his wife trailed through Abby's mind. He had looked half-killed with shame and lustfulness when he'd said it; he had been agitated. Abby set her fingertip near the image of Sondra's face. She couldn't put this woman together with this cabin, couldn't make sense of any of it.

Abby put the photo back, knocking over a smaller photo in the process. She fumbled to rearrange things, feeling clumsy and furious. The awful foreboding, that terrible prescient monster in her mind, was growing, pushing an image at her of Nick and Sondra together. And it seemed so possible. On a certain level, Abby saw Sondra as Nick's sort of woman. All elegance and dazzle, but not flagrant, not in-your-face. And she was adventurous, clearly up for anything. Sondra would take risks; she would embrace them. Nick would go for that. He'd be intrigued by it.

But, no. Abby gave her head a small, firm shake. Nick having a fling with Sondra was no more possible than Nick having partnered with Adam Sandoval, no more possible than the ridiculous notion that the three were involved in some kind of outlandish corporate robbery scheme. That was the stuff of television crime shows or Hollywood thrillers. She crossed the room to the dining alcove and looked out the window. A shed stood in a clearing some fifty feet away, but the woods were reaching for it, would soon reclaim it and the land it sat on, if cutting wasn't done. It relieved Abby somehow to think of the upkeep on this place, what it must cost in terms of time and money. Didn't Nick complain that he never had enough of either? Wasn't it silly to think he would hide himself away here—but suddenly her attention was diverted by a flash of movement.

Abby focused on trees clustered nearest the shed. A person, she thought. But who would be out there? It was so damp and freezing.

Hank joined her, handing her a mug. "Couldn't remember if you took sugar or anything."

"Black's fine." Abby was glad just to cradle the warmth in her hands. "I thought I saw someone out there."

"Hunter, probably. It's the season."

She thought of the fawn again. She started to tell Hank the rescue story, but then she couldn't bear being so close to him. She felt a renewed sense of pity for him, that he was so homely and morose, so dull. *Insurance*, she thought. Why didn't he find a better occupation than selling insurance? He might keep Sondra's interest if he made more money. Or why didn't he join a gym and work out? If he got into shape, maybe Sondra wouldn't have to go off and dance naked for other men. Maybe she wouldn't have to go after someone else's husband. Abby went to the sofa, unsure of herself and the hot, panicked direction of her thoughts. She yanked on the afghan thinking she would fold it or jam it in her mouth before she screamed.

Something came with it. A pillow, she thought. But when she gave the blanket a sharp shake, what dropped to the floor was a jacket. Brown leather, the same as the couch. Bomber style. Abby stepped back, clutching the afghan to her chest as if she might be in danger of attack. Then thrusting the coverlet aside, she went to her knees, putting her fingers on the jacket, pulling it toward her, turning it over, examining it, finally standing with it in her hands to find Hank watching her.

She held it out to him. "It's Nick's. I gave it to him for Christmas last year."

Hank's eyes widened. "Are you kidding?"

Abby said she wasn't. "How did it get here?"

"What do you mean, how? On his goddamn back is how."

Abby ran a hand down one sleeve.

"I guess that about says it."

"It could be something else," Abby said, and when Hank laughed, she hated him for it, for making her feel she was naïve and a fool, for making her think Nick had betrayed her. "But it was at home. After the flood, I mean. I saw it there last summer, in June, or no, it was May, the end of May." *I put it on, wanting him, wanting his arms around me....*

"He must have gone back there for it."

"What are you saying? You think he's alive?"

"I got the impression that's what you've believed all

along. Why else would you contact me and suggest we come up here, if you didn't think there was a chance he was alive? You wanted proof, one way or the other, and now you have it."

Abby couldn't take it in, what Hank was saying.

"Look, you told me you didn't stay at home all the time after the flood last April. You stayed with your mom or with your friend at her ranch. Your husband could have snuck back. He could have gotten his jacket. Maybe he got other stuff. You ever check?"

"Not really," Abby said. She told him how she'd found a window open once, and, on a couple of other occasions, lights had been inexplicably turned on. "The last time I came home, the back door was ajar."

Hank kept nodding, kept repeating, "It was him."

Abby ignored Hank. "The jacket was in the closet in May," she said, trying to sort it out. "I found it and I found this." She dug into the inside pocket and pulled out Nick's checkbook, waving it at Hank. "I hunted for this the other day. I needed a check to pay the plumber, and when it wasn't there, in the closet, I thought I'd moved it myself." Abby held the jacket away from her by its shoulders, staring at it as if it might offer an explanation. "Now it's here and there's no way it's possible. No way," she repeated.

Hank snorted. "Get a grip, woman! Don't you see? Men do this shit all the time. They duck out on their old life, especially when it sucks the way your old man's did. They fake their death, whatever it takes."

"Nick's life did not suck!"

"Hah! You're the one who told me how down he was on himself, how he wasn't acting right. Didn't you say that? So he hooks up with Sondra at work, they get a thing going. Wouldn't be the first time for her. God-dammit!"

"You honestly believe your wife and Nick have been together here, that they're—"

"Fucking each other! You're holding the fucking proof!" Hank stalked into the kitchen and out again. He returned to the window and leaned stiff-armed against the frame.

Abby dropped the jacket onto the sofa, dropped her-self down beside it, dropped her face into her hands and tried to think. She had imagined it was the re-porter, Nadine Betts, who was her intruder, and that had seemed preposterous, but to suppose it was Nick? That he had come home at some point between May and now and taken his jacket and possibly other be-longings? How insane was it to believe that? Abby re-membered her mother saying that when your mind is without an explanation, it will invent one. Is that what was happening? Were she and Hank inventing a story to suit facts that weren't more than conjecture?

Abby uncovered her face. "You don't think they're here now, do you?"

"You see them anywhere? You see a car? Jesus Christ. They're long gone. If they helped Sandoval rob that settlement fund, you can bet all three of them are out of the country by now."

"What about Lindsey? Did they take her? Would they take her and leave Caitlin? You said Sondra was devoted to her. None of this makes any sense."

"It makes perfect goddamn sense."

Abby could see Hank had made up his mind.

"The cops were right about Sondra when they said she'd run off with some guy and made herself a new life. Your husband was the guy; he's done the same thing. That jerk Sandoval, too."

"You're jumping to conclusions," Abby said, but now she felt uncertain. "We should call the police." She looked around for her purse where she'd stowed her cell phone, and when she realized she'd left it in the car, she started for the door. "If it's even remotely possible, what you're saying—" *Was it?* "It means Lindsey is with them. She could be— Oh my God, Hank! She could be alive!"

Abby turned to him, feeling almost manic in her excitement, wanting to see his reaction. He met her gaze, but his expression was troubled, intense in a way that was unsettling. It was as if he didn't see her.

"Hank?" she prompted.

He didn't answer.

His breath was audible and the pulse she'd noticed earlier was jittering under the skin at the corner of his jaw again. She would think later she should have realized what was happening; she should have remembered what he told her about his temper. She might have remembered if he hadn't turned away and rested his forehead against the window, if he hadn't in that moment seemed so defeated.

Abby saw his shoulders heave. She heard a small sound of distress, but that might have come from her. She was still holding Nick's jacket and she lifted it to her face to stifle the noise.

Hank said something about Caitlin and the light she put on for Sondra in the window at home every night. "How can a mother do this to a kid who loves her like that?"

Abby thought he was addressing her, that he wanted

an answer, but when she looked, Hank's back was still turned, his forehead still pressed to the window. She wondered if he was crying, if she should go to him, if she could, but then suddenly he wheeled on her.

"What kind of—?" he began, but then his voice broke and before Abby could register his intention, he spun back to the window and drove his fist through the glass, shouting, "That fucking whore!"

The noise as the window shattered seemed to go on forever. As if in slow motion, Abby saw Hank pull his hand to his chest; she saw herself rise and cross the room to him. And then he was going down, folding, buckling, an injured animal run to ground, driven to its knees. She tried, but she couldn't help him. She staggered in her attempt to brace him with her body. But she was too light. He collapsed to his side, drawing himself into a knot, good hand cradling the injured hand. She knelt and spoke his name. His gaze locked with hers, and she saw the anguish in his eyes and something else. Something manic and furious, a rage so profound that it shook her worse than the sight of his blood.

"Hold on," she told him. She straightened, and using what mental strength she could muster, she went into the kitchen and found dish towels folded in a drawer. As she dampened the top one, she saw that it was hand-appliquéd with the patchwork figure of an old-fashioned girl in a bonnet hanging out the wash. Under her tiny feet, a lilting row of embroidery spelled: *Laundry on Monday*. It had probably belonged to Sondra's grandmother, Abby thought. And then she thought: what a shame it will be ruined now, as if the loss of a vintage dish towel could matter.

She found tweezers in the bathroom, and back in the dining alcove, she knelt beside Hank again and grasped his elbow. "Can you sit up?"

He obeyed docilely, like a child. She set the damp towel to one side and draped a dry towel, *Visit on Friday,* over her forearm, waiter-style. He balanced his palm on it. Delicately, she picked out the slivers of glass she could see. Then, with the damp towel, she began dabbing at the wounds, applying gentle pressure. A jagged gash running roughly perpendicular to his knuckles was especially deep and continued to bleed each time she drew the cloth away. "I think you need stitches."

He didn't answer.

She began wrapping his hand in a fresh towel, leaving his fingers free, tucking the loose end near his wrist. Then, keeping his hand in both of hers, she squatted in front of him. His eyes were unfocused. His face was gray and beaded with sweat. What if he was going into shock? She felt pulled toward that edge herself, and she fought it. "Hank?" she said.

No response.

"We have to get you to a doctor. Can you stand up?" She slid her hand under his forearm.

He jerked his elbow as if her touch offended him. "I'm all right," he said, and rising unsteadily to his feet, he went into the kitchen, leaving her to watch in disbelief as he unwrapped the bandage she'd made, turned on the tap, thrust his injured hand under the water and groaned.

Hank wouldn't let Abby drive. He'd rewrapped his injured hand himself in a clean towel, *Mending on*

Wednesday, and he used his left hand to steer. They were headed down the winding road. Toward Bandera, Abby guessed, although they hadn't discussed where they were going. She pulled her cell phone out of her purse.

"I doubt you can get a signal this far out," Hank said.

Abby punched in the Bandera County sheriff's office number and hit send, but as Hank predicted, there was no reception.

"The local cops won't find them anyway, if that's who you're calling, not if they've left the country."

Abby looked at Hank. He was pale and haggard, but he seemed calmer now; he seemed all right or as all right as he could ever be. She thought she could talk to him; she had to talk to him. "I want to let Sheriff Henderson know we found the jacket. I want him to know what you suspect. It could mean Lindsey's alive, Hank." She repeated what she had tried to tell him earlier, before he put his fist through the window.

He thought about it. "I guess, yeah. She'd have to be."

"It would mean they're fugitives, is that what you're saying?" It sounded preposterous—it was preposterous. Still, Abby's mind skipped past reason, seizing on the possibility. Thoughts crowded her brain: that she would immediately begin her search for Lindsey and never give up. If it took the rest of her life, she would find her daughter. But even as hope shimmered, a cooler sensibility prevailed, that she had no real idea what finding the jacket meant. Abby stowed her phone.

She had tossed the jacket into the backseat, and she felt its presence there, world-shattering, incendiary. Evidence at the very least of Nick's infidelity and betrayal. But was it also evidence of embezzlement and abduction? Could he and Sondra have helped Adam steal the missing settlement money? Could Nick have taken their daughter, basically kidnapped her, and involved her in some horrible scheme? The questions careened around the walls of Abby's brain. All of it and none of it seemed plausible.

Suppose Nick had taken Lindsey, where were they? Living it up with Sondra and Adam on some tropical island? Lindsey would never go along with that. Was Nick holding her prisoner?

Could he have involved himself in such a bizarre scheme, one that was so heartless and cruel? If something had happened to her daughter because of Nick, Abby thought, she would—

What? Kill him?

She stared out the window at a narrow ribbon of silver light on the southern horizon that was all that remained of the day. Her stomach growled, and she remembered she hadn't eaten anything substantial since last night, other than the cheese and crackers she'd shared with Hank. But it was peculiar, wasn't it? Vaguely sickening, how the body could go on no matter what, demanding food, sleep, a hot bath. Comfort. It was like a machine—

"Abby? Abby!"

She turned blankly toward Hank, who regarded her with some impatience "That's your cell phone, isn't it?"

The tinny chords of *Ode to Joy* came from her purse on the floorboard. Abby could see the Caller ID. *Jake.* Her heart fell, and she shrank against the car door, not wanting to answer, to have to confess where she was and the terrible possibility that had surfaced as a result.

Why hadn't she walked out on Hank while they were still in Houston, when she'd had the chance? Why had she started this to begin with?

Hank repeated her name. Abby retrieved her phone.

"Jake?" she said. "I'm in the Hill Country, but I'm on my way home now. Can you meet me there? We need to talk."

"No, Mom! You aren't going to believe this!"

"What? What's wrong?"

Abby darted a glance at Hank and found him staring at her.

"They think they found the car, Mom! Some old man found your Cherokee."

For one dizzying moment, the world stopped. Abby felt it recede. Even the air was gone. Her hand rose to her chest. "Where?" she managed to ask. "What old man?"

"A creek somewhere south of the Guadalupe. The guy was fishing."

"Lindsey?" Abby pressed the back of her hand over her mouth, afraid of herself, that she would lose it.

"No one's gotten close enough yet to see inside. The car's jammed up in some rocks. The old guy wouldn't have noticed except—"

"How did you find out?"

"Sheriff Henderson called me. He said you weren't answering your phone."

"I was—"

"I know. Gramma told me."

Hank pulled over onto the highway shoulder.

"They found my car," she told him.

His eyes widened; he said something Abby didn't catch. Jake talked in her other ear. She couldn't pay attention. Even sitting still was an effort. She wanted to open the car door and run. Anywhere. Just go. And the sense of her urgency mystified her. For seven months she had wanted nothing more than the truth; she had asked for it, begged to know it, but now, rather than confront it, she wanted nothing more than to run away from it. She thought of Nick's jacket. If she threw it away, she would still have to tell Jake about finding it. If she lit it on fire, reduced it to cinders, he would have to know it had been located and where and what it might mean. How could she tell that to Jake? How would she frame in words what seemed unspeakable?

"Mom, listen, I'll be at Aunt Kate's in about an hour. Go there, okay? I talked to her. She knows what's going on."

"But I want to go where the Jeep is."

"It's dark. You'd never find it. Just go to Aunt Kate's and wait for me."

Abby agreed reluctantly and Jake started to break their connection, but she stopped him. "We'll be all right, honey. Okay? No matter what happens, what we find out, we'll fine, do you understand?"

"Sure, Mom. You have to believe it, too." He sounded bright and calm, and Abby knew he wanted to reassure her, to help her hold herself together, hold them together.

He wanted to preserve the very world she would have to dismantle, or so it seemed to her then, and dread coiled like a wire around her heart.

CHAPTER
21

Kate ran down the front porch steps as Hank pulled to a stop in the driveway.

Abby got out of the car. "Tell me everything Dennis said."

Kate pulled her into a tight embrace. "It's not much."

"Other than the car is light in color." George came up behind Kate.

"The same as my Jeep," Abby said, stepping back. She nearly collided with Hank, whom she'd forgotten. He caught her elbow with his good hand, mumbling something that sounded to Abby like, "Take it easy." There was a silence while Kate and George looked him over, while they registered the hand wrapped in its kitchen towel, then looked questioningly at Abby. The moment was awkward, but she managed the introductions.

"Mama called you," Abby said to Kate.

Hank shifted his weight. George cleared his throat.

Kate said, "You should have told me. I would have gone with you."

"He's not Charles Manson," Abby said. Kate eyed Hank's wrapped hand before ushering them inside, into the kitchen, where she had coffee and brandy waiting.

Abby sat at the table, not trusting her legs.

Hank held up his cell phone. "I should call Kim," he said and stepped outside, pulling the door closed.

Abby wondered how much he would tell his sister, if he would say they'd found Nick's jacket, if he would tell Kim he'd put his fist through the window. She found her own cell phone. "I should call Louise," she said.

Kate offered the brandy. "You should probably have a shot of this first."

Abby shook her head. She couldn't swallow.

Consuelo answered and explained that Louise was ill, that she had the flu. Abby could hear Louise in the background, asking who it was, then insisting Consuelo give her the phone. Louise did sound terrible, and Abby explained the situation as briefly as possible.

"I'm coming there," Louise said, and Abby could hear the struggle it was for her to find enough breath to make the words.

"No, you shouldn't be out of bed," she said. "Just rest, do what your doctor says. I'll call as soon as I know anything."

For once Louise didn't argue.

"She must be really sick," Abby told Kate, stowing her phone.

Hank came through the back door, rubbing his ear as if it ached.

"Is everything all right?" Abby asked.

"Caitlin's upset that I won't be home tonight."

"Who's Caitlin?" Kate asked.

"My daughter," Hank said. He pulled out a chair and sat down.

"What's going on here, guys?" Kate put a mug in front of Hank.

He stopped her when she'd only half filled it with coffee and reached for the brandy decanter. "Could be one of two things," he said topping up his cup. "Assuming that car is Abby's, they'll either find nobody in it or they'll find her husband and my wife."

"What?" Kate's head jerked comically.

"Her husband and my wife were fucking each other, that's what."

Abby set her jaws together and stared into her lap.

"Abby?" Kate sat down by George.

"We found Nick's jacket, the leather one I gave him last Christmas, at the cabin."

"How did it get there?" Kate was incredulous. She exchanged a quick glance with George, a glance that struck Abby as furtive and full of alarm.

Her stomach lurched. She said, "I don't know."

"Bullshit." Hank drank noisily from his mug, then refilled it with brandy. "Don't mind her. She's just having a little trouble facing reality."

Kate found Abby's gaze. "Is he trying to say Nick is alive?"

"I'm not *trying* to say anything. The fact is unless they find the bastard in the car, I'd bet every last nickel I have that he and my wife, and quite possibly that bastard Adam Sandoval, used the flood to fake their own deaths."

"Are you kidding?" Kate was in disbelief. "What about Lindsey? Did she fake her death, too?"

"Oh, for Christ's sake." George sounded as if he'd had enough. He went to the counter, retrieved a mug and poured himself a shot of brandy that he drank in one swallow.

He looked upset, Abby thought. He looked rattled, and George almost never showed emotion. Fear swelled against Abby's ribs. It rang in her ears. She had the sensation that she was going to find out now, the terrible truth that everyone else had known all these months.

George was lecturing Hank about talking out of his head and giving Abby false hope. He was saying what utter crap Hank's theory was. George leaned against the counter and said, "I'm not even going to address the ridiculous business about folks faking their own deaths. The bottom line is a man doesn't take his daughter along when he's involved in some escapade with another woman. Nick wouldn't be that stupid."

Abby was comforted by George's defense and she might have pursued it, but just then she heard a car door slam.

"That's Jake." She shot up from her chair so fast it teetered. "Don't say another word about this in front of him, not until we have the truth. I mean it."

Footsteps came across the porch. Kate opened the door. Jake appeared, followed by Dennis, and Abby's heart loosened; she hadn't expected him, hadn't expected the sight of him to bring her such relief.

Jake hugged Kate, then George. Then he walked into Abby's embrace. "There's nothing we can do until morning," he told her.

"The car's wedged up in some boulders next to a

stream on the old Anderson place," Dennis said. "The water from the Guadalupe must have carried it up there. The river runs pretty close to the highway along that stretch, and that area did see some of the worst flooding." He took off his hat and rested his eyes on Abby. He was still in uniform, still on duty.

"That's in Kerr County, right?" George said. "I heard Lon Anderson sold out not long ago."

"His daughter made him," Dennis said. "I guess he set the place on fire, nothing too serious, but she told him that was it. He had to sell and move in with her family or go into a retirement home. He chose his daughter's place."

Abby was swept with impatience at the folksy details. "What does any of this have to do with my car?"

"Lon's old place is close enough to his daughter Marcy's place that he and that old mule of his have been sneaking back there to fish. All this time Marcy thought he was camping on the Guadalupe."

Kate said, "Last I talked to her, she was telling me he's a worse trial to her than her kids."

Jake straddled a chair. "You said he saw lights. That's how he knew."

"Yeah, but his daughter thinks he imagined it." Dennis shifted his hat brim in an uneasy circle.

"What do you mean he saw lights? Like car headlights?" George asked before Abby could, and she thought she heard Dennis sigh. She thought when he answered he seemed reluctant, even chagrined. He wouldn't meet her gaze.

"That's what he said when I interviewed him, that he wouldn't have seen the car at all if the headlights hadn't been blinking. He said it went on all night and spooked him so bad, he left the next day."

"How would it have kept battery power all this time?" Jake asked.

George said, "Were they on when you got there?"

"No, but I talked to the old man myself, and he seems convinced. It was real to him. But like I said, Marcy's just as sure it was a figment of his imagination."

No, Abby thought. It was no figment. Lon Anderson's vision of blinking lights was an answer to her prayer.

"So what's the plan?" Hank slurred, drawing everyone's attention. He poured another shot of brandy.

Abby thought someone ought to move the bottle away from him. She gestured in his direction. "This is Hank Kilmer."

"He brought Abby here," George added.

Dennis set his hat on the counter.

Jake asked Kate if he could make a sandwich.

Kate said, "Where is my brain? Of course you're hungry. Is ham okay? Anybody else?" She looked at Dennis.

"Thanks, but I should get going. I'm meeting the Kerr County guys in the morning at first light." He found Abby's gaze. "You'll be all right here?"

"Yes." Abby smiled as if she understood his meaning, but she was completely at sea. Why wasn't he doing his job? Asking about Hank, his injured hand, what she was doing with him, why he'd been the one to bring her here?

But Dennis only nodded once and retrieved his hat, and as gentle as the gestures were, they seemed ominous to her. He went to the door, then paused and turned back to her. He gave her his promise that he would call. "The moment we find anything," he said.

"My wife is what you'll find. Or nothing…"

Hank was belligerent in the way drunks can be, and Abby realized he'd had enough to drink that he might say anything. She looked at Jake, completely engrossed in eating his sandwich, chewing methodically, as if he were alone. He didn't want to know what Hank was talking about any more than Abby wanted to explain it.

George walked Dennis outside. Kate closed the back door after them and hesitated there, brows raised, expectant. Of what, Abby couldn't have said.

Jake scooped up his dishes and brought them to the sink.

"We need to talk," Abby said to him.

"I'm tired, Mom. Can it wait until tomorrow?"

Kate checked her watch. "It is tomorrow. After one already. We should all try and get some sleep."

Abby rubbed her arms.

Kate told Hank he was welcome to sleep on the sofa in the den, but he said he was fine where he was.

Jake disappeared, and Abby heard the door to the hall bathroom close.

He was gone a while, and when she went to see if he was all right, she found him stretched out on the sofa in the study, elbow over his eyes. She paused a few feet inside the room. Light from the hallway marked the sweep of his brow, limned the curve of his cheek. She controlled an urge to go and sit beside him, smooth her hand over his hair. If he were younger, she would hold him. "I could get you a pillow," she offered.

"I'm fine," he said.

"You should take off your shoes."

"They're not touching anything."

Abby didn't pursue it; she didn't want to argue. She had thought she and Jake would talk. But about what? Hadn't she warned the others against exposing him to all the speculation, the outlandish theories? What else was there? She looked over at George's desk, the papers scattered across it, the fax machine. She'd sent the message that had brought Hank Kilmer into Kate's kitchen, into their lives, from there. But it was ridiculous to blame him. The car was found, and tomorrow Dennis would discover what was inside it. The truth, the answer to the mystery. Or not. Abby didn't know and until she did, she wasn't going to worry Jake with her questions and her fears.

"Is he asleep?" Kate came to stand beside Abby, arms filled with bedding.

"He was up all last night cramming for a test."

"I brought him a pillow and a blanket." Kate carried them past Abby, and she heard sounds of their whispering; she heard Jake's shoes hit the floor one at a time, the creak of the sofa as he settled the pillow under his head. Kate shook out the blanket and dropped it over him, and Abby was envious, a little hurt, that Jake would allow Kate to tend to him. She said good-night, then drew Abby into the hall, walking her toward the kitchen. "We need a hot toddy."

"Where's Hank?"

"On the sofa in the great room. I'm pretty sure he's passed out. He had a lot to drink. Abby, what happened? How did he hurt his hand?"

Abby sat down at the kitchen table. Kate eyed her intently. "He's kind of a weird guy."

"Did George go to bed?" Abby asked.

"Yes." Kate wheeled, impatient. "Is hot cocoa with Kahlua okay? I'll heat some milk."

There was the sound of the refrigerator door opening, the wink of its light, snuffed when the door snapped shut. Kate found a saucepan; she ignited the burner, and Abby studied the ring of flame, somehow soothed by the sight of it and by the pervasive quiet and semidarkness, everything in shadows, soft-edged, dreamy.

"He freaked out," she said in a low voice.

"Freaked out? What do you mean?"

Abby described going into the cabin, finding Nick's jacket. She said, "If you could have seen Hank, the look on his face…it was as if he wasn't there, wasn't present, and then the next thing I knew, he'd punched his fist through the window."

There was a pause between them, and then Abby continued.

"I don't understand any of this, how the jacket got to the cabin, the odd things that have happened at the house, the phone calls—" she looked up sharply "—and please don't tell me again that I'm imagining things because I know what I know, what I heard. Those calls happened."

"Maybe tomorrow you'll get some answers." Kate stirred the milk.

"Nothing I want." Abby realized now that her hope that Lindsey was alive had begun to loosen. Something warned her. Her instinct knew it wasn't possible.

"No," Kate agreed. "Probably not."

A long note of silence between them filled with the brush of the spoon circling the pan.

Abby hugged herself. "One thing I know for sure, my marriage was in a lot more trouble than I thought."

"Based on what?" Kate turned from the stove. "What that weirdo Hank says? He's crazy, Abby. He's got issues. I mean, really—people faking their deaths? Do you really think Nick would do something like that? When he had Lindsey with him? There's no way. She'd never go along with it in any case."

Abby was surprised. "You're defending him?"

"I might not be Nick's biggest fan, but I know he loved his children. He wouldn't hurt them. You don't think he would, do you?"

"I wouldn't have. Maybe I wouldn't now if it weren't for Lindsey's call. I'm talking about the one she made from the gas station in Boerne. She sounded scared, even hysterical."

"I thought you weren't sure."

Abby rubbed her eyes. "I'm not. I go back and forth. I drive myself nuts. It's like this special corner of hell I live in."

Kate attended to the milk.

"She memorized Nick's closing argument."

Kate switched off the burner and looked askance at Abby.

"The one he made at the end of the Helix Belle trial. Hank told me Sondra knew it by heart. Jake and I were in court that day; Nick was fantastic. His argument might well have won the whole thing, but I couldn't quote a word of it to you now."

"Abby, honestly, so what? You were there for him. You supported him. You were a good wife."

She didn't answer. It wore on her to remember how little she had made of Nick's performance, his victory.

Looking back, all she could see was his vulnerability in the wake of the accusations that had been made against him, and how much he had needed her, and she had turned her back. She'd left him alone. Left him for someone else to find and comfort.

"Come on, Abby. Sondra sounds like she's as big a lunatic as Hank. She was a stripper, for God's sake. Would Nick go for someone like that? Besides, he adored you."

Abby thought of the photographs of Sondra, beautiful and elegant. "Well, she looks a whole lot better than me in a bikini."

"Oh, Abby." Kate's whisper was full of regret.

The scope of the mystery, and her own failure to question any of the troubling signs that had led up to it, was too much to bear. Abby lowered her forehead to her crossed arms. She would never forgive herself if she learned Nick had involved their daughter, if he had taken Lindsey into this mess. But what was the mess? What would Dennis find in that car tomorrow?

Abby felt Kate drop into the chair beside her and scoot close. She felt Kate's arm come around her and Kate's cheek against her hair, and they sat together for a while, hip to hip in the dim silence. Because there weren't words but only presence, only Abby's fear and her grief and Kate's love to receive them.

It was late in the afternoon, and Abby was alone in the great room staring from the window when the phone rang. She heard George pick up in the kitchen. Jake and Hank were in there, too, Abby thought, having a sandwich. Kate was unloading the dishwasher, but that clatter stopped abruptly. Abby rested her forehead against the window. She felt empty of everything, even the sense of waiting. But as moments passed, she became impatient. What were they doing? Abby straightened. *Whispering.* She could hear them, and she started across the room.

George appeared in the doorway. "It's Dennis," he said and held the cordless phone out to Abby, his big, work-roughened hand shaking, his face crumpled with sadness and concern.

She wanted to say something to reassure him, but the most she could manage was to take the phone. "Dennis?" she said.

"Abby, I'm so sorry."

"It's my car, you're sure?"

"It's a Cherokee, same make and model. The license plates are a match." He paused, then continued. "Abby, from the clothing and so forth, it appears there was one adult male and one young female inside."

A sound came, a low moan. Abby flattened her hand over her mouth. Her eyes found Jake's, who along with Hank and Kate had joined George. Kate brought her arm around Jake's waist. Abby saw his shoulders heave and closed her eyes. Dennis was talking about the remains.

She interrupted him. "I want to see them."

"You really don't," he said gently. "You shouldn't."

"There's nothing to see, is there?"

"No. I'm sorry. It's a long time now since the flood."

She returned to the window, bending her head to it. As recently as last week, yesterday, in the minutes before Dennis's call, she'd had hope, slim as it was. Now she had nothing. Just the endless agony of questions and the more agonizing reality that she would never see Lindsey again. Her beloved daughter, her darling girl, was gone. Abby's heart shuddered. She clenched her teeth fighting the cry that rose. If she gave in to it now, if she allowed the enormity of her loss to overtake her, it would break her in half.

"The adult in the car is definitely male," Dennis said, "and there is definitely only the one."

Abby heard Dennis repeat himself; she registered the note of disbelief in his voice, but she didn't hold on to it.

"If you need anything," he went on when Abby didn't respond, "you or Jake...."

"Thank you," she managed to say. "We'll be fine. At least it's over. At least now we know where they are and we can bring them home." Abby glanced at Hank.

Dennis explained what the procedure would be from here, and Abby picked out certain words like *coroner* and *morgue*. She got the impression there were legal obligations to be fulfilled. He made certain Abby had both his cell phone and office numbers in case she had questions and elicited a promise from her that she would keep in touch. He said, "I'll let you know when the lab results are ready."

She thanked him and ended the call quickly, set down the phone and cleared her throat. Composing herself, steeling herself. But Jake looked so beaten, so defeated and sad, it almost undid her. She went to him and held him, murmured things she would never remember, and then Kate came, and George, and the four of them huddled together, but Hank stood apart. Abby felt badly for him. "They didn't find Sondra," she told him. "She and Nick weren't together, after all. We were mistaken."

Hank didn't say anything; no one did.

A frisson of unease snaked up her spine. "Oh, my God! Jake, I'm so sorry." She took his hand. "I should have told you. I was going to, but you were so tired last night and I… When I was at the cabin yesterday, I found your dad's jacket and I thought maybe he was—"

"I know."

"What? How?" Abby looked at Kate. "You told him? That's what all the whispering was in the kitchen, wasn't it?"

Kate started to answer, but Jake talked over her. "I already knew, Mom. I heard you and Aunt Kate talking last night."

Abby said she was sorry again, that she hadn't meant for him to find out that way. "I thought your dad and Sondra were—I was wrong, though." She laughed and put her fingertips to her mouth. Her relief didn't feel right. She didn't feel right. Her knees were weak. She wanted to sit down, but Jake was watching her with such—was it pity? Fear? Remorse? Something felt so off, so peculiar.

He said, "But if it's Dad's jacket—"

"It is."

"Then how did it get there?"

"He knew Sondra," Abby said. "She was working for Judge Payne when your dad filed the suit against Helix Belle, so I imagine they knew each other pretty well. He must have loaned it to her. It's possible, isn't it? Then I was thinking about when he came out here to Bandera last winter. Sondra might have come with him or met him there. I know Kate says she didn't see her, but suppose when he mentioned the bit about property, he was referring to Sondra's cabin? She told Hank she wanted to sell it, and maybe she hired your dad to look into doing that. She thought so much of him." Abby stopped. She gave her head a slight shake. She wanted this to make sense, to come together, and it wouldn't.

She glanced at Hank. He looked sick. Beyond hang-over sick, she thought. He had wanted closure and didn't find it. His sister Kim wanted Sondra's dead body, and she hadn't gotten what she wanted either. Abby was sorry for them. But they had nothing to do with her. Sondra had nothing to do with her.

"Mom? I think we probably have to face the facts." Jake said this tentatively, but then he stepped toward her as if he meant to force the issue.

She twisted away. "I'll call Nina. She'll know about Sondra. Nina can look in Nick's files, find his notes. Under the circumstances, I don't think confidentiality will apply, but if it does, Dennis can get a court order, don't you think? Isn't that how it's done?" She waved her hand. *Abracadabra*...

No one answered; no one looked at her. Abby's stomach knotted.

Hank said he should leave.

Kate offered an invitation to dinner; he turned it down. Abby followed him out of the house, matching his quick, impatient stride. She wanted to let him go, to leave it alone, but she couldn't. Not until he spoke to her, not until he looked her in her face and admitted he had been wrong about Nick and Sondra. Shouldn't he do that much after all his accusations and drama? He'd put his hand through a window, for God's sake, over nothing.

"Hank?" she called after him. "I'm very sorry you don't know where your wife is, but I can't help but be relieved that she wasn't with my husband and daughter."

He stopped and looked at her, and she saw his pity for her and his contempt. "Sondra was fucking your husband, Abby. I know it in my gut, just like I know they were together when the car crashed. I don't know why her body wasn't found with his today. Maybe she was thrown out; maybe some animal got her, but she was damn sure there when they wrecked, I know she was. I know she's as dead as he is."

"But why do you want to believe that? You should be thrilled. You could still find her."

"Not alive. Ask them." He jerked his thumb in the direction of the house. "Ask your son. He knows the truth. They all know. The sheriff, too. The only reason they won't tell you is because they don't think you can take it." Hank went around to the driver's side of his car and started to get in, then he squinted at her through the metallic glare off the car's roof. "Take your little theory about the jacket, that crap about how your husband loaned it to Sondra. Sometime last winter, you said, a jacket he didn't have until Christmas Day, I might add, and then what? You're the one who swears you saw it in a closet at home in May. Do you see where I'm going with this?"

"No," Abby said, but she did see, and she clenched her teeth against it. "Nick would not have involved Lindsey—"

Hank stabbed his skull with his index finger. "Think about it. If Sondra wore the jacket to the cabin last winter, how did it get back into your closet where you saw it last summer?"

He waited, but Abby didn't answer; she wouldn't.

She hated him, the disgust so evident in his eyes, the curl of his lip.

"That coat didn't get into the cabin on Sondra's back, Abby. It went in on your husband's back. He didn't come out here in April to go camping with your daughter. He came out here to meet my wife and maybe even Sandoval. Hell, they could have all been in that car together. We'll probably never know."

Abby shook her head vehemently.

"Fine, don't believe me. But you might want to go back inside and ask your son about the woman he saw with his dad in February."

"What woman?"

"The same one your husband was seen with again last April at the gas station in Boerne."

"There was no woman. Someone—the sheriff would have told me," Abby said. "You're crazy."

"Oh, yes, there was. And just like every other fucking guy in the world, the kid behind the counter couldn't keep his eyes off her. It was Sondra. He described her to a fucking T. He got a good long look. He told the sheriff he saw her get into your Jeep, Abby, and he never saw her get out."

"You're a liar, Hank! I feel sorry for you." But doubt riddled her words; the bitter taste of it coated the margins of her throat.

He started to get into his car now, and Abby felt a rush of relief. Then he paused as if there was more he wanted to say, but she shook her head, warding him off. Ducking into his car, he drove away.

Dust from his tires drifted in his wake as lightly as feathers. Abby took several steps toward the house, walking blind. It would come together if she looked at it; if she paused for one moment to consider. If she were to turn around now, she would see the facts, the cruel reality lingering in that drift of dust. And now, abruptly, as if it were there, a physical entity that clubbed her from behind, she bent at the waist, braced her hands on her knees. Her breath came in shallow spurts; her heart swelled painfully against her ribs. She thought it might burst. She prayed that it would and kill her. She was a fool, that was the "something more" Hank had wanted to say to her.

She thought of the looks she'd been getting from Jake and from Kate and George; she thought of their odd silences and the ways she had been manipulated, even patronized. They had treated her as if she were incompetent and weak. She straightened, eyeing the house. Her brain felt on fire. She was hardly aware of climbing the stairs, flinging open the kitchen door hard enough that it bounced off the wall. The three of them, Kate, George and Jake, broke apart from where they'd been gathered at the window as if they could somehow make it appear they hadn't been watching her every move. "You knew," she said.

No one answered. Seconds passed. They might have been frozen.

Finally, Jake said in a low voice, "I didn't want to tell you, Mom. I didn't want you to be hurt anymore."

"You saw them in February? Where?" Abby's throat was so tightened by grief, by her fury and disbelief, that she scarcely knew how the words could pass.

"At his office." The words tumbled out of Jake. "You know how much Dad liked it when I went there. It always put him in a good mood."

"You needed money."

"Yeah, and I figured if I asked him for it there, he wouldn't yell at me like he did at home."

"So?"

"So I'm in the parking garage going to the elevator and I see them in Dad's Beamer and they're like—" Jake reddened "—all over each other."

"Did they see you?"

"I didn't think so, but then Dad came after me and caught me on the road. He tried to play it off that it was all her. He said she was, like, obsessed with him. He said he was only trying to reason with her. It was shit. He was lying." Jake's voice broke.

"You lied to me! I asked you and you lied. How could you?"

"I knew it would kill you, Mom, but you can't let it. Okay? You can't let him win."

She didn't answer.

"I told you to go home, to leave it alone." He was accusing her now. "Why didn't you?"

"Because I have to know the truth." Abby looked at Kate. "You saw them together, too, and you told George, but not me." She laughed. "It's true what they say about wives being the last to know."

Jake's eyes shone with tears. "I thought you had it figured out, Mom, I really did when I heard you found his jacket."

"Obviously, I'm an idiot. I didn't want to believe it, to think he could do that to me, to us." Abby bit her lips. She was sorry for Jake. Sorry for them both, but she was too angry to comfort him. "You should have told me, Jake. And you—" Abby raised her finger at Kate "—you knew last winter. How could you? But then why should I wonder? You've done it to me before."

"That's enough, Abby." George said it gently, but clearly he meant it. He went to his wife's side.

Jake took Abby's arm. He wanted her to stop, but he didn't understand. He didn't know the history she and Kate shared. She shook free of him and confronted Kate. George put out his hand. Abby ignored it. "Has it occurred to you that if you'd had the courtesy to tell me you saw Nick with that woman last December, I could have done something about it?"

"I didn't—"

"That was such a sweet story you told me, that he was looking at land for us. It wouldn't surprise me in the least if you knew the whole time what he was up to, that he was helping Sondra sell that cabin. I'm sure it's worth a fortune, more than enough to finance their getaway." Abby's laugh was harsh. "Too bad for them Mother Nature had other plans."

"Oh, Abby, don't you think you're way out on a limb—"

"No! The gas station attendant saw them together. Hank said he identified her."

"That's an overstatement, Abby," George said. He added something about Lindsey, the bit about how Nick wouldn't have taken her. He said, "Don't you remember? The kid described Lindsey to Dennis, too, but he couldn't say that he saw her with Nick."

Abby heard George. She registered the rationality of his argument, but she was too seized by the fruit of her bitter imaginings to grasp that he was offering her another alternative, a different outcome, worse or better, from the one she was bent on believing, which was that Kate had betrayed her, and she, Abby, had allowed it to happen—again. "You did this," she told Kate. "If you had only picked up the phone and called me, if you had told me you saw Nick with another woman, I would never have let Lindsey go with him. My daughter would be home now and safe—"

"Oh, don't say it!" Kate reached her hands toward Abby. "Don't say I'm to blame. Nick was alone when I saw him. I swear it!"

A stunned silence grew cold and stiff, as if all that had ever connected them had died.

Abby turned to Jake. "Who else knows?"

He shook his head. "No one."

George said, "Abby, none of us is guilty of anything except trying to protect you. Maybe Jake wasn't right. Maybe telling the truth would have been better, but we acted out of love for you and genuine concern."

"But what is the truth, George? What do you know? Because I would be willing to bet that you still are not telling me everything."

He sighed.

Kate went to the sink. She filled a glass with water, sipped it and set it down, and without looking at Abby, she said, "This is what I know, all I know: Nick was alone when I ran into him last winter. He told me he was there about property. If he had a woman with him, I didn't see her. The only other thing I know is that when Dennis went to interview the gas station attendant, the kid thought he remembered Nick from a picture Dennis showed him. He remembered Lindsey getting the restroom key, and he also said Nick was with a woman and they seemed close. The kid thought the woman was—he thought she was the man's wife or girlfriend."

"So Hank was right." Abby felt exultant.

George said, "The kid was seventeen. He was stressed. There were tons of people there that day all milling around because of the weather. I mean, it was all so iffy. It just didn't seem right to talk about a bunch of maybes. Maybe it was Nick, maybe it was Sondra, maybe they were together."

"Well, there's no maybe about what Jake saw, or what Nick told him, is there? There's no maybe about Lindsey's phone call to me from the gas station or that she was deeply upset about something that was happening. Something to do with her daddy."

A pause hung like old dust.

"None of us had all the pieces until today," Kate said. "Even now, how can we be sure?"

"I'm so sorry, Mom." Jake raked his hands over his head.

"This is why you've been avoiding me like the plague. How long were you going to keep it up, Jake?"

"I wanted to tell you. I just couldn't figure out how. Then when Dennis called about finding the car, I asked him if there was, you know, a woman inside."

It took a moment, but once Abby realized that Dennis had known the truth, too, the sense of her humiliation mushroomed. She felt light-headed. Dennis knew things about her. About Nick and her marriage. She'd spoken of her family as if it were sacred. She'd let Dennis see inside her. See her love for Nick, see into her most vulnerable, soft, tender places. And the whole time he must have been stacking up her words, her pretty fairy-tale speeches, her tears and her grief, against his knowledge of her husband's betrayal. Dennis had assumed her frailty along with the rest of them, and he didn't even know her.

Abby's mouth felt full of chalk. She could use a glass of water herself, but she wasn't asking these people for anything. "I look like an ass," she said. "It's a mystery how you've kept from laughing."

"Nick's the fool," Kate said. "But honestly, Abby, would you have believed me or Dennis if we'd told you what the boy at the gas station said?"

"Whether I would believe you or not, whether I could handle it, that wasn't for you to decide."

"You've been through so much," Kate said. "I couldn't see adding to it. Even if Nick was up to something, he's still gone along with whatever his reasons were for his behavior."

"She's right, Mom."

Abby switched her glance to Jake. She was angry enough to kill. But whom? "I want to go home," she said.

"Now?" Jake said.

"Yes," she said. "Now."

On the way home from the ranch Abby told Jake to stop at the sheriff's office in Bandera.

"Dennis won't be there," Jake said. "It's too late. He's gone home by now."

"I'll take a chance," she said. "You can wait in the car."

"I won't ask what you're planning."

"No," Abby said. "Don't."

Dennis was on his way out of the building, and when he saw her, his face opened with such pleasure that Abby felt herself nearly come unhinged from her purpose.

"Is there somewhere we can talk?" she asked.

He motioned her into a nearby office and closed the door. A desk and three filing cabinets nearly filled the tiny space. The only decoration was a row of black-framed certificates that hung in a crooked line on one wall.

Dennis offered Abby a seat.

"I'll stand, Sheriff, thank you," she said, and his eyes widened as if her formality surprised him.

"What's wrong?"

"Why didn't you tell me what you learned from the attendant at the gas station?"

Dennis frowned.

"My husband was traveling with a woman last April. The gas station attendant told you that, but you didn't tell me. Why?"

"You were under a lot of strain. Kate was worried about how much more you could stand, and, in any case, it was hearsay."

"I've heard all that, but you're the police. You're supposed to report the facts, and you didn't. You asked me a lot of questions, you came into my home, you got plenty of information out of me. You knew where I stood, how I felt about everything, and you let me go on thinking—believing—" *That my life was real, that my marriage was solid.* She wanted to say it, but if she did, she would lose her composure. She walked toward him, intending to move around him. He caught her arm. "Don't," she said, and he let her go, stepping aside.

"You didn't deserve this," he said.

"Which part?" she asked. "Being lied to or being kept in ignorance?"

Dennis didn't answer.

She had nearly reached the exit when he said her name, and she stopped.

"You're right," he said. "You were entitled to the facts. I just couldn't find a way to say them. I don't think Jake could either," he added.

She waited a moment and then walked on. She didn't look back.

Jake and Abby didn't speak until they reached the Houston city limits and then she gave Jake directions to Hank's house where she'd left Nick's car. Nick's car that was hers now. She was his widow. Everything was hers. If he'd lived, she would be his ex-wife instead of his widow. To think that less than a year ago, she had thought their troubles centered on their finances, the length of Nick's commute, all the upkeep on their property. She'd thought a move into town would fix their lives right up. It was laughable, heart-wrenching. He'd made such a fool of her. But if only she'd known, if she'd been told the truth about Nick and what he was doing, she would have kept Lindsey home with her that weekend. She would still have her daughter. Abby bit her teeth together to keep from crying out.

Jake pulled into Hank's driveway behind the BMW, and Abby got out. "Hold on a second, Mom." He fished around in the backseat and handed her Nick's jacket through the open window. "Hank gave it to me this morning."

Abby folded it over her arm.

"Will you be all right? Can you drive?" he asked.

She nodded and glanced toward Hank's house that was dark except for a solitary lamp burning in one window. Her heart constricted. Caitlin's beacon. She

was still waiting for her mother. Dennis had promised they would search the area where Abby's Jeep
had been found for Sondra's remains. He would do it
because Abby had told him about Caitlin, her need for
her mom to come home. He hadn't commented when
she'd mentioned Hank's theory that Adam Sandoval
might have been in the car, too, that he might also
have died in the accident. That was a police matter;
let them figure it out.

Abby bent her gaze to Jake's. "Thanks for bringing me. Maybe you'll come home for the weekend?"

"I'll try." He looked away and as quickly looked
back. "I kept waiting to hear from him that he'd told
you. He said he was going to. He promised me he
would."

"Is that why you didn't go with them to the Hill
Country? It wasn't because you had to study, was it?
You were angry at your dad."

"I didn't want to be around him."

"Was Sondra invited?"

"No! I don't know. That's what I can't figure out.
If that was really her at the gas station, why was she
with him? Dad wouldn't have brought her along, not
with Lindsey. Uncle George is right. He wouldn't have
done that, no way. He told me it was over, Mom. He
swore it was."

Abby shook her head. She was cold and too tired to
think. She wanted to lie down.

"I wonder what happened to her. Seems like if she
was in the car, she couldn't have lived, could she?"

"I doubt it."

Jake chewed his lip and contemplated the view
through the windshield. Abby got out her car keys.

Down the street, someone whistled. For their dog, she guessed.

"Dad didn't take the settlement money, Mom. He wasn't in on that; he wasn't Adam's partner. You know that, right? I mean, he was a bastard, but he wouldn't steal from those kids."

Abby thought about it. "I don't want to believe it, Jake." But she didn't know. She wasn't sure anymore who Nick had been, who they had been as a couple. She wondered if she even knew who she was, if she would ever trust herself again, and that was possibly the worst feeling in the world.

"Was Dad acting different? Were you guys, like, fighting?" Jake asked.

How did it happen? That's what he wanted to know. How had his world, the one he believed in, with two parents who loved each other, come apart this way, seemingly without warning? "I think he was more troubled than we realized, in ways we didn't understand," Abby said. "He was unhappy, maybe. He didn't talk to me, or I didn't listen. I don't know." She smoothed the folds of Nick's coat over her arm, absently, feeling sad and awkward, feeling tiny licks of anger heat her temples. Ask your father, she wanted to say. Ask that woman. *Sondra.* Abby didn't want to think about it… the possibility that she had survived, while Abby's own daughter had not. She did not want to live in a world where such a horrible injustice could be a reality.

"After the flood," Jake said, "when I realized you didn't know about her, I figured, why should you have to? Dad was dead. It was over."

Abby didn't respond.

"It is, Mom. It is over, right?"

Abby said, "I hope so," but she wondered, if that was true, why did everything feel so unsettled?

She was turning into her driveway when her cell phone rang, and, thinking it was Jake or her mama checking to see if she'd made it home safely, Abby stopped to answer.

"Hey, I'm here," she said, but instead of the warm affectionate response she'd anticipated, what greeted her was silence. Her heart froze. *It's not Lindsey*, warned a voice in her head. *It can't be.*

"Hello? Who's there?" she demanded.

The silence was cut through by faint static, then a drift of words, something soft and singsong that sounded like, "Are you happy now?…Are you happy now?…Are you happy now?…."

"Who is this?" Abby demanded, but she realized the connection was severed, that she was talking to empty air. She brought the phone down, checked where the call was from, but the record gave her nothing. Out of Area, it read. She peered into the path of headlights. It wasn't Lindsey. Of course it wasn't. Common sense told her it wasn't. Even if it had been Lindsey, she wouldn't have asked such a question.

Abby's impulse was to call Jake or her mother, but she didn't act on it. She knew what they would tell her, that it was a prank, and in the end she would be sorry she had involved them.

The house was dark, and it filled her with foreboding to go inside, but she did. She even slept for a few hours on the sofa in the den. She didn't bring Nick's jacket inside until the next morning and it was when she was hanging it back up in the hall closet that she saw Lindsey's pink-and-green striped hair ribbon, the one she'd tied at the end of her braid last April, lying on the closet floor.

CHAPTER
22

Abby ran the length of taffeta through her fingers. It was the same ribbon, wasn't it? It was wrinkled as if it had been tied, then come loose and slipped off. Lindsey often lost her ribbons that way. But how had it come to be here, in the closet of all places? Abby parted the collection of jackets and sweaters; she fished through the assortment of shoes and boots on the floor. She didn't know what she was searching for. She'd already done this once when she hunted for the checkbook that was in Nick's jacket. If the ribbon had been here, she would have found it then, wouldn't she?

The phone rang, the landline, and her head came up. Her heart hammered in her ears as she raced to the kitchen to answer it. But it was Joe, according to the Caller ID.

Still, she said hello, as if she had no idea who it was, and studied the ribbon in her hand.

They exchanged pleasantries, and then Joe said, "Abby, listen, there's been a development, something I thought you should know, although I'm sure it'll be all over the news shortly, if it isn't already."

Abby straightened. He was going to tell her Nick had done it; he'd stolen the money from those injured children. The sense of this snaked through her mind, vicious and cold. She closed her eyes.

"Adam Sandoval's been found."

"Dead?" Abby said and caught her lip because she wished it. She wanted it to be true. She couldn't have said why.

"No, alive. He's in jail, in Amsterdam. They didn't like the look of his passport there when he went through customs, so they detained him. Then when they searched him, they found he was carrying nearly a quarter million in undeclared cash."

"The money from the settlement."

"Minus a few thousand, but, yeah, it's mostly there. And it's good, too, because eventually, it'll come back into the fund to support those children. Nick's winning that case, all his hard work, it won't have been in vain after all, Abby."

She pulled out the desk chair and sat, pressing her knuckles to her mouth.

"Abby? Did you hear me?"

She swallowed. "Yes, thank you, Joe. Thank you for letting me know."

"No problem," he said.

"Joe? Was Adam alone when he was arrested?"

"A woman was with him, his wife, I think."

Or Sondra, Abby thought. Was it possible?

"Listen, we should get together soon. We'll need to

address the probate of Nick's will and his equity share in the partnership. You'll probably still want to consider working, but I think together with his life-insurance benefits, you're going to be in a good position financially." Joe paused.

He sounded so satisfied. Abby sensed he was waiting for her to voice her satisfaction, too, even her gratitude. It was as if what Nick had left was better than the man himself, as if he was worth more dead than alive. Abby toyed with the ribbon. Was it the one she had tied onto Lindsey's braid? She held it up. She guessed it could as easily not be the one. She was going to have to watch herself, the tricks her mind might play.

"Well, I guess that's it," Joe said. "You'll call if there's anything I can do for you?"

Abby said she would; she thanked him again and hung up. She thought he probably knew about her trip with Hank into the Hill Country, why they'd gone, what they'd discovered, even though she hadn't mentioned the circumstances. Abby imagined Nina would have found out about all of it somehow. Maybe, Abby thought, she should ask Nina how Nick's jacket had managed to make its way to Sondra's cabin. Maybe Nina had the answer.

But what difference did it make? Whether Abby ever knew or didn't? It wouldn't bring Lindsey or Nick back; it wouldn't make the house payment, either. Resolutely, Abby stowed Lindsey's ribbon in a desk drawer. She would have to find a job, and soon, but she couldn't call on Hap again. Chances were he'd forgive her, but only after she explained, and she was sick of that. She felt as if the entire world knew her business.

That night, lying on the sofa in the den, Abby

thought of her new life, the one that she lived now without her daughter, without so much as the comfort and grace of her memories, because all of those were a total lie. Abby flipped onto her back. Suddenly, she couldn't breathe for the heat that came. She felt suffocated by it. She felt as if she had swallowed fire.

Everyone had said the worst was over, that time would soften her grief, but she didn't feel grief. She felt hate. It pushed against the walls of her brain, huge and destructive. Flinging the cover to the floor, she got up, found the keys to Nick's BMW and headed out to the freeway. The speedometer edged eighty, then eighty-five. Now ninety. The light-haunted scenery blurred, and then all at once she let go of the steering wheel and let go of sense, too, and it was terrifying and exhilarating. She was shaking when she took control of the car again and steered it cautiously onto the road's shoulder. She fought for breath and reason. Who was she trying to punish? *Them,* she thought. Nick and Sondra. But they were beyond her reach. At least Nick was. And if Sondra wasn't?

Abby stared into the gritty path of headlights, unable to imagine what she would do if Sondra were to somehow be found alive. She wanted to go back in time. Inside her head she felt at war. She felt herself waiting for something else awful to happen.

Finally, when she felt calm enough to drive properly, she started the car, and it was when she reentered the freeway that she noticed the dark-colored sedan parked on the feeder some distance behind her. But it didn't register; she didn't take the memory with her, and a few days would pass before she would think about it again.

* * *

Jake came home that weekend ostensibly to do his laundry, but Abby thought he had come to check on her, and it both pleased and annoyed her. He was heaving a tangled mass of jeans mixed with bath towels into the dryer when Abby walked in with the groceries.

"How many times have I told you not to overload the machine?" she asked, kicking the door shut.

He took the sack from her, bringing it into the kitchen. "That machine can take it," he said. "Trust me." He popped a couple of grapes into his mouth.

She held the rest of the bunch under running water.

"I've been thinking, Mom." Jake leaned against the counter.

"Uh-oh." Abby sounded lighthearted, but inside she was dismayed. She knew what he was going to say, that he was dropping out of college. She braced herself for it.

"Ha, ha," Jake said, "but, seriously, I've been thinking how Dad said you could wait too long to figure out what really matters, you know?…and I think he was talking about finding out what you want to do in your life, not what someone else wants you to do. Like, he wanted me to be a lawyer, but that's not what I want. I can't live his dream anymore."

Abby finished rinsing the grapes and started scrubbing the sweet potatoes she'd bought to go with the pork roast they were having for dinner. She knew she couldn't stop him, not on her own, not without Nick's support, and it infuriated her to think that Jake's degree would be lost, too, one more casualty of the calamity that seemed never-ending. She needed to stay calm, but inside she felt like screaming.

Jake said, "I want to transfer to Sam Houston State. I want to study law enforcement."

Abby glanced sidelong at him. "In Huntsville?" The university was just up the road, maybe a thirty-minute drive. She'd see more of him.

"Yeah," Jake said. "Dennis told me the criminology program there is one of the best."

"Dennis?" Abby turned off the water, picked up the kitchen towel and dried her hands, unsettled at how the mention of his name brought a flush of warmth to her face, but she wouldn't call it pleasure. She couldn't. "You talked to him about it?"

"Yeah. He's a good guy, Mom."

Abby didn't answer. She couldn't give that to Jake, her validation.

"Look, he's really sorry—"

"I'm sure he is," Abby said, adding, "It's fine, Jake." And because she didn't want to talk further about Dennis, she brought up the coroner's office. "They called the other day," she said gently. "They want to know what arrangements we've made for the remains."

"I'm so angry," Abby said to her mother a couple of weeks later.

They were in her mother's kitchen, having just finished planting a few dozen ranunculus tubers. The ruffled, brightly colored flowers with petals as thin as crepe paper were one of her mother's favorites, and Abby brought fresh tubers every year in November and helped her mother plant them.

"I'm just mad enough to kill, and it scares me. I've never felt such anger in my life." Abby finished washing her hands and turned off the water.

It had been misting earlier, and outside the window, fat pearls of moisture dripped from the eaves. A robin fluttered to perch on the fence post that held the mailbox and sat preening in the somber light. Ordinarily Abby would have called her mother to come and look, but not today. She scarcely registered the robin's presence.

"Who are you angry at?" her mother asked.

"Nick, and at Sondra, but mostly myself. I knew something was wrong; I knew Nick was unhappy, but I ignored it. I thought it would pass."

"You're too hard on yourself," her mother said. "When you're running around after two children, you're so busy doing, there isn't a lot of time or energy left to pause and reflect. You trusted him. You've always been trusting. It's your nature."

"Not so much now." Abby came to the table and sat down. "Hank Kilmer called the other day."

"Do you think it's wise, keeping a relationship with him?"

"At least he never lied to me."

Abby's mother looked startled. "But you must realize Jake never meant to lie. Neither did Katie. She feels awful for what's happened. Just dreadful."

Abby averted her glance.

"She is so sorry, honey. We are all so sorry."

"Do you know how sick I am of hearing that?" Abby pursed her mouth. She felt her grief swell hard against her ribs. It rose into her throat, bitter-tasting and as black as ink, and she was frightened by it. The tears came in spite of her, brimming over her lashes, scalding her cheeks with their pent-up fury. She bent her face into her hands, shoulders heaving from the force of her sobbing.

Her mother brought her a warm, damp dishcloth and rubbed her back again.

"I don't want to hate Nick, Mama." Abby forced the words through labored hiccups.

"It isn't in you to hate."

"You don't think they were wrong? Kate and George and Jake? They knew things, each one of them knew different things about Nick and kept them secret, when if they'd told me, I might have stopped him. At the least I would have kept Lindsey home with me."

Abby's mother sat down. "Maybe they were wrong and maybe they weren't, but it's in the past now and you can't change it. What matters is they acted out of love for you. They wanted to protect you. They still do."

Abby rose and returned to the window. The robin was in the grass now, pecking among the flattened yellow blades.

"What will you gain by blaming them?"

Abby didn't answer.

Her mother tried again. "You're still here, Abigail. Kate and Jake—"

"Don't say it again, Mama. How I have to go on for Jake's sake. Don't say I have to live for him or Kate or you so you can be okay."

"No, that isn't—"

"Your granddaughter is dead!" Abby wheeled, voice rising, shattering. "He took her. Took my daughter from me, Mama, to be with that woman! Maybe you can get over it, maybe you can forgive him, but I can't!"

"You think I don't feel Lindsey's loss? That it isn't the gravest pain to bear? Seeing you, what you and

Jake are going through? You think I don't grieve, as you do, for the loss of our precious girl?" Her mother's voice broke.

Abby knelt at her side. "I'm sorry, Mama. I'm sorry."

It took several moments, but Abby's mother gathered herself, and once the air between them settled, she said, "Can't you see? If you dwell on the injustice, you become the victim of his mistake, his cruelty."

Abby straightened. "But he was cruel."

"Yes, and I deplore his actions, but hating him only hurts you."

"But isn't it so convenient? Nick dying? If you ask me, he got off easy."

"He might argue that point," her mother said dryly.

The sudden smile that twitched on Abby's lips felt unnatural. Hideous. She touched her mouth.

"Forgiveness is hard," her mother said. "Harder than anger, but forgiveness is what heals. Forgiveness and love."

Abby reached out with her hands. "He's taken my memories, Mama. Even those I can't trust."

Her mother rose and came to Abby and pulled her into an embrace. "Give it time, sweet," she murmured.

CHAPTER
23

A dark blue sedan was parked behind the house in Abby's spot when she came home from visiting her mother's, as if it belonged there. Abby braked for a moment, considering, and then pulled in behind it. Nadine wasn't leaving until they had it out. If Abby had to call the police on the reporter, she thought, she would do it. She pulled her keys from the ignition, got out of the BMW, and walked around the blue sedan. It was an Impala, not a Taurus, and it was empty. Abby started for the house and then looked back, suddenly remembering her wild drive the other night. She'd seen the blue car then, too, parked behind her on the feeder. It was ridiculous. The woman was following her, obviously. But why?

"Nadine?" she called, rounding the front of the house. There was no answer, no sign of the reporter.

Abby took her cell phone from her purse as she

retraced her steps, but then she was unsure whether to dial Charlie's number or 911. She'd never changed the locks as he'd advised. And she should have, she thought, when the back door opened without the assistance of her key. Somehow she wasn't surprised, although she distinctly remembered locking it when she'd left. She pushed the door a bit wider even as she told herself it might not be the smartest thing to go inside on her own. But she *was* on her own now, right? She had to learn to take care of things by herself, and certainly she could handle Nadine Betts. Abby gripped her phone tightly in one hand and her keys in the other.

"Nadine?" she called and she didn't bother keeping the annoyance from her voice.

"No," a woman answered.

Two steps took Abby into the arched doorway that divided the den from the kitchen, and she knew that instant whom she would find instead of the reporter. Abby knew just as surely as if Sondra had announced herself.

"You." The word out of Abby's mouth was an accusation, an indictment.

"Yes," Sondra answered. She was sitting on one end of the sofa, all blond elegance in her oversize white linen shirt and slender jeans. A smooth turquoise medallion framed in ornate silver hung from a chain around her neck, a vivid splash of color against the warm honey shade of her skin. There were bracelets on her wrists, rings on her fingers. Her feet were as narrow and slim as the rest of her and cased in pale blue flats that tapered into points at her toes. She looked relaxed, sitting there with her legs crossed at the knee, one flat dangling. She looked as if she belonged on

Abby's sofa. She had even pushed the bed linen Abby slept under to the opposite end.

"How did you get in?" Abby demanded.

Sondra held up a key.

"Where did you get that?"

"Nick gave it to me."

"I doubt it," Abby said, because she didn't want to imagine that he would do something so unconscionable, so heartless. "You need to leave. Now."

"I will when you give me Nick's jacket."

Abby stared, nonplussed.

"You took it." Sondra sat forward. "Out of my cabin the day you came there with Hank. I want it back."

"I saw you!" In her mind's eye, Abby recalled the view from the cabin's back window, the fringe of woods, the figure she'd seen slipping among the trees.

"I nearly froze my ass off waiting for you to leave."

"Well, that's not my problem. Please, go."

"Nick gave the jacket to me," Sondra said matter-of-factly. "It's mine now."

"You're out of your mind."

Sondra grinned smugly and reached for her purse, a huge soft-sided tote, the same shade of blue leather as her flats, and pulled it onto her lap.

Watching her fish through the contents, Abby wondered in a distracted corner of her mind what she was hunting for.

"You met Kim, right?" Sondra glanced up at Abby. "Hank's idiot of a sister? She'd love to see me committed, or better yet, dead. But never mind that. I've been in here before, did you know?"

There was a spark of glee in Sondra's voice now, as if she were pleased to announce this, to share the good news. But something else was swimming in her expression, too. Something darker and frayed.

Unbalanced. The word appeared in Abby's mind. Her heart paused. She held up her cell phone. "Leave. Now. Or I'm calling the police."

"Oh, I know how angry you must be."

"You don't know a damn thing about me."

"Really. Well, I know what happened to Nick and your daughter. I was there."

Abby's breath left her; she felt as if she'd been blindsided. "Tell me," she said, and her need to know, that had haunted her for months, was as searingly hot as it had been when it had been fresh. Nothing else mattered; nothing else was in her mind. Shaking, she dropped her cell phone onto a side table and gripped her arms above her elbows.

"It wasn't my fault." Sondra was maddeningly cool.

"What wasn't? Screwing my husband? Involving my daughter in your dirty affair? Driving her off a cliff? Which?"

"I don't particularly care for your—"

"Oh, my God! It was you, wasn't it?" Abby was struck by a fresh realization. "Those times on the phone, when I thought it was Lindsey, it was you pretending to be her." Abby didn't know how she knew; she just did, that the phone calls she had believed in and treasured for the hope they brought her had been a prank just as Jake had suggested. There had never been a chance of finding Lindsey alive, never a moment when Abby might have saved her. "How could you be so cruel?"

If Sondra heard Abby or cared, she didn't respond. She was intent on her search through the contents of her purse, muttering to herself. Then, suddenly, her hands stilled, and she looked up and smiled unnervingly.

Abby's heart stalled; a tendril of fear hooked her spine. "You should go now," she said.

But Sondra remained where she was, blandly smiling, as if the upturned corners of her mouth were secured by a series of tiny hidden stitches. "I wanted Nick to tell you about us," she said. "I hated always having to sneak around. That's partly why I came today. I want Nick's jacket, but I also thought you, of all people, deserved to know the truth. I mean, we both loved him, right?—and he's dead now."

She lifted one hand in a vague gesture, kept the other hidden inside the purse. Abby looked there as if she might see through its leather walls. Something was going on, something worse than seemed apparent.

"Of course, you had him longer than me. I didn't even know who he was until the Helix Belle case came to trial."

Abby remembered Hank telling her how obsessed Sondra had been with the case.

"When I saw him the first time in action in the courtroom, I was amazed. Mesmerized. He had such a—a—" She looked away, and, bringing her fingertips to her mouth, she apologized. She said she could scarcely speak of him without losing her composure.

A fresh wave of panic broke in Abby's mind. Her ears were ringing and she wondered if she was in some kind of shock. Otherwise, wouldn't she do something? Pick up her phone and call 911? But she had a sense that Sondra could go off at the slightest provocation. She looked relaxed enough, sitting there on the sofa. She might have been a neighbor who had dropped in for a short visit, but there was a kind of tension in her posture, a certain hyper alert quality about her that struck Abby as unnatural. And there was her hand tucked into her purse.

Abby was awfully afraid of what might be hidden there; she didn't want to think about it, the possibility that Sondra had brought a gun into the house. It couldn't be. People—ordinary people—didn't do that.

Sondra said, "I was there for him every day of that trial, every day court was in session, but you—you," she repeated with sharp disgust, "only managed to come for the closing arguments. Nick said you had no interest in his career, that you mainly saw him as a paycheck."

"He wouldn't have said that." Abby defended herself without thinking.

"Did you even know the man?" Sondra set her purse aside, and Abby's worry over it eased a bit. She eyed her cell phone.

"I tried to save him when those bastards accused him of stealing the settlement money. I did everything I could. I went to everyone I knew—the mayor, the district attorney. I called the governor. Nick didn't want me intervening on his behalf, but somebody had to." She scooted to the edge of the sofa, bracing her elbows on her knees. "Judge Payne fired me over it."

Hank had said Sondra quit her job. Had he lied or was Sondra lying now? Abby looked at her. She fiddled with her bracelets.

"People never want to face the truth," she said. "Have you noticed? Even the judge said he was letting me go because I was unreliable. The asshole suggested I get help, but the truth is that he disapproved of my relationship with Nick, our—" Sondra touched her upper lip delicately with the tip of her tongue as if, unlike Abby, she couldn't bring herself to say it, the word "affair."

How did I not know, Abby wondered. How could I have been so blind? She remembered her impatience with Nick and his mood swings, and her decision to leave it alone. *This, too, shall pass.* But maybe on a deeper level she had known there was something more beyond the trouble with Helix Belle. Now that she thought about it, Nick had been cleared of suspicion within a matter of days. Less than two weeks had passed when Helix withdrew its allegations, yet his moodiness had dragged on through the holidays, into spring. He'd not been himself on the day he left for the Hill Country.

Sondra said getting fired was probably the best thing that could have happened to her. It had forced her to leave Hank, she said, to open her design business. It sickened Abby to listen to her go on about her intention to divorce Hank and marry Nick. Sondra mentioned the sale of the cabin, that Nick had promised to help her arrange it. "There would have been enough money then that we could have gone anywhere and started over. I wanted that desperately," Sondra said. "I tried to explain it to Nick, that he couldn't—" She broke off.

"Couldn't what?"

Sondra twisted her bracelets. "The thing is, he kept stalling and I ran out of cash. What else could I do but go back to dancing at the club? Nick was furious; he stopped taking my calls, but what did he expect?" She looked up at Abby and her eyes swam with tears, heartbroken shadows and a softer light of blank confusion, bemusement…some horribly wrong, discordant note that seemed out of place. She sat back and drew her purse onto her lap again.

Abby's pulse tapped in her ears, light and paper-thin.

"If only he had listened to me last December, he would be alive now. I want you to know that. I want you to know that I gave him every chance then, just the same as I'm giving you every chance now."

"What do you mean?" Abby asked carefully.

"The last time we met, before the flood, was in Bandera. It was near Christmas. Nick didn't want to come, but I said if he didn't, I would call you and tell you everything about us."

"You were there, with him, at the courthouse in Bandera?" Abby was thinking of Kate's December sighting of Nick.

"There was a problem with the title on my property. I needed Nick's help to fix it, but then he ran into some friend of yours, or so he said, and it freaked him out. I don't know because I was in the restroom, so he could have been lying."

No, Abby thought. He hadn't been lying, but neither had Kate, and Abby felt a tiny ripple of relief.

"He just wanted to get out of town after that," Sondra said. "He swore he would take care of everything from home, that he'd be in touch after Christmas, but he wasn't. It pissed me off. I went to his office one day and waited by his car. He had to talk to me then, but he was so cold. He said we were a mistake."

Had Nick broken it off? Abby wondered. Had there even been a relationship between him and Sondra, or was she making it up? But she had Nick's door key, his jacket had been at her cabin. She was here now as if she had some kind of claim on Nick, however bizarre that seemed. What did it add up to, if not infidelity?

"I didn't speak to him again until the gas station in Boerne. Oh, you should have seen the look on his face." Sondra clapped her hands together the way a child might if she were thrilled with herself.

"I thought you were in the car with him," Abby said, but Sondra seemed not to hear her.

"Fucking weather screwed up everything—" She stopped, and her gaze drifted as if she were studying something in her mind.

Glancing at her cell phone, Abby considered whether she could grab it and run out of the house. She didn't know, couldn't decide. What did Sondra intend? Suppose she *did* have a gun?

"I only wanted to tell him he was going the wrong way, but he wouldn't listen." Sondra's voice rose. "He kept shouting, 'Leave me alone, leave me alone,' over and over. He made Lindsey cry. He scared her."

At the gas station, Abby thought, the Shell station Lindsey had called from, when Abby heard her daughter crying. She bit the inside of her cheek.

Sondra said she had taken Nick's cell phone from the Jeep. "He left it in plain sight, left the car unlocked. The phone would have been stolen. I took the map, too, and some other stuff, change from the cup holder, a ribbon, I think it was Lindsey's. I don't—I'm not sure why I took the other things—" Sondra frowned.

Abby's mind gave her pictures, unwanted pictures, of Sondra handling Lindsey's hair ribbon, something Abby herself had cherished, of Sondra inside Nick's jacket, where Abby had sought refuge. A sound broke from her chest, and she put her hand there. Her eyes clashed with Sondra's.

"I took the map because I wanted to show him the right way to go, but he pushed me. He called me a crazy bitch. There was no need for that." Sondra's voice caught. She pressed her lips together.

"What did you do?" Abby spoke over the heavy frightened thudding of her pulse, even as her sense that Sondra had done something to hurt her family grew in her mind.

"When he left the gas station, I followed him. I only wanted to talk, you know? I drove beside his car and motioned for him to let down the window, but he sped up, so I had to speed up, too. I only wanted to talk." Sondra rubbed her upper arms briskly. She repeated it, "I only wanted to talk," once, twice, three more times, a slurry of words. "I tried to keep up, but he kept going faster. It was raining so hard, and I was screaming at him to slow down, but he didn't and the curve came and he started to slide and then he—the car just—went through the guardrail down into all that water—"

"You ran them off the road!?"

"No, it was him, all him. He wouldn't stop."

"Get out!" Abby seized her cell phone and tried to tap out 911, but she couldn't see the numbers, her fury was so all-consuming, so blinding. She thought if Sondra did not go, she would kill her; she would choke Sondra by the neck until she was dead.

"Stop!"

Sondra's shout pierced the hide of Abby's rage. She looked up. The gun Sondra pointed at Abby was small, snub-nosed, ugly. Abby felt her breath go. She felt her knees weaken.

"Put down the phone."

Abby dropped it.

"Mom?"

"Jake? Get out of the house!" Abby heard his laundry basket hit the mudroom floor and then his car keys hit the kitchen counter. She bit back a cry. She had forgotten he was coming home this weekend.

He appeared in the doorway. Abby looked at him over her shoulder, watched as his eyes widened, taking in the scene. But otherwise he gave no sign of alarm, and Abby marveled at that. He was wearing Nick's jacket, and she thought that was good. Maybe if he gave it to Sondra, she'd go.

"What is she doing here?" he asked.

Sondra gestured with the gun. "Get over there next to your mother."

Jake said, "Okay, but why don't you put the gun down?" He came slowly to Abby's side, and his presence steadied her even as she felt terrified for what might happen to him.

"No," Sondra said. "I came here today because I thought your mom—you and your mom deserved to know the truth about what happened to your dad and your sister, and it was hard for me having to relive it. But I thought, it's not about me, you know? Now your mom is blaming me. She was trying to call the police like I'm some kind of murderer—"

"She ran them off the road," Abby said.

"Shut up!" Sondra said.

Abby clenched her jaw.

"You weren't in the car with them?" Jake asked Sondra, as if their conversation were normal.

"I followed them from here." She reflected Jake's

ease, and Abby realized it was a ploy, that Jake's calm demeanor was deliberate. She wondered at his presence of mind, his courage.

Sondra went on. "I had called Nina, you see. That's how I knew Nick was going camping that weekend. I planned to surprise him at the campsite, but then he got off the interstate in San Antonio and checked into a motel."

"Because of the rain," Jake said.

"It was terrible," Sondra said. "Coming down in sheets; it was like driving blind. The next morning, when it was still raining, I thought he would turn around and come home, but he went the wrong way—"

"He must have missed a turn somehow and he ended up in Boerne at the Shell station," Abby said, putting it together. "She must have followed them from the motel."

"I didn't—" Sondra's voice stumbled. "He wouldn't stop, if he'd only stopped." The words came hard. Tears brimmed in her eyes. She pressed the back of her free hand to her mouth. She looked lost, frightened, as frightened as Abby felt.

"I only wanted him to love me again," Sondra whispered.

Jake said, "Why don't you give me that gun?"

She gestured wildly with it. "I didn't have to come here. I didn't have to put myself through this."

"No," Jake said.

"She wants the jacket," Abby said, hoping to distract her.

"You want this?" Jake opened out the jacket's front edges.

Sondra nodded. "I thought it would be nice of your

mom to let me have it. I loved your dad, too, you know? He hurt me. Very badly. But I still love him."

Jake eased his arms from the jacket's sleeves.

"When he left me, I wanted to die. I wish I had been in the car with him. I wish I had gone over the cliff, too. I don't know why I didn't." She looked at Abby. "Don't you wish you were dead? How can you stand it? Living without him?"

Abby didn't answer. She couldn't.

"That's why I bought this gun, because I can't stand it. You must feel the same, right? I can help you, help us both. I can help him, too." She pointed the gun at Jake, and what sounded like a squeal rose in Abby's throat.

"There are six bullets in here," Sondra said. "Enough for all of us."

Jake held out the jacket as if he meant to hand it over, but at the last second, when Sondra stepped toward him to take it, he swung it at her, making her stagger.

The gunshot that followed exploded into the room, deafening Abby, even as it seemed to suck the very air from her lungs.

Jake rushed past her, and in a blur Abby saw him hurl himself at Sondra. She lost her grip on the gun; Abby saw it fly; she heard it skitter across the floor.

Jake dove for it a split second ahead of Sondra.

Abby grabbed her cell phone and managed to pick out 911 and give their location.

Jake and Sondra rolled over the back of the sofa in a tangle of limbs.

When the gun went off a second time, Abby couldn't hear her own scream, but she felt the force of it burn her throat. Flinging her phone aside, she went to Jake, dropping to her knees where he lay underneath Sondra, unmoving, pale. Abby shoved her. "Get away!"

Sondra scrambled to her feet.

"Jake?" Abby put her hands on his face; she touched his shoulders looking for blood, an injury. His eyelids fluttered. He took in a huge shuddering breath.

"Are you hurt?" Abby asked when his eyes opened fully.

He looked dazed, but shook his head. "Got the wind knocked out of me is all."

Abby saw the gun then. It lay partially concealed under Jake's leg, and she grabbed it, turning on her knees, leveling it at Sondra. It was heavier than she had imagined, and it felt cold in her hand, like something foreign, evil. Abby felt distanced from it and from herself. She felt as if she inhabited a different world now than the one she had wakened to this morning, but she would not allow this woman to take any more from her than she had already taken. Abby stood up. "The police are on their way," she said.

"I don't care what happens to me." She ordered her hair, straightened her shirt. She didn't look threatening or off balance now. She didn't look anything more than exhausted and unhappy. But somehow that felt even more disconcerting to Abby, like the hush after one storm has passed, but you know there is another one coming. The air felt electric.

"My life was over when Nick died." Sondra went to the sofa and retrieved her purse.

"Sit down," Abby said.

But Sondra didn't. She got out her car keys and looked hard at Abby. "You didn't love him. I see that now and I hate you for it. Why couldn't you let him go?

Why should you have all this?" She jerked her arm in an arc, indicating the house. "You have his son, too. And what do I have?" Bending abruptly, she scooped Nick's jacket off the floor and brandished it at Abby. "This! This is what I'm left with."

"You have a daughter," Abby said.

Sondra looked blank as if she didn't comprehend Abby's meaning, and then she turned and swiftly left the room.

"I'll stop her." Jake took the gun from Abby and went after Sondra. Abby followed him.

"Let her go, Jake," she called. "The police will get her. Let them handle it."

But Jake didn't respond; he didn't do as Abby said, and when she heard the back door slam behind him, her heart dropped. Where were the police?

Sondra was backing down the driveway when Abby got outside, and Jake was watching her go. Abby joined him. "She won't get far."

"What is wrong with her?" Jake ran a shaky hand over his head. "I thought for a second we were goners."

"Why don't you put that thing down?" Abby indicated the gun.

He said, "The safety's on. It can't hurt anybody now."

"I think the reason we're standing here is because of your cool head." Abby's voice slipped.

Jake put his arm around her shoulders.

They heard the approach of sirens.

"Thank God." Abby felt limp with relief.

Sondra was halfway down the driveway when the first patrol car pulled in behind her, blocking her exit. The two officers were outside the vehicle in moments.

One had his hand on the butt of his holstered gun and was cautiously approaching the driver's side of Sondra's car.

The other was just as cautiously coming up the drive toward Jake and Abby as if he questioned which of the three of them was the danger. Abby would never know why, but some intuition made her turn to Jake and say, "Let's go in the house," and she had started that way when, all at once, she registered the hard rhythmic revving of a car engine and the sudden squeal of tires on the asphalt. She heard the police officers' warning shouts, and now Jake was shouting.

"Holy Jesus Christ, Mom! Run!" He pushed her, herding her in front of him across the drive.

Abby wasted a precious moment looking in the direction of Sondra's car as it hurtled toward them, but Jake's fist against her back was insistent. They had nearly reached the porch when the car rounded the corner of the house, coming straight for them. Abby, with Jake on her heels, flung herself toward the porch; they half fell up the back stairs.

She waited for the collision and instead felt the wind when Sondra's car veered at the last second and tore past them; she smelled the exhaust, the burning rubber. Lying on the porch, breath gusting from her chest, Abby imagined she could smell Sondra's lunacy, her maddened rage. Or maybe it was the stench of her own fury, her own hysteria that burned down through her core. She couldn't have said. She was clinging to Jake.

One cop car flew past, siren screaming, and then the second. Abby heard the screech of metal when they broke through the fence.

"Holy shit!" Jake lifted his head off the porch floor.

"Are they in the pasture? Where does she think she's going? She can't outrun them."

Abby didn't answer. She didn't think outrunning the police was Sondra's intention.

Moments later, the sound of the crash was horrific, otherworldly. Neither Abby nor Jake saw it happen. They were getting to their feet, dazed, half in shock, but one of the officers told them when he returned from the scene that Sondra had hit the utility pole at the north end of the pasture and was ejected from the vehicle.

"She was going straight at it like a bat out of hell," he said, "and she wasn't wearing her seat belt. Not much way she was going to survive driving like that."

Hours passed while the police and other rescue workers did their jobs. The coroner came, and a tow truck was brought in for Sondra's car. Looking on from the back porch at the emergency traffic strung out over her property, Abby was reminded of Kate's ranch after the flood. The sight was as surreal now as it was then. It made her feel light-headed.

Charlie came, and Abby was glad for his company, his support. It was some time after he heard what had happened, when he had digested the enormity of the danger she and Jake had been in, that he said, "It's like that movie. What was it?"

"*Fatal Attraction?*" Jake said.

"That's the one," Charlie said.

Standing next to them on the porch, Abby said, "A movie isn't real."

The officer who took her and Jake's statements said that he'd contacted Hank, and that Hank had said Sondra had shown up one day out of the blue around a month ago. According to what Hank told the police, he had no idea his wife had fixated on Nick and then on Abby. He hadn't known she'd bought a gun. He'd said there were psychiatric issues.

It took the police little more than a week to conclude their investigation. Someone from the department called and explained to Abby that, from the information they were able to gather, it appeared Sondra had for many years struggled with being bipolar. She had a history of going off her medication, and when she came to Abby's house, she was in all likelihood suffering the effects of some kind of psychotic break.

Abby wasn't comforted. She felt raw inside and panicky. She kept thinking of Sondra's last phone call, the one where she'd asked: *Are you happy now?* Abby hadn't understood then why Sondra had asked that question, but she did now. She thought if Sondra were here she would ask her the same thing: Are you happy now?

Jake went back to school on the Tuesday after the incident. Abby helped him pack his car, and she couldn't stop fussing over him. It worried her that he wasn't taking enough time to process the trauma they'd both endured.

He insisted he was fine. "Really, Mom. It's you I'm worried about."

"No," she protested, and she was annoyed. She was sick of being worried over.

"I'm just glad you didn't pull the trigger on that gun."

"I would have, if Sondra had made one move toward you." Even as she spoke, Abby realized it was true, that she would have done whatever it took to save Jake or herself.

He wrapped his arm around her shoulders. "You're tough, Mom, you know it? You'll make it. We both will." He sounded so confident. Abby hoped he was right.

She wanted to talk to Hank, and in the days leading up to Thanksgiving, she picked up the phone a half dozen times to call him. She wasn't sure of her motive, whether she meant to question him or to berate him, and in any case, something stopped her. Some higher part of herself, and in one corner of her brain, one sane, lovely corner, she was grateful for that. Finally, she purchased a card and wrote a brief note expressing her sympathy for him and for Caitlin. Abby's mother said that was sufficient, that Abby didn't owe Hank one thing.

"Not even forgiveness, Mama?" Abby asked, smiling.

"Oh, Abigail." Her mother sighed. "Only saints can walk on water, you know."

It was after dinner on the Saturday following Thanksgiving; Jake had gone down the street to play basketball with friends, and Abby was headed into the den to read when the phone rang, and for a moment, she froze. Her stomach churned, but then she shook herself, half in irritation. Her mother had told her she needed time to mend, but Abby wondered how much.

Glancing at the Caller ID, her breath caught. "Katie…." she said when she answered, and the name was carried on a sigh that was partly sad, but mostly love and gratitude and relief.

"Oh, Abby, your mama said I should give you a bit longer, but I just couldn't wait another second. I've been worried sick about you. Are you and Jake all right? Truly, I mean—" Kate's voice hitched.

Abby carried the cordless receiver to the table in the breakfast nook and sat down. She said they were fine and asked how Kate knew.

"Dennis heard what happened and called me. He was going to come there, he was so concerned."

Abby's heart paused. "Really?" she said and slid her finger along the table's edge. Whatever anger she had felt against him, or embarrassment or whatever it had been, those feelings had evaporated now. She wondered if she would ever have the opportunity to tell him; she wondered if it mattered to him at all.

"I can't believe Sondra was stalking you, too."

"I thought it was Nadine. They drive the same color car."

Kate said, "It's terrible, but I'm glad Sondra's dead."

"You're in good company," Abby said. "Even Mama is having a hard time."

"I'm just so sorry about everything. I should have told you about seeing Nick. If I had—"

"No, let's not go there."

"But how can we not? You think I saw them together and I didn't."

"I know. Sondra told me she was in the courthouse, in the restroom, when you ran into Nick. She said it shook him up."

"It should have."

A pause perched as light and anxious as a tiny hunted bird.

Abby broke it. "Not all of it was a fantasy. He was with her, Kate, I mean, as in—"

"I know what you mean, chickie." Kate's voice was full; she felt Abby's pain. She would hold Abby's heart while it broke or until it mended or both, if she could.

"I finally talked to Hank the other day."

"Did he know where Sondra had been since the flood?"

"Not really. He said she had friends in San Antonio and she had the cabin. Apparently, she didn't say much about anything when she first came home, but she did see a psychiatrist, and he prescribed medication. Hank said she took it for a while, and it seemed to make her better. Clearer, at least, until she went off it. He said they talked in a way, were honest with each other, in a way they hadn't been in years."

"How nice for them." Kate was darkly sarcastic.

"I know, but that's when Sondra told Hank it was only twice that she and Nick were together. She said he wanted out after the second time. She told me the same thing, that Nick said it was a mistake."

"You didn't deserve any of this, Abby," Kate said, "any more than I did."

"Everyone says that, but I think maybe when a bad thing happens, it isn't a matter of what we deserve."

"What is it then?"

Abby thought for a moment.

"You aren't ready for that discussion."

Abby said she wasn't.

Kate said she thought Abby knew anyway, and Abby smiled because sometimes the way they could read each other was as if they were two halves of the same battered heart.

Kate said, "I think what's important to remember is that Nick was coming home. I think you should trust that. He made a terrible mistake, but he was getting his act together; he was coming home to you."

As if Kate could see her, Abby shook her head. It was another place she couldn't go yet, and maybe she never would be able to look at it, the wonder of what might have been. She said, "I'm so glad you called."

"Me, too," Kate answered, and the skip in her voice matched Abby's.

"I never can stay mad at you."

"You're a better person than me, Abby. You've always been."

"No," Abby said. "Don't burden me with that."

"But you're my idol," Kate said, and the smile in her voice made Abby smile, too.

In the den later, Abby spread a bottom sheet over the sofa cushions, dropped her pillow into place and then, holding the coverlet to her chest, she stood looking down at the bed she was making for herself. Sleeping here was ridiculous. If she kept on, she would become permanently crooked. Still, even as she carried the spare bedclothes upstairs, her heart was anxious. She'd scarcely been inside the bedroom she and Nick had shared since last April, much less slept in their bed. She thought of Jake, that when he came home he would see she wasn't on the sofa but asleep in her own room. He would be reassured, she thought. He would think things were finally getting back to normal, and imagining that kept her resolve in place.

The freshly changed sheets were cool as she slipped between them and turned on her side. Moonlit shadows fiddled over the walls. There were small noises, the familiar night noises, amplified in the silence. She heard the owl; the branch of the old bur oak scraped the bedroom window. Nick had wanted her to call someone to take down the tree, but Abby kept forgetting. She loved it, loved the sound of the branch gently tapping as if it were a dear friend seeking to come in. She tucked her hands beneath her cheek.

And felt his presence there, not inches from her. She felt Nick shift toward her, and in her memory, she was facing him. It had happened just that way the last time they had made love. It was the night he'd been so late coming home, Abby remembered, when he'd been upset about their finances and Lindsey's sprained ankle. The same night he'd mentioned the crazy client, whom Abby now knew had been Sondra.

They had gone to bed, and once the light was out Nick had reached for her. He'd pressed his face into the hollow of her shoulder and whispered against her neck, "I'm sorry I'm such a bastard. You deserve better."

She'd traced the line of his brow when he'd lifted his head. "You know you can talk to me?"

"Yes, but not now," he'd said, and he'd lowered his mouth to hers, and his kiss had been long and slow and full of need. He'd teased a trail of kisses from her lips up to the corners of her eyes, down to her chin, from there to her collarbone. Levering up on one elbow, his gaze never moving from her face, he'd unbuttoned her oxford shirt, an old one of his that she wore. He'd slid her panties from her and Abby had opened herself to him, moaning softly from sheer relief and desire.

He'd been fully present with her then, the earlier tension between them forgotten, and they'd been together in that hot, sweet way they had always shared. *We should talk about this.* She remembered thinking that in a corner of her mind. She remembered thinking they couldn't let the stuff of life, their work, finances, the children, get in the way of their commitment to each other.

We are the heart of the family, she had thought that night. Our love for each other is the heart.

Abby remembered wanting to say this to him, but she hadn't. Instead, when he'd released her, when their breath had slowed, she had been so drowsy and content that she'd turned her back and curled into his embrace, settling herself into the cup of his lap.

After a long moment, he had said her name: "Abby?" and he had inflected it with such wistfulness and doubt, and when she'd answered, "Hmm?" he'd said, "Nothing," and "I love you," and she had thought it was enough.

She would have to live with that now. The memory of his wistfulness, his seeming regret, and her failure to pursue it, to find out the source of what was troubling him. She would have to learn to live with all of this. Live the mystery, the questions, and somehow it would have to be okay. *But not all at once,* that's what her mother said.

And it was true, Abby thought, because tonight it was enough that she could lie here in her own bed and remember, and the pain wasn't quite so awful.

CHAPTER

24

Toward noon one Sunday in March, she took the broom and went out onto the porch. The air had a dancing effervescence, as if it were thrilled with itself. A light rain before dawn had left behind beads of moisture. They glimmered like opals scattered among pale green shoots of spring grass. Abby imagined she could hear it growing and felt her heart ease inside her chest. Winter would give way, she thought. It always did.

She poked the broom into the porch corners, swept the accumulation of leaf trash and dust toward the steps. Soon she grew warm enough to take off her sweater. When she heard the car coming up the drive, she stopped what she was doing and shaded her eyes. She didn't recognize the car, but she recognized Dennis Henderson when he parked and got out. He waited, looking at her over the car's roof, and she had the feeling he was asking permission. She lifted her hand, a half wave.

He came to the bottom of the wide concrete steps. "Is it okay?" he asked, and she knew he didn't mean because of her sweeping.

"I was about to make lunch," she said. "Would you like a sandwich?"

He nodded and joined her. He was wearing a faded blue windbreaker over a T-shirt, jeans and work boots. Even out of uniform, he had an air of stillness, of immovability and strength, that was as compelling as it was reassuring.

He took off his sunglasses, held up a book. "For Jake," he said.

"What is it?"

"It's about law enforcement, the different fields. He said he was interested."

"He is."

"From what I hear, he's definitely got the nerves for it, a cool head under pressure."

"He does. I might not be here if it weren't for him, but I'm not sure I like the idea of him making a career out of encounters like the one we went through."

"Maybe you'd rather I didn't leave this for him, then."

Abby shook her head. "He's grown up. It's his decision."

She glanced into the near distance. What would Nick think of this man bringing their son a book, another man giving his son advice? She set the broom beside the door. "Give me a minute," she said to Dennis, "I'll make the sandwiches and bring them out here."

He handed her the book. "I've wanted to see you

again ever since the night you came by my office. I almost did come after that. When I heard what Hank's wife did, I— my God, Abby, when I think what might have happened to you and Jake." He looked off, mouth working. "I wanted to try and explain, but I figured I'd just make things worse."

"It was a bad time," Abby said.

Dennis nodded.

Abby looked at the book in her hands. "We had Nick and Lindsey cremated and scattered their ashes out back where the bluebonnets grow under the oak trees. We used to picnic there when the kids were little."

"That's good. They're at rest now," Dennis said.

"Yes."

He looked out toward his car. "When I ask Kate, she says you're okay, but I had to see for myself." He brought his gaze back to her.

Abby didn't answer. She could see that he was worried she was angry with him, that he'd maybe offended her by coming here without warning.

He put out his hand but stopped short of touching her. "Are you?" he asked.

"So far."

"I should have told you."

"About the boy at the gas station, the woman he saw Nick with." She glanced up at him. "I doubt it would have changed anything."

"You were entitled to the information. I thought I was sparing you."

She looked down. "I feel like a fool."

"You aren't a fool, Abby. I know my saying so won't take that idea out of your mind. But in time you'll see—" He broke off, his glance drifted.

She knew he'd thought about her situation, the speech he could make about it, that he was still thinking, trying to put it together, an explanation to comfort her.

"Men get wound up in their egos sometimes. They're more apt to act like animals in their behavior than women. They tend to run when they're scared. They don't talk about the fear."

"Sometimes it scares me to think how needless their deaths were, how preventable. It's the futility that gets to me." She looked at him, and he nodded. He understood.

After a moment, she retrieved the broom and held it out to him. "If you'll get the corner over there by the window, I'll make lunch."

He shrugged out of his jacket, took the broom from her and set to work. As she went into the house, he was whistling softly, some fragment of a melody she didn't recognize. But the sound of it was pleasing to her.

In the kitchen she laid the book Dennis had brought for Jake on the countertop and then went out the back door to stand on the steps. The rich scent of pink jasmine saturated the air, and she drew it deep into herself. She'd planted the vine near the door on purpose so she could do this at every opportunity, stand here in early spring and immerse herself in its fragrance.

Her gaze drifted beyond the pasture to the thick fringe of trees crowding the back of the property. The branches were a mixed network of angles and thicknesses, a pattern of inky bones supporting a delicate green lace of unfurling buds. But the bluebonnets beneath the trees—where she and Jake had scattered the mingled ashes of their family—were what drew her wonder. The flowers robed the ground in lush folds of blue. Sure and beautiful evidence of life.

And she did nothing to encourage them. Year after year, they came through earth that was hard-packed and matted in layers of debris, and each spring they appeared thicker and more glorious, or so it seemed. And each spring, like the old Indian chief in the legend, the sight filled her with awe.

Standing here, feeling her heart lift in the old familiar way, she wondered at herself. She wondered at the confusion of her emotions, how it was that in the midst of such profound sorrow, she could feel her ribs part with such sweet joy. But she was enough of a gardener to know that survival was seeded into the nature of death as well as life. Even her survival. If she chose it.

In the kitchen, she made sandwiches and glasses of iced tea, and gathering everything onto a tray, she brought it onto the porch. Dennis leaned the broom near the door and, taking the tray from her, set it on the table she indicated.

Turning to her, he said, "I noticed some porch boards were loose when I was sweeping."

She made a face and said she knew. "I have a laundry list of chores to do around here."

He grinned at her. "I'm pretty good with a hammer and I work cheap."

The errant breeze loosened fine strands of hair from her chignon, and they fluttered over her face. She lifted her hand, but Dennis was there before her. She felt his fingertips graze her cheek, draw toward her ear and around it, slowly, so slowly, as if he were intent on not frightening her.

"I want to help you, Abby, to be here for you," he

said, and her mind wrapped around the safety that seemed inherent in his offer, his very presence, and she wanted to hold it; she wanted to lean into it, into him, but she wondered if she dared, if she could trust a man again.

She held his gaze, searching for the words to express what she was feeling, but it was impossible, and she gave her head a slight shake when she couldn't find them.

But he seemed to know, to read her mind. He said he didn't care how long it took. He said, "I just don't want to lose you."

Her heart rose, and she smiled, and when she flattened her palm against the center of his chest, he took it in his own.

* * * * *

Turn the page for a sneak peek from
Barbara Taylor Sissel's upcoming novel
SAFE KEEPING
Available soon from Harlequin MIRA

CHAPTER

1

My son is a murderer.

The words hovered in Emily's mind.

She said them aloud, "My son is a murderer."

But they sounded no more believable than when they were rattling around in her head. Why did her mind do this? Why did it conjure up the worst of her fears? One that was neither logical nor possible? So far, like Tucker, the girl, Jessica Sweet, was only missing, not dead, and whatever more dire connection might exist between them was a figment of Emily's overactive imagination, the result of too little sleep and too much worry. It was the uncertainty that was killing her. If only she could know Tucker was safe.

She stared over the foot of the bed, beyond the circle of lamplight, into new morning light that was as pale as a milky eye. Behind the closed bathroom door, the sound of the shower was a muted hiss. The sharp crease of light on the floor under the door assured her Roy was in there performing his morning routine. Even in retirement, he was a man of routine, of habits that were as predictable as moonrise.

Heart thudding, she looked at the telephone on the nightstand near her elbow and then at the bathroom door. Was she prepared for what would happen if she went through with it, if she dialed 9-1-1? Was there time before Roy was finished? The sound of the shower clattered in her ears. She lifted the cordless receiver from its base.

Impossibly his fingers closed over her wrist. "Don't, Em."

Her gaze bounced. A breath went down hard. "Someone has to—"

"No."

"Tucker's been gone almost two weeks, Roy. It's not like him."

"What do you mean? He pulls this stunt all the time, his damn disappearing act, and the hell with us left behind to worry."

"But never for this long. I think we should call the police."

"No," Roy repeated.

"What if he's been in an accident?" Emily asked. "What if he got mugged or someone took him? He could be lying somewhere hurt." Her voice picked up speed; it caught on her panic. "He could have amnesia."

"You're making yourself crazy." Roy sat beside her. "He's making us both crazy." Emily started to answer, but Roy talked over her. "He's thirty-four years old, for Christ's sake, a grown man. Why is he still living here? Why isn't he out on his own?"

"He's tried, Roy. You know he has." Emily stopped. They'd had this discussion so many times; she knew it by heart. If she were to go on and say the rest of it, that some children took longer to grow up, that if they were patient Tucker would eventually find his way, Roy would say she was making excuses. She would be moved to defend herself. They would go back and forth, making an endless loop of words that would re-solve nothing.

He picked up her hand and met her gaze. The wan circle of lamplight silvered the gray bristle of his closely cut hair. With the tip of her finger, she traced a darker line of fatigue that grooved his cheek. He was exhausted from the stress; they both were. "I want some peace and quiet in our lives," he said. "Is that so much to ask? Haven't we earned it by now?"

"Yes," she said. "And we'll have it, you'll see. When we find Tucker, we'll sit down together—"

"God help us if it's happening again, Em." He looked hard at her.

But she wasn't having it and looked away. "Don't be ridiculous," she said, even though only moments ago, she'd been in the same place, entertaining the same anxiety. She thought of reminding Roy that Tucker had been furious when he left, and given his mood, it wasn't terribly unusual that he hadn't called. He'd walked out angry any number of times before, and while it was true that he didn't ordinarily stay away this long, it was still possible that was all this disappearance amounted to. Except it wasn't, and something inside her knew it, knew that this time was different.

It was like a crack in the earth, imperceptible to the naked eye, but there all the same, a warning, an omen. Setting the phone receiver on the nightstand, she pressed her fingertips to her temples. "I want him home," she said, putting her feet over the bedside. "I want to know he's all right."

"I think it's a mistake to call this his home, Em." Roy was in his closet now, pulling on a pair of jeans. "I think when he shows up, we need to set boundaries, set a concrete date that he has to be out of here. We've done all we can for him, more than most parents would."

"It might be different if you wouldn't lose your temper," Emily said. "If you could give him the benefit of the doubt the way you do Lissa. If you could just—"

"Just what, Em?"

She didn't answer; she was out of energy, suddenly past the wish to explain. She looked at the floor. *If he'd been our first, he might have been our last.* The old joke, one she'd heard other parents make, drifted through her mind. She didn't find it particularly amusing even though she'd resorted to it on occasion herself. Would she have had another child had it been Tucker and not Lissa who came first? No one could have asked for a lovelier or more obedient child than Lissa, and Evan, the man she'd chosen for her husband, was a godsend. Emily and Roy relied on him, his steadiness, his kindness and good sense. Even Tucker seemed calmer and more content when Evan was nearby.

"What would you tell the police if you called them?" Roy emerged from the closet. "What evidence do you have—of anything wrong, I mean?"

"How do you know they don't have him already?"

"We would have heard."

"The girl who disappeared," Emily began, because

it was impossible, after all, not to voice the fear that was uppermost in both their minds, "the one everyone is looking for, Jessica Sweet, I think I recognize her name. What if Tucker knew her, dated her like he did Miranda?"

"Like I said before, God help us if that turns out to be the case." Roy stuffed his shirt hem into his jeans and threaded his belt through the loops. "I'll tell you right now, I can't handle that again."

The drama, Roy meant, the horrible way it had ended—in Miranda's murder of all things. Emily picked at her thumbnail. She and Roy had welcomed Miranda Quick when Tucker first began dating her in high school; they'd grown fond of her. They knew her family from church, knew her to be a sweet girl, the very sort of girl Emily could imagine as a daughter-in-law, but after graduation Miranda changed, becoming restless and unhappy. She went out nights alone. Tucker had no idea where she was or what she was doing, and when he found out, it devastated him. But he loved her, and he was determined to stay with her even after she proved herself unworthy of his devotion.

He remained faithful, while Miranda broke his heart over and over. Emily had never felt so helpless and frustrated. Then, just when she thought it couldn't get worse, Miranda went missing and Tucker was the one who found her body. A day later, the police came for him. They questioned him for hours. His picture was everywhere in the media; he was labeled a person of interest—in a murder investigation. How? Emily still couldn't wrap her mind around it, how her son had become involved in something so horrifying. She blamed Miranda. Miranda was the cancer who had gotten her hooks into Tucker. She was the blight of their lives, and if it was possible, Emily believed she hated Miranda more now that she was dead, and she truly didn't care if she went to hell for it.

Switching off the bedside light, she felt the mattress give when Roy sat down to put on his shoes, felt the heat from his palm when he flattened it on her back. He said he would make the coffee. "I'll bring it up to you with some toast and that marmalade you like. How about it?"

Ordinarily, she would have been delighted. Roy wasn't the sort of man who was comfortable in the kitchen. A construction site was more his domain; hard physical labor was his refuge, and providing a good living for his family was his contribution, his source of pride. Or it was until last fall when he retired. Emily encouraged it. She imagined they would do things together, finish building the lake house, plant a vegetable garden. She'd dreamed of more exotic possibilities, traveling on the Orient Express or learning ballroom dancing, but in a very not-funny way, there was just something about having your son's name—their own Lebay family name—linked to a murder investigation that caused such visions to lose their luster.

Pushing aside the bed linen, she told Roy she would make the coffee, that she needed to get up, to be busy. But then she was sorry not to have accepted his invitation, because when they came downstairs, he didn't accompany her into the kitchen. Instead, he disappeared into his office.

Emily heard the door close, the click of the lock, and she sighed. Standing at the counter, she parted the checked curtains at the window over the sink. The view

was as familiar to her as the image of her own face.
Her great-grandfather had built this house, and it had
come down to her through the generations. She grew
up here and could recall the very year her parents re-
modeled the old carriage house to accommodate two
cars and the workshop, where, like her dad, Roy would
go to putter. Beyond it, there was an alley. Closer in, a
huge old elm tree centered the bit of backyard, housing
a picnic table that Roy built and a wood-seated swing.
After they were married in the spring of 1972, on his
good days, Roy had pushed her in that swing.

"Higher!" she hollered at him, laughing. "Higher!"
she shouted.

And later, he pushed her while she held their children as infants in her arms.

They had been happy, hadn't they? They weren't different from other families in the neighborhood. They
shopped and vacationed and participated in community
events. They attended church. And like their neighbors,
they'd had their share of good times and bad.

Emily started the coffee, and while she waited for
it to brew, she collected the Monday editions of the
two newspapers they read from the front porch. Their
small-town newspaper, the *Hardys Walk Tribune*, was
lighter in weight and folksier in tone than the *Houston
Chronicle*. On her way back to the kitchen, she paused
at Roy's office door, and putting her ear against it, she
listened and heard nothing. Only the sound of the tall
grandfather clock on the landing in the front hall. The
rhythmic *tock tock* was magnified like heartbeats in a
row. Gunshots fired in evenly spaced salute.

She straightened. In her mind's eye, she could see
Roy sitting at his desk, and on the wall opposite him,

she saw the gun case that housed his collection. The glass front would hold a faint reflection of his image, doing whatever it was he did in there these days. She hoped he wasn't brooding. The guns worried her. She didn't like thinking it, and perhaps it was only a temporary effect of retirement, but there was something in his demeanor in recent weeks that was beginning to remind her of the wounded man he was when he came back from the war in Vietnam. He'd tried hard to hold in the horror, closing himself off from her, not wanting to burden her, he said. They worked through it eventually, but it had taken a near-tragedy to bring him around.

She tapped on the door. "Coffee's ready," she said through the panel, and she was relieved to hear his acknowledgment, to hear the leather creak as he rose from his chair. He followed her into the kitchen, and she thought the drag of his step sounded more uneven than usual. She wanted to turn and look, to ask if his pain was worse, but he didn't like her fussing over him.

She unsheathed both papers from their plastic wrappers and set them, still folded, on the table, and that's when she saw it—a piece of the missing girl's, Jessica Sweet's, face. It was looking out from the front page of the *Chronicle*. Above it, Emily glimpsed two words: *found* and *dead,* and her heart slammed into the wall of her chest. Any moment now, Roy would see it, too.

She brought the toast to the table and sat across from Roy. She was aware of the newspaper between them and was seized by a sudden, heated and irrational urge to tear it to shreds. She imagined Tucker coming through the door. He would put his arms around her; he would say how sorry he was to have caused her such concern. She would tell him about the dead girl, show him her picture, and he'd be sorry for her, too. But he wouldn't know her. He wouldn't have loved her or shared a messy, emotional history with her the way he had with Miranda Quick.

Emily picked up her slice of toast and then set it down, thinking if she had to sit here through another day without word from Tucker, or about him, she would come out of her skin.

She caught Roy's glance.

"What?" he said.

"Why don't we ride out there?"

"Where?" he asked, but she was certain he knew.

"Indigo Lake."

"What for? There's nothing to see," he said. "A slab, pipes, a frame. I ought to get Evan to send a crew out there to pull it down. I'll sell the land."

Evan had worked for Roy in the family construction business long before becoming Lissa's husband. Evan and Lissa ran the company now since Roy's retirement. Tucker would have had a share in running it, too, if he was in the least reliable.

Emily touched Roy's hand. "I think you should finish the house. It would take your mind off—" She didn't want to say Tucker, so she said, "Things, you know. You need a project. Once it's finished, if you don't want to keep it, you can always sell it then."

"Why the sudden interest? You've already said you won't move out there."

"I could change my mind."

"Why would you?"

Emily looked into her coffee cup. *For you,* she thought. But if she were to say that, he'd think it was out of pity. "A change of scenery," she said softly. "I think we need a change of scenery."

Roy made a sound that could have meant anything. He took his cup and plate to the sink, thanked her for the toast. It was only after she heard his office door close behind him that she realized he'd taken the Houston paper with him, and her head livened with a fresh buzz of anxiety. He was bound to see the photo and the article now, she thought, and she closed her eyes. It was happening again just as Roy feared. She could feel it to her core. And this time, when Roy insisted they cut their ties to Tucker, he would mean it.

ACKNOWLEDGMENTS

I love books. Each one is a gift, and for me reading them is essential. So it is a dream come true that I have been given the means to pay the gift forward. And while I did author this book, the dream of sharing it with readers would never have come into being without the help of so many wonderful people. First among them are my critique partners who are generous listeners, tireless readers, and creative sounding boards, and who, each in their own right, are incredibly astute as editors and authors themselves. I wish every writer could find such a remarkable group. Thank you Midwives for all the Friday-night sessions and for always cheering me on: Colleen Thompson, Wanda Dionne, Joni Rodgers and TJ Bennett.

I owe such a debt of gratitude, too, to my sister, Susan Harper, and to my dear friend, Jo Merrill, who generously read the manuscript and helped me brainstorm multiple times, and who never lost enthusiasm. I am living proof that you can go a long while on such generous amounts of steadfast loyalty and constant reinforcement.

Thank you again to my brother, John Taylor, who has never once wavered in his faith that I could do this or most anything else. Sometimes his voice in my ear has been the spur and I'm so grateful for it. Also, I am deeply appreciative of my niece, Heather Wilson, who has this uncanny ability to know the exact right time I need a wake-up call and a dose of encouragement. Thank you to Christy Kliesing and her sweet certainty and belief in me, and thank you to both my sons, Michael and David, my big pillars of support, my teachers. They have never doubted I could do it and when it's darkest, they always know how to make me laugh.

There will never be enough right words to say how grateful I am to my mentor and friend, Guida Jackson. The wise counsel, the support and the opportunities to learn and grow as a writer and editor that I have received from her have been invaluable. Her faith in me has given me the confidence and will to keep going. I'm so grateful, too, for her celebration of every small and large victory. She has generously nurtured and nourished so many of us fledgling authors and is herself a remarkable author and teacher.

On my own with my manuscript, I can touch the lives of a handful of people, but for an author to bring an actual book into being, to extend her reach beyond that initial closed circle, requires help from publishing professionals, not just any sort of professionals, either, but people who conceive a passion for your story, who see the potential and who are seized with a vision, who love the story as much as you do. I would like to convey my heartfelt thanks to the entire, incredible MIRA team, everyone who has helped to bring the book into being, from sales and marketing to art and publicity. I am especially grateful to Erika Imranyi, my editor at MIRA, for her perception that is unfailingly accurate, and for the many hours she has invested that have shaped, honed and immeasurably enriched my work, and for her support and encouragement, which she offers in liberal quantities right when I need it most.

Huge, profound thanks to my dream agent, Barbara Poelle, who saw the potential and whose early faith, enthusiasm, friendship, and editorial guidance gave the manuscript the exact right polish. I wish I could convey in words what her support and encouragement mean to me. She's a gift of herself and I will always be more grateful than I could ever say for that day when she decided that rather than email, she would give me a call. Thank you, B2, for helping my dream come true beyond anything I could have imagined.

And last, a big shout out to readers everywhere. Books wouldn't happen without you.

Joy to everyone, many thanks, and love to you all.

EVIDENCE

OF

LIFE

BARBARA TAYLOR SISSEL

Reader's Guide

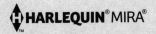

Questions for Discussion

1. Abby goes to great lengths to find her family, including going to the Hill Country with Hank, a stranger. Do you think she was brave or foolish? What would you do in similar circumstances?

2. Is Nick's vulnerability at the time he met Sondra a mitigating factor in his betrayal of Abby? Can there ever be mitigating factors in the betrayal of one person by another? Do you think Nick and Abby's marriage would have survived if Nick had lived? Could you forgive an unfaithful spouse?

3. Many times throughout the story, Abby is surprised by the behavior of people she believed she knew—her husband, her son, her best friend; she learns she doesn't know any one of them as well as she thought. Have you ever been surprised in the same way? Do you think it's possible to know someone completely, even those with whom you live?

4. Abby and Kate are two very different people. Kate is outgoing and verbal, while Abby tends to be more solitary and introspective. Would you say their friendship proves the old adage that oppo-

sites attract? What traits do you admire in your closest friend? In what ways does the relationship enhance who you are? Do you feel, as Abby does, that you and your closest friend are two halves of the same heart?

5. Many of the characters keep information from Abby in order to protect her: Jake, about seeing his father with Sondra; Kate, about running into Nick at the courthouse. Should they have told Abby about the incidents immediately or at least once Nick was dead? Or is ignorance truly blissful? What would you have done?

6. It takes Abby a while to recover her will to move on, and when she does, it is partly through observing nature. Where do you find comfort and healing in times of great heartbreak?

7. What do you think is the significance of the scene where Dennis and Abby come across the injured doe and her fawn? What about the old Indian chief's sacrifice in the legend of the bluebonnet?

8. Discuss the significance of the title.

9. Motherhood and sacrifice are strong themes in the book. Discuss the sacrifices Abby made for her children. Do you feel she did enough to protect

them and to steer them in the right direction in life? How do you feel she handled Jake's troubles with school? Is there anything she could have done to prevent what happened with Lindsey?

A Conversation with Barbara Taylor Sissel

Evidence of Life is the story of an ordinary woman in an extraordinary situation. What was your inspiration for Abby's story, and how, if at all, do you relate to her?

I certainly relate to her as a mother, in particular when it comes to her abiding concern for her children. And I can relate to how quickly the ordinariness of life can detour into calamity. I think most of us can. I hear a siren and it gives me pause. It's a signal that somewhere something has changed. Someone's day, someone's life is irrevocably altered from what they planned when they woke up that morning. In Abby's case, too, I was looking at the question of whether it is possible to ever really know someone. Human nature is so unpredictable. We wake up next to someone for years on end, but do we, can we, truly know every thought they're having, every decision they're making that could have consequences for us down the line? But for me it is the very mystery of all of this that makes life uniquely beautiful and compelling.

The Texas Hill Country is a captivating, picturesque locale. Why did you choose this as the setting for the novel?

I live in Texas and yet never truly bonded with the state until I began visiting that part of it. It seems to me to have an energy that's singular. The very air has an effervescent quality and the land itself has a presence, an aura that is energizing and yet peaceful and serene. And it's such an improbable location for a flood. They don't happen often there and when they do, they can be epic in the truest sense of the word, perfect for storytelling.

When you began the novel, did you have Abby's character and journey already mapped out? How did she surprise you along the way? Were there any interesting surprises from other characters?

Not completely mapped out, no. She strengthened through her evolutions and her journey became more focused. I think one surprise for me was her friendship with Kate, what those two women shared, the sometimes troubled nature of the events in their lives and how their friendship managed to survive in spite of them...I didn't plan any of that. Another interesting surprise was the old man. His chapter just fell into the book one day, fully formed. What's odd is that shortly after I wrote it, a friend and critique partner who was familiar with the story told me she heard of a similar event on NPR that actually happened in England. Blinking headlights led to the discovery of a car in a remote location and a subsequent investigation found that it, and the family inside it, had been missing for six months. Strange but true!

What was your greatest challenge writing *Evidence of Life*? What was your greatest pleasure?

I think the greatest challenge was bringing Abby through her grief, through her dark night, and the greatest pleasure was finding out that there was hope for her, that she could recover and choose life...I liked that she did.

On your website is the tagline "At the heart of every crime there's a family, someone you love..." What is the significance of this line in *Evidence of Life*, and is this a running theme in all of your work?

I became interested in the impact of crime on families when I lived with my own family on the grounds of a first-offender prison facility. It was a remarkable experience to interact with the inmates and their families and to see and hear firsthand how their lives were altered, often irretrievably. There isn't a whole lot said about these people, how they manage in the wake of learning that someone related to them, whom they love, has committed a devastating crime. How do they carry on, get up every day and go to work, care for their children? Shop for groceries, survive? How do they talk about it, think or feel? Can they forgive? Suppose they believe their loved one is innocent? Suppose they think the victim deserved what they got? Suppose they're divided within the family about their feelings? In each of my novels these are the questions I seek to find answers to. I don't focus so much on the legal issues and court procedures that come about as a result of a crime, but the emotional impact on the family. And the crime may not be legal but moral in nature, as in Evidence of Life, which centers more on the crime of betrayal. It's not necessarily punishable in a court of law, but the conflict that rises, the nature of the collateral damage that occurs as a result, is the same.

Your previous books (*The Ninth Step, The Volunteer, The Last Innocent Hour*) were indie-published. How was your first experience being traditionally published different from your previous experiences?

With indie publishing, the sheer number of details I kept up with in addition to simply writing the next novel were daunting. It's a "many hat" occupation that's, in part, balanced by the satisfaction of almost total control of the project and fast publication. With traditional publishing, the wait is of course longer, but what I've experienced is the enormous benefit of razor-sharp editing by my editor, who cares as much about the novel as I do. I really like that, having a partner who is so careful, who is as devoted to how good the book is as I am. As of this writing, I haven't yet experienced the power of marketing and distribution that a traditional publisher has, but I can only imagine that it will be far different, and wider-ranging, than what I have been able to accomplish on my own, although I'm very proud to be an indie author. I'm elated, and consider myself very fortunate, to have the opportunity to write in both worlds.

Can you describe your writing process? Do you write scenes consecutively or jump around? Do you have a schedule or a routine? A lucky charm?

I begin every morning by revising yesterday's work and then go on to write new material, usually working for four to five hours. When it comes to writing the story, I do work consecutively. For me, one detail hinges on another. The slightest change can unhinge everything that comes after, like a domino effect, so the story has to be right from the beginning, or as right as I can get it on that day, before I move on. As for a lucky charm, I think it's my muse, whom I envision as an adorable but capricious child and often, when I get stuck, when I can't find her or the inspiration and creative flow she brings me, I go out into the garden and find her there, waiting for me.

Can you tell us something about the book you're working on now?

The prison where I lived with my family was for first offenders, and, when it was possible, the inmate's family was a key component in the inmate's rehabilitation effort. As a result, I met some of the family members and got to know the ways in which their lives had been altered in the wake of the arrest, conviction, and incarceration of the young man they loved. The families were usually good people, ordinary people. In the story I'm writing, a man is accused of a brutal murder, and his family is left reeling. His mother and sister marshal themselves and unite in the effort to find the truth, which proves to be shattering in ways that are as shocking as the crime that launched their journey. Family loyalties are tested beyond endurance, and in the end, it isn't only the one family member's life, but all their lives that will hang in the balance, in a way that is both terrifying and unexpected.

BARBARA CLAYPOLE WHITE

Bestselling author Will Shepard is caught in the twilight of grief after his young son dies in a car accident. But when his father's aging mind erases the memory, Will rewrites the truth. The story he spins brings unexpected relief…until he's forced to return to rural North Carolina, trapping himself in a lie.

Holistic veterinarian Hannah Linden is a healer who opens her heart to strays, but can only watch, powerless, as her grown son struggles with inner demons. When she rents her guest cottage to Will and his dad, she finds solace in trying to mend their broken world, even while her own shatters.

As their lives connect and collide, Will and Hannah become each other's only hope—if they can find their way into a new story, one that begins with love.

The In-Between Hour

Available wherever books are sold.

New York Times Bestselling Author

Heather Gudenkauf

When teenager Allison Glenn is sent to prison for a heinous crime, she leaves behind her reputation as the golden girl of Linden Falls forever. Her sister, Brynn, carries the burden of what really happened that night, and faces whispered rumors every day in the hallways of their small Iowa high school.

Now their legacy of secrets is focused on one little boy. And if the truth is revealed, the consequences will be unimaginable for the adoptive mother who loves him, the girl who tried to protect him and the two sisters who hold the key to all that is hidden.

Available wherever books are sold.

Be sure to connect with us at:
Harlequin.com/Newsletters
Facebook.com/HarlequinBooks
Twitter.com/HarlequinBooks

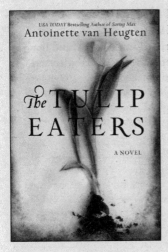

AVERIL DEAN

With haunting prose and deft psychological insight, Averil Dean spins a chilling story that explores the dark corners of obsession— love, pain and revenge.

Alice Croft is a young woman with a damaged past and a dark agenda. Ten years ago, someone ruined her life. But now she has a chance to right that wrong. Her plan is simple: seduce Jack Calabrese and convince him to do the crime she can't commit….

Alice thinks she knows Jack. She thinks she can use him to get what she wants. But she's wrong—and being wrong about Jack could be deadly.

"Crisply written, wickedly suspenseful…[*Alice Close Your Eyes*] reads like a dark, sensual nightmare….Don't miss it."
—David Bell, author of *Cemetery Girl*

Alice Close Your Eyes

Available wherever books are sold.

REQUEST YOUR
FREE BOOKS!

2 FREE NOVELS
FROM THE SUSPENSE COLLECTION
PLUS 2 FREE GIFTS!

YES! Please send me 2 FREE novels from the Suspense Collection and my 2 FREE gifts (gifts are worth about $10). After receiving them, if I don't wish to receive any more books, I can return the shipping statement marked "cancel." If I don't cancel, I will receive 4 brand-new novels every month and be billed just $6.24 per book in the U.S. or $6.74 per book in Canada. That's a savings of at least 22% off the cover price. It's quite a bargain! Shipping and handling is just 50¢ per book in the U.S. and 75¢ per book in Canada.* I understand that accepting the 2 free books and gifts places me under no obligation to buy anything. I can always return a shipment and cancel at any time. Even if I never buy another book, the two free books and gifts are mine to keep forever.

191/391 MDN F4XN

Name _____ (PLEASE PRINT) _____

Address _____ Apt. # _____

City _____ State/Prov. _____ Zip/Postal Code _____

Signature (if under 18, a parent or guardian must sign) _____

Mail to the **Harlequin® Reader Service:**
IN U.S.A.: P.O. Box 1867, Buffalo, NY 14240-1867
IN CANADA: P.O. Box 609, Fort Erie, Ontario L2A 5X3

Want to try two free books from another line?
Call 1-800-873-8635 or visit www.ReaderService.com.

* Terms and prices subject to change without notice. Prices do not include applicable taxes. Sales tax applicable in N.Y. Canadian residents will be charged applicable taxes. Offer not valid in Quebec. This offer is limited to one order per household. Not valid for current subscribers to the Suspense Collection or the Romance/Suspense Collection. All orders subject to credit approval. Credit or debit balances in a customer's account(s) may be offset by any other outstanding balance owed by or to the customer. Please allow 4 to 6 weeks for delivery. Offer available while quantities last.

Your Privacy—The Harlequin® Reader Service is committed to protecting your privacy. Our Privacy Policy is available online at www.ReaderService.com or upon request from the Harlequin Reader Service.

We make a portion of our mailing list available to reputable third parties that offer products we believe may interest you. If you prefer that we not exchange your name with third parties, or if you wish to clarify or modify your communication preferences, please visit us at www.ReaderService.com/consumerschoice or write to us at Harlequin Reader Service Preference Service, P.O. Box 9062, Buffalo, NY 14269. Include your complete name and address.

SUS13R

An irresistible new installment in the
Swift River Valley series from
New York Times bestselling author

CARLA NEGGERS

**Unlikely partners bound by circumstance...
or by fate?**

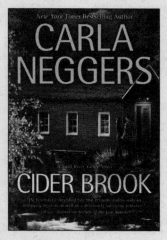

Rescued by a sexy bad-boy firefighter isn't how Samantha Bennett expected to start her stay in Knights Bridge, Massachusetts. Now she has everyone's attention—especially that of Justin Sloan, her rescuer, who wants to know why she was camped out in an abandoned New England cider mill.

Samantha is a treasure hunter, returned home to Knights Bridge to solve a three-hundred-year-old mystery. Justin may not trust her, but that doesn't mean he can resist her....

Available wherever books are sold.

Be sure to connect with us at:

Harlequin.com/Newsletters

Facebook.com/HarlequinBooks

Twitter.com/HarlequinBooks

www.Harlequin.com

MCN1588